R

"I'm trying to forget what a horrible day I had." Dany clicked Jack's glass with hers and then sipped her drink. "Today Eleanor hated a hat. One hat! She had the milliner in tears. I have to think of a way to stop that behavior."

"Forget it, what can you do?" Jack replied. "After she's driven everybody crazy for a month, the costume house somehow saves her. The show opens out of town and she's taking bows, accepting congratulations."

"I suppose it's worth it if the result is exciting."

"Dany, you can't mean that."

"I do. How can you miss the thrill of it when you see it on stage and it is perfect?"

"I can miss it. It escapes me and it always has." He put their glasses on the windowsill. "But I love your excitement. I love watching your reaction, what I saw when we were in Philadelphia, how it affects you. You know why? Because I love you, Dany."

"No, Jack, no." She didn't want him to say it. "Not yet, please."

She wondered if he ever had any doubts, if he'd ever been denied the toys he wanted as a child. His arms went around her waist, lifting her off her feet and she couldn't answer him, couldn't deny him.

"Finally," he murmured, kissing her again and again, carrying her to the bedroom.

Silk

Robert Mackintosh

PINNACLE BOOKS
WINDSOR PUBLISHING CORP.

For
Mildred
and
Lee, Mervyn, Ross, and Geraldine.

PINNACLE BOOKS

are published by

Windsor Publishing Corp.
475 Park Avenue South
New York, NY 10016

First printing: January, 1992

Printed in the United States of America

Prologue

The limousines crammed into the narrow street blocking the honking taxis trying to get in line at the front of the Hellinger Theatre. Spotlights blazed, lightbulbs flashed. Television cameras, autograph seekers, rubberneckers crowded the sidewalks up to the police barricades. It was the night of the thirty-fourth Annual Tony Awards.

Out of the cars and into the jammed lobby, people waved, laughed, kissed, and jostled one another. The air was buzzing with tension. In the theatre, commotion and confusion reigned. The ushers battled pandemonium, trying to lead people to their seats.

First, the television monitors flashed on. Then, the sound of scattered applause filled the room before the following announcement from the stage: "Nominees are seated on the aisle. Come to the stage as quickly as you can. Accept your award, go off to the left. The press will be photographing backstage. You will be escorted back to your seat. There is not much time. About your thank you speeches, please, please make them as brief as possible. There is very little time. I urge you. Brevity, please."

The houselights dimmed. The orchestra began, the applause grew louder. Colors brightened the television screens, the evening had started. . . .

The fifteenth row. Dany wasn't used to sitting this far

5

back. How long some of these acceptance speeches took. She was dying to look at her watch but she'd have to grope in her bag to find her glasses and she could imagine the sharp poke in the ribs she would receive from her daughter sitting beside her if she tried. They attended the presentations every year. It was expected of them. To dress up, put on evening clothes, to be seen. It was good for business.

What was that man on stage saying, the fellow from Hollywood in the dreadful dinner jacket? Before the announcements of best play and musical there was to be a special award.

"Hello. I'm Augusta Parker. Tonight we are saluting a phase of our business, a category that is often overlooked. We are honoring a woman who has for more than forty years made a magnificent contribution to that very, very special world. The artistry of executing costumes. For the ballet, television, film. And the theatre! Always here in our city, our bailiwick, she has tirelessly worked and created magic. Tonight we honor the great talent of this great lady. We love her in her fitting rooms, we admire her in our dressing rooms, we're furious with her before dress rehearsal when she is late delivering our costumes. And then we gasp with wonder when we see the beauty she has created.

"Tonight, ladies and gentlemen, after too many years, this long overdue tribute—this special Tony award to Dany Mounet."

To think that she almost cancelled this evening, that she had groused about coming, Dany thought. "You knew about this!" She leaned to kiss her daughter Veronique's cheek. "Oh, *chérie,* what pleasure!"

She is not very tall. Her walk is slow as she starts down the aisle. She is a Sargent painting, a Lautrec lithograph. Her hair is cut short, a fringe of dark curls at her forehead. Her black dress glitters with jet. She is in her early

6

seventies and she looks fifty. She walks faster as she nears the stage, with the gait of an Ellen Terry, a Duse, a Lynn Fontanne.

This has been earned, Dany said to herself. And what a long time it has been. But she was going to have the award. Her daughter had known and kept this a secret. How difficult to keep surprises in their workroom, in their business. And Veronique looked pleased because this meant something to her, too. This honor. Now to get up the little staircase to the stage and to do it gracefully.

Augusta Parker stood there waiting, the statue in her hand. With her stencilled smile. Ready to give the warm embrace, to bestow the customary kisses on both cheeks. All the years had led to this. A walk down a theatre aisle. To receive this from a comparative stranger, a woman she knew only in the fitting room and backstage, across the tables at Sardi's. What was she wearing, who made that dress? It looked like a monk's robe in silk. Beige raw silk, too heavy for a warm June night. The folds at the neck-line, the turn of the cuffs—Dany had seen such a dress once before. . . .

The applause sounded tumultuous as she reached the stage. They had asked for brief speeches and that was all she could manage. An elegant bow and thank you. Dany's long, slender fingers brushed back a curl from her brow—and a smile.

Yes, she'd seen a dress like Augusta's once before. It had been in lavender.

One

1980

Mounet. The letters on the brass plate were etched in Roman type. A discreet sign, not immediately apparent at the side of the massive oak doors of the brownstone house. If you were in the theatre it was understood that you would know. Dany Mounet. For costume fittings. On West Forty-fifth Street. Between Eighth and Ninth Avenues.

Dany had bought the house in the nineteen-forties when a magazine publisher went bankrupt. For over thirty years she spoke of it as her atelier, her studio. Sometimes she called it the workroom but never the "shop." A shop was where cars were repaired, where carpenters built bookcases. Dany had her affectations, they were a part of the aura she created from the first moment she started working in the house. She wanted the name Mounet to be famous in the world of the theatre. She disliked the term "show business," she never used it.

The curtained walls of the main hallway had been backcloths painted in the early thirties by Alexandre Benois and Rex Whistler for the Ballet Russe. An ornate and chipped writing table, two Victorian sofas covered in worn horsehair and three velvet chairs from a row of seats salvaged from an old theatre made the entranceway an eccentric reception room. Behind the carved mahog-

9

any doors to one side, a staircase led up to apartments.

"Instead of living above the store," Dany once said, "I live alongside it."

Fitting rooms were beyond the doors on the left, then the workroom. A track of sewing machines went down the center of the long, narrow rooms, the legs of old dining tables showed under muslin covers, wooden horses held plywood tops that were worktables piled with pattern paper and rolls of cloth. Metal bins tilted under the weight of bolts of fabric shoved into slots in a patchwork of colors: red to pink, purple to blue, green, gold and yellow, brown and beige. The flashy wall was a slapdash arrangement of crêpes, brocades, chiffons, taffetas. Dany's treasure of fabrics accumulated through the years on Forty-fifth Street. "My rainbow of silks," she usually said.

The morning after the Tony's, Dany came down the stairs from her apartment, her white cotton smock starched and crisp as always, ropes of pearls and jet around her neck. But today she was greeted by a round of applause from the workers; the seamstresses, drapers, tailors who had been with her for years, many of them since she'd opened the business in the old brownstone. They were thrilled to have seen her on television last night, they were a part of the acclaim she had received. She stopped to accept congratulations. First the shopping staff, the eager group of youngsters who went out every morning to look for the unusual pieces of fabric, the ribbons, beads and sequins in offbeat colors to be approved by Mme. Mounet and the designer of the current production being made in the workroom. The atelier, as Dany said. They were her "gnomes," the talented ones hoping to become designers she called "cocoons."

"Let them work in my atelier," Dany had said, "you'll see. After a year or two I'll show you butterflies."

Dany walked through the workroom gesturing for the applause to stop. She walked quickly, the long stride of an actress sure of her place in her own theatre. She nodded her head to the side, smiling to acknowledge her audience.

"*Buon giorno . . . si, si, grazie . . . Danke schoen . . . Gracias . . .* wasn't it wonderful? Yes, of course I was surprised." Dany stopped to make corrections on a dressmaker dummy, her eye infallible as she pulled at a skirt she wanted redraped. "No, no!" A gentle scolding, a shake of the head as if the draper were a naughty child. "And baste the hemlines, we'll finish them after the fittings. *Merci, oui, merci mille fois,* yes, I know. Thank you, all of you . . . no, now steam this, don't press it too hard." Dany's fingers ripped the collar. "No, my pet, redrape it, please. It's not sculpture, it's a fichu—*leger, leger,* light like a cloud . . ."

Dany stopped at the tailor's section. "Where's Veronique?" she asked, returning the embrace of a tall, bony man. "Benny darling! The award wasn't only for me, it was for you, too. For all the perfect suits you've made." Benny wouldn't let her go. Emotional Benny, kissing her cheeks, her forehead and talking too fast. "After all these years, can you believe it? Thank you, dear Benny. What?" She'd never learned Romanian but Benny assumed she had.

"Veronique! Where is she? Ah, there, *chérie!*"

The embroidery department was under the skylights that had been the solarium at the back of the original house. "*Chérie,* my phone started ringing at seven! Congratulations, first thing. And I haven't finished packing . . ."

The three Italian women sitting at the embroidery frames dropped their crochet needles on the stretched fabric pinned to the clamped wooden slats and sang out their praises. "*Brava signora! Bravissima! Ben fatto—*"

"*Mille grazie, cariné . . .* Veronique darling, maybe I shouldn't be going."

"I told you, Maman, I'll help. I knew you wouldn't

11

finish your packing." Veronique Mounet leaned over a frame scattered with ruby beads to receive her mother's kiss. "We have a lot to do today."

She is sleek as a jaguar, Dany thought. But what cat never purred? Veronique was in ivory and beige silk, quite a change from her usual jeans and cotton T-shirt. Her breasts under the silk blouse as she bent for Dany's kiss were firm and high, her neck smooth—not at all the skin of a woman just past forty. Dany smiled at her daughter. After all, it's in the genes, it's inherited!

"A lot to do? Why should today be different, when do we have enough time? Why are we still beading, what is all this?"

"The new second act costumes. This is the last bodice. You wanted to remake it, remember?" Veronique spread the beads and stones, fitting them over the chalked pattern marked on the taut satin.

Dany moved a few of them, twisting a length of bugle beads. "There! Outline the rubies in gold, make it bright. It will be divine." In Italian she asked the embroiderers if they could be finished by noon. *"Subito, cara?"* Dany's voice was syrup. "For me, for my last day? Give me a present. Work quickly." Dany took Veronique's arm. "Let's fit together in the big room, shall we? Let's do everything together today—we won't be seeing each other for three weeks!"

As they walked to the fitting room Dany stopped at a sewing machine.

"What are you doing, *liebchen?* Forget making button holes. Mark them with pins; we're fitting in half an hour! Why did they add another set of costumes at the last minute? Years ago we'd go out of town and make changes after New Haven or Boston, now it's previews here in New York. *Diamonds*—what a title for a musical! Ed Billings is asking for trouble. The critics can always say 'Rhinestones'." Dany laughed. "More apropos to call it *Paste*, which is what we'll be doing instead of

12

sewing if we don't hurry! All this last minute chaos . . ."

"The room looks quite calm to me, Maman. You're always edgy before we're ready to ship out a show."

"I should leave tomorrow. I'll postpone. I'll send wires. A day later, what's the difference?"

"Maman, of course you won't."

"Do you mind, *chérie?* Are you sorry that I'm leaving?"

"You decided all this three weeks ago," Veronique said. "You said you deserved a little extravagance, a gift to yourself. Remember?"

"I can call Alix in Cap Ferrat, you know. It isn't too late."

"Did I start this, Maman?" Veronique asked. "You're play acting and I just said the show isn't packed out yet. Don't give your performance before the curtain goes up."

"This is my stage!" Dany waved her arm out into the air. "And I'm *not* giving a performance." Veronique wasn't a child, but didn't she deserve a slap? "Don't be so serious, Veronique." Dany hadn't slapped her when she was a child. How could she do it now? "Maybe I shouldn't go —"

"Maman, this is your first holiday in years. Look at the perfect timing, you've won your award and you're going away!"

"You're right, *chérie.* After all, how many of my old friends are left? Alix won't ever tell her age but it's getting late, she's not going to be around forever and you know that Renee has been pleading with me for years to come to Provence. Renee who hates to write letters. You read what she said. Absolutely begging me to come for her *bir–s–s–day.* I can hear her saying it. It must be a milestone, eighty-five or ninety — imagine! She wouldn't acknowledge anything but a round figure . . . ," Dany giggled. "I can imagine how fat she is now with the food down there! Oh, Veronique, haven't I earned this?

13

I haven't seen Renee in years and I'm not getting any younger myself, dear daughter!"

Dany reached across a worktable to pull a jacket away from a draper. "No, no, don't finish that lapel! Such confidence, suppose it doesn't fit?"

"And we haven't all day!" Veronique chuckled.

"Are you laughing at me, Veronique?"

"Well, aren't you funny?" Veronique headed into the fitting room. Flowers crowded the doorway, spilling out into the reception room. "What's all this?" she called out.

Nancy Elmont, the office manager Dany called "sparrow," came into the room with a stack of papers. "Hello, Veronique. Good morning, Madame. Do you believe this? It hasn't stopped, phone messages, telegrams. And all these!" The sweep of her arm took in the plants and floral arrangements on the reception room floor.

"It's going to look like a funeral parlor," Veronique said.

"Madame, haven't you packed?" Nancy asked. "I have to get to the bank for you but I've been signing for all this for an hour."

"I'm speechless!" Dany squealed like a child about to open her toys, pulling at the cards on the wrappings. "It's better than Christmas."

"You have fittings, you know," Nancy said. "And no time now—"

"Don't be a girl scout leader, sparrow. Not today."

Nancy Elmont was nearly sixty, short and scrawny, without any particular style other than her pleated skirts safety pinned in gold. "She hasn't bought anything since 1948," Dany often whispered when she saw Nancy come to work in the morning. "And that gray hair in a pageboy! She's worn it that way since she started here."

"You'll have to leave all this till later, Madame," Nancy said. Her voice was small and shrill, a peep. She kept the books, did the clerical work. She filed, orga-

14

nized the schedules, helped the shoppers. Anything not to be exiled from the glamorous disorder that had seduced her the moment she walked through the brownstone doors thirty years ago.

"Nancy, you're right," Dany said. "Oh, look who's here! Has something gone wrong at the theatre? Children, you're early!"

The dancers were coming into the hallway. First a dark-haired boy in faded jeans and sweat shirt with a huge canvas bag over his shoulder, then another in washed-out army fatigues, a shiny duffle bag strapped across his back. They offered Dany flowers wrapped in green paper.

"You darlings, perfect roses, how thoughtful! I'm ecstatic!" The first girls arrived, more jeans and sweatshirts, jersey tights and T-shirts, each holding a single rose. "We're in the big room today, girls and boys together. Call Benny, the dancers are here. And, Nancy, no phone calls," Dany said. "No interruptions and I hope no criticism—designers, nervous designers! Where is that Jones woman? These are her final fittings, her last chance to pick!"

"This way to Bedlam," Veronique said. Thank God it was dancers' costumes being finished at the last minute. Dancers had humor and enthusiasm. They were usually understanding about the problems of costumes. And how kind and considerate to have stopped to buy the roses!

Veronique hated the fitting room. Before she began to work with her mother, she had been awed whenever a star arrived for a fitting. She was a child then, growing up in the workrooms, stagestruck as far back as she could remember. Her favorite actresses had come into the atelier: Katherine Cornell, Gertrude Lawrence, Lynn Fontanne. Veronique wasn't allowed in during the fittings, but sometimes the fitting room doors would swing open. The draper, the seamstress, the women who had

15

worked on the costumes would be called in to see what magic had been wrought. It was then that Veronique saw the finished ball gowns, the bustle dresses, the elaborate crinolines. Dany worked the lights, her special combination of amber and pink, called out *voilà!*—and Veronique saw them. The leading ladies of Broadway: Tallulah Bankhead, Ina Claire, Ethel Merman, Beatrice Lillie, Kate Hepburn, Helen Hayes, Mary Martin, Ruth Gordon, Shirley Booth.

When Veronique began working for her mother and doing her own fittings, her view of actresses underwent a change. When an actress arrived from rehearsal, dressed sloppily or in expensive bad taste, and proceeded to complain and criticize as if she were the Empress Eugenie, Veronique often wanted to push the pins directly through to the flesh. Instead, she watched, learned control and discipline, even affected Dany's splendid manner in the fitting room. Veronique called it the ego center. Dany could handle it because she was co-starring there; it was her center, too. Mother and daughter both laughed when Dany said it was easier to make scenery—at least the sets didn't talk back.

Veronique loved the workroom. Draping, watching the costume develop from muslin to final fabric. Cutting, supervising the stitching, the finishing. All of it delighted her—if only someone else went into the fitting room.

"Now Belinda," Dany said, "no carping today. A little enthusiasm, please. You're going to love it. And if you don't, then pretend that you do. It's my last day! You can complain to Veronique in the theatre tomorrow."

"And she will," Veronique said.

"Chérie!"

"Belinda, aren't you warm?" Veronique asked.

Belinda Jones wore ponchos and serapes to camouflage her large figure, orange yarn to hold the top-knot of her mouse-brown hair in place. A purple challis poncho reached to the hem on her black cotton dirndl skirt.

"You know how I detest air-conditioning," she said. Belinda was inarticulate about her work except for absurdly sensible malapropisms that usually gave the best laughs of the day in the workroom. She was notorious for the misspelling of her sketches but she had a brilliant sense of color and absolutely no intellect to get in her way.

Dany considered working with Belinda a near perfect collaboration. Famous for her interpretations of designers' sketches, Dany enjoyed going beyond suggestions; her ego was nourished as she chose the laces, ribbons and soutache for what Belinda brushed in on a drawing as Lucia's "Bridle" gown.

"Oh, dear," Belinda muttered, seeing the pieces of costumes carried into the room. A tutu not attached to the bodice, skirts and blouses not yet together. Benny wheeled in a rack of doublets and shirts, tights hanging over his arm.

"You said you believed in blue. Well, here you have it." When they were selecting the colors, Veronique had laughed and said Belinda acted as if she'd discovered blue. Now Veronique saw it was more effective than she'd expected. Belinda had chosen a range of color from the palest powder blue to hydrangea and the deepest royal and midnight.

The dancers howled their approval as they started to undress. Sweatshirts were peeled off, bras and T-shirts and jeans tossed to the floor as two girls squeezed into tight velvet bodices and the boys wriggled into their tights.

"They're not neat but they *are* pretty," Veronique whispered to Ryan, her assistant.

One girl grumbled about a tight armhole, a waistline

17

that pinched. Dany slapped her behind lightly and said, "Behave!" She pulled and pinned, ripped and tweaked at the blouses. "Beautiful, no? Belinda, they're gorgeous. Say something!"

"Lovely. Yes, they're very pretty," Belinda mumbled.

Two of the boys stood in their dance belts, waiting for Benny to find their tights.

"Look for them later," Dany said. "Fit the jackets anyway!"

"Belinda is blushing," Ryan whispered to Veronique. "Are there sexy thoughts going on behind those pink cheeks?"

Belinda turned away from the boys, then looking in the mirror, she pulled at one of the girl's skirts. "Isn't this one awfully skimpy?" she asked.

"You think so?" Dany asked. "We'll cut a new one."

"Oh no," Veronique said. "Ryan, get a length of bias, the fabric's on my table."

Quickly Veronique slit the skirt, draping a panel at the girl's waist. "Belinda, really! One skirt out of twelve? With the lights and the music no one will ever know."

"I'll know," Belinda said.

Veronique was on her knees, cutting the edge of the skirt.

"Ryan, will you finish this for me?"

Ryan took Veronique's scissors. "Belinda boring!" he said, pointing the scissors toward the designer's back.

Ryan was sharp and as crisp as his white shirt that seemed painted on his copper skin. Brown wavy hair, a short, narrow nose and dark eyes—Dany had called him the Caravaggio boy until the wide, innocent mouth slid sideways into a mocking smile.

Ryan worked with Veronique, draping and cutting with thick hands more suitable for carpentry or plumbing, but he had the touch of a couture-trained tailor. Having come to New York from an Iowa trade school

18

to live with one of Dany's shoppers, he had found the costume house too enticing to leave. He had been a skinny, inquisitive kid unafraid of work and long hours. Veronique was charmed by his unusual curiosity and now four years later he was her cohort. His body had been remodelled, but his humor had always been as scissor-sharp as his ability with a length of silk.

"You're going to need a little holiday yourself," Ryan whispered to Veronique. "Want to come out to the beach for the weekend?"

"Hush, you two!" Dany said. The problem skirt was forgotten, the boys were elegant in the ink blue doublets. The girls' tutus were attached to the bodices, feather light as they twirled to show off.

"It's the sky," Dany cried out. "Clouds, glorious clouds!" The pinning was minimal, the costumes fit. "When it's done at the last minute it's always the best! What is the time, am I late? Veronique, isn't it beautiful? Belinda, Belinda, well?"

"Thank you, Dany, Veronique." Belinda wiped her brow with a piece of muslin. "It does look good."

Veronique was on her way out of the room, helping Ryan carry a heap of costumes.

"Can you spare the superlatives?" Ryan wisecracked to Veronique.

Her mother was leaving for three whole weeks. Veronique pressed her palms against her worktable, shutting her eyes for a second. Tomorrow was dress rehearsal, and she'd be taking Belinda's notes because the foolish woman wouldn't have an assistant. Tomorrow afternoon. Long hours in the dark. Well, at least the show was at the St. James, the theatre was close enough to run back and forth to the workroom if disaster struck. Veronique dreaded the prospect. It was always the first time, as if it had never happened before. A dif-

19

ferent cast, new music and hopefully a new plot. Certainly the pain of apprehension would be in the air. Belinda would be scratching under her cotton serape at tomorrow's rehearsal, her nervous itch before her headache. Anxiety would tingle through the theatre. As if none of them had been through it before, as if it was the first time.

Oh Lord, she was tired, Veronique thought. She hadn't talked about it and if she did Dany would scoff. Veronique hadn't allowed herself to put it into words before but the routine was stale. Other colors, other fabrics. New sketches from one designer, then another designer and another. A year went by quickly, then another and another. Belinda's designs had been truly beautiful. It was never less than perfection. Dany saw to that, but wasn't it trite and worthless? All the hours spent selecting and choosing, then torturing the cloth into new life, were unimportant. It would be foolish to discuss it. Maman wouldn't take it seriously. She probably wouldn't listen. How many years had it been since Dany stopped listening?

When Dany decided to accept Renee Hugo's invitation to come to France, Veronique likewise had been longing to get away. To be away from Dany. No, it was more than that. She'd hoped for a month at the house in Watermill, Dany's little place near the beach. And if maman was going to be there then a rented house further away. Near Montauk or at the Vineyard or Nantucket. Veronique wanted to set up an easel again, to paint and to be alone. Away from Ryan and his young friends, those frantic weekends at the Pines. Because she was just filling time at Ryan's rented house on Fire Island. She knew she wanted to be alone and yet she was afraid at the last minute. When Friday was approaching and Ryan asked if she'd come away for the weekend she accepted him without hesitation. She couldn't say no, not because she'd be disappointing Ryan and his pals, but she was afraid of being alone.

She didn't have the courage to be by herself, holed up in her top floor apartment. Knowing Dany was alone too, one flight downstairs in her own apartment. *And happy there.* Maybe that was part of it. A weekend with Dany meant more superficials again. They never talked seriously and if she was going to deal with frivolity she might as well do it in the sun, without any critical glances when she drank another margarita, lit another cigarette. It was comfortable to be in Ryan's laughing crowd—even if they were too young for her.

Dany enjoyed her time by herself. After long hours in the workroom Dany relished her Sunday morning in bed with the newspapers and magazines. She looked forward to her afternoon walk on Ninth Avenue visiting her favorite shops, the bakery, the Italian grocers below Forty-second Street, the old delicatessen where she bought her chunk of paté for dinner later, alone in front of the television set.

No, Veronique couldn't bear that. It was a tasteless picture in her mind. Mother and daughter, lonely parent and lonelier child sharing their books and the music on the stereo. What did they have to talk about? The week's gossip had been exchanged while they were working everyday. But was serious talk that important, Veronique suddenly wondered. She whispered the question even to herself. As if she were afraid someone might be listening.

"Veronique, I'm going to open my presents. What are you doing, *chérie?*" Dany called out.

"Looking for the tights Benny was missing. Did you know Nancy hadn't dyed them? What color should they be? I know they're blue but what blue?"

"What color is on the sketch?" Dany asked.

Veronique flipped through the sketches on her table. "Pencil color!"

21

"Then *dye* them pencil color!" Dany pointed a finger at Belinda. "Naughty girl, why do you draw your last minute sketches without color? We'll do it later, Veronique. Come sit with me."

"We'll be into the first preview before the tights are done." Veronique walked to Dany's table wishing she could hit Belinda.

"What shade of blue shall I pick?" Belinda mumbled. "Oh God, I wish I could invent a new color."

"Yes, Belinda, of course. Picasso wanted to invent a new color too. Go through the swatch book and find a tone you haven't used—a clear blue, nothing too grey, not too subtle." Dany fluffed the soft curls on her brow. Her gesture. A bit of business before her next line. "A lively blue, Belinda, with life!" Dany wanted to open her telegrams, to unwrap her gifts. This was her scene and she was going to enjoy it. At her table, her corner, her walls covered with framed posters of all the plays, the successes and failures of more than thirty years. "We'll have tea earlier today. Come on, everybody. Time to stop now. You know you're all working tonight?"

Late every afternoon whenever overtime was necessary Dany served tea to the entire staff. It was one of her rituals. She poured from a huge old samovar set on her table, platters were brought in with sandwiches, paté, cheese and pastries, the specialties prepared by Dany's "United Nations" and in minutes the worktable became a groaning board, all work stopped for an hour.

Nancy came in with two shopping bags. "Ooh, Madame, someone sent champagne," she said. "And caviar."

"From me, sparrow, to all of you. My bon voyage treat." Dany knew what Nancy was going to say.

"Really, Madame, what extravagance!"

"Nancy—" Dany had expected it. "You've never been impoverished in Paris as I was!"

"No," Nancy said. "I've never been to Paris, you know

22

that. Elsa Groueff called, she's going to be late."

"Yes, I spoke to her, too, Maman," Veronique said. "She *is* sorry. She can't get here until six. You won't see her."

"Oh, what a shame. My darling Elsa. Well, it *is* going to be your show, Veronique, and you love Thirties clothes. It's the period you adore—and a small cast. It won't be difficult. And you love working with Elsa. You won't miss me at all, will you, *chérie?*"

"No," Veronique answered. Dany was being cute now, waiting to be told she was truly indispensable. "I won't miss you."

"Knowing Elsa, it is probably all designed."

Veronique couldn't resist. "And with no pencil sketches! The author is coming with her. Since when does the playwright come with the designer? Honestly, what a bore!"

"Noel used to come. I was mad about him," Dany said.

"This one is English, too," Ryan said.

"Ryan, you know everything!" Dany said.

"When Gruff Groueff came in looking for the color swatches—"

Dany slapped at the air, hoping she'd reach Ryan. The boy was fresh and Elsa didn't deserve the nickname.

"She told me the play was about a trial. A murder case."

"Ryan!" Veronique wanted to stop him but he loved hearing gossip before Dany did.

"Young man, you're in the wrong business. It isn't too late, you can change. Go to work for Liz Smith, or maybe to California for Hollywood Variety!" Dany opened a box letting the tissue paper fly.

"Where's Blackpool?" Ryan had to go on. "Elsa said the play was done there. It was part of their rep season and the critics were mad for it." He almost spat as he talked, making sure he wasn't going to be interrupted

23

again. "They called it the best new play of the season."

Veronique understood why he annoyed Dany. He was too pleased with himself when he had news about a forthcoming production.

"Ah, Veronique, look!" Dany pointedly ignored Ryan. "Roses from Angela and Peter!"

"Your favorite shade of pink," Veronique said. "Too bad they're not a new shade of blue."

"*Chérie,* what's wrong?" Dany reached across the table to touch Veronique's hand.

"Ryan irritates you?" Veronique flinched, Dany rarely showed affection. "Belinda annoys *me* and you treat her like an overprotective nanny." Veronique pulled her hand away from Dany.

"Shhh, *chérie,* she'll be back in a second. The minute she sees the caviar."

"I'll behave." Veronique sighed and handed a small box to Dany. "Here, open this. It looks fragile."

"Look at these divine buds! Rosebuds from Cecil! If he were in the workroom you'd be cheerier."

"Oh, would I?" Veronique asked. "For sure the fitting room atmosphere would be more enthusiastic. Go on now, open your telegrams."

"When I think how afraid I used to be before opening a telegram," Dany said.

"You? Afraid?"

"Oh, there were times in my life . . ." Dany ran her fingers through the curls on her forehead. "Well, never mind that. Look what's here!" Dany tore at the envelopes. "Pour some wine for us, darling. Nancy, Benny, Miss Jones, come along now. Everyone gather round. Have a drink, a little sandwich. You'll miss me soon enough. Three weeks without me nattering at you!"

Veronique drank her champagne and poured more. "Caviar, Maman?" Veronique watched her. Dany was like a diva surrounded by her claque.

"From Jerry, the sweetheart, and Helen, how lovely!

Isn't this wonderful?" She opened a formal arrangement of carnations, iris and roses. "Veronique, look from Peter Ingolls! Our lawyer sent flowers!"

"Mmm, they look like they were ordered by phone," Veronique said.

"He's a very busy man, *chérie.*"

"And we're a tax deduction for him."

Dany opened more envelopes. "From Oliver and Diana in Hollywood. Barbara and Arthur, the dear children! And Claudette!"

Veronique was too critical. Dany didn't want to look at her. Are we suddenly becoming enemies, Dany asked herself. Was Veronique resenting all this admiration, this tribute?

Did Veronique resent her own mother? Dany had respected Veronique's independence and Veronique wasn't a child, she was a woman now. Dany hadn't interfered, not ever. Perhaps she should have said more instead of allowing Veronique to go her own way. It wasn't pleasant listening to Veronique's sarcastic gibes these days. Veronique never understood the flashes of temperament, the antics of the peacocks in front of the fitting room mirrors but that was an essential part of the business. It was exciting, it was being a member of the company. And this was going to belong to Veronique one day, this entire house. Being in charge for a few weeks was going to be good for her. Perhaps Veronique might tolerate the ego and learn to laugh at the affectations if she ran the atelier alone.

Dany read the messages and opened more presents. "Alexis! And Celeste, Veronique, read this! Albert Costume Company! The hypocrites, they'll never have a Tony award for their assembly line costumes! Jack Albert, I haven't seen him in years. The nerve, the gall! What flower means jealousy?"

Did Jack Albert sit with his feet up on the old desk the way his father had before him? Was he fatter now?

Why was she wondering? Memories were jumping around, clicking on and off like flashing traffic lights. What was this? It had started last night and she thought it was a dream, after all the wine.

Did it take only a split second to know that you were old? Dany thought about her disdain of sentimentality but these people of the theatre had remembered her. Oh, she knew she was name-dropping. Maybe Nancy, Benny, all of them, were laughing at her but she was touched. Albert Costume! Had that done it, that arrangement of red roses? Good wishes from the competition she'd ignored for years — and surpassed. She'd sworn she'd do that a long time ago. Was this an homage to a very old woman — a final curtain?

Impossible. Dany thought of the mornings after a dress rehearsal, after an opening when she walked into the empty workroom. The airlessness, the coldness of the bare tables and the cleaned-up room waiting for a new production to begin.

There always was another play. Thank God! There *was* new color. Every day she'd find a new tint, a shade that she saw for the first time. That was it. Being able to see. Foolish Belinda Jones wanted to invent a new color! Didn't Veronique see color? You'd never know looking at her apartment. All that clear unmuddled white, her favorite beige cotton. Sparse was what it was. Veronique called it minimal. Yes, that was it. The least! Veronique ought to have more, she should do more. Maybe looking after the workroom on her own was going to help. If only she'd find someone to become close to, had she inherited that trait from her *perfect* mother? Was it contagious to watch someone being alone? It wasn't true intimacy Veronique had with Ryan and his crowd. They weren't significant enough for Veronique. Too flitty, too promiscuous, Dany thought. Yes, new colors were what Veronique needed, too. If only she'd look. Dany knew her old eyes weren't going to stop seeing. Oh no, not yet!

"I'm going to be away from these satins, these brocades and laces! At last I'll be seeing real color." Dany spread some caviar on a slice of toast. "The sky of France, the Mediterranean for the first time!"

"You went back once." Veronique was snapping again.

"That wasn't a holiday, it was to tend to your grandparents' graves. And that was long ago." Veronique remembered such trivia. She knew her grandparents were buried in France, how often she'd been told about a cemetery in Amiens. "Veronique, you were only a year old."

"Why have you never gone back?" Belinda asked.

Dany sipped some wine. Questions now, she thought. "Because I was starting a business, making a reputation." Her sharp tone was surprising. "And I had a daughter to raise." Dany smiled at Veronique. "More wine, *chérie?*"

She didn't like this at all. Clearer than any dream Dany saw herself in a cemetery. Standing at her own grave covered with flowers, fresh, moist with dew, and she began to pick them up. To run away as white cards fell from the bouquets and she didn't stop, she went on running. Faster and faster.

"Maman! The car's going to be here in half an hour! We have to get moving—"

"I won't take long, I promise," Dany said. "This is a twist, *chérie,* sending mother off on summer vacation!" Dany pointed to a box on the floor almost under her table. "Look, another present. I bet Nancy didn't see it." She tore away the tissue paper. "Oh my, Veronique. Cornflowers!" Now it was blue flowers, *les bleuets.* Last night a lavender robe. *Mon Dieu.* The colors were vivid in her mind. She saw them in an instant, the colors of memory. "Veronique, how I remember cornflowers."

27

Two

Dany read the note many times. Mme. Gerard Dessaux. The signature was in purple ink on lavender paper. She had seen the name before, but where? Maybe she'd read it in a newspaper. The stationery was expensive, the address on the envelope was in the seventh *arrondissement* and that meant wealth. The note asked Dany to call for an appointment, Mme. Dessaux wanted to order dresses. Plural. Not one dress but dresses. Dany thought she might have seen the name in one of the fashion magazines she thumbed through when she stopped to buy the morning newspaper. She couldn't afford to buy *Femina* or *L'Officiel*, any of the costly fashion periodicals. But she scanned the pages quickly at the kiosk hoping to spot some new detail, a collar, a pocket for one of the dresses she made in the small apartment up the stairs in Passy.

The afternoon she went to the Dessaux apartment on the Avenue Bosquet she was indeed curious. The circular foyer was something to see, it seemed awfully eccentric at first and Dany knew nothing to compare it to. She had never been in such a room. The stark white walls were lacquered almost like mirror, pieces of sculpture were placed haphazardly between stacks of books on tables with green marble tops and gracefully curved brass legs. The rough, carved wooden pieces and the gnarled bronze figures must be sculpture; childish, primitive deities from some unfamiliar country. Were these things of beauty or were they strange objects collected by a peculiar woman who wanted equally peculiar clothes? Then looking at the titles of the books, old, finely bound volumes of dramatic history and anthologies of nineteenth century comedy, Dany remembered in a second. Of course, she had seen the name in the newspapers, on posters. *Dessaux.* Gerard Dessaux was the well-known theatrical producer.

The tall woman coming through the wide doors was in her early thirties. She wore no makeup, her skin was pale but slightly flushed, her blond hair brushed back from her brow fell to her shoulders in a smooth coif. Only the pendant earrings, silver and amethyst, kept Dany from thinking she was looking at one of the younger sisters in the convent back home in Amiens. Certainly her simple robe was an ecclesiastic style.

"Good morning, I'm Charlotte Dessaux, please come in."

What world was this, Dany wanted to know. The enormous room was bright with afternoon sun and paintings on every wall. Lively, cheerful pictures. Still lifes, confusing abstracts and seascapes. Paintings of sailboats and beaches, water and sky. This woman must love the sea. Dany recognized the Matisse, a Miro and a sterile Mondrian against the dove gray walls. The flowers in the room were white, waxy lilies curling out of porcelain bowls, heaps of roses in crystal bottles. The windows were curtained in a crisp fabric. Those colors, it had to be! Dany appraised silently. They were silk prints by Dufy.

Three years ago Dany had expected to see a city blazing with Dufy colors. The day she arrived in Paris the mist and chill had covered the sky with gloom. She had anticipated brightness, glow, and music. Pianos pounding to a crescendo when the train pulled into the Gare du Nord. But everything was the color of fog, the familiar drab color of Amiens.

Three years and now the color was on the silk covering Charlotte Dessaux's windows.

"I've just come back from a holiday in North Africa and Italy. It was beautiful, as always." Charlotte Dessaux spoke in a low, gentle voice, breathing on her words, almost successfully hiding a stammer. "I'm an insatiable shopper as you can see and I couldn't resist the clothes the country people wear. They weren't easy to come by." She showed Dany the skirts, blouses and vests carefully spread over the charcoal velvet sofa. "I love the ease and comfort of these things. Look at this embroidery, feel the texture of this cotton. I thought we might copy some of them in other fabrics. I have to have new clothes for all the parties coming up. If only the couturiers understood the elegance and style of folklore. When we're finished and I wear them then they'll understand. They will, you'll see." Charlotte Dessaux held a skirt to her waist and turned, swirling the pleated cotton. "That is if you agree with me. Can you help me, Mme. Mounet?"

Help? The woman stood in her rich circus of a room, surrounded by her paintings, zebra-covered ottomans and tapestry-covered chairs, suedes and velvets and pale Aubusson rugs. Yet with a glint of mischief in her lavender eyes, she was asking Dany to be an ally in a game of dress-up, a masquerade. She had no concern about the costs. She wanted ravishing clothes unlike anything being worn in Paris. She held the skirts from Calabria, the vests from Agadir like stashes of loot. She behaved as if only she and Dany knew the value of the secret treasure and like a child she was asking for help.

* * *

30

Dany wanted to remember that gray September day in the railway station. She never wanted to forget it. For all the dreams she'd had before she came to Paris were possible. She had never talked about her dreams, not a word to anyone for the year after she married Simon Mounet in Amiens. She waited for him to finish his first courses at medical school, waited for his scholarship and the apartment he would find for them. Simon was practical and realistic; she was sure he'd be reluctant to talk about his dreams. But he had them, she had to believe he had his dreams.

When she saw him standing on the railway platform under his black umbrella, in his old, tan raincoat, she knew it was a beginning. He looked taller that day and thinner. He'd forgotten to wear his hat and his light brown hair was too long.

"Simon! At last!" she called out before she ran to him, laughing as she threw her arms around him. "You need a haircut! Oh, darling, Paris is somber and gray!"

"Not for me! God, I'm happy to see you!"

Then there were no words, only kisses and he couldn't stop. "You'll see color in the spring," Simon said, "but Dany, you're here and we're together now!"

Simon had found a flat in Passy, he thought it important for Dany to live in a decent neighborhood. The rent was more than he'd intended to pay but they'd economize on other things. He wanted his wife to be safe and comfortable. Passy was like a village, Dany would feel at home there.

"It's very plain, my love, but the Avenue Marceau will come later," Simon told her and she wondered what he meant. The few pieces of furniture had been delivered from Amiens, the cartons were still packed.

"I was afraid the van would be late," Dany said. "When did it arrive?"

"This morning when I came in from the hospital."

31

Dany was in the bedroom, opening the empty armoire, seeing the bare bed. "But, *chéri,* where did you sleep?"

"In the chair. For only a few hours." He came into the small room. "I worked all night." Simon didn't seem sure where to move, what to say. His smile was sheepish. "And I wanted to wait for you." His hand touched the floral ticking on the mattress.

Dany stretched to hug him. "Oh, Simon, then find scissors and we'll unpack the linens!" She had been waiting too. Shy Simon. Lean like a poet, his mother said, and reticent. He'd been waiting for this day, too. He was as impatient as she was but he was too modest to admit it. They hadn't been together for months and now, at last, this was their new home. Not the bedroom in Papa Mounet's house in Amiens. This was theirs.

"Quick, not a moment to lose!" Dany was laughing. "Get the pillows! Our bed, Simon. *Ours!*"

The plain little flat was easy to keep clean and Dany found the shops for marketing. She prepared the meals and went for walks, roaming the streets, learning the ways of Paris. Down the steps from the Trocadero, along the river, across the bridges. Dany found new places every day before returning to the apartment to wait for Simon to come home from the hospital. Across the Pont d'Iena to the Eiffel Tower, the Pont Royal to St. Germain, along the Boulevard Haussman, the Avenue Marceau where Simon hoped to live some day. She stopped at the bookstalls and made conversation with the vendors, sometimes finding a book she could afford to buy. She became a familiar figure to the booksellers, the young woman in her navy blue topcoat, her boucle tam pulled down over the tawny bangs, the amber eyes wide with curiosity, with eager questions and quick responses. She wrapped her blue knitted scarf around her neck and faced the cold wind, the cloudy sky. Dany be-

32

gan to know Paris.

Simon's schedule was difficult. He was spending more time at the hospital and endless hours studying when he came back to the Passy flat.

"Simon, I want to find a job." Dany poured their morning coffee. "I cannot be the lazy wife waiting for my husband to come home from work."

He didn't seem as surprised as she'd expected. He put down the piece of baguette he neatly dipped in his coffee. "In this depression? Do you know that the unemployment rate is worse than ever, Dany? These aren't easy times. What do you think you can find?"

"I can sew, can't I? If I could do it in Amiens, why not here?" She poured more coffee. "I'm used to working, Simon, and wouldn't it help to have more money?" Stitching inexpensive shirts at a factory back home had been the only available work for two years but she was efficient and faster at the machine than older, more experienced women. There had to be such opportunities in Paris.

"I suppose there is no harm in trying." Simon dabbed Mama Mounet's plum preserve on his bread, studying his knife, not looking up.

"None at all," Dany said. She wondered if Simon was ashamed of being poor. Surely it was no time to talk about dreams and she wasn't sure they were dreams now. Dreams were to be set aside, aspirations were something else. Something practical. She wasn't going to think about acting classes, she had to forget about drama school. There'd be no visits to a movie set on the other side of the city where she might find work as an extra. That meant being away from Simon for too many hours of the day. No, a sensible job was what she had to find. She mustn't dream as she did in Amiens when her foot interminably tapped the treadle under the sewing machine month after month waiting for Simon to

33

send word from Paris.

He wanted an office on the Avenue Marceau and she *had* dreamed of walking into his stylish reception room. The doctor's wife, the famous actress, the patients would whisper as she waited to see him for a few minutes before rushing off to her dressing room for a matinee performance.

No dreams now. Simon would accuse her of childishness and naivete.

"Be patient." Simon held out his cup for more coffee, trying to smile. "In a few years, my darling, all this will be forgotten. We'll live in the sixteenth *arrondissement* and you'll go to a dressmaker to have your clothes made."

"Dressmaker!" Was he giving himself away? He *did* have dreams! "Not for me, *chéri!*" She had to humor him. "On the rue St. Florentin there is Patou, on rue Cambon at Chanel—"

"It's fine to walk around the city, to look in windows, Dany, but don't have too many fantasies. The doors to Chanel don't open for people like us."

She walked the city with a purpose. She'd prove to Simon that she was able to find work despite the hard times. Forget the Great Depression that devastated the country. She walked and asked questions, climbing stairs and knocking on doors of factories and shops and she listened to the negative responses.

"Nothing available," a personnel manager said at a department store. "We have no openings in any section."

"Business is worse than ever," a factory foreman told her.

"No, nothing at all, mademoiselle. Nothing." The *chef d'atelier* was sympathetic but despairing. "We are suffering, the Americans have it worse and their buyers do not come. Not even to steal ideas, to make their own

34

copies of our dresses. I'm sorry, perhaps in the spring, for the next collection we might hire some temporary hands."

From the swank shops on the Faubourg St. Honore to the cheapest manufacturers in the Quartier de l'Europe, Dany heard the excuses, the same sad stories. In the late afternoon she went home to cook for Simon. She was tired and discouraged but determined not to show it when he came in. He didn't believe she'd find a job and he was quite content to see her waiting for him.

"We see too much sickness every day," Simon said. "And, Dany, there is so much more I have to learn. Sometimes I think the patient has more fortitude than the doctor. Let me tell you about one case. We must do blood counts every few hours. It is a rule and with this patient it is futile. He's going to die, he knows it as well as we do but the rules must be followed. If you could see the smile, the plaintive smile on the fellow's face. How he indulges us in our fancies."

"Are you surprised by courage, Simon?" Dany asked. "I think it's a quality we all have. But how often do we know how to use it?"

"You must be careful, Dany, try to keep warm when you are out all day. There is much pneumonia going around."

"I am careful, Simon." She cleared the table and he moved it closer to the floor lamp near the window where he kept his books. Before studying he helped her with the dishes, rinsing a plate under the hot water before drying it. When he finished wiping the cutlery he lined up the forks, knives and spoons systematically on top of the small counter. Dany stared at him.

He looked at her, his big eyes wide with embarrassment. "They're quite sterilized," he said very seriously.

Dany laughed, reaching up to kiss him. "Oh, Simon, this is not the operating room."

35

He prepared his papers for studying and Dany went to the bedroom to look at the newspaper, checking the employment columns to see if she had overlooked any possibilities that morning.

"You'll find something," Simon said. It was late when he turned off the bed lamp. "I'm sure a job will come along." He was soothing her, allaying her fears and at the same time he was making himself feel better. "This is a very bad time for everyone." He stretched under Mama Mounet's goose down quilt, nestling against her, timidly undoing the top buttons of her flannel nightgown. "Please don't worry."

"No, I'm fine, *chéri,* and I will find a job." She pulled at her nightgown, yanking it over her head. "I know it." She undid the string of his pajama bottom, stroking him and covering his face with kisses. "Dr. Mounet, are you warm enough now?" Her voice was low, teasing him. "I do hope so, doctor, because I'm much better. I have no problems at all."

Simon rolled over, letting the bedcovers fall. "Dany, my beautiful Dany."

"Simon, don't ever stop. Love me. Oh, your skin is so smooth. Never stop, Simon—" She was going to go on murmuring, to prolong the moment but he covered her mouth with a long, urgent kiss. Now it would be over, in a moment, and she wouldn't go on talking. He'd be satisfied. Was Simon embarrassed by her talking?

It may have been the lashing February winds that made her walk faster. In and out of alleys on the Left Bank, through the side streets off the Rue de Rivoli, to sweat shops up flights of stairs behind the Madeleine. Was it to keep her teeth from chattering that she talked faster, brazenly asking for work at Vionnet, Patou, Molyneux. She needed a job, she was determined and hurt. Nothing was available.

The rainy morning she applied at the factory near the Quartier de l'Europe she was impatient and angry.

"These few positions are temporary, you must be aware of that!" The austere *directrice* announced in a belligerent cackle. They were hiring hands to complete an unexpected order for English stores. "I need an expert draper, these are couture models we are copying."

"I drape!" Dany shouted back at the woman in a voice equally belligerent.

"Oh, Simon, I told you I'd find a job! I know it has been six weeks but I'm going to work!"

The stacks of medical journals had mounted on the table. He was absorbed in his notes, the papers spread under the lamp lit in the dismal afternoon grey. Hadn't he heard her?

"I'm glad, *chérie*."

"Can we celebrate, Simon?" Wouldn't he smile, wasn't he pleased? "Can we go to the Buster Keaton movie on your day off?"

"If you'd like. I must have this paper finished for my morning class." He hadn't looked up for more than a second. "Dany, I'm happy for you."

A month went by very quickly and Dany was walking again, knocking on doors and looking for work. She had passed the knitwear shop on the rue St. Honore, stopping quite often to admire the sweaters in the window. She took a deep breath, what was there to lose? She had the courage now or was it desperation to ask if they'd be interested in anything like the ribbon cardigan she had knitted every evening while she waited for Simon. No, they weren't putting any new styles in stock but if she could knit sample stitches, show a customer how to make a sweater . . . half an hour later Dany had her second job.

The first Paris spring came but without the promised

color. Dany was working, one job after another. Alterations for the dresses that were too expensive in a tiny shop on the rue Royale, at another factory making less expensive versions of Patou's couture collection. The salaries were absurdly low but she was saving money to buy a sewing machine. She had decided to work at home. There were women in Passy needing dresses altered or new ones copied from last season's couture model. She'd work from the apartment. She had a few acquaintances from the St. Honore shop, the women she talked to at lunch. A *vendeuse* could easily whisper a recommendation to a customer longing to find an inexpensive dressmaker.

Dany assumed she and Simon were happy, but what comparisons was she able to make? When the women at work stopped for lunch and talked about their families, their husbands, their parents they spoke with an exuberance and spirit she found difficult to match. It seemed bad taste to brag and boast about a husband who was going to be a successful doctor. Not when the woman at the next sewing machine was married to a garage mechanic, not when the girl opposite her talked about her father who was a postal clerk.

She hadn't met many men in Amiens, certainly none who had been interesting. Then Simon walked into his cousin Clara's shop one morning, delivering Mama Mounet's *tarte tatin*. Dear Clara with her vague pretentions, her somber store growing shabby without much profit from passé blouses and old-fashioned hats. The worn brocade settee, the chipping teak vitrine and counter, the dated tortoise combs and dull pieces of fake jewelry, the mirror darkening from age and not enough washing. Tall, well-mannered Simon on holiday from the university. Appealing, gentle Simon. He found a reason to visit the shop every day before he went back to school and then Dany met his parents. Mama and Papa

38

Mounet had heard about the girl from the convent who embroidered blouses in the shop. Cousin Clara's favorite. Dany felt at home with them from the start. One night before supper she heard Mama talking in the kitchen. "Dany has energy and spunk. She'll be good for our Simon."

Now when the sewing machines stopped, when her coworkers were finishing lunch they talked about movies, an evening sitting at an outdoor cafe, a Saturday night at a dance hall. Simon didn't like dancing, it was expensive to sit at a cafe. He had a goal, though he didn't talk about an office in the Avenue Marceau anymore. He said they were working for the future. Simon rarely talked about his colleagues at the hospital with any enthusiasm but he was eager to introduce her to Jean Paul Beaudry.

"He asked us to meet him for supper after work one night. You'd like that, wouldn't you?" Simon asked.

"Oh, Simon, yes!" She was delighted. "We haven't been anywhere."

"He suggested a restaurant near the Odeon, a very simple place." Simon wrote the address on a slip of paper. "Will you be able to find it?"

"Simon, do you think there's a street in Paris that I don't know by now? I'll find it."

Lemon color light gleamed below the dark blue canopy of the restaurant. The stalls at the side of the front door sparkled with oysters and clams on beds of cracked ice. Was it because she hadn't been anywhere or was it really that enticing? White tablecloths and hubbub, waiters in ankle length aprons, sawdust over white tiled floors. Noise and clamor. She was out, meeting her husband for dinner in a restaurant!

"At last, Madame Mounet." The man with Simon

smiled. "As I expected, you're beautiful," Jean Paul said. "It seems like all Paris is eating out tonight. Our table isn't ready. Will you have a glass of wine, an aperitif?" He was short, stocky, and pale; his complexion as grey as Simon's. Didn't doctors ever see daylight or sunshine outside the hospital? "I've been trying to get this fellow you've married to agree to this evening for months now. He studies too much and works too hard, your Dr. Mounet."

How well I know, Dany thought. What a cheery man Jean Paul was. And he loved to talk.

"I'm going to suggest renaming the emergency room Lourdes. When Simon is on duty there he wants to work miracles and, you know, I think he can."

"Come now, Jean Paul," said Simon.

"No, it's true. That old woman with the broken elbow? A cantankerous old bird griping about the world. She probably stepped in front of the car hoping to collect some insurance money but her pain was real. And did she make noise, until Simon got to her! He had her purring like a kitten while he applied the cast to her toothpick arm. As meek as a lamb she was. As I said, it's Dr. Mounet's Lourdes."

Dany looked at Simon. Was he aware of the affection and admiration Jean Paul was giving him?

"Enfin, our table is ready," Jean Paul said leading the way. "If you saw the monstrous accident cases we get in the emergency. No, it will be better if you never have the experience. What shall we have? The bouillabaisse is superb and the duck in unbelievable." The waiter took their order. "I want your opinion about the orthopedic department, Simon. I am very serious about specializing. Think of it, an office somewhere in the Alps! The money to be made in the ski season. Perhaps I can open my own Lourdes, a lucrative spot for healing rich broken bones."

40

"But so short a season." Dany sipped her vermouth cassis. Jean Paul enjoyed teasing even more than she did. "What will you do for the rest of the year?"

"Rest," he answered quickly. "Along the Mediterranean, in the sun. And, who knows, maybe I'll have the same clientele. Patients having swimming accidents. One could have a worse life, no?"

Dany joined Jean Paul, laughing at his silliness.

"Mmm, to bilk the rich," Simon muttered. "You were telling me about the new ulcer medication, Jean Paul, and the diets. What do you think?"

Dany had her onion soup. She remembered the advice of a sister at the convent. To be a good listener may be more important than being a good speaker. If this meal were a test she would be passing with the highest grade. Jean Paul loved to talk about their profession and he had humor, but Simon was very serious.

"And your day, Dany? How is your new job?" Jean Paul asked as they ate their dessert.

"I am copying dresses for an inexpensive manufacturer." She was pleased he had asked. "A Lucien Lelong. It is beautiful in a new silk fabric that is going to be all the rage. It is called *crêpe marocain*."

"It sounds like something we'd prescribe for a sore throat." Jean Paul laughed loudly. "And what does it look like, this copy you're making?"

"Jean Paul," Simon interrupted, "those bacteriology reports you spoke of, can you send them over to me in the morning?"

Dany asked for another coffee. How odd for these two to be friends. She thought of Jean Paul's sense of fun and liveliness compared to Simon's rudeness. There was no joy in Simon and it worried her.

Yes, it might be better if she worked at home, perhaps she could make him laugh then. After long nights at the hospital she could give him breakfast when he awakened in the afternoon. She could be with him when he needed coffee after hours of studying. She could put aside her scissors, her needles and threads if he wanted to talk. She'd be at the kitchen table marking her patterns when he came out of the bedroom, his bathrobe hanging loose over his thin, hard body. And if his arm moved over her back, if he bent to nuzzle her neck, she'd stop her work. They'd make love before he went to the clinic, to classes, to begin his rigid daily schedule.

The first days of summer brought sunshine that hardly reflected into the rooms of the Passy flat but when Dany finished a dress she rushed out to deliver it in the bright daylight. Off she went to unfamiliar, hot streets and strange buildings, beyond a hallway and a dour concierge. She peered at the clothes in the shop windows remembering the cut of a skirt, the drape of a neckline and she rushed to her notebook when she was back home, roughly sketching some intricate detail. Her work improved, her customers were satisfied.

The wives of the well-to-do businessmen in Passy did not keep secrets. "There is a most interesting young woman in the neighborhood, she can copy anything. And, *chérie,* so inexpensive!"

"I will tell only you," a matron would whisper at a lunch table when gossip was the main order, "but what a discovery, a find! I defy you to tell me if this is my Maggy Rouff or the copy that little Dany Mounet made."

Word was spreading and Dany had as little time as Simon.

The droning fan Dany had to buy for the kitchen table was a reminder that summer lingered on though it was September. The heavy tweed she was cutting made her hands sweat. The ice chilling the champagne she had splurged on was melting. Simon came in late and they drank the warm wine to celebrate the anniversary of

Dany's third year in Paris.

"The days get longer and longer, don't they? Are you sure you're not working too hard, Dany? You've been at it all night, haven't you?" Simon raised his glass. "To us, *chérie*. May the next year be successful."

"It will be, Simon. I know it will and I don't mind working at night. It passes the time for me. Madame Cassel wants a lace dress. I cannot imagine lace covering that huge body. Where will I find enough of the same design? But she is insistent; she saw a dress at Patou and—"

"Fat women indulging themselves in rich food and expensive dresses!" Simon said. "A boy was brought in today who had diphtheria. In 1934! We will treat the disease but the poor child is suffering from malnutrition. Imagine, a child starving in these times, in this city. And your fat lady with her ego! Well, what do you expect but frivolity from some rich Jew?"

"Simon!" Dany winced. This was new, this name-calling. The pain was like a dagger in her stomach. How cruel to brand someone he didn't know. She'd heard such temper once before, when she was going to work in the shirt factory in Amiens. Rich Jews, a sister from the convent had said, we're in their thrall. She'd never forgotten the expression in the sister's eyes, the disgust on her lips. Unreasonable hatred and now she was hearing such words from Simon! She wasn't sorry she had tried to lighten the mood with an inane story. It had been this way for weeks, for months. This gloom.

"Simon, you bring home your grief along with your stethoscope. You work too hard, I know, but you have to find a way to leave your sorrow behind. And, Simon, Mme. Cassel is not Jewish. If she were, what difference would it make to you? You lose your objectivity, Simon."

"I can't help it. What I see! I'm not working at some

43

fashionable sanitarium treating idle women for eczema or prescribing foolish diets. You want me to listen to details of a neckline or the shape of a skirt? The people I see are sick because they're poor and they're exploited by the rich. By the foreigners who have overrun this country and made too much money. The very people who need help are being used, and we're losing the best of what we are to these barbarians! And you want objectivity?"

"Simon!" Dany drained the last wine from her glass. Where had this come from, this tirade? "Shall I look for classes in political science at the university?"

Dany brought Charlotte Dessaux's peasant clothes to Passy, hanging them over the door of the armoire, the backs of the kitchen chairs, wherever there was space. She traced her patterns before beginning to transform the pieces into new dresses for Mme. Dessaux. She carefully pinned muslin over a vest, to the cotton blouses, taking tailor's chalk and rubbing off the intricate embroidery designs, the appliques of ribbon, guimpe and braid.

The legendary fabric houses, Bianchini, Racine, Colcombet, were pleased to deal with Mme. Dessaux and her new dressmaker. If a piece of silk was very expensive, but absolutely right for the copy of a skirt, then Charlotte had to have it. Dany Mounet became a welcome customer in the showrooms that had not been available to her when she was sewing dresses for her Passy clientele. A new buyer was not to be ignored, not when Mme. Dessaux paid her bills as promptly as she did during this time of very lean business. This young woman was irresistible in her plain blue coat, her crochet tam tilted over her brow, looking like a schoolgirl on a holiday shopping spree with her attractive, tall blond sister.

They met every morning. Charlotte, always wearing a lavender polo coat, her Hermes scarf tied over her head, leading Dany through new doorways. Charlotte loved poring over the samples at the buttonmaker, rummaging through the rolls of antique ribbon in the trimming shop, sharing her sense of discernment and selectivity. Dany was watching, then making her own choices and her instincts were right. Dany had taste, perhaps not developed, not quite rarefied, but Charlotte could see. Dany had an eye.

The Calabrian skirts, the Moroccan vests, the blouses from Catania were translated into Charlotte's new wardrobe. Dany found a part of Paris that seemed like a new home.

She coaxed the pleater into using a method dating back to the turn of the century. She wheedled and cosseted a temperamental old shopkeeper to make passementerie that was not used in the current fashions. Dany learned to inveigle and persuade. It didn't take long. Soon the craftsmen and dealers in the old shops along the rue d'Alesia were pampering the young woman who was sewing for Mme. Dessaux, the wife of the well-known impressario.

Dany made a skirt in royal purple, the velvet ribbons almost black, the satin edging shiny as eggplant; the lilac batiste top so pastel it was almost white. The beads Charlotte called caviar glittered on a mauve satin vest. Dany stitched silk floss in the gossamer blouse enlarging the muted jacquard design.

What a season it had been. . . . Charlotte Dessaux had become her best customer and her tutor. Dany didn't mind the cold, she wasn't bothered by the blizzard. Simon worked every night at the hospital and she was rather ashamed to welcome his routine. She left a hearty supper for him when he came home in the morn-

45

ing and she went out to do the shopping. She began her sewing in the afternoon when his sleep was so deep the hum of the machine did not disturb him. When deliveries were necessary she made them late in the afternoon and days went by without seeing Simon. Sad, Dany realized, to be avoiding him but there was no other way to maintain any spirit of her own. She could not bear being deflated while working. She was beginning to see a future in a world she never knew existed. There *were* Dufy colors in the Paris streets.

Sometimes she could coax Simon to see a movie on one of his infrequent nights off, an old Chaplin comedy or the new Eddie Cantor musical. It surprised her to see him laughing at the slapstick antics on the screen. He rarely laughed and it was good to know that he could forget his arduous hours at the clinic. But then when they were home he had to study again before starting his weekly routine.

"We should ask Jean Paul to join us next time," Dany said. "We ought to reciprocate. It's been months since we saw him."

"Hmm, *chérie,* what did you say?" Simon looked up from his book. "You know, Dany, these new experiments with insulin are fascinating. I am convinced there is a different effect if the injections are given in the morning. In the afternoon the result —" He didn't finish the sentence, he bent over the book again.

Dany stood at the back of his chair, putting her hands on his shoulders. "Oh, Simon, how many times have I said you should have married a Marie Curie."

He looked up, closing his notebook. "Do you think you'll be Mme. Vionnet instead? Is that one of your thoughts, Dany? What ambitions are you nurturing? I'm surrounded by calamity and poverty, and what are you seeing? Gloss, caprice. Your new client filling your head with dreams. I've told you before, Dany. Dreams aren't for us."

"Oh, no?" Maybe he wasn't studying when he turned the pages of his medical books and made his notes. Maybe he was listing his resentments and frustrations. "Do you work on dreams at the hospital, Simon? I had one, let me tell it to you. I was walking down a street. The Cours la Reine. I saw you on the other side and I called out to you but you didn't hear me. I waved and you didn't see. The light grew stronger and brighter. Suddenly they were clear, bright colors. I shouted louder and louder because it was so beautiful. You didn't see, Simon, and you didn't hear me." Dany went to the window, looking at the dark rooftop across the way. "We're walking on different sides of the street, Simon."

Where had it come from? She'd had no such dream and she tried to forget her dreams these days. But she'd said it, blurted it out and it might as well have been a dream. One that had come true.

Sometimes Dany stayed for a cup of tea with Charlotte after a fitting in the Avenue Bosquet apartment. Often she and Charlotte had coffee in a cafe after searching hours for the right shade of plum jersey at Racine, a particular tone of violet chiffon at Gourdon. Charlotte persuaded Dany to take time off, assuring her that a few hours at the Louvre was just as important as sewing. Dany's vision was changing, her scope was widening. Her curiosity was more intense as she looked at displays of china and crystal, furniture in the antique shops. She saw Lalique and Cristofle, Jean Michel Frank's chairs, Cartier and Van Cleef. She was measuring her own judgment, trying to define the integrity of what she admired. It wasn't idle window shopping now but questioning the design of what she looked at. It pertained to what she was working on; the jabot at the

47

neck of a blouse, the folds of a cowl she draped in a supple crepe for one of her Passy customers. Dany's perception was keener, as sharp as the point of one of her needles.

"I love to watch your reactions, Dany." Charlotte insisted they stop at the Galerie Charpentier to look at the paintings, then walk for a few minutes in the Tuileries. "You don't procrastinate. You looked at the canvases just now the way you look at a piece of cloth. Instantly you know how that cloth will cut and you see a finished dress in your mind. Either you caress the cloth or you drop it. You dropped the Miro when you saw the Pascin portrait next to it and I saw the pleasure on your face. It was as if you owned it."

"I'm learning," Dany said.

"I want the Pascin, can't you see it over the mantel in the library?"

"It would be beautiful on any wall." It was obvious that Charlotte would have the painting. It was nothing more than another cut of silk, the equivalent of a trinket. "The man paints with agitation and energy. I understand that, I'm impatient too."

"I've been that way since I was a child." Charlotte stopped to light a cigarette. "I was brought up in a world of adults. My mother took me with her wherever she went. By the time I was twelve I'd seen all the museums, I knew all the important galleries. I was taken to the ballet when I was six, Ida Rubinstein was like a page out of my Arabian Nights. The most exotic creature I'd ever seen. We were in London, my father had relatives and friends all over the continent. I wanted to go back to the ballet but Maman already had seats for the pantomime, for new concerts and she dragged me along. There was no time to see anything a second time. Oh, how Maman loved England. I was terribly spoiled. The only child always is, I suppose."

48

"Yes, I was an only child too." Dany didn't want to tell Charlotte about her father, the memory was too painful. He'd come home from the war eager to start his life again and the automobile shop represented a new spirit for him. Applying the knowledge he'd learned in the army, he was skillful with the intricacies of an engine, repairing motors and he was free of the poverty of Amiens when he was in an automobile. It didn't matter if it wasn't his car. And all that spirit burned up with the flames of gasoline when the garage exploded. Dany understood her father's spirit, she saw it in the Pascin painting that Charlotte wanted to buy. "I think we grow up faster when we're the only child in a family."

"My mother thought there was no child good enough to be my playmate." Charlotte stopped at one of the benches. "Shall we sit for a while, Dany? I couldn't wait to grow up. When you came to the apartment that first day I expected to see someone much older. After our accountant's wife recommended you I pictured one of the spinster ladies who work in those very proper Passy shops. Imagine my surprise. You *do* look like a schoolgirl. The expression on your face, Dany when you looked at the African sculpture in the foyer. You were startled but in an instant you recognized the charm. You have perception."

"Thank you. It is a compliment, isn't it?" Dany watched the children walking to the carousel. "Until I met you I didn't know any of this Paris that you've shown me. I know there's more and I want to see all of it. But I can't share it when I get home. I can't talk about my work." Dany took off her tam, the afternoon sun was warm and pleasant. "Simon comes home from the clinic with all the pain and poverty of his patients. He rejects any bit of joy I try to bring to him. He won't allow himself to see color, to look at paintings on his day off. This is a lonely pleasure I'm having." Dany clenched her fists. "How can it be so frustrating?"

Charlotte didn't answer for a while. "Because you're impatient!" She looked at the children spinning on the merry-go-round. "See how simple it is for them to have a happy time." Charlotte said. "You'll make your husband see, I'm sure of it. We do grow up too quickly but Dany, you know, I think you're the friend I was forbidden to play with," Charlotte stammered. "You're the little sister I never had."

"I hope you're free on Thursday at one o'clock." Charlotte rarely called, they usually fixed their appointments after a fitting or after a stop at one of the fabric houses. "We'll meet in the bar at the Ritz."

The Ritz! Dany had never gone further than the lobby. It must have been over a year ago on a spring afternoon. Restless and longing to see what she'd never seen, the lobby of a luxurious hotel. The men and women she saw there looked as expensive as the jewelry, the handbags and antiques displayed in the vitrines. She had been embarrassed and rushed out after a minute or two. "We'll have lunch," Charlotte was saying now. "And I have a surprise."

"What?" Dany asked.

"How can I tell you if it's a surprise? See you Thursday." And Charlotte hung up.

Dany's umbrella wouldn't stay open in the wind as she rushed down the rue Cambon, the rain splattering against her as she crossed the street. How odd, to be aware of the beauty of Paris in the rain. She hadn't noticed before but it was true; Paris had a shimmer, a kind of majesty in the rain. She winced at her reflection in the store window. She was soaked. Why had Charlotte chosen the Ritz? What was the surprise to be?

She knew she looked like a wet ragamuffin seeking cover in the warmth of the entranceway to the bar.

They'd probably ask her to leave. Charlotte waved to her. She was at a small round table with two other people. The man coming toward her wasn't much taller than Simon but he was as thin. *"Enfin,* Mme. Mounet. I am Gerard Dessaux." If Simon were as thin as a starving poet, this man had the slenderness of wealth. He inhabited a casual manner that matched Charlotte's nonchalant poise. His gray flannel suit was a shade lighter than his hair, his heavy brows were black strokes above friendly gray eyes. Charlotte moved to make room at the table. Dany knew there had been a reason for her nerves and apprehension. She recognized the woman opposite Charlotte.

"Dany, may I present Renee Hugo."

She was as famous as Marie Bell and Moreno, another of the famous faces from magazines. Renee Hugo extended her hand, the black glove soft as marshmallow. Her round face was dusted with pale powder, her large eyes elongated by black kohl and bold blue mascara. The voice was light and cheery, fluttering bird's wings.

"My dear, the dresses you've made for Charlotte are dreams! Glory, utter glory! Have a glass of something, you must be chilled. This weather, do you believe this rain? Have a Dubonnet, I'm going to have another and then we'll go to lunch. I must be at the theatre, Gerard. To hear the readings so let's have a quiet lunch near the Chatelet. We have much to discuss. All of us, we four. And as for you, Charlotte my pet, no trips, no holidays. Promise for I'm going to need you here for support." Her suede finger tapped Charlotte's chin, the black eyes narrowing in a mock threat. Or was she really teasing Charlotte? Dany agreed to the Dubonnet, she hoped it would stop the pounding in her throat.

Renee asked for a Montrachet rouge when they went to her favorite bistro. "To ward off the cold. We must have no sickness, none!" She monopolized the conversation, stopping only when a bite of food was being chewed. She gestured, she chattered with a brio Dany sometimes didn't understand.

"Ah, it is going to be exciting. Acting again and a real part. Who cares if it is in one of the smaller houses, we'll make it big! *Phedre,* my classic! No more stale mannequins in another boulevard comedy! A bare stage. Well, almost bare, remember, you promised me, Gerard. You know that stage hand at the Columbier was right." Renee turned to Dany, tearing a chunk of bread to sop the last of her coquille St. Jacques. She was telling a secret, a profound bit of wisdom. "The man said when there was no scenery you were able to see the words. True, no?"

Charlotte listened, Gerard nodded as Renee chattered on. Her conversation was directed to Dany and Dany had nothing to say. She wondered about Charlotte's surprise.

"How many producers do we have nowadays, except for you, Gerard?" Renee pursed her lips like a silent screen vamp. "You and Jouvet and Guitry. The glorious father, not the son. The son makes movies now! Do you like the cinema, Mme. Mounet?" She didn't wait for an answer. "Second rate! Except for the Americans. And Duvivier and dear Rene Clair. And *Mayerling!* Have you seen *Mayerling?* That man, the sex of that Boyer!" Renee motioned to a waiter. "Tst, tst, no fork for the marrow," she scolded.

Renee ate her pot au feu and when the waiter returned she spread the marrow on a slice of bread. "As for the couture! Will the skirts go any longer? What Patou did to us! We who must now hide our legs. Ten years ago it was another story. I wore Chanel! Not any more, I don't like her anyway. The woman is mean!" Renee's hand shot out to Gerard, pointing to his briefcase, a bread crumb bouncing off her blood-red fingernail. "Who is there in all Paris to execute my costumes for *Phedre?* Gerard, show her!"

Gerard brought out a roll of paper tied with a silver ribbon, untying the textured watercolor papers and giving them to Dany. She saw drawings resembling the Grecian figures on an ancient urn but the sketching of the draped costumes was contemporary, the lines of the body were elongated. The drawings were so light it seemed the brush had hardly touched the paper. Each sketch was initialled L.O. with a scrawled sunburst after it. Louis Ostier. His drawings were often on the cover of *Femina,* his designs in the pages of the fashion magazines. The costumes were sketched for someone quite tall. They might have been perfect for Charlotte Dessaux, but Renee Hugo was short. Beneath her black tunic, under her full skirt, Dany saw a plump body.

"You're asking me to—" Dany tried to hide her astonishment.

"We think you are the perfect choice to make Renee's costumes," Gerard Dessaux said.

"I told you there was a surprise!" Charlotte said.

"You have created brilliance for Charlotte. For her parties and dinners, for real life. Think of the magic you can make for the stage!" Renee grasped Dany's hand. She pursed her lips. "Please?"

Months later Dany heard that she had been selected for the assignment because no costume maker, no couturier or dressmaker would execute any designs for the temperamental Renee Hugo. They started working in a dressing room at the theatre that Gerard Dessaux had set up for Dany. How high-strung Madame Hugo was; no wonder she was not wanted in any fitting room in Paris.

"No, no. This will never do," Renee Hugo pouted. "Give me a waistline! Let me have a piece of ribbon, something to tie!" Louis Ostier was tired and annoyed.

53

They had been in front of the mirror for an hour. He sighed and gave Renee a length of seam binding. She twisted it around her waist and stepped close to the mirror, puckering her lips and squinting as she preened. "No, damnation, it is no good." She began to pull at the dress. "I hate it. I look short!"

"Permit me," Dany said. "You want to define the waistline but there is no waistline on Monsieur Ostier's sketch. Now if we drape up to the shoulder and bring the panel around to the front like this," Dany quickly draped the jersey. "*Regardez*, are you not now the tallest of goddesses?"

Renee Hugo looked at Louis in astonishment. "She is right!"

"If you have loose sleeves ending above the wrist," Dany cut the tight, pointed cuff Mme. Hugo had insisted upon, rolling back the sleeve. "Now won't your hands look longer?"

Renee stretched her neck and extended her arms, taking an imaginary curtain call, admiring her new image in the mirror. "It is so simple," she exclaimed. "Louis, this woman has genius!"

"Renee is not beautiful," Dany said after a fitting. "But what an aura she gives with a mere gesture. Her walk, the way she stands. It is miraculous. She's really not temperamental. It's what she sees in the mirror that she doesn't like. Why is she so fat?"

"You've seen the way she eats!" Louis Ostier declared. "When there is no lover she gets fat."

"Then you must find her a man. We'll have less trouble."

"There will be no more tantrums," Louis said. "She respects you now because you are direct with her."

"And Louis, you must speak up more often," Dany said. He may be the most talented designer but he is timid. "We have no time for timidity, do we?"

Charlotte called Gerard's little theatre a candy box but to Dany it was more like a precious jewelry case. She avoided leaving through the stage door, if the work light was on she crossed the stage and went out the front way. She went up the aisle in the dim light, past the burgundy velvet seats, the gold rococo boxes out to the ormolu mirrored lobby. Dany didn't believe in ghosts but she heard a hum when she walked through the dark theatre. She wasn't sure if the whispering was an echo of the past or the sound of expectation.

"Hello!" Charlotte had come in from the street. "I was backstage talking to Renee. She's very pleased. Are you?"

"Yes," Dany said. "Though she does fuss a lot. I think she enjoys scaring people but it is only a performance, isn't it?"

"Then you are on to her." Charlotte laughed. "That is good."

"Are they always nervous and worried? Actresses, I mean," Dany asked.

"I'm afraid so. This is quite a gamble for her," Charlotte said. "For Gerard, too, and he is not much of a gambler. Renee hasn't appeared in anything but comedy in years and now she wants to play this tormented woman. I suppose there is a desperation when you've turned forty. She wants to prove she can still do something important."

"You do not sound very optimistic," Dany said.

"It will be a curiosity for a few months. Gerard will not get rich with this one."

"I don't understand," Dany said.

"I'm not sure audiences will be queuing up for an ancient tragedy. These days it isn't the play to see as much as it is the play to be seen at. A comedy with an elegantly dressed star is more like it. The curtain goes up at nine, the audience has had dinner and they can parade to the bar during the long entr'actes. All very civilized," Charlotte hesitated, stammering a bit, "And mindless. We shall go one evening, you'll see. Ah, here's Gerard. I've been trying to explain your boulevard theatre to Dany."

"Not my production of this great classic? If Racine had known Renee Hugo he'd have written for the Grand Guignol." Gerard said it seriously but his gray eyes were mischievous. "The prima donna loves to have her own way. Is she behaving?"

"Not really." Dany smiled. "But she's coming along." Dany was grateful for Gerard's protectiveness. When she saw him backstage he was a respectful guardian. Was that the role of a producer? Was each department in need of chaperons and caretakers? She certainly longed for one in the dressing room with Renee.

"We're driving to the Avenue Foch, Dany. May we drop you anywhere?"

"No, thank you," Dany said. "I have some stops to make." She'd take the Metro to Passy.

The reality of a deadline was frightening. Two weeks to finish the costumes for Renee Hugo. Dany had to stifle her sense of elation, the peculiar intoxication she felt. The tantalizing peril that was waiting for her every time she had fittings with Louis. Dany was out of breath and yet she didn't want to stop running.

"Simon, I thought you'd be asleep." He was putting on his raincoat, getting ready to leave. "You haven't had a night off in months."

"I have a paper to turn in before I go to work." His kiss was merely polite and he seemed distracted. "I was about to leave you a note." He took off the coat. "Dany, you're not going to work now, at this hour?"

"I must, *chéri*. The fittings took longer than ex-

56

pected."

"Dany, I've been wanting to talk to you." He looked worried. "I've been accepted in the new lecture series. That means another few hours in the morning but it's important and I'm fortunate to have been accepted."

"You'll have no time off at all. You'll never rest. Simon, do you have to?"

"I'll be fine." She could tell he had been waiting to tell her something, trying to muster up his courage. "I want your opinion. I'm thinking about going on with other studies, specializing in hematology. It means postponing many things we've wanted to do. It means no private practice for a while."

She had expected it, she'd been sure of it. "Haven't I said you must do what you believe in? Haven't I tried to convince you of that?"

"Yes." His touch on her cheek was tentative. A gentle apology. "I'm letting you down. No elegant apartment on the Avenue Marceau. No couture dresses that I promised you."

"Oh, Simon, I don't care about dresses. I can make them."

"I don't like to see you driving yourself." He sat on the kitchen chair, folding his coat neatly on his lap. "I have a lot of studying to do. There are very interesting formulas coming in from a group at a hospital in Nuremberg." He looked more like a nervous patient than a doctor. "Think of new facilities, new treatments but it means a lot more studying, Dany."

No exhilaration, no light in his eyes as he talked about whatever these plans were going to be. Was he so overworked, so fatigued, that he couldn't even show enthusiasm about his new prospects?

"I have studying to do as well as you, Simon. I'm learning every minute of the day and it's why I have to go to the theatre at night. To see what is being done, how the costumes are made, how they're worn. This is all very new to me but I know the feeling of accomplishment from my work, *chéri*. It's a sense of stimulation, do you ever feel that way?"

Dany leaned against the table, facing him. "Other physicians have wives who go to work, I'm sure of it. Women who don't stay at home waiting for the end of the day when her husband comes home. What is there to cook a meal? To clean this flat? It's clean, isn't it?" She looked at the bolts of cloth, the pattern paper and the rack of dresses. He might complain but it *was* clean and neat. "I respect you, Simon. You must continue your studies, become a specialist in whatever field you want. But try to be happy. You can't take on the social problems of the world." She didn't want to criticize him now, he thought he was failing her. "Take a night off, please. To relax? In two weeks come to see Mme. Hugo in the play?"

"No," he said. "It's impossible."

"You could ask Jean Paul to take your place for one night. Or one of the other—"

"No, I won't ask Jean Paul! I don't want to go to the theatre with you. Do that on your own when I'm working!" He got up to put his coat on. "And don't talk about it! All your superficial garbage, meetings and fittings backstage, costume sketches!" He bent to pick up a magazine that fell out of his coat, rolling it up to put back in his pocket.

Dany caught the caption quickly. "France and the Foreigners." Simon did read more than his medical journals.

Renee Hugo won the accolades she had longed for, the critics approved of her performance as the tragic Phedre. They said she was a revelation in Racine's version of the play. One of the first comediennes of the theatre now took her place with the foremost dramatic actresses. Louis Ostier's decor was imaginative and Renee Hugo wore his costumes with style. But as Charlotte had predicted the crowds were not lining up at the box office to buy tickets.

"Will you have time to make three gowns for a new play?" Louis asked Dany to come to his studio, he was working but he wanted to talk to her. The sunny room was not as large as Dany had expected, though the high ceiling, the stark white walls, and floor gave the illusion of space. Clever Louis. He had covered the narrow sofa and two chairs in a pattern of indigo batik, the chests and tables were of pale fruitwood. The sparseness was a trick; it looked like a big room. Louis perched on a high stool at his drawing table. Did he want to be above his audience when he showed his drawings?

"You are so neat, Louis," Dany said.

He leaned forward, wiggling his finger in front of Dany's nose. "The mess is behind the screen," he whispered as if someone might be listening. "I loathe disorder. I have to hide it as best I can." He gave Dany some drawings. "There won't be much money for you. The studio theatres never have enough, but look, you'll see they're not difficult dresses to make. I'll give you the play to read. It's obscure but I think it can work. A little Cocteau, some Henri Bernstein with a dash of mysticism to make it avant-garde." Louis patted Dany's hand. "Otherwise, it would not be for the Left Bank."

Dany nodded, as if she understood. Yes, she had a lot of reading to do.

"Who knows?" Louis shrugged. "I can give it a style and we must go on. We have to keep working."

Dany looked at the sketches. "They're divine!" She caught herself, she sounded as effusive as Renee Hugo. She wasn't experienced enough to be imitating Renee.

"Of course, I'll have time." She was flustered, not sure how to behave. "I'm honored that you've asked me."

"And I'm very pleased," Louis said. "They're quite chic, no?" Louis rarely smiled. Short, round men were generally quite jolly but Louis was solemn as an undertaker. "You understand me, Dany. From now on I want you to execute all my work."

Soon, Dany said to herself. Soon she was going to need a workroom. Louis had said only a moment ago that he had to keep on working. It was true. She, too, must turn nothing down, no one. Not even Mme. Cassel's friends who wanted their clothes altered. Dany had to find women who were willing to work at home, who would follow instructions and understand her patterns. And if she could go on using a producer's available dressing room for the fittings, she could save money. For a small workroom. For her own atelier.

"Can you figure the cost of making these?" Louis was asking. "By tomorrow? We could meet for lunch, walk to the theatre after and I'll introduce you to the managers. Then it will all be settled. Let's meet at the Dome, it's nearby."

Dany walked across the Boulevard Raspail holding Louis's sketches as carefully as a treasured Renoir, a Degas pastel. She passed the Dome and wondered if she'd tell Simon she was going there for lunch with Louis Ostier. Simon. He'd look up from his book, mumble something vague and go back to his studies. Better not to speak, not to expect any interest and if he lost his temper again. . . . No, she'd leave the *pot au feu* to warm on the stove and she'd say nothing.

Dany thought of Louis Ostier's designs. Three evening gowns to make for three thin actresses. Louis made his little joke about the cost of the fabrics. Three for the price of what had been needed to cover Mme. Hugo! But were the three actresses going to be as amusing as

60

Renee Hugo? As warm and generous with their praise?

The silks at Bianchini would be perfect for the dresses, the jewel color chiffons that she'd seen a week ago. She'd stop there in the morning and have the fabric swatches ready for Louis's approval.

Dany ordered the silks, decided on the prices to charge for her work and she accepted another commission. Louis designed a dress for Lulie Amant's recital of poetry. Another studio theatre. Every week she listed her orders in the ledger she bought for bookkeeping. She sewed while Simon slept, wondering why the drone of the machine didn't disturb him. After the sapphire, ruby and amethyst gowns were prepared for fittings, she packed them into boxes and rushed off to meet Louis at the theatre. She ran to the stage entrance of the Theatre de Paris, the Porte St. Martin and backstage she was called Dany *mon amour,* Dany *mon chou.* The people she worked with were unreserved and genuinely warm.

She realized she had become two people. The dutiful Mme. Mounet preparing a meal for her husband before he went to the night clinic and Dany darling, Dany my love. Rushing in and out of stage doors, rushing from fitting to fitting, appointment after appointment, folding her work into her leather satchel and hurrying to meet Louis for a coffee at Cafe Flore, scurrying across the Boulevard St. Germain to join Charlotte for a quick lunch at Brasserie Lipp.

She wanted to shout with abandon, scream out with enthusiasm but the other Dany Mounet had to stifle her exuberance.

She longed to tell Simon about the Giraudoux play she'd seen with Charlotte and Gerard. What an actor Louis Jouvet is! Gerard says Jouvet is rejuvenating the classics. Think of it, Simon. You remember Jouvet, we saw him in the movies! But Dany wouldn't tell Simon, not when he was making his charts for the laboratory.

61

She knew it was futile to say that Charlotte had introduced her to Berard. Christian Berard! The designer who is considered a genius. Louis is a wee bit jealous of him. It was impossible, she couldn't tell Simon any of it.

"La Weygaud is the oldest costume house in Paris." Louis was the perfect guide, leading Dany through the racks of old costumes. "They are used again and again," he pointed to the cloaks and jackets hanging in front of them. "They may be rented for productions all over France or Belgium or Switzerland. A Moliere revival in Bruges then returned and altered for a Shakespeare in Avignon or a Rostand season in Bordeaux. They're supposed to be cleaned after each use," Louis said, making a face, "but don't get too close. This may be a robe for Shylock and with a change of collar, some fresh trimming, it can go off to Antwerp for *Macbeth*." They edged their way down aisles crammed with dresses and hoops and crinolines. "A gown for Marie Antoinette, then change the petticoats, turn back the neckline and who knows? It may be quite reasonable for Camille."

"Fantastic, Louis. This is fantastic." It was all Dany could say after seeing hundreds of worn, old clothes hanging in double rows and from pipes over her head.

"But not for you, Dany. You will make new costumes in your own way." Louis sounded prophetic. "I'm sure of it. You don't want the expense of a business this vast. It takes years to accumulate this stock, this graveyard of catalogued drama. Designers, producers can't do without it but it is not for you."

Dany laughed. "I'm not thinking of it, dear Louis."

Then he wanted a simple lunch, an omelet and cheese at Androuet. He liked the noise and the country food, the delicious bread before he went back to his studio to plan the scenery for the new Jacques Deval play.

"Didn't I tell you?" Charlotte asked. Her description had been accurate, the entr'acte of the boulevard comedy was worth more than the play. Nothing in the bar was still. The chandeliers seemed to tremble above the crowd, the gilt angels framing the mirrors quivered. No one seemed to care about returning to the theatre. It was this procession of scrutinizing, the parade, and the wine that they had come for.

"Look at Mme. Achard," Charlotte was a well-informed announcer. "And Mme. Lopez, in the Chanel." A woman in stripes of moire ribbon was unconcerned that her bosom was ready to bounce out of her flounced decolletage.

"It's a carnival!" Dany said. "More dazzling than the Cirque d'Hiver last week."

"You can be sure these acrobats are more agile," Louis said. "This is one performance I don't tire of."

"Mme. Mounet!" A short, stout woman pushed her way to the table, leaning over the velvet covered chair. "Charlotte, my dear." She wasn't too subtle eyeing the tucks of Charlotte's crepe shirt. "Wasn't I right about this girl? Didn't I say you'd thank Louise Cassel for the recommendation? I hope you're not too busy, Dany. I have a Patou, it's in green and I'd love to have it copied in black." She poked Charlotte's shoulder. "Is this something Dany made for you, *chérie?*"

Dany was embarrassed but flattered. Was there a woman in Paris without an evening gown? Was there no longer an unemployment problem? Charlotte had said it was all quite mindless and she was right. This was a sight, an irresistible spectacle.

Now Louis was waving. "It's Bébé, he's trying to catch your eye, Charlotte."

Dany looked over to the bar, seeing Bérard's shy smile. His clothes hung on his heavy body like damp laundry, perhaps that made him more noticeable. His carelessness was almost slovenly. And Louis was so perfect in his stiff collar, his immaculate tail suit. Louis didn't look like an artist at all. He looked like a director in a bank.

"Who is the tall man with him?" Dany asked.

"The Englishman, Cecil Beaton," Charlotte answered. "Attractive, isn't he?"

"Do you think so?" Dany saw Gerard coming to the table. Their table near the wall, on the edge of this dazzling world where for the first time she was a spectator. In a minute they'd be returning to the auditorium. He came through the crowd without brushing against anyone's shoulder, moving with ease and assurance. A word to Mme. Achard, a nod to Arletty who tried to engage him in conversation. Was the brazen woman flirting with Gerard? He moved effortlessly, unaware of the heads turning as he passed. Gerard was the most attractive man in the bar, his face tan against his white collar and tie, his eyes amused and friendly. Yes, he was the best looking man in the theatre. Dany watched him as he came to the table. His expression changed, he was serious and a bit proprietary. Why not? It didn't matter how many beautiful women were in the theatre, Charlotte surpassed them all. And now Gerard took her arm, leading the way in for the third act.

"Jean Paul has been accepted at the Institute in Geneva," Simon said. "And I'm going to join Dr. Colbe's laboratory team."

It was what he'd been hoping for, the goal he'd set for himself. Yet his tone was reticent and he showed no expression of satisfaction. "It's what you've wanted, Simon, isn't it? I'm happy for you. And for Jean Paul."

"He wants us to celebrate next week. At La Coupole, can you make it?"

"Simon, I'd darken every theatre in Paris, declare a holiday to see you out for an evening!" She wished he'd smile. How long had it been since they'd gone anywhere? How long since she'd seen Jean Paul. It didn't seem possible that more than a year had gone by. "At last, our orthopedic specialist in the Alps. How wonderful. We must get a table in the bar, it's the only place to sit!"

"Oh, you know that?" Simon asked. "You sit there when you're with your pals?"

"Well, yes. I have been there a few times, Simon." He was pale and glaring at her.

"But not on the sidewalk! I've read that one of the few things to be thankful for after the financial disaster of 1932 was that the degenerates were off the streets around the Dome and those other bohemian cafes."

"Don't spoil it, Simon. Don't ruin the evening before it happens!" He turned to pick up a book from the windowsill. "Where does it come from, all this hate and name-calling? Where, Simon?"

"From reading and talking to people you wouldn't understand. From seeing unfortunate cases night after night."

"Do you select your cases?" she cried out. "Do you turn away the foreigner? Do you reject a Jew who sits at a cafe you don't approve of? Is your clinic for the select few with a proper identity card? Do you investigate ancestry in your new lab classes?"

"I don't mean to hurt you, Dany, but—"

"You don't?" Dany looked at him, gaunt against the fading afternoon light. "You know how your rheumatic patients can predict rain, that's how I feel when I'm coming home. I'm expecting disappointment. Everytime

65

I see you, whenever we talk I can feel this gloom of yours and," she swallowed hard, unable to control her voice, "and this bigotry!"

Louis resented making changes, especially when the actress knew more than he did. Or thought she did. Lulie Amant wanted to wear solid black though the deep eggplant satin he'd originally chosen would have been better.

"She seemed to be pleased, didn't she?" Dany put her scissors and pin cushion in the satchel with the black gown.

"Very," Louis said. "Why she wanted to change the color is a mystery. If she's reading Verlaine and Rimbaud she must have black. Silly Lulie. She'll be compared to Moreno anyway and the critics will be ready to pounce." Louis sighed. "Dany, don't go rushing off. Walk with me for a while, this old place is too musty and I have to talk to you."

The afternoon sun was glaring through the trees along the boulevard. "Dany, you must start to look for a studio. You have to find a workroom." Louis sounded as if he were reading a news report. "Gerard will be calling you. Now don't tell me that Charlotte hasn't dropped any hints."

"Not a word. Why, Louis, what's going on?" Dany asked. "Charlotte has gone to Copenhagen and she hasn't told me anything."

"What's in Denmark? Porcelain? Some day Charlotte will run out of cities with new shops to discover." Louis stopped in front of Deux Magots. "Wouldn't you like a cool drink, a lemonade? I'm awfully thirsty."

They found a shaded sidewalk table near the windows. "Gerard is going back to Boulevard theatre. He's reviving an old comedy, a farce really and I'm going to design it. I don't want the costumes made at one of the old houses. I don't want Weygaud's conservative heaviness. I want you to do them. All of it. I want it to look sleek," he gestured a silhouette to Dany, "and glossy. So you must find a place to work, my pet."

"But, Louis—"

He didn't let her talk. "You'll have to hire people. Drapers, seamstresses, finishers, a tailor. I'll help you find a fine tailor and perhaps you should have a milliner."

Louis ordered the lemonades. Dany listened, looking past his shoulder at her reflection in the cafe window. Whose face did she see? Not the naive girl just off the train from Amiens five years ago. The image in the glass wasn't any older, the face wasn't any different. She watched the double image of the waiters tending to their tables, the blurring traffic mirrored in the window. And she knew. The reflection wasn't accurate; the strain and tension didn't show and she was seeing someone new in the glass.

"It is a turn of the century comedy called *Le Gout du Vice,*" Louis was saying. "Robert Venard will direct, he did the *Feydaux* last year. Renee's going to do her first character role. Back to the Boulevard where she belongs, in a comedy. I'll lend you all of my Belle Epoque research. Study the period patterns, the corsets, the underpinnings . . ."

"Hello," Simon called from the bedroom. He was tucking his shirt in his trousers. "We're meeting Jean Paul in an hour."

An hour. It was impossible to be calm and composed. She couldn't wait. She had to talk to him now though she'd been avoiding him all week. And she knew she wasn't to be deterred when she heard his negative reaction. She'd thought of nothing else since she left Louis at the Pont Alexandre. Thank God they were meeting Jean Paul tonight. She could count on his optimism.

"You've made coffee, do you want some more? Simon, listen!" Her hand was shaking as she picked up the pot. "I'm going to have my own place, my atelier. A costume house! Gerard Dessaux is going to produce a new play and I'm going to make it for Louis Ostier. Louis explained it all to me. Just now. This afternoon. He wants me to execute all of his work from now on. In my own atelier! And Gerard will speak to his bank. He'll arrange for financing. A business of my own, Simon!"

"Slow, Dany. Go slow, please."

"Nothing grand, a small space. I'll find something cheap to rent but, Simon, a beginning!" There was so much to tell him but would he understand?

"And what do you know about business? To open this, this house?"

"What do I have to know? They say I have a touch. Louis, Gerard, the other producers I've been working for. They say I have flair!" Simon was at the window, staring out at the street. She saw his hands trembling in his trouser pockets.

"I caress the cloth when I drape, when I sew. I can learn the rest. If someone is thrown in the water he instinctively swims, doesn't he? Do you hear me, Simon?"

He turned, gaping at her. She was too excited to stop talking. His face was blank. Was it fear she saw? "Oh, throw me out the window, Simon, and you'll see, I'll fly! Chanel has a touch and Schiaparelli, too. They make fashion. I'm going to make theatre. Isn't that more magical? Give me a drawing, a twelfth century tunic or a Regency negligee. I'll make it. I have a touch!" She put out her hand. "Touch me, Simon. Touch me!"

His hands were hot and he didn't move slowly as he

68

usually did. He grabbed her, reaching out like a blind man moving too fast and misjudging his footing.

"Touch you? Is that how it's been, they've all been touching you?"

"This too, Simon? Besides your prejudice you've been suspicious, too? You haven't trusted me! What have you become, Simon?" She tried to push him away. "What are you now?"

His mouth was wet, his arms burning as he pressed her against the table, pushing her to the floor. "Ateliers! Dreamworld, that's what it is! Get your credit from the decadent's bank, let yourself be used!" He was biting her, furiously clawing to tear her blouse, ripping her skirt. He was scraping her neck, his fingers scratching her face. No words now, only a raging whimper. He was gasping for breath, leaning over her and lifting her off the floor for a moment. "I'll use you, too, slut!" Then he was on top of her, relentless and demanding. And quickly he was finished.

Her body throbbed. Tears welled up. As she wiped her cheeks, she saw blood on her fingers. She wouldn't cry, not now. "Go to meet Jean Paul," she cried out. "Tell him what you've done." She heard the bedroom door slam. "Will you have the courage to tell him?" She was shrieking. "You're haunted, Simon. Do you hear me? And you'll never come near me again!" She pressed her head against the kitchen wall; she couldn't get up. "Never!"

Dany found a shop on the Left Bank, in a street behind the Rue du Bac. Small, but ample enough, and it was on the ground floor; she liked that. Besides, it was cheap. She lost all sense of time setting it up. Organizing a new workroom, planning the division of space. Gerard arranged the bank loan, Louis's carpenters and painters started to work. Sewing machines, tables for cutting, steam irons; all the equipment was ordered. Charlotte sent furniture that she said had been sitting in a storage room, it would be useful now. A few pieces for the entryway, a refectory table, two chairs, and a divan for the fitting room. A divan that was more like a bed.

"A campaign bed," Charlotte said. "You'll need it for a little rest now and then after dealing with all the belligerent actresses who'll be lining up for costumes in the next year."

Dany wondered how intuitive Charlotte was. A bed. How useful and what perfect timing. Could Charlotte tell? Didn't Dany's new shade of powder cover up the bruises on her cheeks? As soon as the renovations were completed, Dany was going to sleep in the fitting room.

The books, old magazines, cardboard patterns; all the period details Louis had sent were spread across the new table, waiting to be studied. Dany had to learn every nuance of shape and silhouette before beginning to execute Louis's designs. She had decided that the ideal way to make the costumes was to imagine that her shop was a dressmaking salon in this same quiet street during the 1890's. She was about to make clothes, real clothes, not costumes; though they'd be worn on the stage. Louis liked the sound of it when Dany told him her strategy. He said it was a perfect conception.

And sleeping on the divan in the fitting room would keep her away from Passy, away from Simon. The preparations for the new atelier came first. Creating the new production had to keep her from thinking about him. She mustn't relive that last evening. She had to forget it. She said it to herself, over and over, as a litany. Don't think about Simon. It was an invocation. Forget, forget. She was frightened being in their flat alone, terrified that his schedule might change, and she'd come home to Passy late at night and find him there.

70

Two weeks later she found a note on the kitchen table:

Dany dear, can you forgive me?

She held the sheet of ruled note paper for a long while before tearing it up. No explanation, no reasons, and without any apology he wanted to be forgiven. The conceit of Simon! Forgiveness after that raging fit! Where had it come from? That burst of anger must have been seething for too long. He'd been stifling his feelings, whatever sick and furious emotions they were. Could he despise the world outside of his clinic and his laboratories and classes? Did he hate her that much?

She'd been trying to forget but it wasn't possible looking around the Passy rooms. Seeing the books on the windowsill, knowing that during the day Simon slept in the bed she used at night. Dany had a hurried bath, changed her clothes and went back to the empty workroom with bed linens packed into her leather satchel. It was impossible to respond to Simon's terse note and she wasn't able to spend another hour in the apartment. Not until she decided what to do about Simon. And she couldn't think about that now.

"Merveilleux, little one! *Charmant!"* Renee had stopped by one afternoon to see what progress was being made. "I cannot wait to be the first in this fitting room. To see you and Louis exchanging those glances of consternation. 'What do we do with the fat body now?' But I'm going to surprise you. I'm dieting and wait until you see me in those period corsets! Ah, to be doing comedy again and what a part it is! I wanted to work out a new makeup," Renee said. "I wanted Mme. Dessaux to help me but she's gone off again. To London. Just when I need her! Honestly, that girl and her jaunts

71

all over Europe. She calls it shopping!"

"Renee, what do you mean?" Dany asked.

"Never mind, *chérie,* I must run." Renee patted Dany's cheek. "I'm very impressed with you, little one. This is going to be wonderful, your atelier!"

Wonderful. Yes, it had to be. To prove so many things. She must do more than instinctively swim now that she was in the water. She couldn't just flail about to stay afloat. She had to have technique and a direction, to move ahead and go fast.

The carpenters and painters were finished. The work-room was ready! Before rehearsals began, the cast came in and measurements were taken. Fabrics were selected, embroideries and trimmings were ordered. The staff was hired and ready to begin work. Drapers and seam-stresses, a young woman to run errands and go to the shops, a tailor and assistants to make the men's clothes. The charts were tacked up on the wall over Dany's table. Long sheets of brown paper marked into squares by Louis, in each box fabric swatches pinned and noted for every scene of the play. Petticoats, skirts, bodices. Jack-ets, trousers, waistcoats. Laces, ribbons, braids.

Louis rejected the first lengths of coq and ostrich boa that came back from the dyer. "No, no. They're too dark. Dany, they'll have to be done over."

"Can we send them back again?" he asked a few days later. "Now they are too light. Besides the color swatches maybe we should send the sketches. Let them see the value of contrast in the total costume. I know, it's only a tint off but it's very important."

Dany realized that perfection was necessary. No detail could be considered trivial.

"It's small, isn't it?" Gerard asked, following Dany through the narrow spaces between the sewing machines and the cutting tables. "Will you have enough room?" He was glum and frowning. "You're sure you're not understaffed, Dany?" He sounded irritable. She'd never heard him sound gruff before. "I hope you'll get finished on time. Am I in my right mind doing this? I didn't know enough to stay away from the classics so I come back with a Boulevard comedy. A sex farce." There was no mischief in Gerard's eyes today. "What a joke! What do I know about sex?"

Dany wondered why he was mumbling. It was as if he was talking to himself.

"This isn't one of my best days," he said. "Forgive me." He managed a smile. "Charlotte will be happy seeing all this when she gets back." His eyes were sad when Charlotte was away.

Not a day went by without a calamity, a blunder, some unexpected setback. Louis arrived in the workroom early in the morning to watch the seamstresses stitching. He watched Dany as she draped, sometimes taking her pins to show how he wanted the puff of a sleeve reshaped or correcting the neckline of a bodice. In the early afternoon he went to the scenic studio, then he stopped at Mme. Doucet to inspect the millinery. Late in the afternoon he came back to work with Dany, to supervise the fittings. It was easy to lose patience, to fret over details that went wrong.

"The fool!" Louis exclaimed, holding the lengths of taffeta from the pleaters. "It's all too wide. Did he think he was making tennis skirts for Molyneux? Much too contemporary! I want petticoats with tiny little pleats. Narrow! Clusters of them, to rustle and ripple!" Louis twirled, wiggling his hands at his hips. "Froufrou is what I want!"

"Why, Louis, what a good dancer you are!" Dany said.

Louis was blushing and suddenly quite solemn. "Send the pleating back, will you, Dany, please?"

The slender ingenue was disturbed and nervous. "Oh, I've never worn period clothes before." Her corset was nipped in properly, her waistline minuscule. She clutched at her decolletage, blushing and tears beginning to run down her cheeks. "And I'm afraid I haven't very much to show here."

"Don't worry, child," Louis said, "we'll give you a bosom."

Dany cut rough half circles of organdy, basting quickly. "Don't fret, *chérie*." She loosened the strings of the corset. "Push these underneath, now lift. Go on, try. You'll have a bosom!"

Claude Rimber, the leading man, tried on the cream color flannels and the navy blazer. He tried putting his hands in the pockets of the jacket. "Look at this. The pockets are too high!"

The tailor shrugged, not knowing what had gone wrong.

"Have you no eyes?" Louis was furious. "Didn't you use your tape measure? You didn't write anything down?"

"I'll lower the pockets, M. Ostier, and—"

"And shorten M. Rimber by three inches? This coat is too short. You've left no allowance at the hem!"

"We'll cut a new coat," Dany said. "Don't worry."

Flaps on the existing pockets would have covered the alteration, a bit of camouflage. But no, Louis wouldn't have it. On the next show, Dany resolved, she wasn't going to be this acquiescent. It was a waste of time and money. These fitting room surprises must be avoided. It was bad enough when the actor was temperamental and moody and asking for changes to be made. What was worse was someone in the atelier making a mistake. Surprises. *Always the unexpected.*

She had been trying to put off any decision about Simon, trying to convince herself that she could forget. A note was in the morning mail. Simon asking her to meet him for lunch or for coffee in four days, Thursday, 2 P.M. A little place on the rue de l'Ancienne-Comedie. She wouldn't call him to say no, she wouldn't ignore him this time or defer it. If Louis wouldn't schedule fittings that afternoon, she'd go.

Simon was at a table in the back of the little bistro. He stood as she walked in, extending his hand and then the tentative gesture. He bent his head—that dreadful moment—he leaned forward expectantly. Did he think she'd welcome his kiss?

"You're very thin, *chérie.*" He held her hand, not letting go. "Are you hungry? What shall we have?"

"Coffee, only coffee," Dany said. He was paler than ever. She wasn't sure how to behave.

"Dany, don't you eat?" Simon ordered the coffee. "It's been more than three months since I've seen you."

She stared into the coffee cup. Was she expected to be solicitous and concerned?

"Will you ever come home?" he asked.

"Home?" She didn't have to peer into her cup. "What home?" She had the courage to look at him now. "I spend all my time in the atelier. There's a bed in the fitting room. I go to the apartment to bathe and I try to get there when I know you'll be away."

"I'm so sorry, Dany. I promised you too many things and I let you down."

75

"Let me down? Do you think it's that trivial? Simon, the last time you saw me I was on the floor, bleeding. You left me there. And you say you're sorry about promises?" He laced his fingers over his chin, shutting his eyes for a second. "Sorry about your hate and your prejudice? And your temper? Where does that come from?"

His hands shook against his cheeks before he answered her. "From watching the sick night after night. Treating the hungry and diseased. Even the petty thieves who are running through our streets robbing, attacking. They're forced into crime. It's the only way they can exist." He spoke very slowly. "We can't understand that. We've had a roof over our heads. We haven't been cold and hungry."

"No, you had a meal waiting for you every day. You weren't neglected. Did you notice when you were eating roasts, when there was more money to buy food?"

"I didn't object to your work when you were sewing at home. But you started with those bohemians, the decadent foreigners—"

"Again? You don't know these people I work for. They have become my friends. You were never willing to meet them."

"For what? To be approved by a bunch of pederasts? Fakers and poseurs!"

"Who do you talk to? What do you read, Simon, to get all this information? Are foreigners one of your lab topics, a subject in one of those pamphlets you hide in your coat pockets?"

"I read about disease. I see it every day of my life. Incurable disease." He said it with defiance, the enthusiasm she thought he lacked for so long was in his voice now. "The sick, the poor, the exploited. All interrelated, all connected. If cures cannot be found then we look for new methods of treatment."

76

"A few hours in the theatre. To laugh, to forget and lose yourself in another place, in a magical world. That's medicine, too, Simon."

"From the parasites!" he sneered. "The foreigners! Like all those artists, the painters usurping the birthright of our own people. Tearing down France while they sit around the Dome and the Select!"

"Come see the parasites at work, come over to the atelier. Watch M. Ostier who starts at seven in the morning and goes on working into the night. Watch the seamstresses, the tailors—"

"And do they know they're being used?"

"How mean you've become," Dany said. "You resist any kind of joy."

"Joy?" His hand circled the coffee cup, tightly enough to break it. "Women at their dressmakers, superficial nights wasted by sitting in a theatre while the needy are suffering under the bridges."

"Those who want to find work will find it. I did. The Exposition has given more opportunity for work than there has been in twenty years. I pay people every week. Salaries, Simon! From my atelier, my dreamworld that you thought was impossible!" Dany realized he'd never seen her smoke before as she lit a cigarette.

"You left me the day you brought those dresses home from the Dessaux woman's apartment."

"No, Simon, I didn't leave you. I went on hoping that you'd find some pleasure in your life. Our life. But I've left you now."

"I'll see how far you get! Be careful. You may be reported as an illegal alien along with the rest of that crowd you work with."

Dany stood up. "Simon, I can't listen to this! You're without logic or sanity!"

"Sit down." He grabbed her arm, spilling his coffee as he reached for her.

77

"What are you going to do, hit me? Shall I call the owner before you throw me on the floor? Listen to me, Simon. You left me when you began to pity every waif and derelict you had to treat in the emergency clinic. You wallow in pity and that isn't being a scientist. Not to me. It's not altruism to go on the way you do. Driving yourself, taking classes and assignments to justify your inability to move ahead. You bask in hatred and prejudice. You can't understand people." She saw it clearly, if there was clarity to his madness. "You call names to protect yourself from your own inadequacy. That's how you cover yourself. It's like pulling Mama's quilt over your head!"

Dany stood up, she had to lean on the table for balance. "Paris isn't good for you, Simon. It has frightened you from the beginning. Go back to Amiens when you're finished at the hospital. Find work up there. Your parents will take care of you, if you don't hurt them with your new philosophy. You've given up on the sick and needy, do you know that? No one can care and hate the way you do. Make speeches. Go to Rome, Simon, or Berlin!" His brown eyes were wounded and frightened. "Remember when I said we were walking on opposite sides of the street? I was wrong. We're in different worlds. Don't call, Simon, don't write any more notes."

It was raining when she walked out into the street. She didn't mind getting drenched. She was going to walk back to the atelier.

"Three days before dress rehearsal, can you believe it?" Charlotte came into the workroom, looking for a place to put the parcels she was carrying, trying to unknot the scarf caught in the collar of her sable coat. "I saw Louis at the scenic studio, he says you work until

78

all hours without eating." She was opening the packages, taking out bread and bags of fruit. "I went to Fauchon, now stop for an hour. Do you know that it's past six o'clock?"

"Do I know what time it is? I'm not sure I know what day it is!" Dany laughed. "Oh, I'm happy to see you!"

"Do you like my new coat?" Charlotte wrapped the collar high on her neck, turning to show the line of the coat.

"Like it? It's magnificent." Dany remembered the first days they went to the fabric houses, when Charlotte wore a cloth polo coat, not wanting to look like the wealthy client out with the poor dressmaker.

"Now make room here at the table," Charlotte said. She unwrapped packages of sausage, pâté and cheese. "We'll have tea. You'll see, everyone will do better work afterward. Then I want to see every corner of this place."

"Gerard was concerned that I didn't have enough room. He may have been right," Dany said. Unfinished costumes were hanging on racks crowding the vestibule behind the worktable. "Nothing is finished but it will be. I keep telling myself it will be. It has to be."

"Are you feeling all right? You look pale."

"I'm fine," Dany said, "but you know the feeling of swollen glands that hurt when you swallow? I've had that feeling for days."

"Anxiety, Dany. Everyone has it in a different way. Louis sweats, haven't you noticed? Gerard paces up and down and cracks his knuckles. Very unattractive but I'm used to it. And he always starts the week before dress rehearsal."

"Do you get it? What do you do? You seem quite calm."

"What do I do?" Charlotte frowned, as if she was seriously considering Dany's question. "I don't have any annoying quirks or tics. Not obvious ones, anyway."

"Well, London must have agreed with you. You look radiant."

"I do?" Charlotte reached in her bag for a cigarette. "Tea every afternoon, the shops all crammed with delicious things for Christmas and it snowed one day. London is charming in the snow."

The tension in the atelier was a series of small firecrackers compared to the fireworks of the first dress rehearsal. This wasn't the small stage of a Left Bank studio theatre with four or five people preparing for production. Here were bands of people working with authority. Scene painters helped Louis Ostier put the last touches of blue to a Paris sky. Carpenters widened the doors leading to a Japanese garden. Stagehands made the scene changes look effortless, and the actors learned to work in the complex sets, timing exits and entrances through doors and windows, up and down a curving staircase.

Robert Venard shouted directions to the company, a burly figure in the dark, hunched in his seat, chain-smoking. He would suddenly leap to the stage to move a chair, demonstrate a gesture, shoving an actor into a new position. Name-calling and curses were followed by endearments, embraces, and then Venard started shouting again.

"Get that spot in focus! Madeleine, get on stage! Faster! Why can't you get it right? There you go, my darling. See how simple it can be? Now, get off! Go, faster! Get off! Where's Claude Rimber? More pink light on the sofa, Louis!

"Renee, don't reach for the cigar yet! We'll work out the business later. Ah, Monsieur Rimber has arrived. Cruising time in the Tuileries is over!"

80

Often Dany didn't understand, sometimes it sounded like a foreign language was being spoken.

"No!" Venard cried out. "Move after the line, not on it! You're losing the laugh! Get ready to clear! No, don't go to black! I want a soft fade! Louis, where's Louis?"

Venard was tough as a prizefighter but Dany wondered why he used face powder. There were many things she didn't know. Arcs, follow spots, wings, flats. Scrim, house lights, pin spot.

Costume changes were as quick as Venard's temper. An actress came off stage, her dressers found her in the dark. Hands were at the back of her dress, it fell to the floor. Next to it on a muslin cloth was a circle of crushed velvet. She stepped into the circle, it was hoisted up, the waistline was secured, arms reached into sleeves, hooks were quickly slipped into their eyes. Presto, in seconds she was dressed again and onstage.

No time for bewilderment, no mistakes. Dany understood the importance of perfection, what Louis had sought to achieve during the weeks of fittings.

"Very attractive, this Dany Mounet, isn't she?" Dany heard the voice whispering in the wings.

"Forget it, *mon amour*, I've heard there is a husband," came the response.

Dany wormed her way past the stage manager's table out to the auditorium. Yes, there is a husband. She thought of the actors' love of gossip. Even in the dark, before making an entrance at rehearsal, the actors could gossip. Yes, there was a husband not too far away, probably bent over a microscope in a laboratory or at an examining table in emergency. Or having a coffee on his recess and studying a political pamphlet, reading an article on saving the country before the usurious bankers, the parasite financiers took over. Dany ran through the stage door, letting it slam too loudly. She had to

81

join Louis out front, to listen to his notes, his dry comments and sharp criticism. She had to forget, she told herself. Forget there was a husband.

It was over. Rehearsal was finished and notes came from everywhere. From Robert Venard to Louis, Louis to Gerard, the stage manager to the actors. Notes for the wardrobe mistress, the property man.

Charlotte whispered notes to Gerard, Gerard whispered to Venard. Then aloud he gave notes to Claude Rimber and Renee Hugo.

It was over but there was work to be done early the next morning, before the afternoon rehearsal. And tomorrow night—the first performance was tomorrow night.

Dany followed Louis up the aisle of the darkening theatre in time to hear the gasp of approval for the scenery when the curtain rose. Then applause for Renee Hugo's entrance and the warming, contagious sound of the audience laughing.

She knew why Gerard was thin; he couldn't stop walking. He paced when he was worried and the producer always worried. He went back and forth at the top of the aisle and out into the lobby. A minute later Dany heard the crack of knuckles, Gerard was back again standing with Robert Venard. She went backstage with Louis at the entr'acte, listened to his nervous words with the stage manager about the final light cues and then they went out again.

Charlotte left her seat to stand with Gerard, he stopped pacing now. The final moment was near. Gerard waved Louis and Dany over; they all stood together for the last barrage of laughter and the happy wallop of the curtain hitting the stage. A fraction of a second, the curtain was up again and then applause. Rumbling, jubilant applause.

Dany shut her eyes, hearing the shouts of bravo. Louis took her hand, holding her tight. "Thank you, Dany," he whispered.

"This is for you too, Dany," Gerard said. The applause continued. "For all the work you've done."

"Charlotte, you know how to make an aging actress happy!" Renee called out from the foyer. "I said aging, not aged!"

The Dessaux apartment was glowing with candlelight, an opaline shimmer filled the rooms from lamps hidden in corners, rose silk scarfs covering the shades.

"Everyone is here and everyone looks so young! My clever Charlotte using pink," Renee shouted. "I may get quite drunk! I think we have a success, little one," she murmured to Dany.

The rooms were swarming with happy people. It seemed that Charlotte had invited all of Paris, confident that the play was to be well-received. She was at the fireplace waving Dany into the room.

"Did you hear the bravos? Oh, Charlotte—"

"Dany, you don't have to say it. Thanks aren't necessary," Charlotte said.

"I must. And Gerard said I was a part of it. That was very generous."

"A very generous man, our Gerard," Charlotte was beaming.

"Our most cynical naysayers are excited." Gerard was flushed, his gray eyes dancing. "Give them an old-fashioned farce and they squeal with delight! They say we've cleared away the cobwebs, we've given Paris spirit." He held Charlotte's arm. "And an early spring!"

"Dany, you haven't met Arthur Bellamy," Charlotte said, moving away from Gerard.

They had said an American friend was coming to see the play. Arthur Bellamy's reputation was as distinguished as Gerard's. He owned theatres and produced in New York and London.

"I'd like to bring it to New York. The same production, every detail of it," Arthur Bellamy said. "Louis Ostier can have a great career in America. Where is he? I must meet him. And we have no one executing costumes as elegantly as what I saw tonight. Would you consider a shop in New York, mademoiselle?"

"I've never thought about it, Monsieur Bellamy, and it is *Madame* Mounet." Preposterous ideas and grandiose notions were always part of the conversation with theatre people. Dany wasn't used to it but it was as seductive as their use of unrestrained adjectives.

Fanciful thoughts danced in her head all the way back to the atelier. More work, new plays to make. Perhaps a commission for the Comedie, for Jouvet. A costume house in New York. She'd never thought about that, she had never dreamed . . . and a new place to live, an apartment. A small flat above the workroom was going to be available. That would be convenient. But then she had to think about Simon.

The phone was ringing when she came into the hallway. No one ever called after the work day. Had something been forgotten at the theatre? She switched on the lights, running to her worktable.

"Dany? This is Dr. Beaudry. Jean Paul." She held her breath, somehow she knew before she heard him go on. "There has been an accident. It's Simon. Can you get here immediately, or shall I come for you?"

Dany walked through the door of the emergency clinic, down the long passageway to the operating room. The orderly at the desk was wearing a green jacket, the walls of the corridor were green. Past open doors she could see into small rooms divided by overhead rails hung with cotton curtains. Pale, pea soup-green cotton. Dr. Beaudry was waiting for her, the orderly had said. He was coming through the doors at the end of the hall. Jean Paul, too, his cotton coat was green. The color of misfortune. How long ago had it been since Renee Hugo told her that it was one of the old superstitions. Green was bad luck on the stage and Renee believed in all that. Even in real life it was bad luck and Dany believed it, too.

Jean Paul put his hands on Dany's shoulders as if he was going to stop her from walking through the doors to the operating room. His words were faint, hardly more than a whisper. She wanted him to speak louder and yet she hoped she wasn't going to hear him at all.

"Dany, Dany. It's over. The doctor worked as quickly as possible but it was too late." Jean Paul's words came rushing at her now. "The hemorrhage couldn't be stopped. The wounds were too deep."

"Jean Paul, what happened?" She heard herself, fairly shouting at him. "Before you called me. How did this happen?"

"He was walking back from the bakery he went to on his evening break," Jean Paul said. His grip on her shoulders softened. "Who can understand the motives when these things happen? There have been robberies all over the city for months now but usually near a restaurant or a cabaret. Nothing posh or expensive like that around here, but Simon was robbed. He must have put up quite a fight, to have been stabbed that many times. He had to have been damned mad. Or gotten the thief mighty angry."

"You think Simon was mad?"

"He must have fought back, Dany. He was carrying a bag of pastry to have with his coffee. He only had a few francs on him. We never have any cash around here. Simon didn't look wealthy, not in that old tan raincoat of his."

Six years ago Simon was waiting on the platform at the railway station. In his tan raincoat, with his black umbrella. Needing a haircut and smiling expectantly.

"Dany, his face was badly cut," Jean Paul said.

"Oh, no. Do I have to see him, Jean Paul? Will I have to identify him?"

"No, I don't think so. I'll take care of it. There wasn't a single witness, not a soul on the street and he dragged himself up here to the emergency. What irony! Remember when I called this place Simon's Lourdes?"

"Yes, doesn't it seem like a long time ago? Before he changed, before he began to hate." There was no air in the deserted corridor and she needed to breathe. "Poor Simon. Can we go out of here for a little while? Will you walk over to the river, Jean Paul, for just a few minutes?"

She had been taken to the sea a few weeks after her mother died. The sisters had arranged an outing for the class, a trip to the ocean on an early spring day. To see the vast, flat expanse, like an endless lake with no far shore and no strong tide. Only the gentle rippling motion as the ocean met the sky off in the distance. The smooth, lonely sea had brought calm for the first time since she saw her mother die in the hospital. Dany thought her mother had gone to sleep for a while, that happened so often during those last days. Maman fell asleep and Dany sat, waiting until she opened her eyes again, to stare at the ceiling, unable to speak. Then the nurse came in to examine her and she said that at last Maman had found peace in eternal sleep.

Dany wanted to see the river now, she wanted to walk with Jean Paul to see the gentle current of the river.

They walked along the quiet streets without speaking until they reached the stone wall facing the Seine. The dark gray river trembling in the flashing reflection of the street lamps.

"Is this real, Jean Paul? Has this actually happened?" Dany watched the current rushing in cross directions. "Simon was killed by a robber on the street! Simon going on and on again about the needy, the poor exploited souls who came in and out of the clinic, understanding how they could be driven to petty crimes. One of them had a knife and killed Simon tonight! Jean Paul, what kind of crazy justice is there for this to have happened?" What a strange pair they must be standing at the embankment, Dany thought. A doctor with his coat over his work uniform and a woman in an evening gown. The first long dress she'd worn since she'd married Simon. What would a passerby think; that these two had found each other in the Luxembourg Gardens?

"How much did he tell you?" Dany asked. "You were his only friend. Did you share his politics, those rabid ideas he'd rave on about? Did you talk about that when you were together?"

"Talk, Dany?" Jean Paul snickered. "We argued. It got to the point I couldn't listen to him." He took cigarettes from his coat, offering one to Dany. "Poverty became attractive to Simon in the most perverse way, I think. He became obsessed with injustice. It was as if each case, somebody in an accident or some poor soul riddled with disease, had been stricken by the hand of a cruel despot, some devil. It was a mania he had, making the patient into a miserable victim. And he became cruel. When he began to go off by himself to read his fascist literature he withdrew and changed into an unreasonable man I'd never known before."

"I wondered if you knew how many times I wanted to talk to you about him."

"He had it all twisted, Dany. It wasn't the medication, the possible diagnosis or the research for a cure that he was interested in. Instead, he'd finish one of his pamphlets and he'd start attacking the Rothschilds, the bankers. They were responsible for all the anguish and despair he dealt with every day."

"I began to think that I was the reason for this turn he took," Dany said.

"No, I don't think so. Simon was afraid to accept pleasure. And yet he loved you. Maybe he was attracted to what he most feared and had to attack because of that fear. Why, though, was he afraid?"

"I've wondered. And, Jean Paul, we will never know." She wished she could cry but she couldn't. We don't cry, one of the sisters at the convent used to say. It was something that wasn't done. No crying, no coughing. No rude sounds. Had Jean Paul been educated by priests? Strict fathers who taught him discipline and deportment the way the sisters had trained her in Amiens.

Amiens. Simon had to be taken home, to his parents. To the cemetery outside of town, to those cold steps she'd walked along for her father's burial. And then her mother's. She knew the way to that cemetery. She could hear the sounds of a funeral, the voice of the priest, the prayers without passion. Cold, distant words without consolation. She was a child then and now it was Maman and Papa Mounet who would need consolation.

She had to go to the atelier, she had to use the telephone there. Arrangements had to be made.

"I'll have to lie, Jean Paul. His parents in Amiens mustn't know what he'd become. It won't hurt to lie, will it? What will be gained if those sweet people know that Simon had become a fascist? That he was violent? No, they'll know that noble Simon was devoting his life to research and science. Good, brave Simon sacrificing himself night after night in the clinic. That's what they've known and it's enough. A martyr held up in the street by a thief and murdered! They don't have to know that he attacked me, that his mind was filled with hate.

They don't have to know that, do they?" Oh, it was hard to keep from crying now. "Has God done me a favor, Jean Paul? Is this a blessing after all?"

The raucous clamor that had sounded in the atelier only ten days ago was gone. Dany came back to Paris, to the deserted workroom with dust gathering on her worktable and over the cloth hoods covering the sewing machines. Ten long, sad days of futile police investigation and the funeral in Amiens.

It wasn't in the proper sequence of life for parents to live and bury an only son. Dany had thought it unfair for a child to be alone without parents but how much worse this had been. Maman and Papa Mounet, disconsolate but loving and caring. Go back to Paris, Maman had said, back to work, make a success in your new world.

Yes, Dany said to herself, success will make noise in the workroom again. That agreeable sound. Now more than ever before she had to hear it, like swarming bees and noisy traffic. Sounds of activity to help her forget.

Gerard's production of *Gout du Vice* was well-received. Thank God, Parisians talked and theatre people had the most effective grapevine.

"Have Dany Mounet give prices for the ingenue's costumes in the new Deval play," a stage manager suggested.

"The Verneuil comedy is going into rehearsal," Robert Venard told her. "The producer is expecting a call from you."

Introductions were arranged, recommendations were made. Dany spent the mornings on the telephone setting appointments. She accepted all the orders she could get.

Louis had sketches to show her. "A masked ball, another one!" he said. "That American widow hopes to surpass the Directoire masquerade. She wants to outdo Beaumont's costume party and there's money to be made in this. I know it's nonsense. But, Dany, if you don't do it one of the other costume houses will be more than ready to accommodate."

Soon Canaletto-caped Venetians, Fragonard maids and Goya gypsies were flying out of the fitting room.

"I met Edwige Feuillere at the Blanchard party," Renee said on the phone one morning. "I can open a publicity office when my time is up on the stage! Listen to me, little one. I convinced Edwige to come to you for this new play she's doing. It sounds absolutely dreadful but never mind, you're not dressing the words! She must see you, I said. No couturier understands clothes for the stage the way Dany Mounet does. She's calling her producer, he wants the designer to take his designs to Lanvin for execution. Such pretension! So, *chérie*, make a few phone calls. I'll give you the numbers . . ."

A meeting was arranged. The designer brought his sketches. Five costumes for Feuillere. Another order.

Dany hired new seamstresses. She found a draper to train as an assistant. More and more sketches were tacked on the board above her table, lush fabrics whirled out of her hands for sewing. She was working hard, the atelier was flourishing.

Louis often found a reason to stay in the workroom at the end of the day. He said he wanted to watch her set the bias folds of organdy on the Watteau bodice. He wanted to cut the appliques himself before they were stitched on the sleeves.

"Wouldn't you like dinner?" he'd ask. "You must relax for a few hours, Dany." Then he'd invite her to Lipp for his favorite choucroute, to Hazard for a warming plate of paprika chicken on a cold winter night. Dany wasn't sure if he was being a concerned uncle worrying about a bereaved niece or a lonely bachelor seeking company, but it was pleasant to accept his last-minute invitations. Louis enjoyed eating as much as Renee, and if Louis was playing a sympathetic uncle then Renee was a doting governess.

In front of her dressing room mirror, wiping away the geranium blush of the stage before applying her usual ivory powder and kohl, Renee was imagining the tastes of a late supper.

"The chef at Vefour promised to wait for us." She brushed fuchsia lip rouge across her mouth. "Are you working too hard, little one? You have been too brave! I hope you know that I am here for you whenever you need to talk."

"Yes, I know," Dany said, "and when I'm ready I will. Renee, truly I will, but what is there to say? Simon was the brave one. That says it all, doesn't it?" What a nerve, to be lying to Renee. Dany hoped she could fool her.

"And, naturally, no word from the police? Well, it's not surprising. Our stupid politicians are too busy making quotas and identification papers more important than crime. What can we expect?" Renee smacked her lips against the edge of her towel, leaving a deep red outline. "Well, we can have *gigot* tonight. Can you think of anything more delicious? With *flageolets,* little one, and perhaps some lentils! We'll put a little weight on those bones of yours!"

The flat above the workroom was available and Dany had to face clearing out the Passy apartment. She would keep a few pieces of furniture, the old set of china, things that she realized she was sentimental about. Photos, a set of ivory combs and brushes; there were memories to hold on to. And Simon's books stacked on the windowsills, she was sure the University library would be happy to have them.

Dany walked out of Rodier's with a package of woolens for Louis's masquerade costumes. She was happy to have the time to walk. She didn't mind the hazy streets, the murky sky tinged with dull yellow that promised snow. The morning air was bracing, and as she went across the bridge at Sebastopol, the sun came out. The towers of Notre Dame cast mauve-blue shadows.

Wait until spring, Simon had said the first day she came to Paris, you'll have color then.

It happened as quickly as the sun breaking through the dreary sky. Simon, she saw him watching her, an image that she couldn't control. In a flashing moment she thought she saw him. It wasn't the first time; he lurked in shadows on a street, sometimes in the corner of a restaurant. He appeared unexpectedly and she'd sworn she was going to forget. She sensed that he was watching her from behind a lamp on the bridge and she walked faster, rushing down the streets to the atelier. She had to get to the workroom, Simon never appeared there; even as an apparition he wasn't going to step into the atelier. The back staircase off the workroom led up to the new rooms and she vowed never to use the front entrance to the new flat. She was taking no chances, she didn't want to see a ghost in the dark hallway off the street.

Louis came to the worktable the minute she started to unpack the fabrics. Color, she said to herself. Yes, there is color now! "Look at this wool crêpe, Louis," she said, "it's exactly the tone of the blue in an inkwell. Can't you see it as an evening suit?"

"For you, yes. You never make anything for yourself. Promise to wear it when we see Lifar at the ballet next week?" Louis reached for a pencil and began a sketch on a piece of brown pattern paper. "Make Mme. Frenon's domino a bit skimpy and you won't have to buy more cloth. She won't know the difference and

92

you'll have a very chic suit. What is Charlotte going to wear?"

Dany watched Louis sketching. The figure appeared on the paper, he looked at her for a moment and then drew a face. A stylish likeness drawn lightly on the paper. "Does it matter? Charlotte is always the most beautiful no matter what she wears."

"You're not too bad yourself. You never think about it. Dany, don't you know that in your own way you're as attractive as Charlotte?"

"No one is like Charlotte." Dany took the sketch. "Thank you, Louis. I love it."

"It is nothing, *chérie*. Get some of those star buttons from Jean Clement for the jacket. Schiaparelli will never know." Louis giggled. "I must go now. It's late. Don't work until all hours."

"I'll start to drape my new suit. Don't worry, I'll be fine." She walked with Louis to the door.

"Remember, get some sleep." He tapped her cheek. "Good night, Dany."

Dear Louis. She stood at the window, looking at him going down the street. His black coat was too tight, his head almost vanished under his upturned collar. He looked like a dark pigeon scuffling toward the corner. Then he stopped at the street light to greet a tall fellow in a windbreaker and stocking cap. They crossed the street together, the younger man cheerfully putting his arms across Louis's back. If Louis had an appointment with a friend, why hadn't he asked the man to come into the workroom instead of waiting out in the cold street?

"Really, wasn't all that biblical posing pretentious!" Charlotte whispered after the last curtain call at the Opera. "Louis, if you must go backstage, go alone. I cannot lie to Lifar and say I loved it."

"We don't have to go," Louis said as they left the box.

"Charlotte would like *Sleeping Beauty* at every ballet program," Gerard said. "We have to have these new works but she wants only the old romances." Gerard led the way down the marble staircase.

"Louis! Maestro!" A voice called out when they were in the lobby. "You've forgotten all about me, *chéri?*" The accent was Russian.

"Madame Karinska!" Louis was embarrassed. Dany knew the polite but stumbling embrace when he was uneasy. "You know—"

"Ah, beauty!" She kissed Charlotte's cheeks, extended a white gloved hand to Gerard.

"And may I present Mme. Mounet," Louis said.

"So, the new one! I've been hearing about you, Mme. Mounet." Karinska's silver hair was almost blue, her silk suit was navy. "Such pretty clothes. I saw *Gout du Vice,* it is a triumph, Gerard! Louis, you wanted all that reality, I'm sure. The painstaking detail. Admirable, quite admirable! You make pretty dresses, dear girl." Her eyes narrowed. What were the sparkling beads under the blue eyeshadow? Lilac, grey; no, the coolest blue. The most intense light blue eyes appraising like a pawnbroker estimating some old gold bracelet or a brooch with dull diamonds that wasn't worth very much. Dear girl, indeed! What a patronizing tone.

"Thank you, Madame," Dany said. "That was the intention. A romantic reality. Wasn't that what you asked for, Louis?" He was flustered. He never spoke up when he should and Charlotte and Gerard had turned to talk to other people.

Only a few days ago Louis had been talking about the designs for a new *Romeo and Juliet.* Renaissance clothes, he'd said. Young boys and girls in the streets of Verona. Clothes that were worn, truly worn, in the hot

Italian summer afternoons. They sweat in those days the same as we do now, Dany had said to him. You mustn't see the sweat in a theatrical costume. No, not ever. But it's there no matter how often the costume is cleaned though the audience doesn't see it. We can make sweat if you'd like to. We'll spray it on, we'll paint it on any cloth you choose. Open necklines and rolled up sleeves. Renaissance sweat, Louis, on real clothes!

"After all, Mme. Karinska, I'm sure you try for the lightest weight costume on the body of a dancer. Of course, the costume must last. For years, isn't that right? But why always the heavy insides. The muslin, the thick cotton lining to spoil the illusion of that wonderful lightness?"

"Aha!" Karinska turned to Louis. "She has a philosophy! That is good. Stay with it, child."

"There is an impressive woman," Gerard said when they were in the car.

"Do you think so?" Dany hoped her chin went properly high in the air, the way Renee moved when she disagreed with someone.

"Dany, you should be flattered." Charlotte was laughing. "I heard her. The great Karinska was showing a bit of jealousy. You've arrived, Dany."

"Not yet. By no means." Charlotte was probably right and Dany was rather pleased. "Louis, design a ballet. And I'm going to learn to make a tutu, one lighter than Karinska's."

"Do *Swan Lake.* Or *Camille,* glorious Constantin Guys dresses to float and twirl through the air. Can't you see it?" Charlotte asked. "Find a company, call Kochno. Louis you must design a ballet for Dany to show up Karinska! Shall we drink vodka tonight to ward off this damned cold weather?"

The Russian restaurant was crowded, the violinists were taking their bows.

"Oh, we missed them," Charlotte said. "Now wouldn't this color scheme be perfect for a ballet? Talk about romantic. And sexy!" Candlelight flickered over the dark red walls, the crimson banquettes of the dining room. A new shade appeared every second, the waiters' cossack shirts glowed as a flame lashed to the ceiling from brandy being poured over a dessert. Charlotte led the way to their table. "Caviar in blini! You want caviar, don't you, Dany? Did you guess we were coming here? Your suit is perfect in this light."

"Louis chose this crêpe for Louise Frenon's Venetian cape for the Bal des Bluets. I can't resist off-shades of blue," Dany said. "Isn't it the exact color of classroom ink? But I may wear only black from now on. No, no, not because of mourning. Because of Russian women with blue eyes."

"Do I detect a little cattiness, Mme. Mounet?" Gerard asked. "I agree with Charlotte. You made a great impression in a very short time."

Charlotte was nodding to another table, waving to say hello. "There's Eve Curie," she said. "I wonder who she is with."

"Really? That woman in grey?" Suddenly Dany was laughing.

"What is it?" Gerard asked.

"Dany, are you all right?" Louis was startled.

Could she tell them? She couldn't stop laughing. Oh, Simon, are you going to appear now? Who would believe this? I'm in a restaurant with Eve Curie, the great scientist's daughter! Remember how often I said I couldn't be Mme. Curie? Don't you see, Simon, how you had it all wrong? Her tears of laughter were uncontrollable. They wouldn't understand why she thought this was funny. Maybe this was the end of it; maybe Simon wasn't coming back after this!

"Our girl is laughing! Dany, forget about black."

96

Charlotte laughed with her, not knowing why. "Wear light colors, something gay. We'll go to one of those gala parties and dance and flirt. Gerard, are you going to order the caviar?"

He signalled a waiter. "I saw a few flirting glances during the entr'acte tonight." He touched Charlotte's hand. "Did you notice?"

"They were probably for Charlotte," Dany said.

"Dany, men do not flirt with this respectable producer's wife." Charlotte pulled her hand away from Gerard.

"This young woman must go out more often," Louis said. "We have to open her eyes to more than color and what is happening in the theatre. Renee and I are going to the black and white ball in two weeks. Why don't we all go together?"

"I'll be in Monte Carlo," Charlotte said. "Gerard, why don't you escort Dany?"

"No, please," Dany said. "It's too rich for my blood. I forget that I disapprove of all the costume parties when I see the checks coming in but I cannot wear a disguise. I can't put on a mask!" She hated the idea. "I'm just beginning to learn how to wear this face." The intention was well meant but she wasn't up to it. "Besides, Charlotte, isn't it too soon?"

"I loathe costume parties," Gerard said. "Have dinner with me that night, Dany? Somewhere near the atelier."

"But Gerard, we were talking about flirting," Louis said. "You can't flirt with Dany."

"Louis, how naive!" Charlotte said. "He could but he won't."

Dany was uncomfortable and a few minutes ago she'd been laughing. She watched the musicians come out, a spotlight picking out each man around the restaurant, a strain of melody came from one violin, then another and another. The lights dimmed as their music gained momentum. A light and delicate beginning grew richer and more romantic as more violins were heard. A full orchestra of strings playing a lush version of "Dark Eyes" as the lights grew bright again.

"Who else is going, Louis?" Charlotte went on. "Not just Renee and you?"

"No," Louis mumbled. "My friend Stefan will go with us."

"Who?" Charlotte asked.

"You met him at the scene studio." Louis was concentrating on his blini, not looking up. "The new carpenter."

"Oh, yes. The handsome one. Well, I'm sure he'll look stunning."

"He's very talented, you know."

"*Chéri,* I'm sure he is. And strong. All that sawing and working with tools makes very strong arms."

"He won't be a carpenter for long. His paintings are very good." Louis glared at Charlotte, his lower lip quivered. "I said he's very talented."

"I said I believed you." Charlotte patted Louis's cheek. "Now, now, darling, don't sulk. I won't tell anyone."

"Tell what?" Dany was confused now.

"Gerard, we need more vodka." Charlotte lifted her empty glass. "Well, my girl, be prepared for more work when I come back. I'm going to buy cottons in Provence, those marvelous country prints. And we'll make absolutely exquisite blouses and skirts." Charlotte tossed her head back, running her fingers through her blond hair. "Time for a naive look, I think. Don't you agree, Louis?"

"Dany, take the measurements but don't tell me." Renee frowned in the fitting room mirror. "I know that I'm fatter. That's bad enough but I don't have to hear the grisly details. I know that nothing fits me. Ugh, this figure! Do you believe this was once a beautiful body?"

"Stop eating." Dany scribbled measurements in her notebook. "No problem, Renee, there is very little change."

"Don't tell me, I don't want to know. Hide that book!" Renee sat down, crossing her slender legs, her black slip riding up over her knees. "Tell me about last night. Did Lifar dance? Who was there? So Charlotte is going away again. Shopping for a villa on the Riviera. Now, little one, that is what I call shopping!"

"Really? She said she wants to buy cottons in Provence."

"Mm, among other things." Renee opened her purse and took out a small bag of chocolates.

"Gerard was very quiet last night. He seemed distracted," Dany said.

"He's always like that before she goes away. Haven't you noticed?"

"Yes, I have." What was it about a fitting room that made women ready for gossip? Dany had work to do but it would have to wait. "Charlotte was very sarcastic to Louis last night."

"Oh?" Renee wiped some chocolate off her mouth. "It's nothing. She enjoys teasing Louis."

"Renee, I don't understand. Her remarks were cutting and then she changed the subject. But Louis was quite flustered. Sometimes I'm confused by all of you. There were things Venard said at rehearsals. . . . Am I completely witless?"

"You're not witless, little one, but there are things you haven't been exposed to. Now Charlotte wants a house, an important house and she'll take her time to find the perfect place. The curtain has gone up and you are watching a complicated play. Just remember one thing,

Dany. It's a comedy!"

"Louis has asked the theatre carpenter to go to the ball with you. Charlotte was sarcastic when Louis told her. A week ago when Louis left here a man was waiting for him on the street corner. I wondered why Louis didn't ask the man to come here."

"Louis has a sense of privacy, *chérie*. And impeccable taste, as you know," Renee said. "The two qualities aren't necessarily compatible."

"You see!" Dany exclaimed. "I don't understand what you mean."

Renee bit into another piece of chocolate. "He finds the best looking lovers and sometimes he takes one of them to dinner, to the theatre or a cafe and he is seen. Paris is a very small village. He's seen and then surprised if there is gossip. Charlotte teases him about his parade of beautiful young men."

"Renee!" Dany was shocked.

"Men like other men, *chérie*. It is a fact of life. Particularly in our business. Women, too. Though I've never been able to understand what two women do together. We are all caves and hollows, except for these." Renee lifted her large breasts swelling over the lace border of her slip. "I can understand the men, they have more to play with. Pegs and holes. Little one, I've never seen you blush!"

"What are you telling me?" Dany squealed.

"Louis is brilliant but he's a sly one. He is seductive, the little, fat fellow! I don't know how he lures them but the most handsome types appear in that studio on Boulevard Raspail. Unusual, our Louis. Other boys are noisier and funnier and better looking. They love to laugh and gossip. *Chérie,* I'm positive that gossip was created by two men lying on a bed or on the floor of some garret or under the trees in the Bois. They complete the act, they stretch languidly and light cigarettes,

100

look up at the ceiling or the stars, and they gossip!"

"Renee, how can you tell? How do you know who they are?"

"You'll know. I told you, watch the stage." Renee went to the mirror to apply fresh lipstick. "They have a sense of fun and a kind of valor. Innately brave, these men. They have to be to exist and to hide behind their armor." She smacked her lips on a lawn handkerchief. "What an army they'd be! They know how to fight! Louis, too. He can fight. What are we wearing to the ball? Has Louis told you?"

"I saw one sketch. Either Apollo or is it Paris? Quite naked with drapes of white shantung."

"Haha!" Renee's laugh was raucous. "Then, if darling Louis is going as Helen of Troy, who will I be?"

"You must come for fittings more often, Renee. I'll make your clothes for nothing. You teach me things we weren't taught in the convent." Yes, react in a carefree manner. Slightly frivolous but alert. Watch and observe as much as you can. And later, alone in the dark, chilly bedroom under Mama Mounet's quilt examine all the serious facts you've heard. Strange but what she'd just heard was not really shocking. Questions are asked and sometimes the answer isn't truly an answer. Or it was a confirmation of what you already knew. It was all very serious but not for now. Later, at night. There was time then. Dany untied her work apron.

"Careful! I may hold you to that offer," Renee said. "The cheap little restaurant off rue Jacob, shall we eat there?"

"You work too hard." Renee stirred her coffee, adding another lump of sugar. "You must learn to relax."

"I try," Dany said. "I'm lucky to have come this far and it's only the beginning. I must have a solvent busi-

101

ness. No bank loans, no debts. I've a long way to go, Renee."

"All right but I don't want to worry about you. I can read minds, you know. No crystal balls or tarot cards, looking in the eyes is enough for me. Remember that." Renee's kohl edged eyes were warning. "I worry about Charlotte as if she were my daughter."

"You're not old enough," Dany said.

"Thanks for that, little one. God knows, her own mother didn't care."

"Charlotte told me she was very spoiled and protected."

"Yes, when she was young. She was educated and trained for one purpose. To have a rich husband and she has him. Charlotte has said she was sold to Gerard, not married to him. The custom is for the dowry to be given to the bride, but Gerard settled a fortune on his mother-in-law. Oh, what questionable bargaining must have gone on! He wanted the divine little girl he had watched grow up and he got her." Renee swirled the last of her wine in the goblet. "Would you like a brandy, *chérie?*"

"No, I must work when I go back," Dany said. "How much difference in age is there?"

"Almost twenty years. Charlotte is a strange creature and I adore her. She says she is without talent but look what she does. Her eye, her selectivity. She can spot the next prominent painter before the dealers. She finds a new playwright, discovers the new restaurant or a style before the designers have it in the next collection. Like the peasant dresses you made. A talent for discovery, that is what she has. And she admires you, little one, because you aren't afraid of work. Because you are fearless."

"People are so aware of fear, timidity or whatever you want to call it," Dany said. "Why aren't they aware of their own boldness? I've always loved a dare. It's another test to pass, and how bold do you have to be to spend money?"

"Dany, these trips aren't always for shopping," Renee said.

"What do you mean?"

Renee gulped her brandy. "When Charlotte goes away, it is to some place on the sea. A crowded, busy port where she can be anonymous. She is not unlike the women who go to Baden-Baden or Evian or Montecatini for the waters, but she goes to bars, saloons, the docks and she finds men. Unknown men to love her for a few hours or a few days. Many men. And then like a drunk after a binge she comes home, back to Gerard."

"Who knows this? Besides us, who knows?" Dany was angry and astonished. She didn't want to hear but she knew there was more.

"Gerard, of course. He knows. Nobody else. But now her trips are more frequent. When she goes south next week, she'll go to Marseilles, she'll drive to Nice. I'm sure of it. She may be seen, she can be recognized. That's why I am worried.

"Years ago Gerard fell in love with a blonde child, the daughter of his most revered friend. A young Belgian from a rich family teaching at the University. Years after the war they lost their fortune or squandered it, the friend died leaving an impoverished widow with one prize. The daughter." Renee sighed. "Gerard wanted a wife, a treasure, another work of art. An arrangement was made with the mother and then with Charlotte. He could never touch his prize possession."

"After Simon died, Charlotte told me to beware of guilt. Good advice but think of her guilt!" Dany exclaimed.

"You saw her when she came back from England. She is radiant when she returns, like someone who has been to a sanitarium and is cured. Guilty? One cannot shine

103

with guilt."

"And Gerard?"

"He suffers but he has to allow it. She'd leave him and God knows what she would become." Renee tried to blink away her tears. "Gerard does nothing. There is no one else in his life. In spite of it all, this disease, he worships Charlotte. Worship is a malignant condition, too, little one."

"Look at this incredible sketch. One day Louis will be regarded as another Canaletto or Guardi." Charlotte came to the atelier a few times a week, to see what was going on and to watch with fascination. "You cut the silk with bravado, Dany. You attack without any inkling of doubt."

Dany looked at Charlotte, sitting on the stool at the worktable, her long legs crossed, her pastel suit perfect, her white gloves spotless, her eyes bright under the sheer veil of her felt sailor. She was a photograph out of *Vogue* or *Femina*.

How difficult it must be for the actor to listen, Dany thought. To sit or move silently about the stage while another actor spoke his lines. To be attentive and interested. It had to be easier to read the lines and command the spotlight.

A silent performance was difficult but Renee had said she must watch. And Dany knew this was not a performance, it was Charlotte enjoying her time in the workroom before she ran on to her next appointment, before she went home to supervise the packing for her trip to the south.

"I'm going to find a wonderful villa. Someplace on the sea with space and wide terraces so we can watch the heavenly light, the soft evening clouds and the dewy mornings." Charlotte carefully folded her veil back to smoke a cigarette. "We may have to wait until next summer but we'll go to a hotel if we have to. You'll have to close in July, you know and a holiday will do you good."

Dany smiled at her. Did she understand practicality? No wonder Renee worried. Charlotte rhapsodized about her own plans, she was on one of the billowing clouds she longed to see on the horizon from her terrace. "I have debts to pay before I think about that," Dany said. "I want to have the same staff working all year long. I don't want to lose the good people because I hire them temporarily."

"You'll do it. Look at this place, listen to the buzz. Doesn't activity make a happy sound?"

Happy sounds. To block out the dark thoughts. Dany shivered at the thought of no work in the atelier. An empty workroom, and upstairs a lonesome flat. Only that morning she was aware of the dull quiet as she drank her coffee. She'd not allowed any memories of Simon to remain; no photos, no framed mementos and the stillness made her absentminded. She left the coffee pot warming over a low flame. How strange to miss the fact of Simon. That was all of it, she was missing a person, she didn't know who. It was simply that she was alone.

Charlotte was right. It was imperative to have the sound of activity. To block out the memory of anger and rage that had been in the Passy apartment. She couldn't tell that to Charlotte. To no one. And Charlotte loved the happy sound of activity; silence threatened Charlotte, too. Oh, why had Renee told her about Charlotte's trips! Dany looked at her neatly stubbing out her cigarette. One set of questions led to many more, other questions that couldn't be asked.

"Dany, it's been almost two months," Charlotte was saying. "You haven't said very much but I know what

105

you've been going through. Doing your mourning by yourself. We don't have to put things into words all the time, do we?"

Are we all mind readers, Dany wondered, and did some puzzles come without solutions? "No, Charlotte, I'm sure we don't," Dany answered.

"I've been trying to call you but your line was busy," Gerard said when Dany came to the atelier door. She had hoped he might have forgotten their dinner date. "I think these are your favorite colors, if you've forgotten about Russian costume makers."

"You're teasing me!" Dany unwrapped the bouquet, leading him into the workroom. "Cornflowers, aren't they lovely?" She hadn't worn blue since the night at the ballet. "I'll forget about Karinska! Here, put one in your lapel." She went to the sink at the back of the room to fill a pitcher. "Take off your coat. I was just talking to Renee, you know how she babbles on. And I love listening to her. Lunch at Maxim's, then an interview with a reporter she detested. Now she's worrying about her costume for tonight. Afraid that she'll look like an old Helen of Troy in black with Menelaus and Paris in white!"

"The Hugo performance. She'll carry it off no matter what color she's in." Gerard looked around the room. "Well, this is a busy little shop." Fabrics were piled on the tables, the racks were crammed with costumes.

"Atelier!" Dany corrected him. "I have to order more racks. It is getting crowded, isn't it?"

"I never doubted that it would be." Gerard was hesitant. "You did remember tonight? Why are you still working?"

"I try to straighten up for tomorrow morning. The girls can't wait to go home at the end of the day and some of them are so sloppy. Most of these things are

106

finished but we have to wait for the hooks and eyes."

"Why?"

"Superstition. The hooks don't go on until the day we're delivering or it's bad luck. I'm not taking any chances. I spilled a box of pins today. That's another superstition, it means a rush. I hope so!"

"If you get any busier you will need more room," Gerard said.

"Not yet but I'm hoping Wakhevitch will show me his Comedie designs. Oh, how I want to work with Jouvet!"

"You will. It all takes time. Let me help you with something. Then I thought we'd walk over to Deux Magots for a drink before dinner. You could do with an aperitif, I think. What is all this?" He picked up a curved piece of heavy paper.

"A pattern, it becomes a sleeve when it's traced on a length of cloth." She laughed. "I sound like a school teacher. Will you help me with these bolts of fabric?" She started to show him how to handle the material. "Gerard, why are you smiling?"

"When I was a boy in Alsace I worked in a textile mill." He twirled the roll of muslin, flipping the cloth without wrinkling it. "This is something you don't forget."

"Very good!" Dany said. "Better than some of the workers I have." He wasn't at all self-conscious but she was.

"Do you do this to make the evenings shorter, Dany? To defer going up to your apartment and being alone?"

He went to the theatre to check the box office sales, to watch a scene in a play. That was how he dealt with his lonely nights when Charlotte was away. Dany wasn't supposed to know that but Renee had talked. "Maybe I do prolong the day," Dany said. Charlotte had been gone only a few days but he was lonely, his eyes verified it. She had nothing to say, she couldn't speak. Oh God,

107

if she was going to wear a mask she would have gone to the masquerade.

"I'm sorry I never met your husband," Gerard said.

"I used to think you were rather alike," Dany said after a moment. "Once. It seems so long ago and it isn't at all. No, don't fold the velvet. It should be rolled." Dany went around the table to help him. She wished they'd met at the restaurant. Maybe she should have been like Louis and asked if they could meet on the street. "But Simon rarely smiled."

Was every word going to be the wrong word, she wondered. She slid her hand over the fabric, smoothing the pile of the velvet. Gerard brushed away a fleck of thread and their fingers touched. Dany didn't move and he covered her hand. She looked at his long, lean fingers, the sharp. straining knuckles, the prominent veins curving up to his wide wrist disappearing under the cuff of his sleeve. A sculptor's hand, sinewy and strong but faltering. She was unable to control the reflex. His hand touched her cheek and she caught her breath. He held her face, his fingers moving slowly over her cheekbones, his thumbs lightly caressing her lips.

Gerard's voice was low and dry. "How often are there things to smile about?"

She didn't resist his kiss, she couldn't speak or pull away. Gerard moaned. A fearful sound, the whimper of a hurt, bruised animal freed from a cage. His lips were firm and his hands gained strength. She couldn't speak, it wasn't possible to protest.

Upstairs in the silent bedroom she thought of Simon. His lean, pale body on those afternoons when she stopped working at the kitchen table in Passy. But this wasn't Simon, this was a sturdier man, his lips running over her body. Darker and hungry like one of the hounds that used to come to the convent courtyard to be fed by the sisters. She hadn't allowed herself to admit it but she was hungry, too. She didn't want to open her eyes, she didn't want to see the pain that was always there when Charlotte was away. But she saw no pain when he touched her a while ago. Downstairs in the workroom the pain went from his eyes when he kissed her and she didn't pull away.

This was an act of the utmost conceit. She was thinking of what she knew and couldn't admit, of everything Renee had told her. And she remembered starved hounds needing to be fed. She was committing an act of mercy.

It wasn't until the first week in April that Dany realized she'd rushed through the end of winter like an Olympics runner. Like someone pursued; a thief or an illegal emigré. Forgetting to look at the workroom clock, she'd been late for everything. Fabric salesmen were waiting in their showrooms, producers were impatient in their offices. She hadn't realized why until the sky was clear and sunny. She thought she could blame it on spring but she'd always been most punctual and suddenly she was embarrassed and full of remorse. She knew why she'd been running; it was as if all Paris had been peering into the bedroom window the night Gerard came by to take her to dinner. Watch the stage, Renee had commanded and instead Dany was afraid that everyone was watching her!

She wanted to hide but it wasn't easy. Not when Renee had seats for the Heifetz concert, not when Robert Venard invited her to the Ballet Russe.

Charlotte had called her fearless but Dany had no courage when Charlotte came back from Monte Carlo and came by the atelier one afternoon to report on her trip. She'd been too busy to find the cotton prints in Provence; there had been only time to look at houses. Thank God. Dany didn't think she could face Charlotte in the fitting room ever again. What a relief and Dany hoped she wasn't blushing as she listened to Charlotte talk about a villa, a divine house in Villefranche but far too expensive. If the real estate broker could persuade the owner to come down on the price she could have it for next summer. A year to wait but nothing to do about it and now she was off to London with Gerard. He had new business in England, a play that Arthur Bellamy was doing.

A stroke of luck, Dany thought. She was afraid to see Gerard. She'd avoided going to the theatre, making excuses when the wardrobe mistress called about remaking some costumes. Dany coaxed the woman to come to the atelier. When Renee wanted supper after a performance, Dany asked if they could meet at the restaurant. Now Charlotte was going to London with Gerard. What luck! Dany didn't have to go on avoiding him.

She couldn't say no to Louis when he invited her to the premiere of *Le Corsaire*. She'd have to be ill in her bed, with the highest fever, to miss a new production that Jouvet was starring in. And the party afterward, Mme. Sert's party! Too bad Charlotte was missing that. Renee would be suspicious if she heard that Dany had refused Louis's invitation.

Renee knew how to gossip. She savored each scandalous tidbit with the same gusto she had for a plate of oysters, her tongue was as sharp as the tines of the fork, her relish as hearty as her last, loud slurp of sauce from the shell. A party with Sravinsky, Chanel and the Rothschilds, Lifar and Berard and the company of the play. Talk about *tout Paris!* Dany knew why Renee spent hours on the phone every morning, that was when she heard the rumors. The stories she would repeat at night, in front of her dressing room mirror, over a late supper, or at an after-theatre party.

"You know what they are saying about Mme. Lopez's

110

husband?

"And Misia! The way she carried on about Roussy and Coco was no help. We'll never know what went on there but look at her!

"The Englishman, standing on the right! I wonder if Cocteau knows he's here, *chérie*. He's the one that. . . . oh, little one, the intrigues in these rooms! Don't look too closely, heaven knows what can be uncovered."

Renee talked about the people who didn't mean anything to her. If she knew about Gerard and Dany, she'd say nothing. Not a word to Charlotte, she'd keep quiet. Protecting Dany with silence and without judgment.

"At least you saw the play tonight, you lucky ones! I got here only to talk and eat. The truth now, what was it like, Louis? Madeleine Ozeray, how was she? And her costumes? Patou did them, no?"

Louis criticized the decor, he'd have done it differently. All the designers were jealous of each other and it was expected that an opinion would be harsh and a bit mean.

"Her costumes were beautiful," Dany said, "but why does Patou want to work in the theatre? I don't want to make clothes for real life. Patou, Piguet, Paquin! And Poiret; maybe if my name began with a P!"

Two months whirled by and Dany stood at the door of the Dessaux library. Gerard's secretary had said it was a late afternoon meeting for the staff of *Gout du Vice* and here they were. Louis and Robert Venard, Charlotte and Renee. Dany wondered why this conference had been called. She waited at the door before making an apology. She was late again.

The room was brighter than usual despite the rainy afternoon. Charlotte had bought new lamps, sleek chrome stilts with white shades lighting new natural

111

linen upholstery on the sofas and chairs. Dany remembered the day she went to the Ritz to meet Renee and Gerard. It had been raining then and it was raining today. And she was superstitious!

"Is there a conspiracy?" Dany asked. The conversation was remarkably muted, even Renee was talking in a hushed tone. "This looks like a scene in a spy movie."

"Conspiracy, little one!" Renee cried out. "We're too excited to speak, if you can believe that. You're too thin! If you were a few minutes later the caviar would be gone. Come sit with me and we'll finish it." She spooned a dollop on a piece of toast. "And listen to the news!"

"You should hire a receptionist," Charlotte said, "if you're too busy to take phone calls."

Oh, perhaps more than apologies were necessary. Dany thought *she* had important news for them but what was going on? She was surprised to see Arthur Bellamy coming into the library with Gerard.

"Come now, Gerard. Tell, tell! Let the little one hear," Renee exclaimed.

"Ah, Mme. Mounet, I'm happy to see you again," Arthur Bellamy said in his precise French. He reminded her of one of the mimics she had laughed at when she'd gone to the Music Hall with Charlotte a few months ago. His obviously new Prince de Galles suit was too close to his stout body, too pressed and his polka dot bow tie was too floppy. "Remember when I said I'd like to produce *Gout du Vice* in New York?" His speech seemed too rehearsed today, a nervous schoolboy unused to reciting in class. "Gerard is going to be my partner. Have they told you the rest?"

"Dany, we're going to America," Gerard said.

"Arthur promises what they call an all-star cast," Robert Venard said. "Like a Hollywood movie and we will introduce a new star!" He winked, his thumb point-

112

ing to Renee.

"New York is very cold in the winter, isn't it?" Louis asked.

"You'll get used to it, *chéri*." Renee held out her empty champagne glass. "My English, my English! I will learn quickly, I promise you, Gerard! I will become fluent. Fluent!"

Gerard filled their glasses. "You haven't heard it all, Dany." He gave her a glass of wine. Dany looked at Charlotte, she was puzzled and she couldn't look at Gerard's eyes. He had turned to Robert and Louis. Was he avoiding her glance? He looked well, his blue striped suit looked new. A London tailor, probably, and not the same one Arthur Bellamy went to. Gerard wore clothes with more style than anyone she'd ever seen.

"Rehearsals in the fall!" Renee hollered out. "September in New York. Oooh, I cannot wait!"

"One detail depends on you, may I call you Dany?" Arthur asked. "I told you when we met that I thought you should have a place in New York. I am prepared to underwrite a work space for you if you agree to make the Broadway production. We need you in New York. You can have a very successful business there."

"It is an exceptional opportunity, Dany," Gerard said. "Isn't it, *chérie?*" Why was he looking at Charlotte?

"You'll be our ambassador in New York," Robert said. "Our connection whenever we may be there again. This may be a beginning for all of us, Dany."

"Why do you think she must stay?" Louis asked with a sulk in his voice. "I need Dany here. Say no, Dany! Say no, please!"

"Dany, say yes!" Renee reached out to slap Louis's arm. "You must go. Without hesitation, little one! What is there here? Paris is getting darker, she is suffering! All these extravagant parties, all the masquerades and the dancing. It is a final banquet before the demise! I cannot bear to see you as another Paris widow working day and night! Getting one of those little, pinched faces, you're too young for that, little one!"

"Renee is right." Robert stood up. He looked angry, his hands pushed into the back pockets of his trousers. His legs spread apart like a Pigalle thug looking for a fight. "It is growing dark here and we can't go on appeasing the German maniac forever—"

"You see! Idiot!" Renee jabbed Louis's knee. "Dany, this is a wonderful chance!"

Dany looked at them, blinking when her eyes met Charlotte's meek smile.

"Renee, enough of the histrionics," Charlotte said. "I envy you, Dany. How often does one have the chance to start again?"

Dany took one of Renee's cigarettes. "This is very exciting for all of us." This wasn't an audition, she thought. This was a real performance she was about to give. She had center stage and she had to prove that she had been watching, that she could carry a leading role before an audience of friends. But she didn't want applause. No, she had to be more than convincing. Please, Gerard, don't drop your champagne glass.

"Yes, I am grateful for this exceptional offer. I would love to work in America. But you see, I was late this afternoon because I've been to see the doctor. I know I waited too long and he verified my suspicions—" Now she must deliver her curtain line. "Do you think New York is ready to welcome a pregnant widow?"

Three

On a late September afternoon Arthur Bellamy's chauffeur met Dany at the Hudson River pier, seeing to her luggage and leading her through the crowd of passengers to the waiting limousine. The autumn wind was sharp, making Dany catch her breath. The first view of New York from the ship had been as exciting as she'd expected and yet she thought she had seen it before. The metallic skyline was clear as the cloudless sky and as familiar as the Eiffel Tower.

Here it was; new streets to walk and a new language to learn. She had become a Parisian in six years, now she must be an American, a New Yorker. *And quickly.* She was going to have an American child who would know these streets the way her mother, when she was a girl, had known every street and alley of Amiens. Looking out the window Dany sensed the urgency and the tempo, the pace of people walking quickly, crowded sidewalks and traffic sounds much harsher than the noise of Paris. In all this hubbub it was going to be easier to lie, to tell the child about a noble father who had been struck down just months before her mother came to America.

Dany sat back as the limousine moved across town. *Home.* She had to be confident, this indeed was going to be her home. This was where she'd erase the

115

thoughts of the painful winter with Simon and, she could feel the blood reddening her cheeks, that impetuous night in the workroom with Gerard.

She *did* feel comfortable, New York wasn't foreign to her at all. She thought she could tell the driver to turn left at the next corner and she'd know exactly where they were.

The car stopped in front of a dignified red brick house, one in a row of austere four story buildings. Dany followed the chauffeur into the vestibule; a directory on the wall listed three tenants' names. Then a fourth said Mennino, Hats. Below it Dany read House of Mounet.

Wasn't Arthur Bellamy silly, Dany asked herself. How pretentious, what house? In Paris she'd never thought of a name for the business with any trick or flourish. Dany Mounet was quite enough, only the name. Like all the other dressmakers and shops around the city.

One night Charlotte had been talking about Arthur Bellamy after he'd left for New York. "The dear man has a streak of pretention that I can't take seriously. Though he turns most of his philanthropies into very profitable enterprises. He yearns for prestige and panache yet he's rather shrewd at the same time. Or he's quite lucky. No, it doesn't ever have to do with mere luck. Arthur is financing you because he wants to introduce someone with a new flair and elegance to the New York theatre world. You'll be a success, Dany, I have no doubt. But don't let Arthur own too much of you." Then Charlotte had hesitated. "And if he gets any pompous ideas, give him an argument! You have better taste and you'll have more stature, after all."

"Hello, come on up!" the woman at the top of the stairs called out. "I'm Peggy Bellamy." Up one flight to an open door, the steps covered in worn, dark green

116

carpet, faded striped-paper walls lit by brass side lamps. "At last. How was the trip?" She spoke in impeccable French.

"Exciting," Dany answered. "Every single minute of it."

Peggy was a plain woman, tall, a bit too stout, and her smile was a welcoming embrace. She was not at all what Dany had imagined Arthur's wife would be. Her genuine manner and her throaty, cracking voice was friendly and attractive.

"I hope you like all this. I didn't want to go too far decorating for you. I told Arthur we had to wait until you got here. He'll be along in a while."

Peggy Bellamy showed Dany through the rooms. A large square parlor led to a smaller room meant for dining with a kitchen behind it. A room at the other side was not very large but bright with sunshine from the windows facing a back garden.

"What's in here can be moved anywhere you'd like," Peggy was pointing to a chest and two bentwood chairs. "This is furniture I had in the country and we can drive down there whenever you'd like to pick up what other things you may need. Arthur said you'd prefer working and living in the same place."

"It seemed the most practical way to begin. I've managed this way in Paris and I want the baby near me all the time." Dany was overwhelmed, all the essential things were in the apartment. It was meager but well thought out. On each table, on the bureau and in corners, on the windowsills were plants and clay pots holding yellow mums. "This is so kind of you and it is lovely, Mrs. Bellamy. Especially the flowers! Thank you."

"The name is Peggy and no thanks, please. You have to be as comfortable as possible in order to work. I

117

don't believe artists have to suffer. Now tell me, how is your English coming along?"

"I'm afraid of it but I try. I read and I talked in English as often as I could on the ship." Dany felt as if she was stepping on stage. She took a deep breath and spoke in English. "If you will be patient with me I shall begin now."

In Paris Dany was used to working late into the night and starting her days early in the morning but that routine was like a rippling brook compared to the torrential waters of New York in the next month. She'd never allowed herself the indulgence of timidity and she had no time for it now. Renting equipment, buying supplies for the workroom that was to be in the front parlor of the apartment, dealing with unfamiliar workmen and tradespeople in the most frugal way took all of her time. She knew her credit was established at the bank but she negotiated her purchases as shrewdly as any old Amiens shopkeeper. The furniture she chose at the Bellamy house in Oyster Bay was borrowed. She was firm about that and she was careful itemizing her bills, keeping her ledger for Arthur Bellamy's accountant.

Peggy Bellamy recommended a doctor and the hospital for Dany. She took her shopping, leading the way to neighborhoods where the best bargains were to be found. The Bowery, Canal Street, the lower East Side became customary weekly stops. Dany soon realized that if she pretended confusion about understanding English, if she reverted to French when she talked to a hostile storekeeper, her accent gave her an advantage before settling prices.

The workroom was set up and behind it the dining

room became a fitting room with an old three-way mirror placed against one wall and a pipe of small spotlights hung from the high beamed ceiling. At night it would serve as a comfortable sitting room. Meals would be taken at a kitchen table. The baby's crib was to be in Dany's bedroom and the small adjacent room was to be for the nanny Peggy insisted must be found. As in Paris, help was not hard to find. Dany interviewed many women with fine dressmaking abilities. Though she wondered how many languages were to be spoken in the small quarters, she hired two Russians who spoke French, an Italian with very little English and a Greek girl who communicated with her in sign language.

"It is ready, the atelier is ready!" Dany said at the end of October. "At last!" The American actresses came to be measured for their turn of the century dresses. Then Renee Hugo arrived at the Algonquin Hotel with Louis Ostier and Robert Venard. Rehearsals started. Dany began to cut fabrics with Louis at her side as often as he could be with her. He was intimidated by New York, uncertain in the scenic studio and too shy to venture out without someone to translate for him. Together they went across town to watch rehearsals and to eat at one of the local French restaurants or to be entertained by the Bellamys.

Dany was amused by Arthur; he seemed like a young boy showing off to impress his friends. At the Colony he was greeted effusively by the maitre d'hotel; at Voisin the coat check girl knew his name and at the Twenty-One Club a table was found for him though he arrived without reserving in advance. He was always the peacock enjoying attention, while Peggy preferred the inexpensive bistros off Lexington Avenue and cozy places in Greenwich Village. Dany saw how oddly matched these two were; Peggy doting on anonymity and Arthur absolutely savoring swagger and flash.

Two days before the company was to leave for Boston, Charlotte and Gerard arrived in New York. In the early evening Charlotte came to Fifty-sixth Street to see Dany and the new atelier, not surprised to find Dany working alone.

"It doesn't seem too far from the Left Bank," Charlotte said, coming into the workroom, looking at the table cluttered with pattern paper and muslin. There were bolts of fabric and unfinished bodices and skirts draped on the dressmaker dummies. "But now *Madame la Directrice* is a bit roly-poly, no?"

Dany returned Charlotte's embrace; how good it was to see her. And she hoped the wince wasn't apparent as they hugged. Yes, the *directrice* is fatter and her doctor says she is quite healthy. Dany wondered where the audacity came from, to stand there facing her best friend, shamelessly happy to see her and wondering if her remorse showed as much as her roly-poly belly.

"Paris, New York. Nothing changes, does it, Dany? You're working late. Gerard had to run to rehearsal to see Arthur. Come on, show me these rooms."

Charlotte nodded approval as they walked through the apartment. "You know we're all dining together? Now, what is this about the pacing of the play? Arthur is worried about Renee's English? Can he be serious that she's unsure of herself?"

"Renee unsure of anything? I haven't heard a word," Dany said.

"Do you get nervous too? How is your English?"

"Oh, I'm a bit bashful sometimes but, Charlotte, I've felt at home here from the first day off the ship. And I've even started to dream in English!"

* * *

"This is more of a conference than a reunion," Charlotte whispered across the table at Voisin. Louis was worrying about the painting of his scenery after a trip to the studio that afternoon.

"Everything here is so big," he said. "They're making too many plays at one time. I can't believe my work will be done in time."

"It will be done." Gerard was reassuring. "It has to be completed on time because the producer will not pay the overtime and the scenic studio won't absorb any extra costs. Arthur explained all of this to me this afternoon. It's not like Paris. It is more of a business here."

"A business!" Renee said. "My second act business should get the same laughs in America as in Paris. I can pantomime in another language, can't I? Isn't laughter universal? Do I need my passport stamped before I make laughter in Boston?"

"The wolf takes off the sheep's costume," Dany spoke softly to Louis at her right. They could go on with dinner, Renee was going to be playing only to satisfy her own ego now.

"This Bellamy is giving too many notes this afternoon. I worry about my accent and he calls a meeting. Suddenly there are storms; sirocco and mistral!" Renee exclaimed. "Your Arthur Bellamy tells me it is a play, not French Music Hall. How does he know I played the music halls? That's where I learned about timing! When we have an audience, I will give laughter!"

"Don't I know what I'm directing?" Venard spoke with confidence. "Your American partner is the one with what is called the jitters. Before every opening we have them, only now he has them too soon."

Renee sipped her wine, holding out her glass for

121

more. Red wine and applause, she always wanted more.

"Bellamy, Bellamy!" she said. "He has no cause to worry. I'll give him a great performance. If my English is not so clear then my accent will charm and beguile the audience. The way you say it works for the shop-keepers, little one! And when Renee Hugo forgets lines, is it not better than most actresses who remember?"

"They are all the same, little one. The lobbies may be different and the seats may be one color or another, the house may be large or small, but when you get back-stage, believe me, they are all alike. There's a scent, al-most imperceptible, of age perhaps and old paint, makeup, sweat. I don't know, can anticipation have an odor? It is the same in Milan or Marseilles or Warsaw. It'll be the same here." Renee had suggested to Dany that they walk to the theatre. She was pleased with the swank of the Ritz Hotel and the Boston Common was covered in an unseasonable light snow. "Be careful, *ché-rie,* we don't want to fall in this and have an unex-pected disaster. Though I've heard they have the finest of hospitals up here." Renee held Dany's arm for a mo-ment. "Somehow I cannot see you having the baby be-fore dress rehearsal. Who will tell me how truly fat I look if you're not sitting out front making your little notes?" Renee was in an affable mood, edgy but agree-ably nervous.

Venard had called dress rehearsal for late afternoon after he worked through the lunch period with Louis on the many props for the third act.

"Chaos awaits along with the Muse!" Renee said as they turned into Tremont Street. "Attention! These pud-dles! They will be sheets of ice if it gets any colder. *Chérie,* one second. Wait." Renee wrapped her sealskin coat tight around her hips, adjusted her muff up to her elbow, pulled the brim of her velour toque over her brow. Now she was ready for her entrance through the stage door.

Again there was a magic in the darkness when Dany made her way down the aisle to join Louis Ostier, her pincushion clamped to her wrist, and her notebook in hand. The short gasp of expectation lasted only a moment. The curtain rose and Louis's set was revealed perfectly reproduced. The American cast played superbly and as Venard had ordered they went through the play without stops, gliding over their errors that were noted and whispered to the French speaking secretary Arthur Bellamy had hired for the Boston engagement.

Louis dictated corrections, most of them for the tailor. She was happy to have made only the women's costumes; money had been saved by using many off-the-rack clothes from Albert, one of the old costume houses. Rehearsal was never flawless, she knew, but this was very close. She thought the hand of a sorcerer touched the stage and the touch was light. That was the magic potion, the lightness of it all.

Dany waited for Louis to come on stage after he gave his lighting notes to the stage manager. The people from Albert Costume Company were coming down the aisle, the older man calling out his notes.

"Fix the valet's coat. And the minister's hat is too big, his pants are too short. Should be at least an inch longer." Cigar smoke spilled out of his mouth with the words spoken in a frog's croaking voice. "The ladies costumes are good. Gotta hand it to Bellamy, he's got an eye. This Ostier guy knows what he's doin'." He kept tapping the shoulder of the lanky fellow coming on stage ahead of him. "That grey morning coat pulls across the shoulders. Christ, Jackie, there are too many

123

alterations. You're gonna have to stay with Benny to watch this crap. I gotta be outta here tomorrow on the eleven o'clock train. I promised your mother I'd be home for dinner."

Dany wanted to call Louis but he was still offstage. She couldn't believe what she was watching.

"Mr. Putnam, before you change, can we get at your jacket? Take it in at the center seam, Benny." The man went on giving orders and the actor said nothing as safety pins were shoved through the cloth of his jacket. Safety pins! "Been on a diet since your last fitting, Mr. Putnam?" He smiled at Putnam as if the man had misbehaved at school.

Dany's face must have reflected her disapproval. The young man watching her was grinning. Could he read her mind? He was tall, lean as a cowboy in a Western movie and he was amused.

"Safety pins don't fall out." His laugh was almost patronizing. "I'm Jack Albert. Have you met my father?"

Renee was right, all theatres were the same backstage, but what would she say if she were out in this lobby? Did everyone in Boston know each other? Did they all come to opening nights together? This audience didn't parade as the crowd did in Paris, there was no bar to rush to and here it wasn't an entr'acte. It was an intermission. Groups of four and six gathered together smoking cigarettes, speaking softly and then turning to greet another couple. The men were in dinner jackets and the women in evening clothes and furs, but they lacked the style of Paris. Though there was a definite excitement in the lobby, it was muted; not a raucous menagerie but a humming apiary.

The Bellamys knew everybody too and the group surrounding them was laughing. A good sign. Gerard had not been pacing at the back of the theatre in his usual worried way. He sat with Charlotte on the aisle in case he was restless.

"Where have you been?" Robert Venard came up behind Dany. "We wanted you to have a drink with us at the bar down the street. It is going smoothly, no?"

"Yes. You and Renee were right. Laughter works everywhere. If you had done it in French they'd be laughing too," Dany said. "You should be very happy, Robert."

"And aren't you?" Robert was very serious, having his own case of the jitters. "It looks exquisite and Louis is very pleased."

"Thank you." Dany took his arm. "Let's find Charlotte. Where is she?"

"Over there, near the door. She was looking for you."

Charlotte was chatting amiably; her plum velvet dress highlighted by shocking pink gloves, her satin hand on Gerard's arm. In a second her gentle touch could steer him away from the strangers they were talking to. Charlotte's control, how aware of it she was. Aware of her value, standing in this foreign lobby. Lustrous Charlotte. Brighter than the new Matisse on the wall of their salon in Paris, more elegant than the thin Giacometti looming over their fireplace. Charlotte was the first treasure, the most adored prize. She knew, and why not? Beauty commands. Wasn't that what beauty was for?

The lights flickered on and off, signalling the end of intermission, the start of act three.

"Arthur is optimistic. I know, we've heard that before but I agree," Charlotte said when she joined Venard and Dany. "The critics will like us. I have a good feeling about it."

"It shows," Dany said. "You look very happy. And pleased, like the proverbial cat."

"Gerard says we can buy the villa in Villefranche. I'm going home before the New York opening to negotiate the purchase. The *Normandie* leaves in ten days. I'll miss the new arrival, Dany. I'm sorry about that, but next summer you can bring your son to the Riviera for his first holiday."

"It will not be a boy." Dany was positive she was not going to have a son. "Don't count on next year, Charlotte. You forget that I've a new business to run. Plans get changed and we know that there are always surprises popping out of corners for us. Did we think a year ago that we'd be standing in a lobby in Boston talking about the future?"

"Plans and dreams are two different things, aren't they?" Charlotte said.

"Dreams go wrong, too," Dany said. She wasn't in the rosiest mood. It was beginning, that deflated feeling that enveloped her when the work was finished. The costumes were done and they were on the actors' bodies, moving around the stage. The peculiar sense of emptiness grasped her as soon as the curtain was up and the performance began. A useless feeling, rather like a dismissal. The music had started, the actor spoke his first lines and she could go home. Her work was completed. Tomorrow morning she was boarding a train to take her to New York, back to the empty atelier. To make phone calls, to introduce herself to an alien world of producers, hoping for a commission to execute costumes for a new production. And in a few weeks she was going to the hospital Peggy Bellamy recommended. "Leroy is the only hospital where one should have a baby." That had decided it. She was told it was the best, and Peggy knew

126

everything about the best in New York.

Here she was, talking about plans and fancies with her best friend, and the one thing she had always believed in—outright honesty—was vanishing into the air. Like a balloon let loose in the Tuileries and floating off into the Paris sky. Soon it was going to be time for the Dany Mounet performance. Tears to be shed when the baby was born, tears for the fatherless child she'd hold in her arms. Mother as played by a widow. Oh, if only Gerard was the one going back to France, it would be easier to play the role.

He was walking toward them as the lights flashed again. "I think I'll watch the last act from the wings," Dany said.

"Have a Manhattan then or an Old-Fashioned," Peggy said. "You look like you need something to warm you up."

"A Dubonnet, please. I can't get used to all your cocktails," Dany said. Peggy had invited her to lunch before shopping for baby clothes. "I love sitting on the bus. Upstairs, you call it the double decker, don't you? But it was cold. Don't I look like I'm carrying twins? God, I hope not. One will be enough, won't it?"

"You're not that big. You're just magnifying the way you feel because it's getting close to the time," Peggy said. "You feel good, don't you?"

"Yes, but I thought motherhood fills you with a sense of jubilance. I'm glum and irritable and I look like a stuffed bear. Of course, I'm hungry all the time. Little wonder I look stuffed!" Dany said. "What's new from Boston?"

"Arthur said business has been good all week. After the wonderful reviews it should be," Peggy said. "You'll feel better when they all come back next week, won't you?"

"Louis has been back for a few days. We went to a restaurant last night. He is not very comfortable in New York, and he will not speak English. He tries but he is too modest and timid. We went to Passy. You know it, don't you?"

"Yes. Arthur loves it. It's too posh and serious for me. Good food though."

Peggy loved the Village; this simple Italian place where the food was probably excellent and Mrs. Arthur Bellamy was an unfamiliar name.

"I lived in Passy when I first went to Paris," Dany said. "The restaurant is nothing like my old neighborhood. And now I am wondering if I am not starting here the same way I did back there. It seems so long ago and it has only been a year. A young woman came in yesterday, she'd been upstairs at the milliner's. She is opening at a club down here, Number One? She wants me to copy a dress. That's how I began; copying dresses for ladies who lived in Passy. Am I starting all over again?" Dany didn't want to think about it. "Peggy, I'm ravenous. What do you suggest for lunch?"

"Spaghetti. A big bowl of it to cheer you up." Peggy waved to a waiter. "You're worrying about work, aren't you?"

"I have to be busy after I come home from the hospital. Oh, how I hope the play is successful. For everyone; and it will help me to find new business if it is, won't it?"

"When dear Arthur made his arrangement with you in Paris, Dany, it was solely for *Taste of Vice,* wasn't it?"

"Yes, haven't the bills been proper?" Dany asked. "I've tried to be careful." Peggy had said "Dear Arthur" quite sarcastically. "He told me no one in New York worked the way I did and I could be very successful here."

"And you will be. I don't want you to worry about this. Arthur spends money rather effusively but sometimes he gets too careful. His theatrical judgment is superb, nonpareil, shall we say? In other areas he wavers a bit. That's another story and I'll tell you about it sometime. Anyway, Arthur's money comes from me, all of it. I don't look like a rich woman but I am. Very rich. You didn't think any further than this one production when you left Paris. Not very intelligent, Dany. And why my husband would allow such a deal I can't imagine." Peggy stopped, laughed suddenly, and pointed a finger at Dany. "Listen. If you have to make copies for singers in Detroit nightclubs or for the Albertina Rasch dancers at the St. Regis, do it. It's business. Before long you'll be doing every first rate play on Broadway. In the meantime don't worry about your rent."

"But, Peggy—"

"Never mind and don't interrupt. I own the building anyway. That's why we put you up there," Peggy said. "You mustn't worry. Arthur shouldn't have brought you over here for one play. He should have signed a contract with you. We'll forget that now. I know what he was counting on." Peggy seemed pleased to lean back against the red leather banquette, before going on. "He hoped you'd be depending on him for help. That is the kind of relationship he hopes for. Because, Dany, Arthur has his eye on you."

"What? I don't understand."

"My dear girl, in a few months when he thinks it'll be proper for you to be going out, he'll behave like a suitor asking you to all the clubs. He'll say it's business and along the way he'll find time to give you a little pinch, what he calls making a pass. Though I don't think you'd classify it as a very serious pass. I don't for one minute think you would entertain such an idea. But just in case, listen to me, Dany. Don't do it. You'll find work on your own and you won't owe Arthur one American cent. I said I'd tell you more someday and I will. Not today."

Dany wanted to ask questions but obviously she shouldn't. Peggy said not today. When Peggy was speaking she was decisive. Dany never knew anyone as resolute and sure. Her husband was a cheat; yet how matter of fact she was. She said it like a radio announcer giving a news bulletin. Dany was not to ask questions. When would Peggy be ready to talk again?

"Now we must get over to University Place. No one in New York has baby clothes like this woman. You'll see. It's worth coming down here. She is a Belgian and wait until you see the stitching she does, the quality of her work."

"I thought I'd make things myself but when was there time?" Dany said. "Now it's too late. For the first time in my life I don't feel like sewing. A magazine reporter is coming to interview me later this afternoon. I've never been interviewed before either. The young Ingolls boy from the press office is bringing him."

"Peter is my nephew. My sister's son."

"I didn't know that. He seem to be a very bright young man."

"But not in love with the production end of the theatre." Peggy seemed rather annoyed. "He'll be going back to school next year. He wants to be a lawyer now." She sighed. "We don't raise artists in my family, I'm afraid."

Dany wanted to ask questions again but knew she mustn't. Like Charlotte and Gerard, another odd kind

130

of marriage. Arthur was a philanderer and Peggy knew about it. She talked about it in the most clear-cut way. Dany decided it was rather nervy for Peggy to assume she'd be interested in Arthur. Dany couldn't wait for Renee to get back. Renee would explain, Renee always knew. Peggy was not unattractive, just rather plain. Not interested in clothes or cosmetics. No children and she didn't like many of the things that Arthur cared about — Twenty-One and the Colony, the smart restaurants and cabarets. Peggy liked coming downtown to 12th Street, to red checkered tablecloths and informality.

Did Peggy expect "suitors" to come calling after the baby was born? Funny, and so old-fashioned. Madame Mounet, the young widow in a nineteenth century novel, longing once more for the sound of wedding bells.

She'd never heard wedding bells at her modest wedding in Amiens. And modesty didn't exist in the world she lived in. Here it was all about bravura and eclat. That was what she had to learn and it took a special frame of mind not to be embarrassed by it. She had expert trainers and she'd master it. Charlotte certainly had, and Renee was the mistress of bravura. Peggy had it too, Dany supposed. An easy, relaxed kind of authority. In spite of her spare makeup, her sandy, uncoiffed hair, the tan cashmere cardigan over the chestnut wool skirt and without any mannerisms, Peggy was noticed. She had presence unless her plainness was an affectation. How else could a tall, stout woman look? No matter, Peggy had authority. That came from being used to money. She said she was very rich. How very American! To simply say it openly and directly. That was bravura, too.

* * *

131

Dany avoided the workroom now that it was empty. The bare worktable, the silent sewing machines, the unoccupied chairs were not a happy sight. Soon, she thought, the clamor in the room must begin again. Peggy said she wasn't to worry. The windows in the little bedroom needed curtains. Without much enthusiasm Dany had to sew. She had to have something new to wear for opening night. She had to force herself to cut the length of silk faille that Louis said she must have as a kind of Renaissance dress to fall softly over her new round figure. It was an amusing sketch Louis had made, an exaggerated version of a Bellini woman with a slight indication of Dany's head. The swollen figure in profile, the face looking straight out from the paper with one eye closed in a devilish wink. *"La Vierge Et l'enfant"* scrawled in India ink across the bottom of the page. Louis was witty sometimes. Was he telling her something? A sly comment on her condition? She must not dwell on what the others were thinking.

The traffic on Madison Avenue was very loud. Nothing unusual, she thought, but she'd never been aware of it before. The noise in the workroom had been loud before she had to fire the small group that had worked so diligently to finish the costumes for the Boston opening.

The kettle was on, the round table was clear of pin boxes and scissors and set for tea. Tea with Charlotte the last afternoon before she boarded the *Normandie* for Paris.

They hadn't seen each other often in the past month. No time for long walks, looking in shops, no visits to museums and art galleries. Rehearsals and preparing the new production had prevented all that; maybe it was for the best. Maybe she hadn't wanted to see Charlotte alone. Maybe she was afraid. Nonsense! Charlotte thought of her as fearless. Hadn't Renee said it back in Paris? It was too late, anyway, to be concerned with suspicions. Particularly from Charlotte. No matter now; the next few weeks would be filled with goodbyes. Only Renee would be in New York. But, oh, what a solace that was.

The downstairs bell rang.

"What are you carrying?" She called as Charlotte came up, with bags and packages. "Have you bought out the shops?"

"Presents! Gifts for the baby, for you and a few for me." She was out of breath. "They have things here we never can get at home. I may leave you a shopping list for the next year. You can send me a package every month."

"Happily," Dany said. "But if the play is a success you will be coming back."

"If." Charlotte took off her coat. "It does get cold here, doesn't it? And the crowds. Fifth Avenue is a mob scene! Where do they come from? But aren't the shop windows glorious before Christmas? I want to be a child again."

Dany laughed. "You are a child. How was the trip from Boston? How is everyone?"

"Fine, fine. Renee is very pleased with herself. Though they are quite nervous about coming to New York."

"I know. Peggy says the critics are very difficult here." Dany went to the kitchen.

"I brought pastries," Charlotte called out. "In one of these bags is a box of the best looking petits fours

133

you've ever seen."

"From the shop on Sixty-first Street? I bought them, too!" She laughed, the apprehension was gone. "I don't have a workroom full of hungry women. There are enough pastries here for a week!"

"Doesn't little mother need her sweets? You can have them every afternoon." Charlotte arranged a plate. "How do you feel? Are you all right?"

"Yes, I'm very healthy but how I wish it was over."

"I envy you. Now let me carry the tray," Charlotte said. "Who in the world but Dany Mounet could have done all this? The voyage over here, a new country, this atelier and the play!"

Dany looked at her. The soft grey suit, sleek and smooth over the thin body, the lavender ruffle of her blouse framing the slender neck. Soignárlotte, envious? It was too funny, slightly foolish. "I do it," Dany said. "That is all. I just do it." She said it without thinking. It was a reflex but it was true.

"Aren't you ever afraid?"

"Lately," Dany said. "I have been a little."

"Don't be, Dany. I couldn't bear it if I thought you were afraid."

"Then I won't be. I promise." Dany couldn't bear the admiration. "May I open my gifts?"

"Of course. I can't wait for you to see what I found."

"Charlotte!" Dany found knitted sweaters, one after another in the first box. White with pale yellow edges, creamy ivory with a pale pistachio green cording, a cardigan with pearl buttons, a hooded jacket embroidered in lavender.

"I couldn't resist the color. For a boy or a girl, it is a beautiful color," Charlotte said.

"And all done by hand. You are mad!" Dany ex-

134

claimed. If Charlotte was suspicious she'd never have done all this.

"There are more." Charlotte reached for another package. "Open this!"

The brushes and combs, the tiny fork and spoon were sterling silver. It didn't matter if Charlotte knew. She probably would be more protective and concerned. Charlotte might consider the child a bond between the three of them; between herself, Gerard and Dany. Lunacy, but Charlotte never moralized. She lacked conscience. Otherwise she wouldn't be going home tomorrow, to buy a villa, perhaps to spend a few days in Marseilles or Genoa or wherever, one of those ports.

"You can't get these Irish and English things in Paris," she said. The blankets were of the sheerest, lightest wool. "Adorable, no?"

"Such largesse, Charlotte. I'm embarrassed!"

"Nonsense." Charlotte poured more tea and lit a cigarette. "I want you to dream about coming back for the summer. You can work ten months and then come over. Think about it. Dany, don't you dream? Have a corner of your mind constantly filling up with lavish, extreme ideas, beyond what is sensible and practical. A holiday in the South of France! A sable coat, paintings. Collect something, something no one has seen yet. Dany, have extravagance. It's the most delicious feeling." She meant it, her lavender eyes were beseeching. Then she went on slowly. "A comfort. You can have it all, Dany. Remember that. It isn't too late for you."

Why did Charlotte think this was true? Was she going to go on? Did she want to talk about her mysterious trips in Europe? Dany wanted to interrupt her, she'd never acknowledged the fact before but now she didn't want to hear any of it. If Charlotte told her then the trips and the danger were facts and Dany didn't want any verification.

"Dany, all of this makes up for something I've never been able to have. These gifts! Imagine if they were Renoirs, a new Matisse. Today I saw a Hopper painting. I want it."

"Charlotte, extravagance requires money. Lots of it." Dany looked at Charlotte's eyes, twinkling with the thoughts of buying more and more. And she saw Gerard's expression next week after Charlotte was gone. The hapless, forlorn eyes, the way he'd looked in Paris when Charlotte went away. These things she mustn't think about now. What a difficult exercise, to block thoughts out of one's mind. Dany tried to laugh, listening to Charlotte.

"You'll have it. I have no doubts," Charlotte said. "I must be going. I'm packing without a maid and as usual I'm going home with more than I arrived with. Are you alone tonight? What are you doing?"

"The theatre with Peggy and some of her friends." Thank God. This was a night Dany didn't want to spend alone. "We're seeing a musical, *I Married An Angel,* did you see it?"

"No, but Gerard did. He'd like to do it in Paris. He thinks American musicals will be wonderful for Paris." Charlotte hesitated. "Well, little sister, goodbye for now. I'll call you in two weeks and you can let me hear the little one cry into the transatlantic phone!" She put on her coat. "I'll carry my hat. I love the feel of the wind whirling around the Plaza." She kissed Dany, holding her close. They walked to the door. "I hope to see you very soon." She was halfway down the stairs when she turned. "Remember what I said, *chérie.* Start dreaming!"

136

Dany stepped out of the stage door into the glaring afternoon sunlight. Venard's last dress rehearsal was over. It had run smoothly, faultlessly and it was completely unnecessary. Louis had sulked all afternoon, sitting in the dark theatre with Dany at his side and the scenic studio men behind him. The problems with the second act staircase were solved but Louis was restless and worried. He hadn't agreed with Robert, wearing costumes wasn't going to keep up the company's energy level before the opening performance.

"Another layer of sweat and more wrinkles in the costumes." Louis said it with a pout and he sat at the run-through like a petulant diva, grunting and complaining.

Louis had a point. The costumes now had to be pressed and ready for the curtain at 8:30 P.M. The wardrobe mistress and the dressers would have no time for a dinner break. On the other hand, Dany understood Robert. He was right, too. Though he did treat the company and crew like cattle when he had his own case of first night jitters.

She hadn't seen Gerard. Arthur had taken him to the barber shop. *"Quel optimisme!"* Renee had said. "And what nerve!" Dany was glad. She hadn't been alone with Gerard since. . . . She almost laughed at herself. Nine months had gone by and she'd managed to avoid any time alone with Gerard. What a relief!

The cold air was bracing and Dany turned up her coat collar, catching her breath. She would walk back to the atelier, have a nap, a hot bath and then she would dress slowly. Indulgences she never had time for. Peggy's car was picking her up at 8 P.M. It was exciting, her first New York opening. The traditional party at Sardi's and the prospect of applause as the actors entered the restaurant. Peggy had explained the custom.

She had arranged the party and Dany prayed for an ovation when Renee walked into the restaurant.

Her first opening night dress was hanging on the door of the bedroom armoire. She had steamed it carefully this morning before hanging it up. She wished she could dress without looking in a mirror. The sight this morning had been a shock. She grimaced remembering the picture in the armoire mirror. How long, she had asked aloud, standing there, looking at her reflection. She had stretched her neck, thought her cheeks were fatter than ever and turned away blaming the mirror. A fun house mirror, distorting the image. No human being could be so fat! She hoped the dress would fit.

At least she had time. It would feel good to walk home though everybody on the street looked so cold, holding their hats, hunching their shoulders, and stiffening against the icy wind.

Louis came out behind her, giving her a kiss and an apology. "I said *'merde'* to Renee and the appropriate good wishes to the company. Robert is such a bitch at times but I wished him good luck. Which way are you going, *chérie?*"

"I want to walk. Do you?" Dany asked.

"No, No. Thank you," Louis faltered. "I will have a drink before I go to the hotel to change. *Merde, chérie, a toute a l'heure.*"

"*Merde,* Louis." She pulled her wool hat down over her ears. Louis turned toward Eighth Avenue and the bar near the corner. He waddled along briskly and from the alley at the next theatre a figure appeared, walking quickly and joining him. A tall, burly young man in a windbreaker clapping a hand on Louis's back as he caught up with him.

Dear Louis, how does he do it? Dany wished Renee was with her. Louis was smiling, his round face almost hidden between the brim of his black felt fedora pulled low over his forehead and the folds of his gray wool muffler wrapped over his chin. A brief hello and the two of them walked down the street to the saloon. Oh, how Renee would go on; Dany could hear her. "What would Louis do if there weren't workmen around the theatre for him to seduce? And Louis thinks he is discreet!" How Renee would laugh!

Dany turned to walk across town. This was indeed a beginning, and tonight was very important. An Arthur Bellamy play was expected to be stylish and elegantly produced. He had a reputation for presenting the most tasteful plays in New York, always stylish revivals but this was something new. A cast of well-known American actors and Renee Hugo. A major debut and all the publicity, the interviews had stressed the distinction of her arrival. It was Venard's first play and the eminent Ostier was making a New York debut, too. Eminent, yes, but would the foreigners be rewarded with approval? Dany walked faster, agitation was contagious. She wanted to be on her bed closing her eyes for a little while. In her bathtub, feeling the tingle of soap bubbles. She was having her own spell of opening night nervousness.

The florist had said she wasn't to worry, the flowers would certainly be delivered to the theatre on time. The bouquets of garnet roses for the women in the cast and the single flowers for the men. Peggy had suggested Constance Spry. They send flowers for opening nights all the time, she had said. Dany fretted now, she hoped they were backstage before the call for half-hour. And the champagne for Renee. It seemed so much more lavish to give Renee her favorite Veuve Clicquot as a good luck gift. She'd probably open it and have a glass before she finished her makeup—if Sherry's delivered on

139

time.

God, she was tired. Dany wished she had taken a taxi but the fresh, cold air had to be good for her. It was only a few blocks more to Fifty-fifth Street. The doctor had said she must walk. He should see the steps from the basement of the theatre up to the stage sometime. Maybe he'd reevaluate his prescriptions for exercise!

The pain in the small of her back startled her as she took her keys out of her bag. Like a knife jabbing into her back. No, it was a butcher's cleaver striking heavily into a piece of meat. She leaned against the vestibule wall looking at the flight of stairs up to the apartment. The pain disappeared, she took a deep breath and went quickly up the steps.

It wasn't a good idea to have a nap; she might sleep through the night. A long, warm bath was a better idea. Much better, Dany thought. She went to the bathroom to let the water run. As she reached for the tap to feel the temperature of the water, another pain struck. Oh no, she cried out. She held the edge of the bathtub, forcing herself not to shut her eyes. A clamp was crushing and tightening against her abdomen. She mustn't faint; not now but the pain didn't stop. She reached to turn off the faucets.

Impossible! This was impossible. There was no one to call. Peggy was at the hairdresser's. Why? She would not look any different after hours sitting under the dryer! Or she was on her way home to dress. Renee was at the theatre. What timing, what terrible timing! She had to get to the telephone. The lamps seemed to be blazing suddenly. The room blurred for a second. She breathed deeply again and sat on the bed, opening her phone book.

"Dr. Ginsburg, *s'il vous plait?*" What idiocy, she was speaking French. She waited, looking at her watch. 4:30

140

P.M. Please God, let him be there. *"Oui, Madame Mounet ici,"* she was doing it again. She described the pains. "Yes," she said. "Yes, I can. No, my friends will be at the theatre. Yes, I can get there by myself. Thank you, I will meet you at the hospital."

She looked at the Madonna dress hanging on the armoire door. "I will never wear that dress!" She was talking French. She was talking to herself! This was maddening. No time to pack the little bag she was supposed to have ready at this moment. Get to the hospital as quickly as possible! And a cold, icy rain pounded the streets.

The blessing was to see the couple getting out of the cab across the street at Chez Robert.

"Taxi, wait! Please," she called out. "Quick, take me to Leroy Sanitarium or I may have my baby in your taxi."

"She stole the show in her own way, didn't she? The little devil!"

That canary could chirp from the highest tree and the voice would be recognized on the ground. Even when Renee whispered she could be heard in the last row of the balcony. Dany had stopped dreaming, the dull aching was almost pleasant and the cheerful voices seemed far away, as if she heard talking out in the corridor. When she opened her eyes Dany thought the room was shadowy and blurred. It cleared and she saw them, Renee and Peggy, far away at the foot of the hospital bed.

"You were conspicuous by your absence, my dear, and we were worried. You can be expecting lots of company, the entire cast is coming to visit," Peggy was saying. "Thank the Lord that Harold Ginsburg called.

141

I'd have been frantic not knowing where you were."

"I asked him to call you," Dany said. "Before they gave me the ether." Was that fragile voice her own? "How exhausting this is!"

"No wonder!" Renee balked now, teasing. "She was a week early, the little scene-stealer!"

"You saw her?" Dany asked. "Isn't she fine?"

"A rather fat little beauty," Peggy said.

"Wrinkled, not a beauty at all. *Jolie-laide*." Renee laughed. "But wait, you'll see. She'll be a beauty."

"I told you it would be a girl. Veronique. Veronique Mounet. It has a good sound to it." It was a struggle to stay awake, but she must. She had to hear about last night. "It is so good of you both to come. Now tell me about the opening."

"I thought you'd never ask, *chérie!*" Renee looked at Peggy.

"We brought you all the newspapers. Atkinson adored it. Better reviews than in Boston."

"Better than Paris," Renee squealed with delight. "Wait until you read them! We are ecstatic. When I heard the applause walking into Sardi's, well, that was the best part!"

Dany shut her eyes. "I'm so happy." What good news. Now to get on with this new life. To be out of here, home with little Veronique. And working. She must call every producer, all the designers. She must get to know every one of them. Her small atelier must be filled with sewing women and noise. It was going to be good. She felt it. She was sleepy, very sleepy, but at last it was over. The wondering, the pain, and now the odd feeling of accomplishment. She had a baby, fragile but healthy. And a week early. What a blessing, little Veronique couldn't wait. Was this a sign? The child was an accomplice, helping with the calendar.

"I think the little thing looks like Simon," Dany sighed. "Is it possible to tell so soon? Simon's child, his daughter. He'd have wanted a boy. All fathers want a little boy, don't they?" Maybe the clientele at Sardi's would applaud this performance. She was weak and tired, so tired but she had to go on with it. "Well, he will never know, will he? But I'll tell Veronique about him. I will, I will. She will know about poor Simon who died too young." She wasn't brave enough to look at Renee. "Peggy, is Venard pleased? Did they like Louis's work?"

"You can read the reviews later. We can't stay too long. You must rest," Peggy said. "Give me your keys and I'll go to your apartment. I'll have the driver bring back your things. You can't lie here looking like a charity case in that hospital gown."

Peggy, bossy and maternal, fixing the pillows, straightening the bed covers and finally a warm pat on the cheek.

They were saying goodbye. Renee, coq feathers and sealskin, bending over her, lips fluttering, kisses and murmuring. "Little one, I'll be here again tomorrow. Shall we read the baby her godmother's reviews? All the raves! Sleep now, *chérie,* sleep."

Dany said goodbye to them. She was going to fall asleep again. It was impossible to fight the feeling of drowsiness, the comfortable sense of allowing fatigue to take over. She had managed it all on her own. Charlotte will be impressed. In a while, a nurse would come in to the room carrying Veronique. In a little while she would be holding her daughter.

Then Dany remembered the surprising image, the face that had hovered in the air over her dreams yesterday. All through the anesthetic, right up to the last minute. The handsome, dark face, lean and smooth with the

143

mocking, amused grin. That fellow from the other costume shop at the rehearsals in Boston. Jack Albert. His face. How curious, how really bizarre, and how blissful it had been to see him floating there. Not quite an apparition, no, he had been clear and touchable.

"Am I Madame Dubarry receiving at Versailles? Look at the flowers, the fruit, and candies! The gifts! And every hour I have been saying goodbye to somebody," Dany said.

"Only one more, little one. How was Louis?" Renee asked:

"Sad. Very sad. Not because he was leaving but because I wasn't going back with him."

He had come in like a shy choirboy, embarrassed by the baby and ill at ease in the hospital room. But dear Louis, he had brought roses, two of a color, carefully selected to make up the enormous bouquet of varied shades of red and pink, yellow and white as if he had been mixing paints on his palette. After all the small talk and platitudes he was silent.

"Come now, Louis. You must be very happy to be going home," Dany had said.

"Yes, but you should be going with me. I have so much work waiting for me. And this is not your home." He bit his lips and sulked.

"It is now, Louis," Dany said.

"You had begun a successful career in Paris. And I will need you." He was petulant and looked hurt. It was selfish of him but he had said it. "Who will execute my work now? Who will understand?"

"You are far too talented to need anyone, Louis. You know how to make the costumes yourself, you can direct anyone in any workroom in the world, *mon chér.*"

Louis tried to hide his satisfaction after hearing that. He tried to suppress his grin and his body quivered with ego and pride. "Ah, but all the same, Dany—"

She didn't let him finish. "This is not a death sentence, Louis. It isn't as if we will never see each other again."

He kissed her brow. "I know, I know." It was the benevolent caress of a charitable priest. "Yes, one day we shall meet again." He took his coat and hat, wrapped his scarf around his neck and shuffled out of the room.

"Louis wasn't happy in New York. Perhaps there is too much urgency here," Dany told Renee. "A pace he'd never get used to."

"I think Paris is safer for him. He can have his hiding places there and pretend that his secrets are well kept."

They must talk about something else now. Renee was too wise. Louis and then Robert had come in alone to say goodbye but now Renee was here to wait for Gerard. Yes, Renee was canny enough to be in the room when Gerard came to say goodbye. Renee was very clever and perceptive.

"Robert doesn't want to go back to France. Did you know that?" Dany asked. "I've never felt that I knew Robert, not at all the way I know you and Louis. He stays the outsider, doesn't he? But the things he talked about today!"

"A peculiar devil, our Venard, but there is so much feeling in the man."

How old was Robert? Dany couldn't tell. The thin layer of powder on that strong, tough face. Was it pure vanity or a useless attempt to disguise the years?

"I'd like to be staying, too," Robert had said. "I hope to be back in the fall. The agent at the Morris office thinks he'll have a play for me."

145

"Oh, Robert, how marvelous that will be!" Dany said.

"Dany, we have friends who don't like to see the truth. They believe they can go along living the way they have since the Twenties. They ignore all the signs, the warnings. They are ostriches. I don't want to be a soldier. I think we will have war very soon and I do not want to be in it. I want to be here in America."

"Maybe I'm an ostrich too." She had no opinion. She hadn't thought about it. She had been too busy to think, that was it. "You must come back if you can find work here, Robert."

"Even if I am running away? Deserting a party that has become too loud and lasted too long to go on to another that promises to be brighter. Given by a younger crowd."

"Have you done that before?"

"Maybe not as often as I'd like," Robert said. "Sorry, I didn't mean to be so serious today. You must have a great success here, Dany. Make a happy life for yourself and your daughter." His heavy boxer's hands were gentle on her shoulders. "I must go now. *A toute a l'heure,* Dany my friend."

Dany propped up the sagging pillows. "Oh, how I want to get out of this bed, Renee!" She pulled at the blanket. "I'm learning about understanding, Renee. Unspoken thoughts."

"I don't think you have to learn, *chérie.*" Renee's eyebrows lifted.

"I hope Robert can come back here. It was very flattering that he wanted to tell me what he felt."

The knock at the door was tentative and light.

"Aha, another one!" Renee lit a cigarette. "Never mind, in a little while you will have Veronique to say hello to and then I think you should have a glass of

146

champagne. Come in, come in! Gerard, look at her! Does this creature look like a mother or a girl of twelve going to her first communion?"

"More flowers! Thank you, Gerard." Dany smiled. She had her cue from Renee. Lighthearted and animated, if she could keep it that way. The flowers were blue, deep blue salvia and almost purple iris. "Oh how pretty they are!"

Where had he found them? Blue at this time of the year! Was he remembering that other time? The night he brought her cornflowers when they were to go to Deux Magots. She had to be careful now.

"Give me your coat," Renee ordered.

"You do look twelve years old," he said.

"Well, today perhaps fifteen." She was playing a coy ingenue. "It seems I have been sleeping for a week and I've never been this tired in my life." The afternoon sun glared into the room. Did he have the doleful look she had expected to see? "Now I feel like going back to work. I wish I could go to the theatre tonight. How are you, Gerard? Just think, in a week you will be home again." She hoped she wasn't going on too nervously. "I haven't learned about impeccable timing, have I? I'm sorry I missed the opening."

"Nothing is wrong with your timing, *chérie*. You had an opening of your own!" Renee squealed. "Look, the child still blushes!"

Dany felt her cheeks redden. "Pull down the shade, please. The sun is too bright for you."

"That's why I moved my chair. Footlights! At my age I need only footlights." Renee went on laughing.

"When will they allow you to leave here?" he asked. He didn't look as mournful as she thought. But he'd been in the theatre longer than Renee and maybe he was giving his best performance today.

"In three days we go home. Peggy has found a nurse and in a month the nanny arrives. I hope she likes the sound of sewing machines."

"Hope they are whirring furiously. You'll need money to support—what is she called? Nanny!" Renee said.

"I'll manage." Dany had thought of extravagance and taking Charlotte's advice. Now Renee was criticizing.

"Dany always finds a way," Gerard said. "I have faith."

"Thank you, Gerard."

"Oh, so do I," Renee said. "This little one will be a star. Remember what I told you, *chérie*. Act like a star and they'll think you're a star."

"And next summer you will come to the Riviera. Charlotte told me she insisted," Gerard said. His face darkened. "She must be in Nice today, signing the papers." His hand trembled slightly as he lit his cigarette. "Next summer we will be together in Villefranche."

"First you must find a new play for me! Something wonderful and new and funny that we can bring to New York again! Why don't you ask Deval to write something like *Tovarich* for me. Or get a new play from Achard." Renee pulled at the brim of her velvet hat. "Something delicious for a fat comedienne."

"Yes, yes," Dany said. "With many costume changes, all very chic!" Charlotte had told her to dream. It wasn't difficult. It never was but she thought she'd lost the habit. Like being on a diet, she'd wanted to dream but she couldn't allow herself the pleasure.

"Talk to Venard about a new play for next year. You'll have plenty of time on the *Ile de France* to plan a new season and Robert is very gloomy, Gerard. He needs cheering up," Renee said.

"He told you how worried he is?" Gerard asked.

"Yes; he told Dany too."

148

"He gets too involved with politics and melodramatics." Gerard seemed annoyed. "He should stick to comedy. To farce."

"He's very concerned. Is he right, Gerard?" Dany asked. "I was surprised to see Robert full of fear and in a way he seemed alienated."

"Did he have to worry you about it? Now? It was thoughtless." Gerard was irritated. "He's a male Cassandra."

"Gerard," Renee interrupted abruptly. "I think he may be right."

"If he is then he shouldn't go home," Gerard said. "We're all afraid." He went to the window to raise the shade, holding on to the string. He stared out to the street. The sunlight was gone, no shadows on the floor or the wall. Gerard's voice was low, as if he might be overheard. "We all feel threatened. We all have our private ghettos and mine is populated by too many ghosts." He let go of the shade; an instant flap of sound and he turned around. "I'll talk to him. As you said we'll have plenty of time on the ship. Now do you think the nurses will allow me to see this little Veronique?"

A simple and innocent request. Oh no, pull the shade down again, Gerard! Quick, make the room dark. She'd never thought he'd want to look at Veronique. She hadn't rehearsed this part of the scene. "Renee, will you take Gerard down the hall to see the baby?"

"You can't sit here night after night reading novels and magazines," Peggy said. "Veronique is very well cared for. You ought to get out. I'll understand it when the workroom is busy and you're exhausted at the end of a day. But, Dany, now isn't the time to be alone."

"That's what Renee said." Dany looked at the little sitting room, neat and pristine. No bolts of fabric, no iron racks of finished costumes. The rug looked sterile without tufts of thread and fallen pins after a day of fittings. Maybe Louis Ostier had been right, she should have gone back to Paris. Peggy didn't understand. It was a simple pleasure to have music playing softly, an American novel in her hand, knowing that Veronique was safe in her crib with Kate Mullaney nearby ready to change a diaper, give her a bottle. Dany could run into the room when the baby cried and hold her and spoil her before Katie came in to take charge.

Dany convinced herself that this routine was temporary, that's why she liked it. Making dresses for a girl who sang at the Number One wasn't a career. It wasn't even a way to make a living. It was unpleasant to go to the theatre now, to sit there not listening to the play, not hearing the music. Only watching and making notes to herself. Uneven hemlines, ill-fitting dresses in shoddy cloth and poorly made. Probably not true but she was envious. She wanted to get started again. This wasn't the flat in Passy. It wasn't the workroom off the street near the Rue du Bac. No, it was her New York atelier, better than Paris. This was supposed to be an auspicious beginning.

"When do you see this Thornton fellow?" Peggy asked. "Arthur knows the owner of the French Quarter and a recommendation wouldn't hurt. They do very lavish revues, you know."

"He's coming to show me his sketches on Friday. Of course a word from Arthur might help but I don't think night club owners go to see plays like *Taste of Vice*. Do you?"

"Dany, don't be a snob. That's so unlike you!"

"It isn't what I meant," Dany said. "I thought pro-

ducers would be queuing up on this street, that the
phone wouldn't stop ringing after the notices for the
play. I expected a bit more prestige, that's all." It was
exasperating. She'd been out of the hospital for over a
month. Fortunately Winnie Olsen had come along with
her night club booking, with the dresses to be copied
and her very rich friend to pay for them. She'd ordered
four more, how she loved her image in the fitting room
mirror. "In Paris everything happened so quickly for
me. I haven't the patience now. Maybe I expected too
much."

"It's a good thing you did," Peggy said. "I'm not
worried about you. I want to see the baby again before
I leave. Oh, why won't you come out tonight? Arthur
is in Philadelphia seeing something. A few of us are going to Chinatown. A place with wonderful food and,
Dany, you haven't been there."

It was easier to say yes than to have Peggy nagging
at her. "All right. I'll have to change my clothes. Will
you wait?"

"Nonsense! It's very casual, you look fine," Peggy
was happier when Arthur was away.

Tom Thornton was an exuberant fellow, younger than
Dany had imagined. There was no doubt from the moment he walked in that she'd have the order. He had
admired her work when he saw *Taste of Vice*. He was
determined to find someone new to execute his designs
and Dany was a dream come true for him. He was energetic and nervous showing her the designs. Dany remembered Louis Ostier's sketches for the masquerade
balls in Paris. These drawings were elaborate, too,
though not as well drawn. But then, who had Louis's
style?

Tom made an agitated gesture, sketching in the air. "Silky and understated. Do you see what I mean?" His hands rippled in front of her. "Diaphanous, the aura of a Paris night." She assumed he'd been there. Then he showed another group of sketches. "Trim, striking and sharp." His long, bony fingers slashed the air in clipped movements. "Sexy. You understand, you're French! I didn't want to go anywhere else. We'll create something new. I'll get lost in the workroom at one of the big houses. They all get so busy."

Dany couldn't resist that. The designs were simple in line but the colors were a bit harsh. She wasn't going to be critical, she needed the work. Forget about Louis and his faultless sense of color. Thornton was a new, young designer eager to make a splash. He had a future to think about. She did too.

"Do you know Frank Norwin, Madame Mounet?"

"No." Dany didn't recognize the name. "Should I?"

"He's the owner of the French Quarter and he spoke very highly of you. I wondered if you'd met him in Paris. He goes there twice a year to see the Folies Bergere. To steal ideas!"

"I'm pleased that he knows about me but I've never met the man." Dear Peggy; obviously she'd asked Arthur to make a phone call. Would Tom Thornton laugh if she told him she'd never been to the Folies Bergere.

"Now Mr. Thornton—" Why was it difficult to pronounce his name? And why was he so sloppy, with his paint-spotted corduroy jacket and that loosely knotted knit tie over a wrinkled maroon shirt? "We should make lists and you must give your specifications. The fabrics you want, trimmings, everything."

"Do you have a good milliner? The hats are going to be very important."

"No, not yet." The woman who had made Louis's

smart turn of the century hats had gone back to her former job in a wholesale factory. She had hated the pressure of the theatre, the temperament and the ego of the actresses. The woman in the little shop upstairs, Mrs. Mennino might be interested, and it would be so convenient. "Trust me, I will find somebody."

This was going to be complicated. Seventy-five costumes to be finished in less than three weeks. The prices—estimates they were called—must be given to Mr. Norwin in two days. Tonight she would make telephone calls to hire back her former workers. Over the weekend she'd shop for fabrics on Rivington Street and she must call Evans Morley, the business manager at Arthur's office. Maybe he would help her with the costs.

"If the prices are approved can you work with me next week, Mr. Thornton?"

"You get your prices ready and I'll tell Mr. Norwin they are cheaper than any of the other houses would be." His voice was higher when he was excited and obviously he was pleased with the meeting. "Everything French represents 'class' to him anyway. In this case he'll be right." He snickered. "And please call me Tom."

"If you will call me Dany." Everything French. She was going to order new labels. Dany Mounet in black letters on white silk and in the left corner New York would be printed, and on the right, Paris. That should have the suggestion of what Tom Thornton had just called "class."

Dany wanted to know what was "classy" about the shouting, squealing crowd at the French Quarter dress rehearsal. Waiters clattering chairs and scraping tables across the floor of the long, narrow room being set up for the new evening show. Bartenders jangling glasses on the horseshoe shaped bar under the faint pink light

153

from the thrusting platform of the first stage level. Behind it was another platform and five feet above it was a bandstand.

Somehow a magnetic tingle was in the air at a theatre rehearsal when voices called out from the darkened rows of orchestra seats to the lit stage. Something was happening; a relationship; a long cord tying the people on the stage to the unseen group working out front. And the efficiency, the determination created sparks that snapped back and forth.

The club looked shabby. The sound of voices from the crew and the crowd of men huddled at tables in front of the stage smoking cigars made it seem tawdry. Not at all the glamorous cabaret she saw the night she brought the estimates to Frank Norwin when the chandeliers were lit, soft music played and the room was filled with a dressed-up audience.

Every few minutes a sharp yellow glare streaked across the front section as the kitchen doors swung open and more waiters came out to set the tables with red cloths, napkins and ashtrays.

"Indigo, please!" was shouted and the club was filled with blue light. The kitchen doors opened again and twelve girls quietly stepped forward. "Christ, what are we gonna do about the light from the kitchen?" The voice was raspy. "We don't wanna see the girls until they get on stage. I want the effect of them coming from out of nowhere. The nowhere being the audience! Where's Frank Norwin?"

"Okay, okay, we'll try to douse the lights. You'd better time it. Shit, Harry, I've got a staff of chefs that have to keep working in the kitchen."

"When you built this place why did you put the dressing rooms behind the kitchen?"

There are no kitchens in a theatre! Dany lit a ciga-

154

rette and sat next to Tom Thornton at a table close to the stage. It wasn't fair to expect performers to walk past the grills and ovens, the busy kitchen reeking with cooking smells. But it would work; the lights would be cued to go out before the girls came on the stage. Food shouldn't be served at that time anyway.

The girls looked sexy in the deep blue satin costumes. Their breasts covered in diamantee chiffon, sheer as spiderwebs. "They look beautiful, Tom," Dany whispered. "It will work. It always does."

It was important to remember that. No matter how much name-calling, yelling and shouting, no matter how serious the problem, a solution was found within minutes or at the most an hour or two.

It always worked and though the specifics varied, each time seemed like the first time. A new show and another deadline to be faced. New designers, new directors and new producers to work with. The temper must be controlled, an attitude of complete and utter discipline must be maintained. No one should see any sign of nervousness or uncertainty. It always worked. To be calm meant to be sure. After all, the work was done by perfectionists. Screaming and hollering was a waste of time. Dany's costumes were executed proficiently. She thought quickly, her fingers moved swiftly in an emergency.

Work! New shows and new deadlines. A cabaret revue called *Bon Voyage* on West Forty-ninth Street, another small revue in the Village on Sullivan Street, the line of dancers at the Maisonette in the elegant St. Regis Hotel.

Two weeks to make scanty, little costumes for the chorus girls called ponies with low necklines, dainty puffed sleeves, rows of tiny ruffles under short, circular skirts. The more exotic showgirls draped and feathered,

155

sequinned and beaded revealing long legs and voluptuous bosoms.

The smoke in the fitting room was heavy enough for a cave in Montmartre. The ostrich feather headpieces were almost as high as the ceiling and the girls gossiped noisily as Dany and a helper delicately placed rows of pearls over nude net covered brassieres. The shriek was piercing, suddenly pearls were flying in the air.

"What happened? I didn't do anything!" a girl cried out.

"Honey, you breathed," another girl said, roaring with laughter. "Your tits are too big, sweetie! Madame Mounet, Sheila needs more pearls." Rows of beads slid off their strings. The floor was a cloud of feathers as the girls knelt to help Dany retrieve them.

"This is the first time I've ever had a complaint." Sheila stood in front of the mirror, clutching her breasts.

"Do these pearls come in a larger size?"

"Open those pearly gates, Sheila!"

"Talk about pearl drops, wow!"

Dany looked at the wheels of the baby carriage moving into the room and then up to Kate Mullaney's totally bewildered face.

"We've had our stroll in the park. What are you looking for?" Kate asked.

"Pearls, Katie, pearls," Dany answered.

"Ooh, look at this adorable child!" Sheila went over to the carriage, her breasts dangling above the baby's face. The pearls were forgotten. The other girls crowded around the carriage cooing with admiration. Veronique reached up, her tiny fingers stretching.

"Look," one of the girls exclaimed. "The baby thinks she has a new rattle!"

"Veronique!" Dany said. "Welcome to the fitting

room!"

Kate had adapted with no trouble at all. She had
been told what to expect when Peggy had sent her to
see Dany in the hospital. Taking care of Veronique was
going to be quite different, not at all like her position
in a big house in Oyster Bay where she lived and
worked after her arrival from Ireland. She had seemed
stern and rigid at first, but the size of Dany's apartment, more workroom than living space, made her relax. Kate found it easy to settle into the casual, frenetic
atmosphere of the atelier, more comfortable without
other servants.

When Dany turned the lights out in the workroom at
the end of the day she went to the kitchen and prepared a meal. She and Kate sat together, eating, talking, and reminiscing. Dany told Kate about Paris and
Amiens, life in the convent when she was a girl. Kate
enjoyed telling exaggerated tales of a childhood of poverty and hardship in Dublin.

Kate was like an older cousin who had come to visit
for a weekend, slightly disdainful and not admitting she
was having a good time but quite willing to stay because she felt sure she was needed.

No child had such a large family of aunts clucking
with admiration and advice. The workroom women ate
their lunch impatiently, rushing to get to the little nursery in the back of the apartment. A few minutes to
visit with Veronique was the brightest part of their day;
affectionate minutes of baby talk in Italian and Russian
and Greek. A sentimental European chorus of ten. Renee and Peggy came in once or twice a week with expensive dolls and toys ready to fuss over the little
celebrity in the playpen.

"Veronique will never know what a man looks like,"

Dany told Renee one Sunday. "Aside from Tom Thornton or one of the other bizarre creatures who come into the workroom."

"Are you talking about your daughter or thinking of yourself, little one?"

"You are a mind reader, Renee, or am I so transparent?"

How many months can go by seeing the same face in a dream? A clear and definite face but probably of pure imagination by now. The face she'd seen only once, at the theatre in Boston. It had to be fantasy by now, not at all an actual human being. Was there a Jack Albert? Why not someone else she had seen just once? She never dreamed of Simon. Or Gerard. No, it was Jack Albert, again and again.

"Dany, you're not listening to me," Renee said. "Who is going to be at the Bellamy's tonight?"

"What? I'm sorry, Renee." Dany stopped daydreaming. "I don't know. Peggy said she wanted to see us before she went to Florida. Arthur wanted to go to the Stork Club but Peggy wanted to have it at home. You know Peggy, she said a small dinner."

"Small to Arthur Bellamy could be thirty people! He is not one for understatement."

"True. They are not at all alike, Arthur and Peggy, are they?"

"No. No, indeed," Renee said. "Have you heard from Charlotte? From any of them in Paris?"

"No," Dany said. "Not a word since her call after Veronique was born. I was going to ask you the same thing."

"If Arthur had his way this apartment would be completely redecorated. He'd have it looking like a house in

158

Beverly Hills. If you want to live in an MGM set, go out there, and build one but don't do it here," Peggy said as they came into the vast foyer. "Tell Maura what you want to drink."

"May I have a Dubonnet, please?" Dany looked into the living room. It was Peggy's room, as cozy as one of her cardigan sweaters. Soft, neutral and not new, like one of her wool skirts, if you looked closely you noticed a fraying seam. No, it was like her mink coat, big, loose, ample and definitely not this season's style, but expensive.

The damask sofas must have been a striking claret color once, now they were faded to a dull maroon. Dark green velvet chairs were rubbed to a shine from too many bodies sitting in them for too long. Lacquered boxes, crystal paperweights, silver lighters and porcelain cups filled with cigarettes, saucers used as ashtrays sat on mahogany and teak tables lit with Chinese urns, jade and quartz vases made into lamps a long time ago. It wasn't a room of valued antiques but all of it was Peggy; treasures well-worn from memories and entertainment.

"Champagne, Renee?" Peggy asked.

"Ah, what a question! Thank you, of course," Renee answered.

"Mes favorites sont ici!" Arthur came toward them. *"Je suis heureux—"*

"Oh Arthur, speak English!" Peggy said. "You sound as if you've had three weeks at Berlitz!"

"It took three years for me to form that sentence. Let me have my fun, my dear." Arthur edged between Dany and Renee. "May I give you a tour of the apartment?"

"No, let them have their drinks and say hello to everyone." Peggy led the way. "You know my nephew,

159

Peter, and Alix. Well, what am I doing? You know everyone except for our dear friends, Ann and Leonard Felman. These two love to invest in the theatre. That means they love to lose money, right, Ann?"

Peggy had kept her word. It was a small party. Evans Morley smiled, his tortoise framed glasses low on the bridge of his nose. He wore the same tweed jacket, gray flannels and grayer pullover sweater that he wore to Arthur's office every day. The same off-white shirt with the badly knotted rust paisley tie. He looked like all the English tourists she used to see at the Cafe Flore in Paris.

"This is my friend, Warren Wilson," Evans said.

Another pleasant smile, like Evans. They looked like brothers, Warren a bit younger in a navy blue suit.

"We met at Sardi's last week. How are you, Madame Hugo?" he asked.

"I'm always marvelous when I have a glass of champagne in my hand." Renee gave Alix Harcourt a warm embrace. *"Mon chou,* it is good to see you. It is too bad our ingenue is so healthy. You never get a chance to go on for her. I watched this child do understudy rehearsals last week and she is very, very good. With the most impeccable French, and Italian, and German. God knows how many other languages. She is brilliant!"

"A bit of very good Yiddish, too." Alix Harcourt was pleased by Renee's compliment. She tossed her head nervously, her straight blond hair flying. "I've considered poison, a bad oyster, anything to make her sick. But no, she is a healthy creature." She laughed, her wide mouth showing large, even teeth. She wasn't as pretty as the girl she understudied but Alix had vitality and an individual kind of flair.

"Oh, look at the view!" Dany went to the windows.

160

She had never seen the park from above Fifth Avenue. "Is there no word for this? In Paris we have *l'heure bleu,* but it is nothing like this! Renee, come look." The light over the trees in the park was mellow, watercolors mixing from blue to mauve to coral in the clear twilight.

"It is something, isn't it? Better than what I'll be seeing in Florida." Peggy came to the windows. "Peter, I hope your mother appreciates what I'm doing this year. Family reunions when I wanted to be in London! We may not have many more chances to go to Europe the way things are going."

War talk. Dany looked at Renee. It was frightening and it made her nervous.

"Have you heard from Gerard or Charlotte?" Arthur asked. "What do you girls think?"

"We talked about them earlier. No, we haven't had a word from them but I don't think we have to worry. They are probably in Villefranche working on the villa," Renee said. "This is the best paté I've ever had. Where do you buy it, Peggy?"

"It's made right here in the kitchen." Everybody laughed.

"What is so funny?"

"We call it chopped chicken liver. I'll tell you how to make it," Peggy said. "Were you changing the subject, Renee?"

"No, no, darling." Renee spread another morsel on a piece of toast. "I don't know what to think. I can't believe we will have war again. But that *cochon* in Berlin, how do we stop him?" Renee waited. "Arthur, will we close next month if your box office doesn't improve? I will have to be going home then."

Dany couldn't imagine New York without Renee. It will be like saying farewell, not adieu, if Renee went back to Paris now. "Gerard will have a new play for you, I'm sure of it, Renee."

"I hope so." Arthur said. "If you want me to tell you the truth, I don't think we can make it through the summer."

"Back to summer stock," Alix said. "Hello Westport, Dennis and Ogunquit!"

"What are those names?" Renee was puzzled.

"What does summer stock mean?" Dany asked.

"We'll tell you about it at the table. Come along," Peggy said. Moira had said dinner was ready. "Now wait until you see our dining room! You'll know what I mean about Hollywood. Arthur wanted a new room and the poor dear, he's lived with my family furniture for so long, I gave in. Now I'd like to murder the decorator and Arthur for allowing it. Come see, it looks like one of the nightclubs you've been working for."

It was more like a photograph in a movie magazine. The walls were stark white with panels of gun metal mirror and Rococo swirl appliques holding gray candlesticks. The same swirl bases held a mirrored table top and the white dining chairs were covered in gray satin.

"I call it bandleader gray," Peggy whispered. "Plain food, everyone! Arthur can dine at Voisin and the Colony for the next month so we're having my favorite simple dinner," Peggy said as they sat down.

Shrimp cocktail and delicious toasted wafers. "We have little theatres in resort towns all around the country," Arthur began to explain. "They open for a season every summer and frequently a good new play is discovered." Renee sitting at his left was fascinated as he described how a resident company worked on new productions every week or two in a New England beach town. Dany listened, wondering what the pressure was that she felt at her ankle. She moved her feet, shifting

162

in her chair and hoping her restlessness was not noticed. There were no dogs or cats in the apartment. Peter Ingolls glanced at her with surprise. She had kicked his foot.

Pink roast beef, baked potatoes and Yorkshire pudding. "Why do you call it pudding?" Renee asked. "It's more like bread."

Brussels sprouts, tomato aspic. Evans was talking about apprentices and how valuable it was to be able to learn all the phases of preparing a production at a summer theatre. Arthur leaned forward to pour more wine for Renee. This time the pressure was at Dany's knee. She squirmed in her seat to change her position. Peter would think it odd if she crossed her legs at the dinner table.

"If Gerard can find a play for you, Renee, to do with the Lunts, it would be the smash of the season. Any season." Arthur went on. Dany looked at the others. Peter was entranced as Alix told about her first summer in Maine at a barn that had been converted to a theatre. Peggy was talking about the new paintings downtown at the Whitney. Suddenly Dany wanted to laugh. This was ridiculous. Arthur was seriously telling them the latest theatre gossip, eating quite properly, and playing with her leg! "I've heard that Sherwood and Sydney Howard want to form their own producing company. Writers should *not* be producers. I'd like to see the faces over at the Theatre Guild when it happens." Now there was a gentle rubbing at her knee. Dany thought of saying something thing to Renee in French but too many others at the table would understand. She mustn't laugh, nothing funny was being said, but she had the uncontrollable feeling she was going to burst into laughter.

"Little one, are you all right? You have a peculiar

look, *chérie.*" Renee came to the rescue without knowing it. The movement under the table stopped.

"I'm fine," Dany said. She'd have been hysterical if he hadn't stopped. "I was thinking that you could do something in one of these stock companies if the play closes." She felt the flush in her cheeks. She must be the color of the jellied tomatoes.

Peggy had been right. Arthur might fancy himself a Don Juan, but wasn't he a clumsy one? When they left the table, would he try to pinch her behind? It was too funny, hilarious really. The silly man. She longed to tell Peggy but she mustn't. Though she'd tell Renee, because Renee would laugh, too.

The chorus girls went upstairs, two at a time, to try on the wide straw hats in Maria Mennino's little shop. When they came back to the fitting room Dany sent two more dancers up to Maria.

"Stunning!" Tom Thornton's twang was sharp. "Exactly what I wanted. They do look lacquered, don't they?"

"Maria is very clever," Dany said. "She spent hours dipping the straw into a bucket of sizing. What patience!"

Maria Mennino was becoming very important to Dany. It was a stroke of luck finding her conveniently up the flight of stairs. There was no room in Dany's atelier for a millinery department and Maria's custom-made business was not too good. That was another stroke of luck for Dany.

"Tom, we can't have the girls sitting here all afternoon." Dany knew the stage manager would be shouting at her on the phone. "Can't we start fitting? Where is that Owen Patterson?"

"He's late all the time. Didn't you know that he goes to the Plaza for a haircut every other Tuesday?" Rancor made his alto voice higher. "Then he has to go to the dentist and to his tailor to fit his new suits. He's a very busy man, Dany, before he starts his day's work. But then you have to remember," Tom's voice became a crafty whisper. "He does work nights, too."

"Tom, behave yourself," Dany scolded. "The girls will hear you!"

Owen Patterson was absurdly perfect; a fashion illustration in *Esquire* magazine, a drawing in a British tailor's album of style, one of the polo players in Old Westbury. He didn't design very often and when he did it was always for a revue produced and directed by Ernest Kester. Kester was well-known for his glamorous revues, for his eccentricities and for hiring the most beautiful dancers and showgirls. He was caustic and sarcastic to those he knew he could frighten and fiercely loyal and generous to the coterie of assistants he used for all the revues he staged. He was most loyal to Owen Patterson.

Months ago Tom Thornton had shown a portfolio of designs to Kester who was impressed. After seeing the show at the French Quarter he was convinced. He wanted Tom to work for him. An agreement was reached for Tom to design two numbers in a music hall revue to open at the World's Fair. Tom was amazed at the fee he was to receive; usually long sessions of arguing and bargaining went on before a new designer finally had to settle for a figure that was too low. Tom's fee was high but Ernest Kester did not tell him until the sketches were finished that all credit in the programs had to go to Owen Patterson. Tom was enraged, wailing about duplicity and chicanery, but he needed the money.

165

Probably to spite Owen, Tom was sloppier than he'd been two months ago when he first came to the atelier, and Owen was as natty as the Duke of Windsor. Maybe that was why he disliked Tom.

"Well, let's start to fit," Tom snapped. "Too bad if he's annoyed when he gets here. We'll have a very cold toast today, that's certain."

"Toast? What does that mean?"

"Oh Dany, you know that Ernest gives all of his favorites nicknames," Tom said. "He calls Owen 'Toast'." Tom imitated Ernest's English accent. " 'Because he's warm as toast.' Couldn't you throw up?" Tom sighed.

It wasn't fair. Tom Thornton was more talented than Owen but Owen wasn't competition for any designer. He worked when Ernest Kester wanted him to work. He didn't sketch, he knew little about fabrics and less about construction. Yet somehow he had a sense of glamour; perhaps it was what he had done about himself, being handsome and obviously attractive. His jackets accentuated his wide shoulders and narrow hips, his shirts were chosen to accentuate his clear blue eyes. He moved like a panther. Had he studied that at the zoo? He was all facade and he had the ability to superimpose his own synthetic veneer on to the bodies of the girls who would be parading in the costumes he dreamed up by drawing vague indications in pencil on a sheet of expensive drawing paper. Or Ernest Kester paid someone else to design for Owen. Ernest and Owen lived together. That was it, Dany saw it clearly. Owen behaved like a well-kept mistress.

Tom had nothing to worry about. "No fretting, chéri. In this business everyone talks too much. They do in Paris and it must be the same here. Gossip will take care of you this time. People are going to know you designed all this for Owen even if your name isn't

on the program. News straight from the fitting room,
Tom? Is there a better way for gossip to start?"

"Arthur Bellamy thinks he's fooling me," Renee said
to Dany on the phone. "He thinks he's the sly one!
Calling to invite me to El Morocco for dancing, using
me as a cover! So be ready, little one, your phone is
going to be ringing within the hour."

"Dancing?" Dany asked. "I didn't know you liked to
dance."

"I do, *chérie,* I love to dance. He's entertaining
friends from the Coast. That phrase—the Coast! Well,
little one, the man is a business manager at one of the
studios. You never can tell. I'd consider Hollywood if I
had the opportunity."

"Promise me that you'll sit next to him," Dany said.
"He'll make me laugh again. I can't take Arthur seri-
ously. He's so unfair to Peggy and he's foolish. Renee,
I don't want to dance with Arthur Bellamy!"

The evening wasn't as bad as she had expected. The
couple from Hollywood were amusing, a bit outspoken
about their new wealth, but Dany liked them. They
were spending lots of money and why deny that it was
lots of fun. Dany was reminded of Charlotte but these
two would never have the Dessaux taste. They were
rather brash, but so was El Morocco. Brash and rich.
Dany liked that. There was another man along with
them, a glum sort but a superb dancer. Renee was at
her best. She loved to rhumba, she told stories about
the French theatre, she sat next to Arthur. And Arthur
didn't want to dance.

"I can't keep time," he said. "I hear it perfectly in
my head but my body won't comply." The mention of
his body made Dany nervous but she danced with the

167

man from California. No, it wasn't a bad evening. Arthur was showing off for his guests and he enjoyed that. The best table, being recognized by the staff, greeting most of the celebrities in the crowded club. But when he lit Dany's cigarette, when he talked about Paris, he looked only at her. Then she had to look away. He looked at her with pining eyes and she thought of Emil Jennings longing for Marlene Dietrich. They were silent screen eyes. No one looked like that anymore. Dany could hear Peggy saying, "No, not now, Arthur!"

The best part of every night was when she came home and went to the nursery to look at Veronique. What a blessing! For a child to sleep so soundly, undisturbed and at peace. The wonder of it. Did she feel that safe and protected in the small room, with Kate nearby at all times? Dany was happy and confident looking at her under the pink blanket. No matter how late it was, whether it was after a long night of dress rehearsal or after the late hours of draping and sewing in the workroom, there was the inordinate pleasure of seeing Veronique asleep. Dany didn't want to analyze it, she wouldn't allow herself to think beyond the precise moment. The feeling of contentment was enough.

Spring was clearer in New York, and the trees in the park were definitely greener. It was not like the spring she used to wait for in Paris, Dufy-color spring, bright and lively. But gentle as she remembered it now.

Ernest Kester had to like her. After the first rehearsal at the World's Fair theatre, he called her "La Belle" and Tom Thornton made a clucking sound and grimaced.

"See, see. He likes you, you're in now, Dany." She was sorry Tom had heard. He was envious and it wasn't

168

an attractive quality. It did make him more aggressive though and that would help. Dany wondered why Tom wasn't comfortable with the Kester entourage. He was as sarcastic as the other fellows, the lighting man and the stage manager. He was as acidly clever as the set designer. Tom was restless and timid around them and Dany knew he was hurt because Ernest hadn't given him a nickname. But he began to make phone calls to arrange appointments with any producer he could get to see. He'd made up his mind. He was going to get a Broadway show to design in the fall. Dany knew that was good thinking.

She wasn't lying to Arthur when he called her every few days. There wasn't time for an evening at the theatre or a quiet neighborhood dinner. Arthur's idea of a place in the neighborhood was the Colony or the Stork Club. Oh, she wished Peggy was back in the city. It was difficult to go on avoiding Arthur.

Dany was startled by the husky voice that asked for Dany Mounet when the phone rang. "This is Albert Costume Company," the operator said. "One moment please, Mr. Albert calling." Dany couldn't believe it. She was going to hear his voice after all these months. Her throat went dry. The face she wasn't able to get out of her mind, and now he was calling. That voice she'd heard only once before in Boston at rehearsals.

"Mrs. Mounet?" She didn't answer. "Mrs. Mounet? This is Joseph Albert calling." It was the father; what was this about? "We met briefly in Boston when you were working on Arthur Bellamy's little play. Do you think you might take the time to come in to my office and talk to me, Mrs. Mounet? It could be to your advantage if you're not too busy." His tone was familiar. She remembered the way he'd spoken to the actors in Boston. "I hope you remember me."

169

Dany could feel the unctuous smile through the telephone. "Yes, I remember. You do alterations with safety pins."

"Well, my dear, I have a new musical coming into my shop." Shop, how she hated that word. "And I was wondering if I could make a little deal with you. If you'll be willing to work on prices with me. You know what I mean? That dirty word, money? I'd like to subcontract some work to you if you're interested. You can find time, can't you? I was hoping you might come talk to me some time tomorrow. It's the new Hy Immerman musical. You have heard of him, haven't you, Mrs. Mounet?"

Of course she'd heard of Hy Immerman. "Yes, I have, Monsieur Albert."

She'd heard of Hy Immerman, but why didn't she know he was doing a new musical? Damn, she didn't understand. She had to know what was going into rehearsals, what was being planned if she was to get work into the atelier. And what was that word? Subcontracting. Now she'd have to call Arthur. No, she'd call Evans Morley. He'd been helping her with prices and he'd know.

"I have fittings at eleven, Monsieur Albert," she said, lying. "Perhaps later in the day?" She didn't believe the sugar in her voice. "Or earlier?"

"Early? How about nine in the morning?"

"Parfait." That was it! She'd use expressions he'd never understand. She'd sound like that French singer, what was her name? That Irene Bordoni! He was talking down to her, calling her Missus, to annoy her before they met. What kind of businessman was he? She'd give a performance for this Joseph Albert tomorrow morning. She'd be more ooh-la-la than Mistinguette! *"Oui,* West Forty-third Street. *Merci, Monsieur*

Albert; à bientôt." She needed the work and he said it was a big musical. How could this man have such a good-looking son?

Luckily it was a sunny morning and mild. She wished she had gray foxes or martens to throw over her suit jacket but then she'd look too obvious. What was she thinking? She didn't want to look too grand, too elegant and not at all flamboyant for the meeting. Neither too rich nor too poor. Jack Albert had seen her in a maternity smock and skirt backstage at the Wilbur Theatre. She must look young and maybe a bit vulnerable. She tilted her navy blue beret over her forehead. A little touch of sauciness would do no harm.

She was excited and not prepared for the commotion she faced when she stepped off the elevator at Albert Costume. She recognized the hoarse voice of the girl muttering into the switchboard at the reception desk. Costumes were wheeled by, tottering hoop skirts bobbing up and down on one rack, men's frock coats on another. A delivery boy carrying two huge rolls of fabric looked lost, not knowing where to go. The hoarse voice waved him down the hall as she told the two girls waiting at the desk that measurements were being taken on the third floor. She looked over at Dany, shaking her head with annoyance. "You heard me, didn't you? Measures are being taken on three."

"Non, non," Dany said, preparing for an entrance. "I am Dany Mounet. I have an appointment with Monsieur Albert?"

The girl giggled, hiding her embarrassment. "Oh, I'm sorry, miss. I'll tell him you're here."

Dany didn't mind waiting. The walls of the long corridor were covered with framed photographs, many faces she recognized, some were unfamiliar but it was a fascinating history of theatre celebrities. She tried not to look too interested. She didn't want to be a gawking tourist. What an old building! The heavy moldings were dark and needed dusting. The overhead lamps gave a musty light and the men and women passing by seemed as faded and run-down. It was like a dilapidated library; the books needed new bindings.

"Sorry to keep you waiting, Mrs. Mounet." He was not too tall and heavier than she remembered. He strutted toward her. A swagger, he was happy to be fat. "So sorry." He apologized and it wasn't necessary. She had only waited a few minutes. This man had been in fitting rooms a long time. His appraisal of her as he spoke was positively lewd. She felt as naked as one of the showgirls in her own fitting room.

"We'll talk in my office and then if you like I'll show you around this establishment. My father bought this building twenty-five years ago, y'know." He was proud of it. The cigar in his mouth was unlit; his straight brown hair, what there was of it, was thinning or he wouldn't brush it forward. His brown suit was expensive. His very wide tie was dull ombre silk. He took the cigar from his mouth; a gold ring was too tight and lost in his fat sausage of a finger. "Jackie, that's my son, you met him in Boston, didn'ya? He woulda been here but I hadda send him down to Philly, some little trouble on the Max Gordon show."

Philly meant Philadelphia. She wasn't going to see *Jackie* Albert today. She needn't have worried about looking young, and vulnerability was a quality his father would not find attractive. The glossy photos of the stars stopped on the wall. There were plaques and framed letters now and what must have been family portraits. A woman in a moiré dress, high collar and leg-of-mutton sleeves. A pretty woman with dark eyes and hair, not happy posing in front of velvet drapes. A

172

tiny woman next to a burly man in a morning suit. Joseph Albert resembled his father. They walked to a dusky office at the end of the corridor, with two mahogany desks and barrel back chairs. The walls were glass covered bookshelves; a collection of costume books older than the furniture were meticulously arranged. Oh, how she'd love to own those books!

"Well, what have you been up to since *Taste of Vice;* been busy?"

"Ah, *oui* Monsieur. I have been what you call very busy." Time to begin, the performance was about to start. "The gowns for Winnie Olsen. You are aware of her great success at Number One? *Quel chic,* that girl! The revue at the French *Quartier.* Pardon, Quarter." She corrected herself. "The Maisonette, *Bon Voyage* and now the World's Fair. The new production for Ernest Kestair—" Again she paused. "Sorry, Kest-er. The show called *American Beauties.* You know him?"

"Do I know him? He wanted me to do the men's costumes but I've been swamped with work here and if I don't do the whole show I don't wanna do nothin'." He sat back in his swivel chair, tilting it so he could cross his legs. "Has he given you a name? He likes to—"

She interrupted happily. *"Oui,* he calls me 'La Belle'."

Joseph Albert ignored what he didn't like to hear. "Well now, let me tell you what I have in mind here." He reached for a black portfolio leaning on his windowsill. "This is a big production. Carl Brandon is the designer, that crazy queen. But I like Carl. He's good. Let me explain this situation." He struck a match against the underside of his desk and puffed slowly, relighting his cigar. He watched Dany, undressing her again. "Ordinarily I'd do this whole thing but I made some prior commitments and there's not gonna be

173

enough time. Is there ever enough time in this crazy business?" He laughed. "Well, I was thinkin' you could help out. I'd farm some work out to you. You're new, and you can probably use it to keep your little shop going."

He didn't appear to be a charitable man. What was he playing at, she wondered.

"Now ya gotta watch your prices, little lady." She didn't want him to see her flinch. She widened her eyes, fluttering with interest. "Hy Immerman is a big producer but he's mighty tight with a buck."

Would a dictionary help her understand him? His slang confused her and his pronunciation, what school had he gone to? She listened to his proposals, curious and suspicious. Talking about money was distasteful. If a deal could be set and she could walk away with the sketches to begin her work, she'd be most pleased.

"Your prices have to be less than mine, ya got less overhead than I do being a little shop and all. So if you do it, watch your costs. Sharpen your pencil when you're figurin'."

The designs were elaborate; witty sketches of harem dancers and Arabian princesses, modern dresses that reminded her of a Parisian couture collection.

"D'ya think you can handle all this?" He wasn't asking her to choose. He had placed paper clips on the sketches he wanted her to execute.

Dany looked at the drawings carefully. She lit a cigarette now, waving it in the air as she gestured. He would not know she was imitating Renee Hugo. "I see silk, raw silk and shantung. Natural pongee! Chiffons!" She pronounced it delicately and stretched the word. "Silk chiffon, *bien sûr,* and from Bianchini! *Mousseline-de-soie, peau d'ange, barathea!*"

"Okay, Mrs. Mounet, hold on. You talk about fabric

174

with Carl. Oh, one thing more. The leading lady in this piece is Iris Keating. She's a great singer, really hot these days. And she has approval of every detail in her costumes." He smashed his cigar out in a large brass ashtray. "Now let me show you this place. It's not like any other shop in the country. I have the biggest stock of rental costumes in America. Every rep company, little theatre group and college come here. Come on, I'll show you around." He stood up, adjusting his tie and preening at his reflection in the bookshelf glass. "When will you wanna get together with Carl? Can you get these sketches priced up tomorrow?"

"Oui," she would call him tomorrow. She was aware of the short time but it was the essence of the business, wasn't it? Never enough time; that made it exciting, *non?* She depended on enthusiasm. It was like champagne! Without it, what was the point? It must be exhilarating to make a show!

"When we have completed what you call 'the deal' then you must come to visit my small atelier, Monsieur Albert." Never, she said to herself. Not the small workroom, the fitting room that became her parlor at the end of the day. No, he would look down his big nose at a nursery and an infant in a place of business.

The black portfolio was in her hand. He led her to the elevator and said goodbye. *"Oui, oui,* I will call you *demain matin*—tomorrow morning, yes."

As the elevator operator was closing the door she heard Joseph Albert. "Boy, does that little dame have great legs."

He was a vain and arrogant man. His good-natured, brusque manner made her suspicious but it was a musical he was offering. It was her first and she needed the order.

When she went back to Fifty-fifth Street Dany called

175

Maria Mennino. "I have sketches for you to see. Many, many hats. Will you come downstairs when you have time?"

They worked together until the evening, forgetting about the time. Maria was astute calculating the costs of labor, breaking down the hours to be involved in the cutting and sewing of the costumes.

"You cannot determine my time," Dany said, shocked to hear Maria's questions. "I drape and cut sometimes until two in the morning. This is *my* business. I am the owner!"

"Then how have you made your prices?"

"I guess." Dany looked astonished. "I know how much the fabric costs, the salaries of my girls and then I add something to make a general price." How could she be wrong? "Isn't that a good way?"

"Listen to me, *cara*," Maria said and she began to make a chart. "I may not have any customers running up the stairs for custom-made hats but I know how to figure prices."

Roly-poly Maria was clever and quick adding the columns of numbers she listed as Dany answered her questions. "How many yards of chiffon will you want for this? Don't you think a rayon lamé will do for these skirts?"

"Never! I'll use silk. Only silk! I have to represent quality from the beginning. I always use the best and after what I saw this morning at Albert, I am sure. They use the trash." Dany waved her arm in the air with disdain. "Such common fabrics!" Dany laughed at herself but she was quite serious. "I must have perfection, Maria, or I will not be able to compete with the other houses!"

176

Renee called from the theatre after the performance. *"Chérie,* I hope I didn't wake you?" she cooed. "Will you give an unemployed actress a coffee or a glass of wine? They put up the closing notice tonight. In two weeks we will be finished. Oh, little one!"

"Renee, I am sorry. Take a taxi as soon as you can. It was expected, you know?"

"But to see it in print, pinned up on the board. It always hurts and I'm very depressed. I'm going to be sorry to leave, little one!"

Sorry was hardly the word. New York without Renee. What a gloomy prospect. Dany had the coffee ready and they drank brandy, too much brandy.

"Surely Arthur will find a play for you, Renee? Or some other producer. And what about Hollywood?" Dany asked.

"One needs a firm offer, *chérie.* I cannot sit in the Algonquin Hotel waiting. I have an apartment in Paris, expenses, bills to pay! And there is that movie for Duvivier, I may do that. I'll miss you and the little beauty sleeping inside. I'll miss seeing her growing up."

"It's not going to be forever, Renee!"

"If there is war, little one?" Renee gulped her Courvoisier. "What will you do?"

"I'm going to become a citizen. My child has been born here. I have no ties back there, do I? Simon's parents? I have them but they will have to wait a while to see their granddaughter."

Renee looked cynical. "Is that kind, *chérie?*"

Dany was sorry she had mentioned the Mounets. "I can't think about going to France now, Renee. It will be a long time before I can think of holidays. Maybe Robert was right. I'm one of the ostriches, too, but if there is war you will come over here. Won't you?"

"Maybe, *chérie.*" Renee filled her glass again. "Let's

177

not be sad. After all, isn't this what life is? Another act, another scene? We move on and haven't I always told you . . . it's a comedy!"

"Madame Mounet, I do think you should be prepared for Iris Keating." Carl Brandon's voice was low and his lilting New Orleans accent was soothing until he said something outrageous. "She sings better than anyone around but she is a bitch! She can fuss about a crooked seam and she can spend half an hour telling you how to fix it."

"But I never make a crooked seam," Dany said.

"Honey, she'll find something to complain about, you just believe me. However, the girl can belt it out. Why she's a real old-fashioned coon shouter." Belt? Dany wanted to know what these words meant but Carl went on talking. "There has been talk about the kind of lollypop she uses to lubricate her vocal chords! She's tough and she has what's called an eagle eye. She's no lady!"

Dany remembered the fitting room in Gerard's theatre in Paris and Renee's first tantrum. "Don't worry, Mr. Brandon. I know how to take care of temperamental actresses."

"I do too, darlin', I surely do." Dany believed him. There was a lot of steel in this Carl Brandon; behind the gentle accent and the slight body under his slender suit. Despite the highly polished fingernails and the soft silk shirt cuffs, there was a rod of iron, a tautness that sent off messages like a staccato telegraph. "Don't fool with me, don't underestimate me" was the message. "Oh, she has a great figure. No taste but a splendid body!"

Dany listened to Carl. He voiced precise demands for

178

the materials he expected, exact specifications for executing his designs.

"Don't sell yourself short when you give in your prices. Allow, please, for changes. I don't change my mind but Iris will. Honey, I guarantee it."

Joseph Albert said the estimates were too high when she sat in his office two days later. Dany crossed her legs, hoping she was subtle as she slid her skirt a bit over her knees. She remembered his comment as the elevator door closed the other day. Perhaps a little distraction would help before she spoke. "Ah, *quel dommage,* Monsieur—"

"I don't get whatcha sayin', Mrs. Mounet."

"Oh, *vraiment?* I am sorry. Quite often I don't understand you, Monsieur Albert. I apologize," she said.

Maria had been very wise when she added up the figures for Dany. "This is the list for Mr. Albert and you keep the carbon for yourself. I've circled the lowest prices in pencil. See? If he gives you an argument then you can come down to the circled figure. There is still profit but not much," Maria said. "And be hurt if you have to do it. Don't cry but be very hurt."

Maria was not psychic but it happened the way she expected. Dany looked at her list with the pencilled figures, pursed her lips and shook her head. "Tst, tst, it is a great hardship, Monsieur, but I will lower them as you wish. One third off is a great deal of money. Please, let's not argue." She hoped she didn't overdo the fluttering of her eyelashes. "I will do it but you must understand that this is a great sacrifice, Monsieur Albert."

She assumed Jack Albert was still in Philly. The other desk top was clear except for a neat pile of unopened mail. She wondered if she'd ever see him. Well, she had the order. And a check. The down payment to cover her first week's payroll.

Renee wanted to see everything in New York before she sailed for Paris. *"Chérie,* you must come with me to see *The Little Foxes* and I want to get seats for the Katharine Hepburn. You can't work every night, little one. It's not good for you!"

It was the worst possible timing but Dany couldn't say no. Her evenings to be alone in the workroom draping new muslin patterns were now to be spent with Renee. The French Pavilion at the World's Fair, supper at the Stork Club, dinner at Twenty-One, the Ethel Barrymore play.

"I could play that part. I must tell Gerard! *Whiteoaks* in Paris. Do you think it would go? It is set in Canada!" Renee exclaimed when they left the theatre. Evans Morley was an attentive escort for a hectic week of theatres and restaurants, too much drinking and too rich food. Arthur jumped at the chance to entertain lavishly and it was unavoidable. Another late night at his favorite El Morocco, another evening ignoring his dark and foolish romantic glances.

"This was one of the best afternoons of my life! Katie allowed me to wheel the pram and the park was beautiful," Renee said one afternoon. "You should have seen the commotion your daughter caused! She is the best looking child in this city and such attention from all her admirers, *chérie!"*

"Seeing a famous actress in the park might have had something to do with it, no?" Dany teased.

"The child is going to be spoiled by all this fussing," Kate said.

"She is adorable and I'm here for only a few more days, Katie." Renee searched her bag for cigarettes, avoiding Dany's look. It was hard not to be sentimental and she didn't want to show any emotion.

Dany hated thinking about saying goodbye, it was going to be difficult. Renee had become more than a confidante and advisor. She was a beloved friend and so much more that was not easily explained. Who would understand the gesture without a word?

"Little one, I must run," Renee said. "Why didn't I move to the Plaza for this week? It would have been nearer. Everything is uptown this week! We're to be at Peggy's at seven. Don't be late, *chérie.*"

Peggy had come home from Florida and Arthur had insisted on cocktails at home before dining at the Colony. Later he thought Renee should see the fan dancers at Jimmy Kelly's. It wasn't fun for Dany sitting in the smoky, crowded club, but at least the shadowy blue light prevented his blatant moon-eyed staring. Wasn't he brazen to attempt to flirt in front of Peggy? Dany ignored him, making Peggy the center of attraction, asking her questions about Palm Beach, her family, the weather. Anything to keep Arthur from being foolish. Was he truly suffering, Dany wondered. This mature man of sixty . . . did he play this role quite often?

"Now you will all be at the boat by eleven. We sail at noon, and I'm having champagne in my stateroom! Imagine, in ten days I will be home, back in my cozy apartment! It seems like I have been away for years!" Renee stepped out of the Bellamy Packard, blowing kisses from the door of the Algonquin.

"She doesn't mean a word of it," Dany said as the car drove off.

The stage manager called early with a change of schedule. Iris Keating had to come for her fittings at 11 P.M. instead of 2 P.M. What a perverse stroke of luck, Dany thought. Now it was impossible to get to the *Ile de France,* no last minute hugs and kisses, no teary farewell. No promises for a reunion in July. She couldn't leave the workroom now and Katie would have to deliver a note and the champagne to Renee's stateroom. Renee would understand, she'd have to. After all, the show must go on, mustn't it? Dany poured a second cup of coffee, taking it to the window facing the back garden. Oh God, take care of dear Renee, she sighed. Dany knew she'd never have been able to handle a goodbye without tears.

"Please, please, shouting won't help! It's a waste of time," Dany said. The wardrobe mistress was near hysteria screaming at the dressers after the rehearsal was stopped. They were stunned by the notes Carl Brandon had just given.

"The joys of a Sunday in Philadelphia!" Carl said. Wrinkled, perspiration-soaked costumes were everywhere, thrown over the racks, tossed over the sewing machines, dropped on the worktable. The grumbling musicians left the orchestra pit, plowing past the muddle and disorganization.

Dany hadn't ever seen a dress rehearsal stopped, cancelled halfway through the first act. The scenery hadn't worked, a scrim had to be repaired before the fast change could be accomplished and none of the dressers were ready for the costume changes. Then, suddenly, Iris Keating developed laryngitis. What a spoiled child she was, behaving so unprofessionally. And why was it impossible to find a doctor?

"You'd think it was some rare disease that will cripple her for life," Carl said.

"A big cup of tea and honey," Dany said. "That would help her."

182

"No, the darling insists on a doctor seeing her. Dress rehearsal postponed until tomorrow," Carl said. "Noon tomorrow, everybody!"

"I will not wear that dress!" Iris had shouted from the stage. "It's . . ." she had searched for the word she wanted, her vocabulary wasn't too extensive. "Bland! That's what it is for Christ's sake! Bland!" Her voice was like a squawking parrot and the next minute she was gasping for breath and crying for help. She needed a doctor! She lost her voice!

Carl hadn't designed the dress in tan but at the fitting Iris had whimpered and pouted until he relented. She had seen tan dresses in Bergdorf's windows and she wanted tan.

"Then go to Bergdorf's and buy one," Carl had said. "I designed a salmon pink dress because I know what the set looks like and what the rest of the cast is wearing. If I wanted tan I'd have sketched it in tan!" Carl's voice was almost as high as Iris's when he was angry and his southern accent got heavier. If Iris's pouting wasn't successful her tears were triumphant. She had the tan costume and now the director hated it. The dance director groaned and Hy Immerman muttered, holding his head in his hands as he bent over the seat in front of him. Carl called out, "Where's Miss Keating? Isn't she in this scene? Oh, there's the darlin'; I couldn't see her in front of the beige backdrop!" Had anyone ever uttered the word *beige* with more venom?

Then Iris began. "This isn't the color I meant! Who okayed this color?"

Now when the company was dismissed and everyone went to their hotel rooms Dany had to recut the dress for Iris.

"Do me a favor, Dany darlin'," Carl had said three days ago. "Bring along the length of salmon crêpe

183

when we go to Philadelphia." Now Dany had to have it ready for tomorrow night—if Iris recovered from laryngitis and went on tomorrow night.

Dany wanted to get away from the havoc, the ill-tempered group trying to organize the costumes that had been dropped and left in the wings when the quick change number had gone wrong. She had to speak to Carl, if he had been backstage at *Taste of Vice* he'd know how lightning fast changes worked. And she had to get to a telephone, she had to call Katie. Veronique had a sore throat before they left New York, she had to know if the fever had dropped.

All day Dany had the uncomfortable feeling that she was being watched. When she had called Katie in the morning, she saw him watching her. When the stage manager gave notes before the lunch break and at the little delicatessen waiting for the sandwiches, Jack Albert had been watching her. He was watching her now, somewhere in this messy basement she knew if she turned around she would see him. The tall, lanky body and the handsome face; intent and serious, not at all arrogant or patronizing. She knew he was watching her.

"What can I wrap this fabric in?" she asked Maria. "I'll cut the dress in my hotel room." She was surprised when she turned; Jack Albert was not there.

"I'll do it," Maria said. "You go and call, find out how the *bambina* is doing. I'll help you cut the dress and then we'll have coffee someplace and finish in the morning."

"Coffee? Where? They say this city is a graveyard on Sundays." It wasn't Maria's fault; why snap at her? "Thank you, Maria. I'll be back in a few minutes."

The phone was picked up on the first ring. Katie was in the sitting room, waiting for the call. Bless her. She was probably listening to "The Court of Human Relations," her favorite radio program. The problems of other people interested Katie. She forgot her own troubles after listening for an hour and she couldn't hear the program when Dany was home. It was too depressing before going to sleep, Dany said.

"Hello, Madame." Why did the Irish brogue make "madame" sound so funny? "Veronique is fine. Please don't worry, the fever is gone. As of five o'clock. She's sleeping like a little lamb. She's fine, I assure you." Katie had spoken and Dany knew that meant the baby was well.

Dany stood at the top of the stairs near the stage door. It was the first moment of relief all day. Now to get back to work, to the pink crêpe dress, the larger hooks and eyes, the heavy zippers to make the quick change quicker.

"You've had a busy day." Jack Albert's voice startled her. "Why are you always in such a hurry? You know, you're even prettier when you're ready to lose your temper."

Where had he come from? He was standing too close to her and he wasn't laughing at her the way his father did. He held her elbow as if he thought she'd fall down the stairs. "I'll bet you've been up and down these steps a hundred times today."

She never felt dizzy, she never fainted but if he let go of her she thought she might. The sympathy in his voice was unexpected. He moved down a few steps until his eyes were level with hers. "Dany Mounet." How odd to say her name. His arms were around her waist; did he think she was going to fall?

"Can I call you when we get back to New York? Will you have dinner with me some night?"

The porter found a taxi as soon as they came out of

Penn Station. Dany tipped him and sat back in the cab, relieved and eager to get back to the apartment. To her atelier, her workroom. *Home.* Driving up Fifth Avenue, looking at the stream of lively people on their lunch hour, the sharp noon light hitting the stone gray buildings, the slick shop windows, she sighed. The snappy breeze felt fresh with the window open; there was a sense of expectation in the air.

Veronique was going to be six months old in a few weeks. Dany hoped she could take her to the park in the afternoon. Katie had said it was only a spring cold. Veronique was fine and it was a lovely day to wheel the carriage under the trees that were beginning to bloom.

Yesterday was a revelation, a miracle of determination. Every second of the day was used to correct the mistakes of the dreadful Sunday. She'd never lose her sense of wonder, seeing everything move into place after that day of complete disaster. The crew had worked miracles. The scrim disappeared in an instant, absolutely vanished, revealing the beige drop gleaming after the scene painter had worked long into the night. The dressers were rehearsed with the precision of a ballet corps, the quick changes moved without fault. And though the doctor advised Iris to whisper at rehearsal, she found her voice. The demanding, spoiled actress really filled the theatre with a sound of elation. A happy sound, that's what it was. And Dany now knew what belting was.

"Dany darlin', can't you stay for the opening?" Carl had asked that morning, but it made no sense. The Albert staff and Maria had left after rehearsal. "Dany, wait until I have my meeting with Immerman," Carl said. "Iris is angling for a new dress in the second act. If they give her the new song, she should have one. It's a red dress song! I'll give you a pencil sketch to take back." The sketch was in Dany's bag and the dress had to be ready for first fitting sometime next week. It wasn't possible to stay for the opening. She reached into her satchel, taking out the envelope she was given at the hotel desk.

"Dear Dany Mounet . . ." The handwriting was precise and a bit childish. "Will you have dinner with me on Thursday? I'll call you and I hope you're not busy that night. Sincerely, Jack Albert."

The taxi turned into Fifty-fifth Street. Yes, she was happy to be home. Tom Thornton was bringing her new designs for the dance team opening at the Rainbow Room in two weeks; Ernest Kester wanted to talk to her and he had invited her to dinner at his apartment. Tom would be jealous about that, but no matter. It had to be about new work and on Friday she was going to see George Lansing, the producer. Peggy said his reputation dated back to the Twenties. Yes, she had many things to look forward to. Especially Thursday night.

"We can meet at the St. Regis bar." Dany said it before she knew why. How odd but she didn't want Jack to come up to the apartment and she realized that it wasn't because she lived in the place where she worked. It was because she didn't want him to see Veronique on the first date. It seemed peculiar and then she was angry with herself. She missed Renee. Renee would know how to handle a situation like this; but then why long for Renee? Not yet; no, it was too soon for him to see the baby.

Jack was waiting when she walked into the hotel lobby. "Hello! I thought you'd be in the bar."

"I didn't want to order my first drink without you." He wore a glen plaid suit, a red and blue striped tie. She wondered why he looked different. It wasn't because he had been wearing a sweater at rehearsal, it was something else. *He had been to the barber!* His hair was shorter, flatter and shiny with pomade. He looked younger and she wanted to laugh, remembering her first day in Paris. So long ago and Simon had needed a haircut. Simon always needed a haircut.

"You look pretty," Jack said.

She wanted to say, you do too. She had to tilt her head up to talk to him as they walked to the cocktail bar. When they sat he turned his chair sidewards, his legs were too long to fit under the table and then he sat back, stretching his legs out in a comfortable diagonal.

"Are you sure?" he asked when she said she'd have a Dubonnet cocktail. He ordered a Dry Martini.

"I know, it is an acquired taste but I can't learn to like martinis."

"I'll make one for you soon, then you'll like it. With Bombay Gin."

"Everyone in New York is an expert bartender," she said.

"You'll see." His eyes were as black as a beetle and she had thought that day in Boston that he looked like a villain, but now his eyes were gentle and laughing. He had asked her about Paris and she felt ridiculously young. How silly to feel like an unsure girl, prattling on, but his eyes were with her.

"And six years later I had my own business on the Left Bank. Now I have my place right down the street here. I love New York," she told him. "I love the theatre."

"You really do. I could tell. I don't love the theatre." He shifted uneasily in his chair. "I grew up with it. It's only a business to me. I don't get any magic from it."

"From the first time I was backstage, the first time I sat out front in Paris watching a dress rehearsal begin,

188

I knew I was being given a present. Something I didn't think I could ever afford. Like something too rare or too expensive, and suddenly I had it. *You don't?"* She found it hard to believe. What had she listened to? What had she talked about for the past few years? Theatre, nothing else. He worked in an important part of it and he didn't love it!

"Have you seen a baseball game? I'll take you to see the Dodgers play. That's theatre for me."

"Will I like it?"

"Dany Mounet," he shook his finger at her, warning her. He had a teasing smile. "You say you love New York. Then you have to love baseball, too. Are you hungry? What about Italian food?"

The restaurant up on First Avenue sounded fine.

"There's an outdoor balcony. It's an old place and a favorite one. I used to think we ate there because it was close to the bridge and that made it easier for Pop to drive home. But you'll see, it's really nice."

"Do you live with your parents, Jack?"

"Yeah," he said. "It's easy and in Italian families, the children live at home until they marry. I know, you're surprised. You don't know my father though."

"Yes, I do." She finished her drink. "I think I do." She hoped the hostility wasn't too noticeable.

"We live in a place called Freeport, we have a big house there," Jack said. "And we have an apartment in the Essex House. Do you know where that is?"

"But of course I know!" Dany laughed. "I've been here for almost a year, Jack."

"The apartment is for the times when we work late or when Mom and Pop go to the opera or somewhere. It's nice." He put down his fork and inched his plate of macaroni away. "You'll have to see it some night."

For an instant, he was shy. She was a Parisian, and

189

he must see her as a woman of the world. What an expression! He thought she was the woman of the world. A widow with a child. Did he think she was older, too? She wanted to touch him, to hold him. Maybe she was attracted only to boyish men. Was that it? Was that the attraction? The boyishness. Like Simon at the beginning. *Woman of the world.* She could laugh! Simon and then for a few hours one night— Gerard. Did that count? Oh, it certainly did. Veronique was the testament to the importance of those few hours with Gerard, wasn't she? And who else had there been? No one. Dear, foolish Arthur who flirted with her. He was rather like a boy, bumbling and clumsy under his coat of pretention. An unattractive boy.

"I thought about asking you over there tonight," Jack was saying. "But then I thought it might seem too pushy."

"Pushy?"

"Yes. Too aggressive. I didn't want to look like some lecher trying to. . . . Well, first date and the guy's apartment. All that."

"Oh, Jack!" She laughed now. She had to or she'd reach out and touch his cheek.

"I was nervous about tonight, Dany Mounet. Not now, this instant, but I was a little bit afraid of you. You're beautiful. You move fast. You think fast and you even have a temper that I like. You scare people."

"Now? Do I scare you?"

"Do I look scared?" He pushed his chair back and stood, leaning across the table. He laughed, too. His long fingers lifted her chin and he kissed her. "Not any more."

"Did you have a nice evening, Madame?" Katie asked as she prepared her morning toast.

190

"Yes, Katie, I did," Dany said. She rarely had her morning coffee at the kitchen table but she wasn't ready for the workroom yet. Pouring a second cup to have with a cigarette wasn't her usual habit but she wasn't moving too quickly this morning. She hadn't slept well, thinking about the innocence of the night before. Walking home after dinner, talking in front of the house, saying good night. Then a few sweet kisses. That was all. Jack Albert was timid; gentle manners and a rascal's face. She enjoyed it. Had she expected him to drag her off to some hotel room when she said he couldn't come upstairs? Yes, it was a rascal's face and she loved to look at him; she was sure of that. She wasn't sure of anything else.

"Katie, what a stack of mail! And so early. Probably nothing but bills." Dany took the stack of letters and she saw the lavender envelope. At last, a letter from Charlotte!

Not a word in all these months. It had to be from Charlotte. She knew the sloping, ornate script on the expensive paper, remembering the first note that had come to the Passy flat. Dany tore open the envelope.

My dear, dear Dany,

Where do I begin? With apologies for not writing before now? You will understand as you read on for I have the most exciting news to tell you!

Dany, I am going to have a baby! I cannot believe I would ever write these words. A baby, Dany! Who would have dreamed! We are both ecstatic. Gerard is euphoric and so very proud. I can't wait to tell Renee who will be here in a few days. Think of it, Dany. Me, a mother!

Some day our children will meet. Our little girls, because I am sure it will be a girl just as

191

you were sure about Veronique. They will play together, grow up discovering the world together. And it will be happier for them, not like our childhood world.

Isn't it all too wonderful? The doctor says I must be very careful. I have to rest for the next few months. When I think of you, walking up the stairs to the atelier, through the snow in Boston, the first rehearsals in the cold theatre. Working as you did and I have to be careful! But, in September I shall have a baby!

I am in Paris for a few weeks, then I'm going back to Villefranche. I want to have the baby there. And wait until you see the new house! It is going to be exquisite. It already is. . . .

Dany stopped reading. It wasn't true! Charlotte was pregnant. It was too ridiculous! She folded the pages back into the envelope. The words were blurring, her hand trembled. She'd finish the letter later. How was it possible?

"Madame, is there anything wrong?" Katie asked.

Dany looked up. "What?" Katie was staring at her from the kitchen door. "No, Katie, nothing at all. Some silly gossip from Paris, that's all." Dany put the letter in the pocket of her smock.

She had been thinking of the innocence of last night. Innocence, indeed! Renee said that Charlotte never let Gerard touch her. Renee wouldn't have lied when she talked about Charlotte and Gerard. Not that night when Renee told Dany to watch the stage.

Dany went to the workroom. She picked up Carl's sketch and compared it to Iris Keating's red dress draped on the form for his approval later in the afternoon. She wanted to run off somewhere, to hide. She

192

hadn't thought about shame before. Now she wanted to cover her face. Foolish to be guilty and late. She had learned how to deal with guilt. Charlotte called her fearless. They laced together, fear and guilt and Dany recognized neither of them. No one was going to know that Veronique was not Simon's daughter. No one would ever know. Maybe Charlotte was right, their two children would be friends when the time came for them to meet. And the children would never know.

Dany went into the fitting room. It looked small for the onslaught of work she was expecting. It was going to be a busy day. Later, tonight she would write to Charlotte. She'd finish reading the letter and then she'd write. A happy letter, full of enthusiasm and good wishes. She had to be happy for Charlotte.

She looked into the nursery. "All ready for the morning stroll?" Katie was tying the bow on Veronique's bonnet. "Let me do that for you," Dany said. "Isn't she the most beautiful? Maman will tie a beautiful bow." Dany took Veronique into her arms. "She's getting bigger by the minute, isn't she? She's going to be very tall. Yes, you are, my darling Veronique."

And in France, Dany said to herself, there is going to be another child. A half sister or half brother, my angel. You may never know each other; we'll have to see about that. But it cannot matter now. No. *Your* father was Simon. Simon Mounet, the legendary figure, a dedicated man who was going to be a fine doctor. A scholar. How sad that he died too young; before he could see you. Oh, he'd have been a wonderful father to you, my baby.

"Enough cuddling for this morning," Katie said, taking Veronique. "We have to get the fresh air in the park. Madame, don't you have any work to do today?"

"Yes, Katie, I have a very busy day." Dany looked at

her watch. *"Mon Dieu,* look at the time!" She had to go to the workroom, the girls would be starting in a few minutes.

What a morning! Later, she had to write to Renee, to ask her questions. But careful questions, light; as if they were in the fitting room gossiping.

'George Lansing presents.' The four walls of his reception room were covered with old theatre posters in narrow wood frames, one after another on the chipping cream color walls. How did the secretary work in such dim light? The brass lamp on the desk gave off a harsh glare under the paper shade and the one at the side of the cracked leather sofa had no bulb. Was Mr. Lansing saving money on his electricity? How many of the plays boasting from the walls had been successful? Dany thumbed through the pages of *Variety* as she waited to see George Lansing. The theatre page predicted a busy fall season, more musicals than any year since 1929. If this was true, there should be many chances for more work. Brooks Costume, Albert and Eaves couldn't do everything. Most of the names listed in the paper meant nothing, she'd have to talk to Evans Morley and she'd buy *Variety* from now on. The frowzy woman bent over the green ledgers answered a buzzer and said Mr. Lansing was ready.

"Honey, do you mind? It's the last door straight down the hall." Dany saw the look of inspection as she passed the desk. Was it approval or disdain? Dany remembered Renee's walk. The long, assured stride and she imagined herself to be taller as she walked down the long, dark corridor. Were these doors leading to rehearsal studios as well as offices? She heard a strain of violin music playing over and over.

She thought it was pointless to knock, he was expecting her. The huge room was quite bare except for the massive desk; a dark green blotter and an ebony pen holder sat on the inlaid leather top. A short, wiry man was closing a violin case at the grand piano in front of the windows. He looked like a jockey, his tweed vest was open and his narrow trousers were wrinkled and old. She knew where the music had come from. He turned and smiled, extending his hand.

"Pleased to meet you, Madame Mounet. You look like you're after an audition not an order." He shouldn't smile, Dany thought; not with such yellow, broken teeth. This was one of the important producers in New York?

"Mendelssohn. I love Mendelssohn. He makes me forget how hard it is to do a show these days. Well, that was some beautiful work you did for Arthur's French comedy. You've done some of Hy's new musical, too, I've heard. Good notices in Philly, huh? Now if that crazy dame, Eleanor Cannon had her sketches ready on time I'd have something useful here to show you, but she promises them for Friday. I can let you see them next week. Have you met Eleanor Cannon? Noisy dame." He laughed at his own joke. "You do speak English, Madame Mounet?"

"If you will give me the opportunity, Mr. Lansing," Dany said.

"Ha, ha, so you have a sense of humor too. We'll get along just fine." He sat at the piano bench and gestured to offer Dany one of the fragile fruit wood chairs near the desk. "Not much furniture in here. Couldn't even salvage anything from the last show. That Reinhardt school of Expressionism doesn't call for much in the way of usable furniture. Well, this time there will be plenty of furniture. Venetian stuff, heavy, but I hope I don't get to use it in here. I hope I get a run out of this one. I can let you read the script. Can't show you sketches, might as well read the goddam play." He went to the desk and pulled a folder from one of the drawers, tossing it on the desk next to Dany. "Now, let me tell you something, Madame Mounet. Eleanor Cannon wants you to make these costumes. So you see, you have a reputation already. On one show for Arthur Bellamy and some nightclubs. They say you have a European touch. So okay, I want no problems. Surround yourself with the pros, I always say. But let me tell you what I'd like for you to do." He didn't lower his voice but his mouth went a bit to the side, his hands went into his jacket pockets as if he were suddenly chilled. He had an intimate secret to share with her.

"When you work up your estimates next week, after you've seen the sketches . . . listen, can I call you Dany?"

"But of course. *Bien sûr.*" A little of the French soubrette for this man. He didn't take a breath, he went on and on, he loved to talk.

"When you make up your estimate I'd like you to puff up your prices by ten percent. Do you get me, Dany?"

"I'm afraid I do not, Mr. Lansing." Dany thought she did but she wasn't sure.

"Call me George. You puff up ten percent and we'll do a lot of work together. When I'm not producing on my own I'm general manager for a lot of other guys. See? The ten percent is for me."

Dany was stunned. "I'll read the script and look forward to seeing the designs. May we make an appointment for next week?"

"You call me on Monday, about this time." He

handed her the copy of the play. "Get an envelope from Connie on your way out. You and I, we can do a lot of business. You take care of me and I'll take care of you. Understand, Dany?" It was the smile of a conniver. If he had been a jockey he'd run a crooked race.

The Mendelssohn concerto began again as she walked down the hall. Games, tricky games, and she must tell no one. She was furious and shocked but what was there to do? It was an order and she needed the work. This was called a kickback and it was dishonest.

"And now, Dany Mounet, you're going to have the very best martini."

Dany wanted to say no but Jack was taking such care, it was rude to refuse him. The right amount of vermouth poured meticulously over the gin in the shaker, then carefully one by one, dropping in ice cubes. At least it wasn't to be a pink drink or a green one, mixed with cream and shaved ice or embellished with orange slices and cherries.

"I can't disappoint you, can I?" Dany watched him stirring the mixture, showing off a bit.

"What do you think of this place? Nice, isn't it?" His beige gabardine suit made him look darker. Light colors flattered him, he should wear them all the time. "It's the hotel furniture. Ma had it recovered. She says if she stays here even one night she wants it to look like home." The cotton covers on the couches and chairs were deep gold and mustard color, a shade darker than the nubby carpet. Dany could hear the decorator or the fabric salesman advising that it was a good, serviceable color that wouldn't show the dirt. Practical. It didn't matter, the room faced the park and the view was glorious.

"The kitchen is stocked with lots of good things for snacks. That's not Ma's doing as much as Pop's. He won't admit it but he's too cheap to pay for room service." Jack gave her the drink. "Salute."

"*A votre santé.*" Dany tasted the martini; it wasn't as harsh as she'd expected.

"How is it going?" Jack sat at the other end of the sofa. "I hope you're not working too hard."

"But I like to work. I don't have any drapers, I do it all myself and I love it. In a few weeks it may be busier." She didn't want to talk about it, not about yesterday and George Lansing's demand for a kickback. That word! It sounded funny but that was what it meant. Kick the money back. It seemed such a funny thing to do if you thought about it literally. "And this afternoon I walked in the park, I don't have time for that usually."

"With your daughter?" he asked. "When am I going to see her?"

"Not yet." And she didn't want to talk about Veronique. It seemed improper. Were they going to discuss business? What were they going to talk about? She sipped the martini hoping he wasn't going to tell stories about his father. Joe Albert probably had no idea his son was here in this apartment with her. In that other room off the foyer, Joe Albert slept with his wife when they were in the city for a night. Did Jack think he was going to take her into that room? That seemed most improper, too.

"Why, Dany?" Jack asked.

"I think it's too soon. I hardly know you." She wasn't sure of her reasons. "It seems, well, indecent. Sitting here with you seems indecent, too."

"Again I ask why, Dany?" He stood up. "Would you like another drink?"

198

"When your parents are here overnight and you're here too, where do you sleep?"

"It doesn't happen very often, Dany." He looked embarrassed. "That other couch opens out into a bed. Why?"

"Oh, I was wondering."

"Dany, you're not thinking . . . would you be considering—"

"No, no. Don't misunderstand." She was sorry that she'd asked him any details at all, she was uncomfortable suddenly. "Please forgive me, Jack. Can we forget about dinner? I want to go home."

Another designer. George Lansing said that Eleanor Cannon's voice was loud, but he should have said more. Dany thought Eleanor was a seamstress looking for work when she first came up the stairs, but then none of the seamstresses was as sloppy as this round faced young woman munching on chocolate cookies and having another cup of tea.

"A deadline is the day when I start to work," Eleanor Cannon was saying. "I think about the play for months and then at the last minute I'm madly rushing to finish my sketches." She put down her cup. "I never seem to finish on time." Her pink brassiere showed under the low neckline of her cabbage rose print blouse. These designers had very odd taste, they dressed very strangely.

"I'll leave the sketches with you until tomorrow," Eleanor said. "I hope it works out because I'd love to work with you."

"I hope so." Dany smiled. The descriptions of the costumes had been vague, the sketches weren't much clearer but they were amusing. The primitive drawings caught an attitude, the stance of a figure told more about the character than the details of the dress.

"These people must not be grand Venetians," Eleanor had said when she showed the sketches. "I want them to look rather vulgar; rich but not stylish."

Was that why she had the assignment, Dany wondered. Eleanor Cannon may not look rich, certainly she wasn't stylish. "I'm to call Mr. Lansing in the morning. If I get the order you won't have to take the sketches anywhere else, will you?"

"Not if he likes the prices." Eleanor's laugh was as raucous as her clothes. "He said he was very impressed after your meeting. He's close with the dollar, you know." She licked chocolate off her fingers and wiped them on her napkin. "I'll give you a call tomorrow."

She tottered from side to side when she walked. She looked rather like Louis Ostier if Louis wore women's clothes. No wonder everybody gossiped, how could you resist it? Dany wished Renee were in New York. How she'd laugh! Well, Peggy would laugh too. These people who came into the atelier were bizarre. *Too bizarre, chérie!* Dany could hear the way Renee would say it. Dany said it aloud. She must call Peggy.

Dany had asked Evans Morley to help her with the prices for George Lansing. "It's a delicate situation and I'm not sure how to handle it." She told him about the meeting with Lansing and the additional ten percent.

"It exists," Evans said. "This kickback business is a necessary evil in some offices. I don't approve. Fine if it works for Lansing, he's been doing this for years from what I've heard and he's never been caught." Evans looked at Dany's price lists and changed most of her estimates. "Well, my dear, you need the order. You have to keep working but it is immoral, isn't it?"

"If I don't go along with him, one of the other

200

houses will do it," Dany said. "He must ask for this kickback on the men's costumes too." She was exasperated. "Immoral!"

Maybe her life was immoral. Being with Jack in his parents' apartment, on a living room sofa, that seemed immoral. And adorable Veronique, the result of an immoral evening in the bedroom over the atelier in Paris.

The friends! Louis Ostier and his lovers; the carpenters, the rough, handsome fellows he met on street corners, who appeared out of stage door alleys. Was Louis immoral? And the way Renee had described Charlotte's marriage to Gerard, his purchase of a beautiful treasure. Now after all their years together she expected a baby. Wasn't there something immoral about it? What was all this?

No, she couldn't think of immorality. She wasn't going to hesitate to give a producer this kickback he had so obviously requested.

"I'll reserve a table at the St. Regis," Jack had said later in the week. "If you'd like we can dance then."

They were quiet, and moving across the dance floor in a slow fox-trot. "Hell, Dany, what are we going to do? I can't go on holding you this way without being rude. I know you won't come to the apartment. I'm not going to ask you that, but what instead?"

"You don't think I'm being one of those demure and teasing women, do you? Please, Jack." She truly didn't know what to say to him.

"The balcony of a movie theatre, a quiet corner in the park, on the grass maybe?"

She had wanted to attempt some level of morality but, looking at him, wasn't it absurd?

"There are hotels everywhere," he said. "I'll register at

the Drake, the Weylin. Next week, tomorrow. Tonight, now. I'll try to get a suite right here! Just say it's all right, Dany. Say it, please!"

"You pick the hotel, Jack." She said it. "Next week."

Summer seemed to be earlier in New York. The afternoon heat was thick and oppressive, hardly a breeze came through the open workroom windows. Dany needed fans to cool the rooms, she'd have to ask Peggy where to find them on sale. The slate she'd put on the wall was damp as she chalked another date on the blackboard. Owen Patterson was coming by in the afternoon to work with fabric cards for a color scheme he was planning to use in Ernest's new revue for the fall.

Appointments, a schedule. The morning heat didn't matter a bit; Dany saw activity in the list on the blackboard. Carl in the late morning to supervise the finishing touches on Iris Keating's red dress. Eleanor Cannon late in the afternoon after Dany's lunch with George Lansing.

The back room of Artists and Writers was empty after one o'clock and Dany knew George enjoyed acting out his own plot, a secret meeting with whispered negotiations and cunning undertones. It was actually very simple to arrange the method for his payments. Checks were to be drawn to cash in three installments before costumes were delivered to New Haven for the tryout of the play.

Eleanor Cannon came into the workroom in the afternoon, always an hour later than she had promised. They began to select fabrics and Eleanor studied a

202

shade of red for twenty minutes, unable to decide on the color, then unsure of the quality of the fabric, she took the swatch to the fitting room mirrors, switched on the overhead spots and stood peering at herself, holding the swatch against her cheek. "I'm not sure, Madame Mounet. Maybe it ought to be a bluer red."

"Eleanor, look at your sketch. It's exactly the same color," Dany said. She wished the woman would stop calling her Madame Mounet.

"I know but . . ." Eleanor Cannon shook her head. "No it must be bluer."

Dany thought of going into the nursery to play with Veronique for a few minutes, to talk to Katie. Anything to avoid the endless procrastination of Eleanor Cannon. No other designer had ever been this difficult to work with. Dany turned to face Eleanor's indecision. At first she thought it was laughable but it wasn't funny after two weeks of vacillation, postponed dates and delays.

"What is that supposed to be?" Eleanor screamed at Maria one afternoon. "I never saw that before!"

"Miss Cannon, this is the turban you draped yourself the other day. You said you adored it."

"I'm not approving that. Take it away!" Eleanor shouted, leaving Maria in front of the fitting room mirrors. "Make a new one!"

"I've done this over three times." Maria looked helpless, staring at Dany. "Each time she says she loves it and then—" She began to cry.

"I don't know what to do about this," Dany said, comforting Maria with a hug. "But no designer is going to make anyone cry in my atelier!" Dany was furious, she had to think of a way to stop this behavior. "I hate tears!"

Dany watched the lights going on in the buildings up-town from the window of the hotel suite near Sutton Place. "Someone forgot to take her laundry in and it's going to rain," she said, watching sheets flapping from a clothesline on the rooftop a few streets away.

"There's no view of the park here," Jack said, "but the restaurant downstairs is supposed to be good and you won't have to think anyone is watching."

"You knew I felt that way?" Dany asked. Jack was stirring the martinis, the room was cool with the windows open and the ceiling lights turned off, only a few lamps lit.

"Yes, Dany Mounet, I knew." He poured the drinks, bringing them to her at the windows. "What are you thinking about, looking at that dark sky?"

"I'm trying to forget what a horrible day I had." She clicked his glass and sipped the drink. "Jack, do you know a designer named Eleanor Cannon?"

"Oh boy, do I know Eleanor! That's why you were off in those clouds," Jack said. "You mean she's got the Lansing play? Has she decided on anything? Is she refusing fabrics she picked the day before yesterday?"

"Yes," Dany said. "And today she hated a hat. One hat! She had the milliner in tears. I have to think of a way to stop that behavior."

"Forget it, what can you do? After she's driven every-body crazy for a month, the costume house somehow saves her. The show opens out of town and she's taking bows, accepting congratulations."

"Then I suppose it's worth it if the result is exciting."

"Dany, you can't mean that. I've told Pop not to work with her. Who needs all that temperament, who cares?"

"I do. How can you miss the thrill of it when you see it on stage and it is perfect?"

204

"I can miss it. It escapes me and it always has." He put their glasses on the windowsill. "But I love your excitement. I love watching your reaction, what I saw when we were in Philadelphia, how it affects you. You know why? Because I love you, Dany."

"No, Jack, no." She didn't want him to say it. "Not yet, please."

"You don't love me?"

"Jack, I'm not sure! I love being with you. I love looking at you—"

"What else then? You love me."

She wondered if he ever had any doubts, if he'd ever been denied the toys he wanted as a child. His arms went around her waist, lifting her off her feet and she couldn't answer him.

"Finally," he murmured, kissing her again and again, carrying her to the bedroom.

Playfully he undressed her, slow and whispering. "Beautiful Dany." Gentle. "Been waiting all this time." His voice lower than she'd ever heard, mumbling as his mouth went over her neck, her breasts. "It's taken so long, Dany, but I have you now." His lips sweet, then all sound seemed to be muted. She lost all sense of time.

The rain had started, whirling the curtains away from the open windows. "No, don't close them yet," she said. She loved the sound, it was a pounding downpour now, spattering on the windowsills. Jack's hand moved lightly on her back, they were breathing together, moving as one being. It wasn't the way it had been with Simon; the pale, eager boy before his anger and insanity. Not at all like Gerard, hungry and silent. Jack was strong and patient, it was as she'd expected, she thought.

At that moment Jack's hands went softly over her

205

neck. "I knew it would be this way. Comfortable, my beautiful Dany. Beautiful, my comfortable Dany."

"Jack—"

"Don't talk. Just listen to me. For such a long time I didn't think it right to call and I couldn't get you out of mind. Then I thought I didn't remember you anymore. I thought what I was seeing was from my imagination, that it was no longer you. Just my fantasy. And then one night I was in a cab going uptown to dinner and I saw you on your way to the theatre. With that French actress, you were going to *The Philadelphia Story*. That did it. You were just as beautiful as what was in my mind, my picture was accurate. You were wearing a little black hat."

Dany listened, running her hands through his dark hair, mussed and slightly wet. She touched his chin, a stubble of beard had suddenly appeared and she kissed the pleased look on his mouth. He had said she was beautiful. He was beautiful, too; his long, firm chest, dark and smooth; his belly flat.

"Dany, Dany." When he said it, his smile was different. It was tender and she knew she'd never forget it.

Peggy laughed, listening to Dany's description of Eleanor's first visit to the workroom.

"Now the woman is impossible." Dany was telling her about the afternoon with Maria. "I think I've found a way to stop her. She comes in every afternoon, changes her mind, denies approving things, colors, cloth; whatever she saw the day before. I can't have a room full of intimidated, crying women."

"What will you do?"

"She has no concept of time. You'd think we had months to make a few dresses over and over. And who

206

pays for the wasted materials, the labor? I want her to sign her sketches after she has seen a fitting and made a decision. I'll mark a schedule on the back of each drawing. First fitting, second and she has to initial them. Like a stamp of approval."

"Can you force her to do that?"

"How will I know if I don't try? She's very ambitious, too. She thinks she designs better than anyone and she makes fun of everything she sees. Where did she come from, Peggy?"

"I have no idea. We've met a few times and I knew her husband slightly."

"Husband? I don't believe it!" Dany said.

"Yes, she divorced him last year. He made a fortune with paper. The gift wrap from Bergdorf's, the box your Wheaties come in. He manufactures it all. Paper and corrugated everything!"

"And she left him?"

"He was foolish enough to get caught with another woman. Same old story. The damn fool played right into her hand."

"What hand?" Dany asked. It was like the first time Renee was gossiping; when she didn't understand many of the words. When she was naive and unsophisticated. When was that, Dany asked herself.

"*Beaucoup de* alimony! She got a lot of money from him. She wanted a career and I hear she now has her eye on someone new. A producer. A rich one. There aren't very many of *them* around. The theatre! She wants to be important in the theatre. Oh, the magic spell it casts! And I hear this new man is very *smitten*."

Dany was surprised. "But she's not very attractive."

"Dany darling, there's magic in the theatre? There is also some unknown siren song certain women sing when they shut the bedroom door."

207

A song. Music playing as a trap is set. A hotel room for an assignation before dinner. She had forced Jack to find the room where she'd be safe and anonymous and away from his father. It was a travesty, but why not?

"Dany, what are you thinking?" Peggy asked. "You're blushing!"

"I am? Peggy, I haven't told you but I'm seeing someone."

"Good, tell me! Who, who?"

"Do you know the Albert Costume family?"

"Not really," Peggy said, "but you're seeing the son? He's the handsome one, isn't he? Dany!"

"He is handsome, isn't he?"

"He sure is. I've only seen him backstage. Why don't you come out to the country with him for a weekend?"

"No, thank you. I don't think so. Peggy, he's not like us. He doesn't love the theatre, he doesn't even like it. He likes baseball, hockey, golf, and he is totally without ambition. Willing to accept what his family has given him. I've never known anyone without any drive at all."

"And? What are you trying to tell me?" Clever Peggy. She could tell there was more to be said.

"I'm mad about him. I love to look at him, to be with him but I have to see him alone. I won't allow him to see Veronique. I've become an absolute puritan about that and I can't see him with anyone else. It bothers me but I think he feels the same way. I'm sure his father doesn't approve of *me*."

"Approve? The old scoundrel ought to be proud. Why do you feel this way?"

"I can't tell you. I sense something, that's all."

"Then you should come out to the country. You know you won't be busy in August. No one is. Nothing will start until September. Come out for a week or two.

Arthur will be in California. Let Katie bring the baby out. I've been meaning to suggest this to you, the city is too hot for a baby. At least let Katie bring her out to me."

How generous of Peggy, as generous as Charlotte but without the complications. What a joke! Her women friends and their husbands. Dany took a devilled egg. Dear God, it was complicated! If Veronique was in the country it would be easier to see Jack more often. That was an enticing prospect.

"May I think about it? It's very kind of you."

"Kind! It'll be fun for all of us."

"Arthur has been in Hollywood quite often lately, hasn't he?"

Peggy sighed, an irritated sigh. Funny, that sigh. It was such a New York sound. "He's negotiating a deal at Paramount. I won't discuss it with him, it's such a hateful idea. Remember the day I told you there were things I'd explain one day? Do you want to hear it now?" Moira came into the living room, dinner was ready. "Moira, will you set the little table in here? I can't bear the dining room and thank God, he isn't here. We don't have to go in there."

Moira moved a lamp on the walnut desk and a maid appeared with plates and cutlery.

"Dany, I don't know what you secretly think of Arthur, and you don't have to tell me. It doesn't matter at all. A long time ago, Dany, there were three sisters. Two of them quite beautiful and one of them was born a 'klutz'."

"Klutz?" Dany asked.

"The clumsy, unattractive one. Not pretty! Fortunately, the klutz had brains. The pretty ones didn't need brains. They were born rich and the first two married men who were richer. The klutz loved painting and

209

books, the theatre, poetry. All the *finer* things in life."
Peggy was usually sarcastic but now her tone was bitter.
"However she couldn't find a man who appreciated the
things she loved. Until one day when she was no longer
young. Yes, the old maid met a man who had marvelous taste, a sixth sense about what made beautiful theatre. She knew nothing about his background, nothing
about his family but he was interested in her. Though
she knew her money played a large part in his interest,
she didn't care. She married him and she was very
happy. He produced plays in New York and London.
He was brave enough to do Restoration comedy and
make it successful. The so-called classics. So what if he
liked to pinch the ingenue's behind, if he liked to go
off to nightclubs and send a showgirl flowers or a small
jewel. He was too silly and very inept with his philan-
dering.

"The klutz didn't like it very much but she had stature. She was married!"

"Oh, Peggy, please—"

"No, don't interrupt me. At first the klutz didn't
mind very much. It was rather innocent. It wasn't like
Mr. Cannon who was caught with the Earl Carroll
showgirl in a clandestine Murray Hill apartment. Clandestine, my eye!

"Now the husband of the klutz wants to make movies
in Hollywood, and do you know why? He has fallen in
love with someone who is utterly uninterested in him
and in despair he wants to move to that dreadful,
sunny cultural desert. And do you know what, Dany?
The klutz doesn't care anymore." Peggy went over to
the desk where dinner would be served, fussing with the
napkins, moving the wine goblets.

"No, I don't care a whit," Peggy said. "I'm a very
grown-up person now. I'm going to divorce Arthur and

210

I'm going to be fine. I'll still be Mrs. Arthur Bellamy; I won't be a spinster, not the old maid, not that other one, you know the sister who never married. Isn't it ridiculous, Dany? The idiotic way we're brought up, all of us girls, who learn that we have to marry. Widows or divorcees, it doesn't matter at all what we become. We gain respect and esteem because once, just once, there was a husband. So that's fine with me; I'll be the ex-Mrs. Bellamy for the rest of my life."

"And the woman who doesn't care . . ." Dany almost said *chérie* the way Renee would have said it. She had to stop doing Renee. It was all right in George Lansing's office or with that gauche Joseph Albert, but not with Peggy. Dany couldn't help it; it was becoming a habit. She liked imitating Renee. "Who is she, *chérie?*" She knew but she had to be sure.

"I told you to beware that day we had lunch in the Village, remember?" Peggy nodded for Dany to come to the desk. "Silly, isn't it? It's you."

The salesman from the lace house was faltering and unsteady as he showed Dany his samples. The workroom was too crowded for one more body, she thought. She told him she'd look at his line in the fitting room. It was better to look at laces in front of the mirror anyway. The pieces he showed were beautiful and very expensive.

Odd, the man seemed so reticent. Didn't he want to make a sale? He looked embarrassed and he was hurrying. "Is there something wrong?" Dany asked.

"No, nothing. It's just that you're so young, and prettier than they said."

What was this about? "Who said?" Dany asked again.

211

"Joe Albert. He said . . . aw, no, Madame Mounet, I'm sorry."

"Go on, tell me," she said.

"He called you the upstart."

"And at Brooks and Eaves, at the other houses? Do they say that too?" Poor man, he wasn't very tactful. She went through the samples again; the over-embroidered chantilly was exquisite. She loved it.

"No. Only at Albert."

"I see. And you weren't sure you should come here? How much is this?"

"That's my most expensive number. It's thirty-five a yard and it's the narrow width, you see."

"I'll take it. Mrs. Cannon will love it and you can tell them at Albert, tell everybody, my competition! Tell them that at Mounet the price is no object!" It was a vain, stupid thing to do but she had to do it.

Dany waited for the light to change at the Park Avenue corner; so deep in thought she missed the signal and waited for the green light to flash on again. Hurt, not enraged or angry as she might have been, but hurt. She didn't care whether Joe Albert liked her or not, but disapproval was damaging and unreasonable. She had to know why. She wondered what he said to Jack. Did he call her the upstart when he talked to his son? That meant she was a troublemaker, an aggressive newcomer. Was Joe Albert so easily frightened by competition, was that it?

She was late. Eleanor had fussed again, trying to delay selecting ribbons, whining and protesting. Dany had cajoled her, blaming George Lansing for the signatures that had to be scrawled on the sketches. No more procrastination and Eleanor thought the lace was divine.

212

Dany picked up the house phone in the hotel lobby. "Jack, I'm sorry. Let's have a drink down here in the lobby. Do you mind?"

She didn't care if he did, and tonight she was not going to the Italian restaurant up on First Avenue. No, tonight she wanted a steak and pommes frites at the small bistro downtown off Lexington Avenue.

"No," she told the waiter after Jack ordered the martinis. "I'll have a Dubonnet please."

"Dany, have I done something? What's wrong?" Jack asked.

"Wrong? You know that something is wrong?" He said he loved watching when she lost her temper. He was going to see anger now. *"Merci,"* she said to the waiter, smiling sweetly as she took her drink. "A salesman came into the atelier today, not a very bright man either." She told Jack what had happened. "I didn't know I deserved so much attention, to be talked about to a salesman. I'm an upstart, am I? Did you know that's what your father has been calling me?"

"No. I don't talk about you. You asked me not to."

"Because I've felt that your father doesn't like me. Oh, I don't care about liking. I care about disapproval."

"That shouldn't bother you either. How can he disapprove of you, he doesn't really know you."

"I'm asking *you*. Don't repeat what I'm saying."

"Maybe he feels intimidated, Dany. Maybe you—"

"Intimidated! Why?" She *was* going to be angry. It was impossible to control it.

"I'm not saying he's right. Pop has old-fashioned ideas. Here you are, a beautiful widow with a baby, just arrived in New York and with a new business of your own. From Paris."

"Paris? What does Paris have to do with it?"

213

"I'm telling you. Pop says—"

"No you're not. Does coming from Paris mean that I'm what you call a gold digger or am I some Pigalle prostitute who—"

"What's that? Pop thinks that Arthur Bellamy . . . well, he helped you get over here, didn't he?"

"I don't understand." But she did. That was it: Arthur Bellamy. He flirted with the pretty girls and he didn't try to hide his flirtations. Peggy knew what Arthur did and apparently everyone in the theatre did too. "Then I'm not an upstart. I'm a dilettante and a courtesan! Do you think I've been lying to you?"

"No, of course not. But Arthur Bellamy did help you and Pop says—"

"Pop says! What do *you* say, Jack?"

"Huh?"

"You're not aware of it, are you? Can't you think for yourself? You always say what Pop said. Tomorrow you tell him! That will be a change. Tell him that I accepted an offer from Arthur Bellamy to start a business of my own. That offer meant making one production. The play we'd done in Paris and the arrangement did not include getting into my bed. I'm paying Arthur Bellamy back, it hasn't taken too long! Tell your father that!"

"I will. I'll tell him. Now, honey, let's go to dinner. Then we can come back here—"

"No!" That's what Simon would have done. The discussion was over for now and he wanted to go to bed. The doctor's prescription, the sedative. Bed! "No! You think it's all right now. It isn't. Your father may think I'm a new threat to his business, that I'm competition. Tell him not to worry. I'm not competing. I'm going to be in a different class and no one will compete with me. No one!"

214

"Good," Jack smiled. "Are you ready for another drink?"

Now she understood the smile. It was a mask, a dazzling, seductive cover. When he wasn't sure of himself he didn't argue or attack, he didn't hesitate to protect himself. None of the tricks that aggressive or uncertain people used. He smiled instead. The mocking, teasing and pacifying smile. The distracting smile that got him his own way. It was infuriating, that damned attractive smile. He wasn't going to win with it now. People had turned, she hadn't realized that her voice was loud. "No, *chéri*. Not another drink!" She walked out of the bar.

"Katie, would you like to take a few weeks at Mrs. Bellamy's in Oyster Bay?" Dany asked the next morning. She couldn't believe that she had slept well, a sleep without dreams and she was full of energy and ideas.

"Without Veronique? Do you want to be rid of me?" Katie's head twitched as if she had been slapped.

"Idiot, no! With the baby, to get away from this heat for a while. I have to go to New Haven at the end of the week and I can meet you at Mrs. Bellamy's later. Next week after the play has opened." Dear Katie, didn't she know how needed she was, and cherished?

"That would be lovely. The little darling can use some fresh country air."

"It won't hurt the darling's mother either." Dany had thought about it when she had her bath. Peggy said there was no work, that nothing happened in August. That meant a few quiet weeks in the workroom, another layoff. She'd have to give the girls holiday pay.

A vacation from Jack Albert, that's what was necessary at the moment. Dany remembered Peggy's house, the long white porch and the lawn sloping down toward the little beach. It was almost a year since she'd been there to pick up the furniture she borrowed for the apartment. Yes, the upstart deserved a holiday. A time to clear the head, to think about what she didn't want to think about. The future didn't frighten her, but Jack; she didn't know about Jack.

"Yes, Katie, it will be good for all of us," Dany said. "If Eleanor Cannon will let me finish these costumes."

Finish the costumes and see them lined up on the racks, ready for shipping. That was what she had to concentrate on for the next few days. A dozen red roses were delivered in the afternoon. She knew before she opened the card that it was without an apology. "You know that I love you when you're angry. Do you know that I love you? Jack." He called later and she said it was impossible to see him.

"We'll work every night this week. No, Jack, not until I'm back from New Haven."

Eleanor was maniacal and all maniacs demanded attention. Eleanor watched every detail and worried as she stood behind the seamstress. She followed Dany around the workroom and she ran up the stairs to sit with Maria who nervously sewed the last turbans.

It wasn't possible to think about Jack. There were costumes to be completed and labelled, boxes to be taped and tied and put on the truck. Did the boxes come from Eleanor's ex-husband? Dany was sure Eleanor had an interest in the Cannon company.

"Pack them like treasures, that's what they are!" Eleanor shrieked the day after the scheduled delivery. "No wrinkles, use plenty of tissue. Careful! Use a box for each one of the velvet dresses. We'll put them in my car. No, we won't be late. Madame Mounet, I promise. We'll be there for dress rehearsal. They'll wait, they'll have to! Trust me, I'm a very good driver."

The company would be made-up and ready to go on stage, hot, bad tempered and waiting. No choice but to drive with Eleanor, with Maria and the seamstresses and all the cartons squeezed together in the car.

Eleanor drove as uncertainly as she chose her fabrics. Dany was amazed when they arrived backstage. Eleanor was unperturbed by frenzy. It was a tonic for her. The woman was mad, but the vivid colors, the odd combinations of fabric, worked beautifully when at last the costumes were seen on stage. Then the weeks of chaos and hysteria were forgotten.

Oh, how good it was to be back! The heat and the glaring sun didn't matter at all, the traffic had been light and the steaming streets were not crowded in spite of the morning rush hour. Dany wondered if everyone left New York in August.

In the workroom the tables were damp. It was a miracle the rolls of muslin weren't mildewed. The empty workroom, how she hated it!

Owen Patterson was to call at 11 A.M. Perfect Owen, where would he take her for lunch? To what smart restaurant? The Marguery or over to the Ritz after he'd shown her the new sketches at his studio. She wondered who had done them this time. Too bad she didn't have a new dress to wear. A cotton or handkerchief-linen dress, dark as ink, cool and terribly chic. A New York dress for lunch with Owen. He'd be poised and elegant until he started describing his costumes. Then he'd stammer and hesitate for fear he was asking for the wrong fabric, making a mistake when he said the skirt must be cut on the bias and it was evident to Dany it had to be on the straight grain. Oh dear, what a pun considering Owen's life.

Owen's beauty was not like Jack's. Owen was glossy; on a hot afternoon like today he'd be dressed flawlessly, not a wrinkle in his clothes. Sleek as a Rolls Royce. Jack had another kind of luster, he could be driving a cart down a Sicilian road.

Dany took some clothes out of her closet. Why worry about what to wear at Peggy's house? The most faded, comfortable dresses would do. Five days in the country—what luck! Time to play with Veronique on the grassy lawn, on the warm sand. She'd buy her a pail and shovel to build a sand castle and she'd wait for it to be splashed away with the tide. Veronique would be walking soon. How wonderful if she took her first steps at Peggy's house. Wouldn't Peggy love that!

Then next week she'd see Jack. She'd be rested and sunburned . . . and she had to go shopping with Peggy out there in the country. She had to buy some new clothes.

Dany jumped, the sound of the downstairs bell was as shrill as a fire alarm. The door was usually open during the work day. Had Maria forgotten her keys, wasn't she upstairs yet? Dany ran into the workroom to buzz back and then she went to the door.

"Yes?" she called down the stairs. "Yes?" she said, walking out into the hall. Why did the sight of the Western Union cap make her shiver?

"Madame Mounet? Madame Dany Mounet?"

The boy stood at the foot of the stairs. Was he too lazy to come up the steps? A telegram. How few of them she had received and yet they frightened her. "Yes, *un moment*. Come up, come up." She needed change to tip the fellow. *"Un moment, s'il vous plaît."*

She was trembling. And how ridiculous, she was speaking French to the boy.

"*Merci, merci.*" She signed quickly and gave him his tip, shaking as she ripped open the envelope. She read Renee before anything else. Renee. What could have happened?

Chérie. Terrible news. Charlotte died today. Gerard arrested. Child alive. Letter to follow.

Four

Veronique looked up from the pile of bills Nancy had asked her to approve. The workroom was the same, the machines were going, the finishers were busy stitching facings and hemlines. Benny was involved with placing epaulets on the doublets. The room was operating as usual. Veronique looked at the time. Was it only two hours since Dany had left?

"Why didn't she hire a brass band to play out in the street?" Ryan asked. "Talk about going in a flurry of excitement."

"Have you ever seen anyone who loves to rush the way she does? She has an absolute fascination for the last minute," Veronique said. "She'll kill time buying newspapers and magazines, then she'll be the last one to go through security. The last one to board the plane. It's a talent to create your own frenzy. Maybe that's what keeps her young. And I'll be old before Belinda is out of this workroom."

"Out of the room? Out of our hair! Did you see the way she went for the caviar? She won't have to eat dinner tonight."

"Want to bet? We're working late, you know. And Ryan, the trim on the velveteen skirts. I almost forgot!" Veronique ran to the sewing machines. "Don't stitch the

220

linings yet." She stopped the seamstresses. "Let me show you. We have to put ribbon on, pleat it first and then stitch it down the middle—"

"Calm yourself," Ryan said, handing Veronique a roll of ribbon. "We'll get finished. Honey, she's only been gone a couple of hours."

"And I sound like her already, don't I? Ryan can you believe she wanted red luggage and did you hear her say she didn't have enough clothes?"

Ryan's brows went up in skepticism.

"Yes, yes, I know," Veronique said annoyance covering admiration. "How can I help it? She is remarkable."

Nancy's voice came over the intercom.

"What now?" Veronique asked, going to pick up the phone. "Mr. Wilfrid is here? Without Miss Groueff?" Veronique glanced at the clock. "Ask him to come back to my table, Nancy."

He could have been one of the actors from the Studio around the corner. David Wilfrid looked like a rugby player as he hurried into the workroom. Did he live in the sun, Veronique wondered. Blackpool was in Northern England, she didn't think the sun shone there.

"I'm sorry to be late." His polo shirt was stuck to his chest with perspiration, his hand was hot and leathery as he introduced himself. Was his dark brown hair really that curly or was it the humidity? "I was to meet Miss Groueff."

"She hasn't come in yet." He sounded impatient; it wasn't her fault.

"Well then, shall I wait outside?"

"No, no, she'll be along in a minute. Elsa's never late." He was tall but the width of his shoulders, the thick neck made him seem shorter. Had he wrestled when he was at school or did he box? Professionally, perhaps. "How about a cup of tea or a coke? We'll work in the fitting room. It's cooler there."

221

"A coke will be fine, thank you." He followed Veronique out of the workroom. "Quite an establishment you have here. Is it always this hectic?"

"I think so." Veronique didn't mean to sigh, the weariness was too obvious. "Especially before we ship out a new musical."

"I'd like to hear about it." His smile was sheepish yet he didn't seem bashful. "Look, I'm sorry about this. Nerves, I guess. You see, it's my first time in New York and there's been a lot of pressure. Elsa wanted you to see this research material today. Now the producers have me going on television at five. I'm intimidated by interviewers with their inane questions and I have a tendency to talk too much." The smile was broad now. "Where is that Elsa? Another thing . . . I have no patience."

"Why have they left you on your own?" Veronique asked.

"You mean I shouldn't be allowed out?" David Wilfrid laughed. "Someone from the press office is meeting me at the RCA building. Is that far from here?"

"Not far at all but we'll get you a cab," Veronique said.

"Look, suppose we start without Elsa? You *have* read the play?"

"No," Veronique was surprised. "Only what Elsa has told me on the phone. It takes place in the Thirties, doesn't it?"

"Yes. Well, I'll see that you get a copy in the morning." He seemed vexed.

"We rarely read the scripts for the productions we make." Was his ego hurt or did the costume people in Blackpool read everything before they began to cut and sew? "But I look forward to having your play, Mr. Wilfrid." Damn Elsa, why was she late? He was right to feel uncomfortable. He was a stranger here and Elsa would have made it easier had she been on time.

222

"We wanted you to see these pictures." David Wilfrid opened his worn attaché case, taking out a black photograph album. "I loaned this to Elsa before she began to work on her designs. These are the people I've written about. I collected them from my family's house in England. It's more than the usual family heirlooms, at least to me. I'm sure you have your own nostalgic portraits commemorating the past. Theatre people are sentimental and I was brought up in the theatre."

"Weren't we all?" Dany's photographs were in frames, her gallery of celebrities she'd collected over the years in the business. They'd had no family. Veronique stifled a sigh of impatience. She was about to have a lesson in pre-war costume history. The Thirties in the North of England.

"Elsa has made something remarkable out of this. You'll see if she ever gets here." He put the album on the round table in front of the sofa, pushing the pin boxes and scissors aside. "Unfortunately there are no shots of the actual trial. I assume it wasn't important enough in 1939."

"I don't understand," Veronique said.

"Sorry. You'll see this more clearly after you've read the play. Don't think I'm a raving egomaniac. The play begins with a trial, in Nice, the South of France. It moves back in time and forward again. A man has been accused of killing his wife but I hope it's more than just another courtroom melodrama. A picture of a rotting society is what I intended. It's called *The Villa Affair*. Now have a look."

David Wilfrid began to turn the pages. The pictures were pasted on the black paper as in any ordinary family album but these were not the common place snapshots taken with some old box camera. Here were shots from the best photographers working in Europe in the 1930's. David Wilfrid was describing the people on the first page. Veronique knew he was talking but she heard him through a ringing in her ears, as if she were under water and unable to clear the droning hum, the clogged hollow echo of his voice.

She looked at the pictures of a couple in beach clothes, the man affectedly casual in his striped sailor's shirt, his white trousers rolled up over his ankles and the thin woman in her fisherman's jacket over a dark bathing suit. These people were familiar and she didn't know why. The same two at a party, he was neat in his white dinner coat, she oddly exotic in a gown cut in the style of a cossack shirt. In tweeds at the races, again in white beach clothes in front of the Carleton Hotel. Cannes, obviously. Veronique stopped David Wilfrid, putting her hand over a photo of the woman in a black skirt, pleated like an Italian peasant dress, a shawl draped over her vest, her blonde hair pulled back showing strong cheekbones and a remarkably fragile beauty.

The sound in Veronique's head stopped, she was suddenly hoarse. "Mr. Wilfrid, this picture is in my mother's room upstairs. This is Charlotte Dessaux! She was my mother's friend, her mentor."

On Dany's round table covered in her favorite *bois de rose* velvet, on the glass top with all those photographs in the silver, enamel and ivory frames. The faces of childhood, Dany's fascinating assemblage of faces. The large picture in the sterling frame, the lovely lady in her oddly elegant peasant dress posed in front of the antique mirrors with her image repeating back and back, out of focus in the surreal and baroque Hoyningen-Huene manner. How often Dany had told Veronique about Charlotte and Gerard Dessaux.

They gave me a place in the world, Dany used to say, they made our future possible, *chérie*.

"I always thought of Charlotte Dessaux as my fairy godmother," Veronique said. "I was told about her when

224

I was little." She couldn't stop, the words were spilling out as she stared at David Wilfrid. "My mother's tradition of stopping for tea in the late afternoon that was because of Charlotte. At the first workroom in Paris Dany forgot to eat when they worked late at night. It was Charlotte who brought in food and she made Dany stop for an hour. This woman is a character in your play?"

David Wilfrid covered Veronique's trembling hand on the photograph. "Charlotte Dessaux was my mother," he said.

Five

When Dany had first seen the story on Alix Harcourt's Cap Ferrat house in *Architectural Digest* she thought it was an exaggeration. Magazine stylists must have brought in the slick, modern sofas, the Breuer chairs, the topiaries and banzais for the luxurious space. It wasn't possible that it all belonged to Alix but now Dany knew it was real. The house was lavish, perfectly kept and as outrageous as the owner.

A strip of the Mediterranean sat above the dense green trees, the color Dany had dreamed about for years. A green-blue line out there in the distance behind the Roman statuary, the white furniture on the marble terraces. All of it flawless and a bit ridiculous. One person, Alix, living alone in this sterile opulence seemed vulgar, but it was lovely sitting on the little terrace off the guest room with the breakfast tray waiting every morning at 8 A.M. and having a few quiet hours before the call to action. Alix usually promised to be up early when they said good night to each other and Dany knew she was awake but not to be seen before eleven. Not without makeup. And Dany got used to the routine. Alix appeared, her floor length terry robe perfectly draped over her black bathing suit, her lipstick and eye shadow perfectly applied and ready for the

226

day's activity. An elaborate tray of drinks was brought to the poolside with the morning newspapers, bowls of fruit and stacks of towels.

And instructions. To the butler, the chauffeur, the cook—and to Dany. They were going to be busy. Out for lunch, guests coming for cocktails, then out to dinner. Maybe a card game in the afternoon. Shopping. Instructions, orders. Dany laughed, it was funny listening to Alix's unfinished sentences in French.

"They love me. Why not?" Alix said the second morning Dany was at the villa. "How often am I here? A few months in summer and they're paid by the year. They worship the marble I walk on." It was true, the servants idolized Alix. It was as true as what Alix had said at the Moulin before lunch the other day. "I'm living proof that if you take the girl out of the Bronx you *can* take the Bronx out of the girl!" Lord and Lady Whatever had no idea what Alix was talking about and after an explanation they didn't find it amusing.

Dany thought about an early swim but the sun and the horizon were enough for the moment. She was lazy and she'd swim a few laps later on with Alix. After 11 A.M. Dany didn't want to move, she didn't want to get out of her robe or off the soft, white chaise. She was content to stare at the sky and the eucalyptus, the cypress and the orange trees. Staring had become a pleasant activity, she'd been staring since her first day in Paris a week ago.

"Why in the world did you want to spend five days in Paris? Who's there now? It's July!"

It was useless to explain to Alix. She expertly turned the conversation around when Dany tried to answer. It was impossible to make her listen to anything that didn't pertain to Alix.

Maybe that was why it was comfortable to stare and let the days, the lunches and dinner parties go rolling by. This was a vacation. This was the way a holiday should be, Dany told herself.

She wanted to see the Cocteau Chapel, the Picassos at Vallauris. But no.

"No," Alix said, "it's closed on Tuesday. And, darling, we can't go on Wednesday!" Alix liked to see paintings on her own walls or at a much richer nearby villa while sipping cool champagne. Dany had to coax and plead to go to St. Paul de Vence, then, what luck! Alix was thrilled to see Signoret when they walked into Columbe d'Or.

Alix asked Dany to postpone a trip to the cemetery. "Go tomorrow, Dany. Charlotte would be the first to understand. We're due at the Dormel's at two. The hairdresser comes at ten o'clock. Darling, my roots are beginn. . . . Auguste has to have the car washed. . . . Go the day after tomorrow. We'll never make it to Menton if you—"

And Dany was convinced, she didn't mind deferring the visit to the cemetery. She was enjoying this laziness and the sight of a mausoleum wasn't the most pleasant prospect. Why was she thinking of death now, she asked herself. How long ago it had been. Maybe this was why she'd never come back. She had worked, year in, year out except for the weekends, the occasional holidays at the house in Watermill. That had been enough to keep her from remembering. Until now. And why now, she kept wondering.

"Bonjour, Dany!" What a surprise, Alix was at the pool. "Darling, how are you? I couldn't sleep. Not a wink. I've been up for . . . did you sleep?"

"Very well," Dany called down to her. "Do you want to swim, I'll be right there!"

"In a bit," Alix went on as Dany walked down the marble steps. "I was just talking to Helena."

"Who?"

"Helena! The English girl, the couple at the Carlton, remember? You admired her dress—"

"Oh yes, the Fortuny. Well?"

"She told me the Cinnons are divorced," Alix said. "He's coming down here next. . . . I wish you'd stay. He's divine. He must have his eye on someone. Otherwise why would

228

he be coming . . . they're always in Porto. Funny, I was thinking only this morning . . . lying there . . . feeling gritty with no sleep . . . the neuralgia . . . the 'meegran,' migraine . . . about those months, the terrible months I had in London. A British divorce! Want some coffee? Did I ever tell you the torment of those days? My hair was standing on end and yelling for help. I'd awaken bright as a marigold but once I was in the attorney's office I'd go wonky! The arguments, the demands I'd be granted, what I mustn't ask for. At the end of a day I was wall to wall tired and, lovie, I was playing every night! Those lines, I should never have done *Ideal Husband* during a divorce settlement. Who'd get the flat, the trusts . . . well, I'd get the skates on and rush to the theatre . . . then home to the bed . . . it simply wasn't fair. Poor Lorraine Cinnon, I can imagine what she's gone through. And only this morn—"

"Alix, get in the pool." Dany was doing her backstroke, not hearing too well through her bathing cap. "The water's delicious." If Helena had been Italian, Alix would have told the story with an Anna Magnani accent.

Alix looked around before gingerly stepping into the water, then she plunged and swam the length of the pool. She wrapped a towel into a sarong around her waist the minute she was out of the water, another into a turban over her brunette hair always pulled tight back into a ribbon-tied chignon. She poured a glass of orange juice and stretched out on a chaise. "Why don't you stay for a few more days? We're having so much fun! What do you want to go to Aix for? Who goes there!"

"Alix! I haven't seen Renee in years and she's old. Very old. You used to love Renee."

"I still do, but she never goes out anymore. You just said she's old and I can't have that—"

"You're not serious, are you? Who do you see at your parties here? Everyone is old except for some of the poorer people. They're the attractive ones and you can't be seen with them too often, can you?"

"Mmm, it's just not . . . well, it's not chic!"

"It has nothing to do with chic, it has to do with habit. The same old faces everywhere you go. Why is that acceptable and Renee Hugo isn't?" Dany was losing patience with Alix. "Renee is my best friend in the world. Besides you. She may not be with us for very long. You know that, *chérie?*"

"Neither will I."

"Alix, you'll be with us forever," Dany said. "You're too mean to leave!"

"I'll ignore that!" Alix adjusted the back of the chaise, sitting up now. "You've been distracted, I've seen it. You're a wee bit morose."

"No, I'm not. I love being here. I've only been a little bit . . . what? Reflective?"

"If that's what you want to call it. You were given a Tony award and you're reflective! I was given mine in 1968 or was it 1967? And I didn't have the pleasure of a holiday immediately after!"

Dany laughed. Alix turned it on again. She wanted to talk about her own awards. "That was before they televised the Tonys, *chérie.*"

"No, dearie, before they showed the bloody bore on the telly! There's a difference, you know? Is the suncream on that table, may I have it, please?" Alix applied the cream to her shoulders and arms. "If you'd like, Auguste can drive you to the cemetery tomorrow. Why don't you go in the morning? I'd go with you but I can't bear . . . they depress . . . then you can pick me up here . . . Menton for lunch at two. Dany?"

"Yes?"

"You were staring into space."

"Sorry," Dany said. "I've been doing that. Old age? We were talking about old people."

"Nonsense, you're not used to relaxing," Alix said.

"Do you think it's too much of a shock for my system?" Dany took a glass of iced tea. "Alix, have you ever sat in

230

the theatre watching a play or a movie and you know it's about to end but you've missed something? You paid attention, you didn't doze for a minute, yet something is missing. Something has been left out. That's the way I've been feeling since I walked around Paris the other day. I can't seem to get rid of the feeling that I've ignored something."

"You're not concerned about the atelier, are you?" Alix asked.

"No, no, Veronique is quite capable. Not too enthusiastic but capable. I've been wondering what I missed. Who? Are there ghosts?"

"In this house? Under this sky? Dany, why do you think I keep the house this way? New things, spare and modern. I'd do it over every summer if I could to keep the ghosts away!" Alix rubbed suncream over her smooth, high cheekbones. "Dany darling, this is so unlike you! We have no age! You've always said that. Maybe you shouldn't go to a cemetery tomorrow."

"Oh, I must go. I don't want to see the old villa, none of that, but I must go. It's a matter of respect."

"Dear Dany," Alix said.

"That's all you can say?"

"Oh, I could say more but I won't."

"Good. I can say more too, Alix, but—"

"But you never have." Alix untied her towel. "Want to have another quick dip?"

"Yes." There was more to say but how to find the words to express the nagging, elusive restlessness? A swim was going to be better than staring. Dany was in the pool ahead of Alix, swimming faster. Funny, the pleasure of beating Alix to the opposite end of the pool. She held on to the side of the tiled gutter. The grout between the bright aquamarine mosaic pieces was chipping. A rusting grey-green color that she hadn't noticed before.

"Alix, look here," Dany said, "the siding is coming loose. You should have the pool man in."

231

It was the first sign of disorder in Alix's perfect house. An unpleasant color. Familiar. It reminded her of another place. Colors again. Chipping grey-green plaster on a wall.

Six

Dany sat in the corridor waiting for a gendarme to come forward, to show her through those heavy, forbidding doors only a few feet away from where she sat. How long was it to be? Renee had driven her over from the Hotel Negresco and the ride along the promenade was extraordinary but this wasn't a morning to admire the azure sea, the palm-bordered promenade. She mustn't allow herself to acknowledge the fatigue from the long but miraculous flight, the tedious trip from Lisbon to Nice. Be composed, Renee had said, and try to convince Gerard to speak. How bizarre! He hadn't talked to his attorney nor to Renee; not a word to any of the investigators from the local police. Yet Renee thought he'd talk to Dany. She waited, opening her bag to find a cigarette but no, not now. She might be called inside at any moment. Did Renee truly think Gerard would? Did Renee really know more than anyone else, as she so often claimed?

Why were the walls of the corridor grey-green? That same pea soup color she detested when she'd gone to the hospital the night Simon was killed. The color of desperation, a depressing shade she didn't understand. Why was this the chosen color for all austere places? Hospitals, official buildings, these courtrooms and jail! Did some sadist decide to magnify the hopelessness of all the patients and victims in such places? The walls hadn't been painted in years,

233

that was quite obvious looking at the chipping plaster. The color beneath had once been the same shade. An old color, with a history, a life she'd never understand.

How many days ago was it when she sat in her New York bedroom talking on the telephone to Peggy with Renee's telegram in her hand?

How long had she sat there waiting for the sound to come back in her head, for the room to lighten after she'd read those words again and again, dialing and waiting for Peggy's busy line to clear. Then the furious screech of the ringing phone!

"I've been trying to get through to you," Peggy said. "Are you there, Dany? Have you seen the *Times?*"

No, she hadn't seen the morning paper, she just came in from New Haven and a boy just delivered a cablegram from Renee.

"What did she say?" Peggy asked.

"Not enough. Wait, I'll read it to you." Peggy said nothing for a long while. Dany held the phone, not expecting a response. She understood and then Peggy said she couldn't send the car. It was the chauffeur's day off but Dany must come out immediately.

"I must go there, Peggy. Can I fly directly to Monte Carlo? To Paris?"

"No, come out here, take the first train you can get. We'll try to get through to Renee when you're here. I'll call Arthur in L.A. We must know more. I can't believe this!"

"I have to know about flights. I have to be with Renee and Gerard." Gerard. Dany couldn't stop saying his name, over and over. Gerard, Gerard.

"Dany, don't be crazy, you can't go! You'd have to fly to Lisbon and I don't know about connecting to France. I'll make some calls. Come here as soon as you can."

"How's the baby?" Dany asked. "How is my Veronique? Oh, Peggy, this is horrible and they're so far away!"

Peggy had been waiting when Dany stepped off the train in Oyster Bay. The brief story on the back page of the *Times* told very little. Dany read it over and over, she'd fold the paper on her lap and a few minutes later she'd picked it up again. Gerard Dessaux had been arrested, accused of killing his wife. Dany held on to the paper as Peggy drove to the house. She looked at it again after she'd unpacked her bag and later when she sat on the porch facing the wide, green lawn. Charlotte Dessaux had died during childbirth at the hospital in Monte Carlo. That was all. No more details.

Was the whole world holding its breath waiting for the phone to ring? There was no breeze, the hedges bordering the stone path down to the beach were motionless. It was still, humid and hot. The call to Villefranche should be coming in any minute. Would the trees move then? Would the leaves rustle back to life? The call. Where was the call? Dany swayed back and forth in the white wicker rocker. The phone had to ring. It must. Renee had to be there, in the house that Charlotte had adored.

"Dany!" Peggy called out at the sound of the ring. Dany ran in to the hallway, Peggy was there with the phone in her hand. "Oh, no!" The look on Peggy's face. What now? "Thank you, operator," Peggy said. "The line has been disconnected."

"Why? Renee without a telephone? It is impossible!" Dany said.

"Reporters asking questions, the house must be overrun with them and, who knows, the police may be all over the place. We'll have to wait for the letter."

"If Renee wrote yesterday it will take at least a week. If!"

"Let's go for a swim. We'll play with Veronique on the beach and we'll try to make this a pleasant weekend. Renee will call, I know it. Goddamn it, why don't we know anyone on the Riviera this summer? That Arthur, he claims to know everybody who's anybody. He says! And we're standing here helpless!"

The phone rang again, an incomplete ring that Peggy picked up instantly. *"Oui, oui.* Madame Mounet." Peggy gave the phone to Dany.

"It *is* Renee." The relief! *"Chérie,* how are you?"

"I'm all right, little one. I was hoping you'd be with Peggy."

"How, Renee? How did it happen?"

"I was in Monte Carlo for the day. She was alone and when I came back Gerard had come down from Paris and he was in the garden. Charlotte was lying on the ground, she'd been struck down. Oh, *chérie,* they'd been so happy. She was still alive when we got her to the hospital but she died minutes after the baby was born."

"The baby, where is he? And Gerard, what has he said? Renee?"

"The child is in the hospital, in an incubator. Very frail but the doctors say he'll be fine. And Gerard, he doesn't utter a word. He will not speak, not to the lawyer, to anyone. His sister in England is going to take the child. Little one, it is too sad. It's as if he's taken an oath of silence."

"What will happen now, Renee? What are you going to do?"

"I'll stay here for as long as he needs me though he acts as if he needs no one. The phone was shut off and the police have closed the villa. I'm at the Negresco in Nice. I talk and talk and, *chérie,* nothing seems to make sense."

"I'll fly over, Renee. As soon as I can get on a plane," Dany said. She had to be there, to offer a hand. She had to go. "Here's Peggy. We'll send you a cable. As soon as I can, Renee, I will be there!"

Dany stood up the moment the doors opened and the gendarme came forward. "Madame, follow me please." She walked through a large, quite judicial looking chamber with many chairs and a long table that reminded her of the convent in Amiens. She followed the man, going through another set of heavy doors to a smaller room with a smaller table and two chairs in the center of the floor. The room smelled of dampness and August heat despite the overhead fan spinning in a whirring monotone.

Gerard turned from the open window. He was thinner.

Oh, so thin, she thought. She'd never seen him in shirtsleeves before, without his usual immaculate jacket. No tie but he'd buttoned his shirt up to the neck in an attempt at propriety. He came to the table, gesturing for Dany to sit. He reached out to touch her, then he pulled back as he sat down, folding his hands on the table. "Dany, you shouldn't be here." He looked over to the closed door, to the long-faced guard. "But I'll never forget this, that you've come, that you've been so impetuous. And brave. The trip must have been exhausting. You flew?"

"Yes, for the first time. It was exciting. I'm not allowed to stay very long. Do they treat you kindly?" She didn't know what to say. She hadn't rehearsed this moment. She didn't expect to be awkward but she was. His eyes weren't pained as she'd seen them so many times before. They were tender and soft as he seemed to wait for her to speak. Dany thought the fan was droning in a louder rhythm. "Gerard, why won't you talk to these people. To your own attorney. You've been accused of something—" She couldn't finish the sentence. "Tell them that you didn't do it. I know you didn't. Don't ask me why. But, Gerard, I know you couldn't. . . ." She wasn't able to say "kill," she couldn't say "Charlotte."

It seemed a long time before he answered. "If I had courage, Dany. But I have none. I wasn't even brave enough to run."

"Maybe you didn't have to run. Gerard, maybe—"

"No, no. Don't try, Dany, please. It is futile." He rubbed his eyes, again and again, saying nothing. The silence was piercing, only the droning of the overhead fan. "Dany, I have to ask you one question," he said. "The child, little Veronique. Is Simon . . . was Simon the father?"

What was the point now? He was admitting nothing yet he wanted the truth from her. Dany didn't say a word, she wasn't able to. Words wouldn't come and she might cry. She who never cried. Like the wild burst of raging tears that day so many years ago, at the cemetery outside Amiens when her father was burned in the explosion. And the sister from the convent saying in her benevolent tone, we do not cry. Oh no, we mustn't cry. Her father had gone on to his rest. We do not cry. How often she heard those four words as she was growing up. But we lie, Dany said to herself. She couldn't answer Gerard. He'd had enough, he was sending a baby off to England to live with his sister. He was giving up his son. And his own life. Dany couldn't speak. She looked at him, his grey eyes wide and pale and waiting for her response. Was Simon the father? Dany nodded. Yes. Was that enough, just to move her head up and down. It had to be. She couldn't speak.

Renee was waiting in the car when Dany came down the steps into the bright street.

"Well, *chérie*, how was he?" Renee didn't wait for Dany to answer. "I can tell by your face, he said nothing. As he has behaved with me. Long silences between the innocuous words? Now listen to me. I know you want to stay longer but the news on the radio! The Germans have marched into Poland. There are reports of bombing. Little one, you must get out now before it is too late."

"War, Renee?" Dany could see Robert Venard at her bedside in the hospital almost a year ago, talking about ostriches. It had come. What he had dreaded, what they all had feared. "We must get to a radio. Oh God! And up there Gerard talks about futility!" She took a cigarette. "What will happen now?"

"He will go to trial in any case. And we will fight the Germans. This time there won't be any appeasement. Light one for me, little one, please?" Renee started the car. "We must call the airline, speak to the concierge. *Chérie*, are you cold? To be cold on the first day of September!"

Dany came back to New York, to the empty apartment and the deserted workroom. To the appointments she'd postponed before flying to Europe, to see Owen and Carl and their sketches for the musicals they were doing for the new season. To hurry to Oyster Bay for two days with Veronique and Peggy. Two quiet, happy days and Veronique

238

took her first steps.

"She's walking!" Peggy cried out, after she poured a glass of iced tea and Veronique, giggling with a sense of achievement, left the cotton blanket spread on the porch floor and extended her arms. She toddled toward the glass in Peggy's hand. "This is the best present I've ever had!" Peggy said.

Soon the workroom was noisy again. The usual morning jabber about crowded subways, the groaning about delayed busses and trolley cars wasn't important. Not when the war news in the headlines, on the radio reports, were worrying and frightening the women coming to work every day. Was the Russian draper feeling any animosity giving work to the Italian finisher, to the Austrian seamstress? The attitude in the workroom became quiet and determined and it wasn't bad, Dany realized. Because there were deadlines, one after another. It was maddening to have to finish the new costumes in such a short time and Dany welcomed the sobriety in the room, it reflected her own mood.

No news from Renee, not a word about Gerard. How many times did Peggy call asking if there was mail? Had she missed an item in the newspaper? Katie brought Veronique home and at the last minute Peggy decided to close the house in Oyster Bay. It was time to come back to the city.

Dany was draping a piece of moss crêpe on the dummy one morning when she knew why she was edgy. For the first time since she'd come to New York she felt like a foreigner. She didn't belong in New York, she was an outsider, another alien.

Weeks had gone by and she hadn't seen Jack. She had made excuses, some valid, some not. And that morning he heard the tension in her voice when he called.

"You're nervous, I can tell," Jack said. "Where would you like to go tonight? Name it, any place at all."

"Somewhere that is very expensive, where we've never been," Dany said. "No, I've another idea. I want to ride on the Fifth Avenue bus, up Riverside Drive. We can see the sky and feel the breeze from the river. Let's eat at that place on the hill beyond Grant's Tomb."

The soothing wind from the Hudson didn't help. The lovely view from the restaurant meant nothing and after dinner Dany asked Jack to take her home. "I'm sorry but I can't control myself. I'm too worried. I may become a drunk, that will make me forget that there's no mail, no news at all. I have no patience, you know that. I want to hear from France!" And she thought of the details she'd left out, the things Jack didn't know. He understood her concern for her friends, the close friends she feared for. She wanted news about Gerard and the trial. When would it be and if he had admitted his guilt or was he still silent? And the child, the little boy in an incubator. Had he been taken to England? To safety with Gerard's sister? To live someplace where he'd never know about another child, a half sister in New York.

The autumn days were shorter and the city was cool again. At lunch time the staff no longer went to the nursery in the back of the apartment to visit the baby. Now Veronique came running to the workroom with sharp-eyed Katie following her. The room full of color was more fascinating and livelier than the toys in the nursery.

"I was at Bergdorf's and I decided to say hello for a minute," Peggy said. "I stopped at Miss Brogan, there was a dress in the window. Wait till you see this!"

"You have to stop spoiling Veronique." Dany knew the words meant nothing to Peggy. "You don't like shopping. Why are you rushing around to the stores?"

"To forget the war news. You've heard the radio? They call it Blitzkrieg, nothing stops those Germans! They march in, they bomb, and they're winning!" Peggy said. "Hell, I wish I could do something. This neutrality, this deadly waiting for some action from our side." Peggy looked at the piles of fabric, the costumes hanging on the racks. "My God, I don't believe what's going on here. What are you going to do about more space?"

"I said I wanted to work, didn't I? There isn't an inch of room to hang another skirt."

"Remember when I said it? I told you so . . . isn't it thrilling?"

Jack said he had a surprise for her when they met at the Italian restaurant. Dany wondered what it was going to be. The things she wanted to talk about weren't exactly surprises, but she did think it was time to talk seriously. He was rushing through the meal, eager to get to it. Whatever it was, wherever it was; this surprise.

"And I hope you're free on Friday, I have seats for the hockey game. It's time you saw something besides a theatre, Dany Mounet."

"Jack, I can't. I'll be in Philadelphia with Carl Brandon."

"You're getting to be a real busy girl. It's great. But Dany, when do I get you to see a game? Come on, finish your coffee."

The taxi stopped at a hotel in the upper seventies off Madison Avenue. "Jack," she kept saying and he didn't answer until they were out of the hotel elevator.

"Now," he said, opening a door into a small foyer, a large living room and a bedroom off a narrow hallway.

"More respectable, isn't it? Less like a hideaway?" He was smiling, the distracting smile. "Are you pleased?"

"It's lovely, but Jack—"

"I can afford it. Don't worry, Dany." His arms were around her. "Want a nightcap? Look." He opened a closet door in the foyer. "We have a bar!"

It was still a hideaway, but a more elaborate one. Dany walked through the rooms. It was attractive with brocade draperies matching the sofa and chairs, a bedspread in dusty rose matelasse. The windows faced the street and a sliver of Central Park.

"*Chéri,* are you sure about this?" She had to say what was on her mind. "Is it going to be worth it for you? I can't see you as often now, the baby is growing up and . . . oh, Jack, what will your parents say?"

Sons left home when they became men or they wanted to,

241

especially here in America. She wasn't going to say it now but he should have found an apartment to fill with his own things; books, pictures, things he had affection for.

"Worth it?" he asked. "Darling, are you kidding? Do you know what you're worth to me, Dany?"

She looked at him, at the dark eyes and his smile.

"My parents don't have to know. We agreed about that." He bent to kiss her and she tried not to hold on to him. "This is ours, honey. Only for us."

He's a boy, she said to herself. A thirty-year-old boy. She wasn't happy with the thought.

Every day when Dany looked at the mail she made the same promise. Tomorrow she would try to get a call through to Renee in Nice. She'd make the attempt though it might take hours, though she dreaded what she might hear. She had to try. Tomorrow. She believed the stories in the newspapers, it was quiet in Europe. A deadly calm. A cut off world. Now they were calling it "sitzkrieg" and she wanted to know if it was quiet in Nice, too. Renee wasn't writing for a reason; she was hiding something. And then Dany wondered why didn't the American press deem Gerard noteworthy enough to write about him?

Dany could hear Charlotte saying that Dany Mounet didn't acknowledge fear. What a laugh, Dany thought. Charlotte, every day was filled with fear. Fear of what Renee might have to tell.

Dany thought of the nights in Paris when she went to the theatre with Charlotte and Gerard, to all the cafes, the theatre and cabarets. Her new routine was like that but New York was livelier, more intense. Dany could feel anticipation in the tips of her fingers, nervous energy rumbled in her chest. She knew why, but was all of New York waiting to hear from Renee Hugo, too?

Running made it easier. Running to the new restaurants, sometimes with Owen Patterson, other times with Carl. To the openings with Peggy. *The Man Who Came To Dinner* and *Too Many Girls,* to *DuBarry Was A Lady.* She knew Peggy would laugh when she told her she'd gone to the Hawaiian revue at the Maisonette, to the new mirrored and mother-of-pearl Ciro's. Dany was being as silly as Arthur Bellamy but it helped to keep on running.

Jack teased her the night he took her to Dinty Moore's to taste corned beef and cabbage.

"It's like *pot au feu,* we had it at home very often," Dany said.

"Did you have opening nights at home very often too?" Jack asked. "I hear you've been going everywhere, to all the smart places."

"Jack! I thought you were working in Boston, have you been spying? And you don't like the theatre. I have to see everything. It's business and—" Dany stopped. Why was she apologizing and lying? "Peggy Bellamy goes shopping. It helps relieve the strain. We all run in different ways. Crazy, isn't it, *chéri,* but we're concerned about people we care for. People in Europe! Can you understand that?"

"Yes, I can. Listen, I'll learn to like the theatre if I can go with you every night."

"No, Jack, you can't. When I'm out with friends, I'm taken home early. When I'm with you we don't finish the evening at the front of my door. We go to the hotel and, well, I can't stay out late every night. Do you understand that, too?"

"No," he said, "but I'll have to try." The dark eyes were sulking, his lips drooped.

"Don't do that, you look like a bruised puppy."

"I *am* a bruised puppy." He exaggerated the expression and started to laugh.

"No. Carl Brandon is right. He calls you the brat."

"Carl Brandon? That little fag!"

"Jack!" She was sorry she'd said it. "What a dreadful thing to say!"

"Talk about puppies, you should see *your* face now. That's what he is, what they all are."

"They?"

243

"Designers. Pop says they're a pack of sulking fags. When one of them can't have a certain piece of silk, when they don't like a color that comes in from the dyer, Pop says it's like namby-pamby kids not getting their own way."

"Your father knows about kids who get their own way, doesn't he?"

"Dany, what are we talking about? How did we get on this?"

"We're talking about how narrow-minded you are. You make money from these people, the artists who create for the theatre. Many of them have become my friends and I don't like to see my friends ridiculed!"

He was a brat. An immature adolescent hiding inside the handsome man she was looking at. He lit his cigarette and she wondered if he was old enough to smoke. Far off in the distance she could hear an alarm, chimes sounding out a warning. She'd heard this before, this name-calling. The easy branding of a group. Pamphlets hidden in medical books that smoked with prejudice, Simon's reading material when he wasn't studying. Dany knew why she wanted to run. This was more than a distant alarm. It was a red light.

Peggy's habit of stopping by to say hello in the afternoon was a subterfuge, but it didn't matter. It gave Dany an excuse to stop working for half an hour. Peggy wanted to see Veronique, that was true but she really was wondering if there'd been news from Renee.

"God, it's cold out today." Peggy shook the snow off her mink coat. "Yes, I'd love a cup of tea. Well, he's back. My husband has come home from Beverly Hills. The Hollywood producer! He's signed a contract with Paramount."

"You expected it." Dany moved a roll of fabric off the fitting room sofa. "What now?"

"I'll get a divorce. I've wanted to for months. I'm tired of being married to an asinine fool. He's staying at the Princeton Club. Don't ask why or how he got in. He never went to Princeton, you can bet on that! It fits into his fantasy world of where the man stays when he's left the little woman."

"Are you sure you know what you're doing?" Dany poured the tea. Peggy looked fine. Controlled and calm but she was an expert at appearing unemotional. And yet she always said what was on her mind.

"Oh yes, I'm sure," Peggy said. "At last I can change the dining room!" How often a laugh was only a millimeter away from a tear.

"Arthur's batty, you know? So don't be surprised, Dany, if you hear any rumors."

"Rumors?"

"He loves to talk about this unrequited love in his life. I don't want you to be hurt by his big mouth."

"No, I won't be, Peggy. I promise."

"It's another way to attain stature. His absolutely stupid values. Like being able to make reservations at the Stork or Twenty-One. Well, almost. At least at the Stork he does get a good table!"

"I feel dreadful abut this. And responsible for what's happened."

"Why? You didn't do a thing. He didn't even set the business up. Properly, I mean. You know, two years ago when I waited for you here in this apartment I was protecting myself. I thought so, anyway. I wanted to see who he was getting involved with, what danger I might have to face. Well, isn't it funny, Dany. Here we are!" Peggy stood up, brushing her hair off her forehead. "This has all happened with him before and it will again. I guess I've grown tired of him and his games. Feelings and emotions don't go very deep with Arthur."

"But you?" Dany asked. She knew Peggy had to feel lost. It wasn't possible not to feel abandoned.

"I don't have love to give out like generous tips to every waiter in town. With me it's a question of giving it wisely. I think! And at this point, it's for friends and what family is left." She took her teacup to the kitchen. "Now can I see Veronique, even if she's napping?"

* * *

It was a sunny spring morning when Katie came into the workroom holding the letter. "Special delivery, Madame." Dany recognized the fear in Katie's voice, the woman had premonitions about telegrams and letters she had to sign for. She, too. "It just arrived, the postman brought it."

The envelope was thick. It should be, Dany thought. After how long? She didn't want to count. Renee, it's about time. She went to the kitchen, opening the letter as she walked. White pages of hotel stationery and newspaper clippings.

My dear little one,

I wait to hear from you and no letter arrives. I scribble a note and wonder if it will reach your door. Here it is chaos and very sad. Alas, I do not have happy news to tell.

Gerard was acquitted three days ago after weeks of an ugly and sordid trial. The jury did not find sufficient evidence and now we will never know what really happened that day when Charlotte died. But imagine the joy at the verdict. Gerard was free! What follows is tragedy, little one, terrible tragedy. We, the attorney and I, drove Gerard back to the villa after his release. He was as quiet as he has been for months. As you saw when you were here. We drank champagne and toasted the future, hoped for victory and tried valiantly to make his first evening of freedom light and as merry as one can possibly hope for in the circumstances.

The lawyer drove me back here to the hotel after our meal at a little nearby bistro and then he took Gerard back to Villefranche. We planned to meet in the morning and my phone rang early. The lawyer. He had gone to pick up Gerard for our breakfast date.

Little one, Gerard killed himself. Sleeping pills. How he had hoarded them I'll never know.

The poor man. Will we ever know what he was feeling? An utterly dreadful sense of ruin? That has to be the reason. His world had collapsed. Hah, at this time everyone's world is teetering on the edge of ruin. I don't think Gerard valued his life without Charlotte. Such a terrible loss. We all have to go on, haven't we an obligation to our fellow man? Oh, I don't know, Dany. Perhaps I do not believe in total ruin. Somehow I think we all fall at one time in our lives but don't we rise up again, reach, grasp and claw to get up? Death makes me angry and I do not believe he killed Charlotte. I'm so mad at him!

His sister came before the trial. She has taken the child to England. It was Gerard's wish to have his son brought up there. Safe in England, he said. Did he know something, a sign, an omen that all Europe is about to fall and the British will survive? Questions, questions. Riddles, little one. Life has too many riddles.

I hope he is at peace now. I hope he is with his beloved Charlotte, that adorable creature he treasured.

I love having your letters. Forgive me for not being better about corresponding. Write to me in Paris, I'll be going back in a few days. How, I am not sure but I will get there. It seems all of France is trying to run here to the south. I have travelled in the wrong direction before in my life and I have survived. Survival! Oh my dear Dany, I cannot write anymore.

Many kisses to the beautiful Veronique and to you. To all my friends, to Peggy and Arthur I send love.

Renee

The clippings were terse and dignified obituaries, a photograph of Gerard, cold and serious and without personality. Then a long list of his theatrical productions, the names of the theatres he owned. Dany read on. "After the not guilty verdict the 56-year-old impresario returned to his villa in Villefrance . . ."

Gerard was fifty-six! Dany had never thought about his

' age, not a specific number. He was older than Charlotte, that was all she knew. The column was cut off in mid-sentence. Renee probably wasn't wearing her reading glasses when she clipped the story from the paper.

"Madame, are you all right?" Katie came into the kitchen with Veronique.

"What?" Dany looked up. "Oh, yes. Time for your milk and cookies, baby? Maman will give it to you." Dany handed the letter to Katie. "You didn't know them but they were the most beautiful people that ever lived." Katie knew about the waiting. The endless waiting and now there was this ending. "I must call Mrs. Bellamy," Dany said. "I have to tell her what's happened."

"Dany, you're shivering," Jack said. "Here, put on my jacket."

"No, I'm all right," Dany said. The wind blew across Central Park rustling the leaves as if it were October. "Has this ever happened to you? A certain light, an odor that reminds you of some other place. It doesn't seem like summer, it was an aroma in the trees. It made me think of autumn in Paris and the Tuileries."

"You must stop this. Honey, you can't stay depressed forever."

"Why not?" Dany asked, looking up at him and wondering. "Aren't you ever in a blue mood?"

"Sometimes. Then I talk myself out of it. I think of something else. I think of you, being with you."

She believed him, it was that easy. "We should have walked on Madison Avenue. The buildings aren't reminders, not like the park. At home there are German soldiers walking under the trees in the park. I don't know how my friends are, where they are. My in-laws in Amiens. . . ." She hated the sound of her cracking voice. The Mounets, she'd kept them out of her mind, for how long? Until the past few weeks. "I have the most awful guilt. I've had it for months. Lights keep going out, one after another on everyone I've known."

"Look, you're doing well. The shop is busy. Come on now, you have to get out of this funk you're in."

"Funk?" Dany laughed at him. *"Qu'est que c'est funk? But the dark is good, isn't it? When we're making love and there are no shadows. I forget then but we can't do that all the time, can we? Oh, Jack, it isn't only Paris that's fallen."*

"You haven't heard of Mac Roth?" Evans Morley asked when he called. "I forget that you haven't been here very long, Dany. He's been around for quite a while, a great promoter. No one can get publicity the way he can. After a string of hits he went out to Metro but now he's back with big plans. And since he needed a general manager, guess who has a new job?" What good news, Dany thought. Evans had been idle since Arthur had moved to Hollywood. "Now, the man does everything with great flash. Larger than life. I think *he* thinks he's Barnum. Never mind. Dany, you'll have to be a part of this. It's going to be a big one."

"And who is the designer? When does it begin?" Dany asked the usual questions and Evans went on. A well-known composer, a famous director. Enough costumes to keep three houses busy for months. It wasn't cast yet but Roth wanted stars. Big stars.

"Big, big, big. Evans, this sounds *formidable!*" Dany said.

"But . . . you know there has to be a but," Evans said. "Hy Immerman is the associate on this, he brings in a lot of money. Now he says that your prices were the highest he'd ever seen for the Iris Keating show. He and Mac want to come over. To see you and your atelier." Dany couldn't tell if Evans was teasing her the way he said "atelier."

"I like this," Mac Roth said. "It has an atmosphere even if it is small." He had walked around the workroom looking at sketches. He picked up a sleeve pattern as if he knew what he was looking at and when he reached into the bin to feel the quality of a fabric Dany could tell he knew it was silk.

"Good idea to have the fitting room look like a living room."

"Because at night it *is* my living room, Mr. Roth."

"Good idea anyway. Relax the ladies before the temperament begins." He didn't stare but his hooded eyes were enveloping. She thought of a book of Persian illustrations and she wondered about his accosting look. "I think there are only a few designers an actress trusts in this business. Gertie had that guy Molyneux and Lynn insists on Valentina. Do you design, Madame . . . hell, can't I call you Dany?"

"Yes, you can," Dany answered, "and I don't design. I'll copy something for a cabaret singer, do some individual pieces but I'm here to execute for the designer you have chosen." She hated the officious sound of her voice. She was self-conscious.

"Well, Hy says Iris Keating trusts you. That's an accomplishment, let me tell you. And good. It eliminates headaches for the producer and the director when the star is comfortable. If you can have Iris in the palm of your hand, you're okay for me. But watch your prices. Right, Hy?"

"This will be a much bigger order, Dany. Not like the last time," Hy Immerman said. "And we can't have those prices again. Not that expensive, please!"

"Expensive, Mr. Immerman? I was called to Joseph Albert's office to reduce my prices by one third and I was very careful to begin with."

"You're not kidding, are you?"

"Non, bien sûr."

"Do you have a copy of your estimates?" Mac Roth asked.

Dany went to her little desk. "Someplace here. Oh, where is that folder!"

"You need a bookkeeper," Roth said when she handed him the papers.

"So she subcontracted to Albert and that scoundrel screwed you, Hy!"

Immerman took the list. "Scoundrel? The son of a bitch took more than a hundred per cent mark-up and he screwed Dany, too!"

"Don't do anymore subcontracting," Mac Roth said. "I'm

250

the one who does the screwing, not old Albert! Right, Hy?"

"Thanks for the visit," Hy Immerman said.

"Thank you." She meant it. More than a year had gone by and somehow she'd known from the start. Joe Albert had cheated her. These men called him a scoundrel. Oh, if they knew . . . the scoundrel's son, the spoiled, handsome, immature son. She went out with the scoundrel's son!

Dany walked down the porch steps to greet Katie and Veronique coming across the lawn from the beach. "Here's your robe, get yourself dry, my darling." She rubbed Veronique's shoulders as she wrapped her in the terry cloth. "Now have a nap, *chérie,* and then we'll all have supper together."

Peggy reached out from the wicker sofa to hug Veronique. "I'm going to have you swimming better than Eleanor Holm before the summer's over, baby." She stretched out, kicking off her sandals. "Well, I said I wanted to have a noisy summer and I'm having one. Now for the best part. Talking about everyone who was here."

"The best part was your delicious lunch," Dany said. "I wish I didn't have to be back in the city tomorrow."

"This is the first time I've heard you sound like you don't want to work!"

"It's because of your wonderful house." Dany lit a cigarette; she needed a breath before saying more. "And your generosity—"

"And lending me your daughter for the summer. I should be thanking you," Peggy said. "Don't change for dinner. We're eating right here on the porch."

Alix Harcourt let the screen door slam as she walked out from the hall. "Boy oh boy, it's good to be back in civilization. I never want to be on the road again. I never want to be an understudy again!" She went to the bar to pour a gin. "I know, you don't have to say it. Until I'm offered the next job."

"We have to keep working, don't we? That's what Renee

251

used to say. Hone the instrument! Did I say it correctly?"

"You did. Another year on tour and I'll be over-honed," Alix said. "And over age!"

"It's good to have you back again," Peggy said. "And I agree. I hope you don't have to go back on the road. Is your agent doing right by you?"

"What a naive question to ask me! You know agents as well as I do. How good are any of them?"

"We should ask if there's a part in the new musical," Dany said.

"What musical?" Alix asked.

"Mac Roth's show," Peggy said. "No title yet. Shall I ask Evans about it?"

"Maybe I should go back to being a showgirl. Who's doing it? If it's Mac Roth it'll be opulent."

"I keep hearing that," Dany said. "He wants to have three shows on in one season. What an ambitious man!"

"And sexy!" Alix poured another drink.

"Do you know him, *chérie?*"

"The world knows that Mac Roth is sexy. Who's designing it?"

"Someone named Harriet Selby. I'm meeting her tomorrow morning."

"Selby! She used to be a dancer!"

"I hear she's his new girl," Peggy said.

"Ah, now the dishing begins," Dany said.

"Don't you love the way Dany pronounces 'deesh'! Say it again."

"Go on, tell me more," Dany said.

"I'd think it's a great order for you," Alix said.

"I have no order. Not yet," Dany said. "The meeting for estimates is two days from now."

"What do you do at the meeting? I've never known any of this."

"Pretend." Dany's guilty look made Peggy laugh.

"Go on," Peggy said. "After all, it is part of the business."

"I make believe I haven't seen the designs before." Dany dreaded the thought of a meeting in Mac Roth's office.

"You want me to go into the details?"

"Tell, tell!" Alix said.

"I give my Renee Hugo impersonation. All the old costume house people will be there, probably that dreadful Joe Albert and I will give my performance! The very, very French accent, the gestures. When I don't want to understand, I talk very quickly in French and I try to sound like Renee."

"But you said you're seeing the designs tomorrow?"

"I am. The designer brings the sketches to the favorite house before the meeting. A sneak look to know how to work out the prices before going to the producer's office. It is cheating but —" Dany's hand went to her forehead, brushing back a wisp of hair.

"You did it, you did Renee!" Alix clapped her hands. "Oh, Dany, it's perfect!"

"But I'm scared. I've never done this before. Looking at a new designer's work, pricing for this Roth person who is so very important."

"You've nothing to worry about," Peggy said. "Come have a drink."

"Did I ever tell you about Joe Albert, the old wolf, that chaser?" Alix asked.

"Chaser? He's so proper, so sanctimonious," Dany said.

"My you-know-what! Listen my darlings." Alix turned from the bar, eager to tell her story. "When I was dancing, back before I became the all-American understudy, I went up to Albert Costume for fittings. All the girls knew about him but I hadn't been warned. I was standing in the fitting room, those terrible cubicles they had."

"I've never been up there," Peggy said.

"A cell with a mirror, not a fitting room! For the chorus anyway, the star went to a bigger room. Old fat Joe came along with some lame excuse to get in the room, some reason to pull aside one of those curtains that you stood behind. Any kind of ruse to have a little peek. You'd think that after all these years in the business the sight of another derriere, another pair of tits would be boring. God, how different are we? Flat or large or perfect, so what. They're just boobies! But not for Joe. He found a reason to come into the room. He'd cop a peek and dear little Mary the fitter was pinning the satin and blushing with embarrassment because the bra was too big. There he was. 'Is that satin you're using?' he asked. 'That beading is very unusual, isn't it?' In a flash he's touching me! Those big, fat hands are moving over my breast! Getting a little feel. And with me, as is apparent, it is indeed little. Well, *mon chou,* he got it from me! A slap, one very firm, hard slap. He's not getting a free feel from me! He was out of that room very fast, I'll tell you. Very fast!"

"Why the filthy beast!" Peggy exclaimed.

Dany was quite still, not really surprised but puzzled. It was only a vulgar little story that Alix had told but it indicated more. The hypocrite. The audacity of the obscene, ignorant man!

"I wonder if he'd remember me?" Alix leaned on the porch rail, one hand on her bony hip. "I'm sorry, Dany. You were telling us about the meeting."

"Nothing more," Dany said. "They'll bargain, ask the costume houses to alter their prices. You lose an order or you get one. I can't do everything. I'm only beginning. But I can try, can't I?"

Harriet Selby didn't know very much and she admitted it but she'd rely on Dany for decisions about fabric and colors. After all, Mac Roth said Dany started in Paris, she had an advantage. It was more experience than Harriet got working in Earl Carroll's Vanities. But the sketches were stylish and this was merely a start, Harriet said and she winked. Dany wasn't sure what that wink meant but she was certain it pertained to working for Mac Roth.

Dany had to resist the temptation to tell Jack about the meeting. No, it wasn't a good bit of conversation for Jack, not the night before she went to the estimate meeting.

"You're like one of the actors you make fun of," Dany

254

said. "Why are you so nervous tonight?"

"I'm not, Dany, honestly. It's just that you've been working too hard and so have I. That's all."

"No, *chéri,* that is not all." Dany looked at the time. *"Mon Dieu,* it is late."

"Whenever you say that instead of Oh, God it means you want to leave." He sat up in the bed. "Come on, I'll take you home."

"You don't have to. The doorman can get me a cab. Stay, *chéri."*

He pulled on his shorts and began to dress. "I have the car, I'll drive you home."

"Don't they ask where you've been, with whom? Aren't your parents curious when their only son arrives home with the milkman? Doesn't your little sister ask you questions?"

"I lie," Jack said. "I'm very good at it."

She hoped he wouldn't smile. They shouldn't have kept their date. After weeks of postponements it had been an unpleasant evening. They rushed through dinner, they were agitated walking uptown to the hotel, and she sensed a clumsiness in their hurried hour in bed. She didn't want to be there and for the first time, she was sure he didn't want to be there either. "Jack, you've lost weight. You're quite thin."

"I lose weight when I don't see you." He smiled. He said he was a good liar and she supposed he was right. Why say what is on your mind when all you have to do is smile? It was too easy, Dany thought and quite irritating.

Sliding into the front seat of the car she wondered what Peggy would say if she was driving home now, disturbed and filled with uncertainty. Peggy would speak up, that was definite but it was second nature for Peggy to say what was on her mind.

Dany had questions but the flippant answers he'd give were going to be evasive. If there were any answers at all. She'd been uneasy for months and she wasn't ready to allow the reason to be on her tongue.

"You're lucky not having to go to estimate meetings." She broke her promise to avoid discussing business but she had

255

to say something. The ride down Park Avenue had never been so long. "I have one in the morning at the Mac Roth office."

"Yeah, Pop mentioned it. You'll see him there." Jack stopped for a red light. "Well, Evans Morley is a friend of yours, isn't he? That shouldn't be too bad."

He turned into Fifty-fifth Street. "You're home. I'll call you tomorrow." He leaned over to kiss her but she turned away quickly, his lips barely touched her cheek.

"Goodnight, *chéri*."

"Forgive me, Evans. I'm sorry to be late but the telephone! I couldn't get away," Dany said. "What a chic office. Am I the last to arrive?"

"They're all here. Come along. Say you're sorry in French." He led the way into a big room, more like a library than an office. "You all know Mme. Mounet," Evans said, shutting the door behind him. As she expected the three old costume houses were represented.

"Don't worry about being late, Mrs. Mounet," Joe Albert said. "It gave us a chance to catch up on our family news. We never get a chance to see one another except for sessions like this when we bid on a big show. And it is a big one, right, Evans?" Joe laughed, chewing on his cigar.

Dany mumbled a polite apology. "We're fortunate that it is going to be a busy season, aren't we?" The men from Brooks and Eaves greeted her, standing to shake her hand.

"This war!" Joe Albert went on. "War makes folks wanna forget, escape from all the rotten stuff that's goin' on. Isn't that the truth? I was just sayin' to the boys that I'd never have thought I'd live to see the day when I agreed with that Red, Norman Thomas, but I do now. He spoke out against conscription just like Lindbergh and everybody else with any sense. Don't you agree, Mrs. Mounet?"

"Oh, Monsieur Albert, I prefer not to discuss politics." Dany took a place offered on a leather sofa.

"Yeah, maybe you're right. Well, I was just tellin' the fellas somebody sure put the *malocchio* on my family. Sure, I know that my father when he first came over here woulda given anything to serve this new land. But that was way back when and times have changed. Don't we have to worry about our own necks now? We got an ocean between us and them Europeans, them Commies always tryin' to get us involved. What luck, hell! I never curse but, oh boy, what I could say this minute. My son drafted! I can't get it outa my mind. My son Jackie's gonna be in the army."

Dany looked at Evans, hoping he could stop this conversation.

Last night she had talked about jitters. Now she had to force her eyes to stare wider and wider, to control herself. She had known there was going to be more. This morning when she was bathing and dressing, she had sensed a distant alarm telling her that she was about to hear more. Jack. He hadn't the courage to talk to her, to tell her.

"Well, like I told the kid, I've promised him the biggest engagement party Freeport, Long Island has ever seen. We'll put it off for a while. Wait till he gets into that uniform and we know where he's gonna be stationed. Then we'll make it a real military weddin' instead."

"Look, Joe. We all have very busy schedules . . ."

"Why don't we make a date for lunch one day . . ."

"Sorry, Joe, look at the time and . . ."

"Yeah, sorry to blow off steam like this," Joe said. "Now let's see these fantastic designs we've been hearing about, Evans. Sorry, fellas, truly I am."

Did the pain show? Dany couldn't take out her compact mirror, she dare not light a cigarette. They'd see her trembling hands. And she had been prepared to impersonate Renee today . . . what a joke!

She came out of the Roth office, out of the elevator and into the hot July sun, thinking of those disturbed people she sometimes saw in the street, gesturing wildly and talking out loud. She must look like one of them now. Here she was muttering and jabbing her arms out into the air like a shadow boxer.

257

Last night Jack had admitted that he lied. Bad enough. But he was too cowardly to talk, too weak to acknowledge anything unpleasant. Beyond his dazzling smile, his bright, dark eyes was a lack of conscience. And he lacked ambition, he hadn't grown up yet, and he wasn't going to. Dany turned into her street, in a few minutes she'd go up the stairs and into the fitting room. She had to hide the anger and the hurt. This was the time for the Renee impersonation. Now!

This was the joke. He was going into the army. *Jackie was going to be a soldier!* It was too humiliating. He didn't respect her enough to discuss it. He'd been drafted! He'd be away from the business he detested, he'd be someplace miles and miles from home, away from his doting parents, his conniving father. She longed to say it. "Jack, this may be a blessing in disguise. *Chéri,* it isn't all bad!"

Into the house and up the steps to the workroom. To hide, mask her wrath. They mustn't see her rage. After all, she had watched Renee, she could imitate her. She had to once she walked into the atelier.

"Katie! I'm going to have lunch with you and Veronique today. I'm not going near my worktable for an hour." She put the portfolio of Selby sketches on the kitchen table. "I don't feel like working today."

And there was work to do. But later, in a little while. First there was Veronique.

She had to make phone calls, set appointments. Fabric salesmen, trimmings, laces. To see a line of satin and velvet.

She draped a sample piece over her shoulders in front of the mirror. "Yes, this quality is lovely. I like it."

What was this pattern in her life, she wanted to know. Was she innately a mother seeking out weak sons who admired her? Back in Amiens, had she been drawn to Simon because of his reticence, before his shyness turned to his manic fascist thinking? Why hadn't she been able to resist Jack though she had plagued herself all these months because of his immaturity? No, not a woman with maternal instincts searching for a son, not an adoring nanny. No, maybe the truth was that she was a sensualist incapable of controlling her desires for handsome lads who were much too young for her — mentally, anyway.

"And how much a yard is this?" Dany asked the salesman, picking up another length of cloth and turning back to the mirror.

There was no place in her life for weakness. Not now. She didn't want a husband, perhaps she didn't need a lover. She wondered every day about Gerard. What had impelled him to kill himself? And if he had lived, what might have been? Oh, dear God, she caught her breath. The weak! Gerard, too. How weak he had been!

She could no longer stand in front of the mirror, folding and draping fabric across her body. It was an unbearable image reflected there. Someone she didn't like at all.

"Thank you," she said to the salesman and she ordered some yardage she didn't need.

This had to stop. Daydreaming. Almost talking out loud while she worked.

The phone rang. And she knew. Running to pick up the phone in her bedroom she was absolutely sure, as if the ring was announcing his name.

"Dany? Honey?" Jack's voice, tentative and uncertain. "Listen, Dany darling," he sounded almost timid. "How about meeting for a drink after work? Will you? I want to talk to you, Dany."

She listened and waited.

"Dany, are you there?"

He was impatient! "Yes, I'm here!" She almost said *chéri*. "Talk, Jack? What do you have to say? It seems that your father speaks perfectly for you. What can you have to tell me that I didn't hear this morning? From him. In an office full of people."

"You know? Oh honey, I wanted to tell you but —"

"But? I'm sorry, Jack. I'm very sorry for you."

"Christ, if I was two years older I'd have missed it. I wouldn't have been taken in the army!"

259

"Jack, the surprise to me is that you're old enough." Then she startled herself, it wasn't difficult to say. "Goodbye, Jack. Good luck."

Two days later Evans asked Dany to come to the office to discuss the estimates she'd submitted.

"Can you explain this, Dany?" Evans gave her two lists of figures. "The prices from Brooks and Eaves are quite compatible and fair I think. Now look at the Albert list compared to your own. I have to give this order out by the end of the day and of course we'll have to use three houses to make it or we'll never open on time. Why are the Albert prices so low compared to yours?"

Dany studied the sheets of paper in her hand, carefully checking the columns of figures. "Evans, I see what he has done. The monster! Joseph Albert knows I can't make the men's suits so his prices for tailoring are accurate. And he knows you're not about to give him an order for the ladies' dresses. After he saw me at the meeting he must have known Hy Immerman was on to him, that he'd cheated me on the Iris Keating show. That's why his prices are absurdly low. He hopes to force me to reduce my figures. That man wants to ruin me, now that I'm just beginning!"

"Dany, I have a budget," Evans said. "We have to work this out."

"May I see the costs from the others? I know it's not ethical, but what in life is? You can't compare the quality of my work with . . . oh, I'll fix him! I'll have a men's department. I'll hire a tailor, I'll steal his! He has the best man and I'll get him. I'll find larger space. I need the room anyway. I'm going to be the best!" She sat up straighter and reached for one of Evans's cigarettes. "The best atelier you've ever seen! As for now, tell me how much you want me to slice off the prices." She silently thanked Maria Mennino for her advice when figuring costs. "And remember, Evans, I am a woman alone trying to make a living!"

The workroom grew smaller as more crinolines and bouffant skirts were finished and hung on racks. More women were hired to drape and sew, a corner of the fitting room became the embroidery section with frames set up in front of the windows. Beads and sequins were going on every piece of chiffon, crêpe and satin. Glitter was added to everything. Dany rented part of Maria's space upstairs and they found a place where a bookkeeper could work. Harriet Selby's costumes were flashy and colorful and expensive. It was Dany's most lucrative order. Despite the opulence, the prestigious names of the creative staff, and the cast, the Mac Roth musical closed in Boston.

Every few weeks Dany was packing cartons, boarding another train to New Haven, Philadelphia, Boston or Detroit. Another out-of-town tryout. Every few weeks Peggy went to Washington. She was going to sell war bonds, she was organizing committees to raise funds for the Free French.

Dany quickly agreed to assist Peggy in any way, wherever help was needed. Every week she wrote to Renee and Robert Venard and Louis, hoping the mail reached them in Paris but there were no replies. Not a word from Maman and Papa Mounet since France was occupied.

Dany hadn't thought about Christmas until Peggy came home from Washington. "Dinner at the apartment. I've invited the world. Five o'clock but you and Katie bring Veronique in the early afternoon. We'll have our own time with presents."

More gifts for Veronique, two weeks after her birthday. No way to stop spoiling the child despite Katie's discipline, not when Aunt Peggy, Aunt Maria, Auntie Alix and the workroom full of women fussed over her every hour of the day.

The holidays were noisy, full of warmth and affection. And Dany realized that the persistent, hollow numbness wasn't exclusively hers. It was lurking around every seat in the theatre, a frantic void at every loud table at a restaurant, in the clamor of a party. Another year of uncertainty and she wasn't alone with it.

Those last words from Charlotte the day before she left

New York came rushing at Dany. Be extravagant, dream; that was what Charlotte had said. Why not? Work was harder now, tension crept into the workroom. With worry. Everyone had a husband, a son, a relative in the service. Death was lurking in the room every day. Dany knew she had to honor what Charlotte had most admired. Fearlessness. In no way was Dany going to allow fear into the atelier. Not when she could keep her staff working steadily. Clothes, costumes, dresses, not a slow week for three swift years. A set of costumes for one musical after another, season after season. The ice show at Radio City, loud, brassy revues, slinky gowns for cabaret singers. And contributions to the USO, costumes for the troupes entertaining overseas. Not a wasted day, not an hour. That was the extravagance.

And a tin box on a table near the bar in one of the bistros Renee had been fond of, where Dany sat evening after evening collecting money to be sent to de Gaulle. She was at the Stage Door Canteen, sometimes in the lobby of a theatre, any place where donations were to be called for.

A house, she wanted a house. That was the dream. A huge workroom with space for Maria's millinery department, a room for the embroiderers. And a men's department for the tailor she'd lure away from Albert Costume Company!

"Alix Harcourt is phoning from Wilmington," Katie announced at 8 A.M. one morning. "She hopes it isn't too early."

Dany came out of the bathroom wrapping her robe over her shoulders. What now, she wondered. Alix went on complaining, calling herself the constant understudy but she wasn't ever out of work for more than a month at a time.

"Of course I'm awake," Dany said on the phone. "I'm in the workroom at eight every day."

"Good," Alix said. "Now listen carefully, Dany *mon chou,* you know that Susan York is a star?" Yes, Dany knew the woman's name, she'd seen her movies and she was about

262

to make her debut in a new comedy. Alix had talked about her for months before going into rehearsal. "We opened last night. My dear, she played the first act and went mad. I mean mad, completely cuckoo! They've taken her away. A sanitarium somewhere. You've heard about stage fright? Well, you've never seen anything like this. And, Dany, I'm taking over the part!" Alix was excited, that was understandable but she talked in scraps, little spurts of information. Like short items in Winchell's column.

"We're shutting down for a week. It's insanity down here. These Hollywood girls simply do not have the discipline, Dany. I've got the part. What a part! Wait until you see! They had a meeting last night, the writer, the director and the producer. They think the play is strong enough to go without a star, so that's me! Well now, Susan York is three inches shorter than I am. They didn't get around to clothes for me, and I'm not being difficult, but I called my agent at three in the morning. I don't want Hattie Carnegie dresses. I said I wanted Dany Mounet to make my three dresses, Dany. That's all—"

"Alix, I'm not a designer," Dany said. "I'll alienate all the designers who come here if I do costumes for you."

"Costumes! I need dresses. Simple, dramatic dresses. You made dresses for Renee Hugo in Paris. Now you can do it for me. And I'm thinner!"

Dany could hear Renee Hugo, on a rainy afternoon at the Ritz in Paris. The call for help. Please? Dany held the phone away from her ear. Alix was cuckoo too, cuckoo enough to be a star.

"I know exactly what I want. Will you come down here tomorrow? I'm going to make it now, Dany. I'm going to be a star! Three dresses, do it for me! Lots of publicity. Call me back within the hour. Think it over. No, don't think, just say yes!" Where was Wilmington, how far away? Another tryout, another train. Dany knew she couldn't say no. "Someone from the producer's office will arrange the details."

It wasn't greed but merely good business, she shouldn't refuse any orders. Why did she need an hour? Alix mentioned publicity. Three glamorous dresses. For a new star. Maybe.

"A bright new comedienne named Alix Harcourt."

"A light and sprightly romp played with inimitable style by Alix Harcourt."

"A new star. Remember, you read it here first. Alix Harcourt is truly a star!"

The critics were ecstatic and Alix had been right. She worked every minute of the day, from Wilmington through a three city tour before opening on Broadway. She rehearsed and she practiced and she studied. She knew what she was doing and Dany admired her zeal and enthusiasm, her total dedication to a play that Alix said was a once-in-a-lifetime opportunity. Her clothes were chic. Alix called it "An American look." That pleased Dany. "None of that Gothic drapery other designers seem to go for nowadays. Simple, comfortable clothes for the stage. Why not!" And Dany had to admit it; Alix knew what she could wear. That didn't happen very often, the actress who knew was a rarity.

"If one order doesn't come in to the atelier then I'll have another," Dany said to the bookkeeper when she was told that she ought to cut the expense of overtime. It was eating up the profit and the profit was small enough.

"I need more space!" Dany cried out again and again. She wasn't giving up, she held on to her dream. Orders did come in, overlapping shows, a small group of costumes for the Ballet Russe. Dany's reputation was growing. Light and elegant execution, she heard the description often now. When Alix was interviewed for *Vogue* magazine she summed it up for Dany, "Perhaps it cannot be defined but you can recognize it when you're sitting in the audience. It's a look, the Mounet look!"

Sardi's was always crowded at night around 11 P.M., when everyone wanted supper, an after theatre drink and a glimpse of the celebrity clientele. Dany came in, surprised to be ahead of Peggy when Evans Morley called from the bar.

"Have a drink with me while you're waiting," Evans said.

"Then will you join us? She's at a Civil Defense meeting," Dany said, happy to have a sip of her Dubonnet. "I saw *Variety* today, the announcement about Mac Roth. Will you be with him again?"

"Yes, we opened the office on Monday. He said he'd never do another show after that last fiasco and he did lose money on it but here we go again. Ah, there's Peggy."

"You must slow down," Dany said when they were at their table. "Peggy, you're taking on far too much."

"Well!" Peggy laughed, enjoying Dany's reprimand. "Will you look who's talking! What have you been up to tonight after you left the workroom?"

"I was at the Music Box."

"To see the play?" Peggy asked, nudging Evans in an I-told-you-so gesture.

"Collecting for War Relief."

"And I get chastised for working too hard. I want a scotch," Peggy said, calling the waiter.

"Evans was telling me about Mac Roth's new plans," Dany said.

"Again?" Peggy was surprised. "The fellow is a glutton for punishment. That flop in Boston should have cured him. But what am I saying? The alternative would be Hollywood, God forbid!"

"He's planning the three productions again. He's determined to have them all on in one season. Are you ready for more work, Dany?"

Dany didn't remember the Miro on the wall in Mac Roth's office. It seemed out of place in the room full of English leather furniture and heavy library tables.

"You've never been here before?" Mac asked, watching Dany look at the painting.

"Oh yes, once before. The last estimate meeting,

265

you missed that one," Dany said. "Lucky man." She didn't want to talk about that morning three years ago, she mustn't ever think about it, she told herself. "But I don't remember the Miro."

"It wasn't here. I may have to redo the office now. Looks out of place, doesn't it?"

Dany felt her cheeks reddening. How did he catch her or was it merely coincidence? "I was just thinking that and I didn't want to criticize."

"Why not? I would if it was the other way around." He flipped through papers on his table, giving her a page. "The schedule. Have a careful look at it. I intend to stick to it. No postponements, no changes."

"Thank you." She wasn't able to look at it, not when she saw him appraising her. He seemed to be checking every inch of what she was wearing. Her shoes, the color of her stockings. His eyes went over her as if *she* was being estimated. It was almost rude. Did he approve of her skirt and blouse, her cardigan sweater? His Arab eyes. She had thought of Persian drawings when they first met but she'd been wrong. She hadn't been aware of it when they were in Boston but now she thought his eyes were those of some slave trader working in a Moroccan market.

"We do the play first, Evans has told you about it. The revue will be the last musical of the season. We'll open here in May. I want to get Merman and Bob Hope. I need stars, a theatre full of stars!" He was smiling at her. "Dany, is something wrong?"

"I hope not." She laughed, she had to cover her embarrassment. "You should be in a fitting room with your x-ray eyes. Do you always do this?"

"Do what?"

And she was sure he knew what she was about to say but she had to say it. "You're like an appraiser! Do you undress every woman you look at?"

"It's not appraising. Just my imagination. I never met a woman I didn't think about nude. Naked, on a bed, a couch. Sometimes the floor. Carpeted, of course. After I have her undressed in my mind I may not want to go on thinking about her. However—"

"And afterward, do they all volunteer?" Dany was astonished that she was going on with this.

"Usually," he said.

It was Evans who knocked on the office door. She was delighted to be interrupted. What a relief!

The first of Mac's three plays opened in New Haven. A melodrama with a cast of five, three men in suits made by Brooks Costume and bustle dresses that Dany thought were tediously realistic. How she yearned for the style of Ostier or even Carl Brandon but Mac had hired an older man who taught costume design at Harvard. His work was effective but drab and without flair. An opinion Dany thought best to keep to herself. The dress rehearsal went on without problems, hardly any notes afterward.

She looked at the time, it was early enough to skip the opening performance in a few hours. It would be a treat getting back to the city in time to have a sandwich with Katie, to read to Veronique before her bedtime.

Mac came through the stage door into the street. "Dany, have dinner with me. Everyone else is nervous because it went so peacefully. Come on, Kaysey's pot roast. It won't hurt!"

"I was thinking of going home. My work is done; hard to believe, isn't it?" Dany said. "You should do more five character plays with three dresses in the costume plot."

"You should do all my shows. Talk about flawless. Wow, lady! Come on, Dany." He took her arm, holding her gloved hand to his lips. "Have dinner with me. I'm the producer!"

"You mean I can't refuse? All right. There is a train around midnight, isn't there?"

"You can drive back with Evans. He has to get back, too. Wait till the musical, Mme. Mounet. You'll have to be around me more often then. Fair warning, okay?"

"Stand still, Alix. One minute for the hemline." Dany was on the floor pinning white jersey. "I'd forgotten that you were on the road when we first did your costumes."

"A year later, can you bear it?" Alix was restless in front of the fitting room mirrors. "When does Veronique get in from school? Dear God, the child's in kindergarten!"

"Not until three o'clock. You'll miss her. Stop fidgeting!" Dany said. "You were better behaved before you became a star."

"Wrong! I'm always perfectly behaved." Alix tossed her head, flipping her hair back from her forehead. "Should I be blonder, do you think?"

"Not if you insist on imitating Tallulah." Dany held on to the box of pins, getting up from the floor.

"Smart, aren't you? Now tell me about this house you've seen. Forty-fifth Street?"

"Alix, it can be perfect. You'll have to see and pray that I can find a way to buy it."

"It isn't the most elegant part of town, sweetie pie."

"I don't care. The block is quiet and respectable. My life is in that neighborhood, *chérie,* five minutes from all the theatres, from rehearsals. And there are rooms. For Veronique, for Katie. Rooms to move around in. Peggy heard about it from her nephew, Peter."

"He's on leave. He called me yesterday."

"Peggy told me. He's going into the law office that handles her affairs when he comes out of the army. It was an officer in his company who is selling the house. He had a magazine that's gone out of business. Now I have to find the way to go *into* business."

"Funny," Alix said. "All my life I've wanted to live on the East Side and now that I'm able to you may be moving way over there. Dany, have I said something wrong?"

"No, but it is strange. In the last letter from Renee, almost five years ago, she said she was going up to Paris from Nice when all of France was trying to get south. Do you know that was the last time I heard from her?"

"Dany, she's safe. They all are. We'd have read about it, if it was otherwise. And it won't be long now. We're going to win. It may be a year, but. . . . You do believe that, don't you, Dany?"

"Yes, yes, I do. Now you won't get this until Saturday afternoon, don't get in a state."

"I won't need it before. Exciting, isn't it? A year anniversary party! Though I don't know why it's at the Essex House. Press agents get the most peculiar deals."

"I thought you said the Hampshire House."

"Maria! I'm surprised to see you in on Saturday." Dany was opening the mailbox in the vestibule. "I wanted to talk to you."

"I came in to finish the Easter bonnets for my nieces. It'll be quiet, no phone calls, no interruptions."

"Except me. Will you have a cup of coffee before you go to work?"

"What's wrong, *cara?*"

"I fancy myself as quite a good actress but you can read my mind better than anyone, Maria."

"It isn't your mind, I only have to look at your face!"

"Let's go in the workroom, it's quiet," Dany said, "and I love the morning sun in there."

Dany brought a tray from the kitchen and set the cups on her worktable. "Well, Maria, I was at the bank yesterday afternoon."

"And?"

"They're turning me down. I'm too much of a risk at this point. I can't believe it! I still owe money to Arthur Bellamy and it comes out of my account monthly to him in California. Outstanding debts, they say. It's not a lot of money, what's a few thousand dollars? But they are the bankers, not I! And I'm not a citizen *yet.*"

"Oh, I'm sorry, Dany," Maria said. "What about Mrs. Bellamy, can't she help you?"

"I've just finished paying the back rent from my first year

269

in this building. I owed her that. She's been incredibly generous, and Maria, I want to do this on my own. She was the one to find the house. She arranged for the real estate broker. Right now, Katie has taken Veronique to the Metropolitan Museum for art classes that Peggy paid for." Dany poured another cup of coffee. "Would you like a cigarette? How much more can Peggy do for me?"

"I'd think mortgages would be easy now. Dany, if I had it—"

"Maria, I know that. Look, there's going to be a millinery department for you in the new place. I know your business is suffering, who is wearing hats now?" Dany lit her cigarette. "And this bank is supposed to be most conservative. But I want that house, it'll be the best investment I can ever make." The phone rang. "I must think of a way—" She picked up the call after the second ring. "Dany Mounet," she announced, forgetting it wasn't a work day.

Maria gestured that she'd go upstairs, they would talk later but Dany took her hand, motioning for her to stay. "Yes, I know your voice," Dany said. If Maria was at the table listening it was going to be easier. "Jack Albert. Yes, I'm very well, thank you."

Four years later, what did he expect her to say, to do? Yes, she was surprised. No, she couldn't see him. It wasn't possible, not even as a patriotic gesture. He had many things to tell her, to explain. There were reasons and now he was going off, probably to the Pacific. He was in the Signal Corps, still a private. And now to be back at the place, at his old desk on a calm Saturday morning. Same old routine, like the old days. It sure seemed funny to walk in and see it all unchanged, to catch up with the old timers. Unbelievable to be sitting across from Pop. . . .

"It's believable," Dany said. She looked at Maria, wondering what more to say. He was unsure of himself and rambling on. "No, Jack, you don't have to explain anything to me. Too much time has gone by. No, I can't possibly see you. Of course I wish you luck."

Her hand was shaking when she hung up the phone. "Is

270

this going to be one of those days?" she asked. "I wonder who he smiles at now?"

Dany assumed most of the people crowding into the Essex House ballroom were investors, happy to be celebrating a success with the producer. Mel Zorin had invited the stars from other shows, then Dany recognized the familiar party faces, usually invited by the press agent, ready to be photographed, eager to sign an autograph. And the men in uniform, Army, Navy, Air Force; Dany knew Alix had conferred with Peggy before convincing Zorin to call the Stage Door Canteen, the Officers Club.

"This is Captain Ingolls," Peggy was proud to be introducing Peter to everyone she knew.

"Yes, I was a kid," Peter was saying. "Yes, I *am* a lawyer. The army needs lawyers, too." He excused himself to get to Alix at the other side of the room.

Peggy and Dany followed him, trying to weave through the crowd. "I'm good at this," Dany said, "just hold on to my arm!" She edged in and out, accepting congratulations for Alix's white jersey dress, returning an embrace, a hug, a kiss and moving on into the ballroom.

"A drink, we need a drink. Where has Peter vanished to?" Peggy was stopped by a couple pleased to see that she was back from Washington. Dany tried to get over to Alix, now holding on to Peter and smiling for a photographer. "The bar, get over to the bar!" Peggy called out.

Drinks before trying to squeeze through this throng. Good idea, Dany thought. Where would they find a table? And not a waiter in sight. Scotch, Peggy would want scotch with soda. If she could get a bartender to pay attention. Where was Peter, she needed him. The heavy figure in front of her turned around.

"Well, hello, Mrs. Mounet," Joseph Albert said. "Looks like this party could be for you as well as for Miss Harcourt's show." He held her hand. "From all the hugs and kisses I seen you gettin'."

"*Monsieur* Albert, good evening," Dany couldn't turn away in the line of people at the bar. Be polite, she said to herself, be civil.

"Me and the family came into the city for dinner down on Mulberry Street and the missus got tired so we decided to stay over. I thought I might as well look in on Mel's party. We keep an apartment here, you know."

"Mister Albert, please." She pulled her hand away from him. "My friends are—"

"Yeah, you got friends all fawnin' around you now. And I'm sure you like that, doncha? Hey, don't try to walk away." He held on to her elbow. "This is what you wanted, all this acclaim, huh? But you can't have it all, can you? I have a feelin' you thought you'd get my Jackie, too. No more fancy East Side hotels the past few years and I bet you miss em. Didn't think I knew about all that, didja?" His voice was low and rasping, almost hissing at her. "Listen lady, don't try to snub me! Wanna drink? You do drink, doncha?" Dany was pinned against the bar as he leaned over, calling for a rye and water. And Jack had said once that his father didn't drink! "What if I got a single room for a couple of hours, Mamselle?"

Dany squirmed, pushing him against the back of a man next to him. In this pack of thirsty people no one seemed to hear! Joe quickly grabbed her hand again, rubbing it along his thigh. "Let go of me," she said, almost a whisper through her clenched teeth.

"You didn't get the son, might as well try the old man. I can give you what you like, I bet. What I got in here'll make you happier than what you got from sonny boy, I'll guarantee that! Anyway, you're gonna lose, Mamselle. Didja know the kid's getting married next week? I took care of that!"

Dany wrenched herself away. "You filthy old fool!" She cried it out as he tripped against the bar. Peter was at her side, holding her. "No, don't touch him, Peter! No more of a scene, please!"

Peggy had found a table at the other side of the room, near the windows. "Now, Dany, what was all that?"

272

She must stop trembling, she had to speak. "Someday I'll ruin that man. I swear it!" Dany vowed.

Dany was sure her appointment with Mac Roth was for 6 P.M. She checked her watch and knocked on the office door again.

"Coming . . . hold on!" She heard the voice. "One second!" And Mac opened the door. "Everyone's gone for the day. Hello! Come on in. You're the one who wanted the late appointment."

"I know. I wasn't sure you heard me knocking."

"I was on the phone. The Coast. This is the best time to get them out there."

She followed him into his office. The antique library tables were gone. "Mac, you did change it!" The room was brighter with beige marble and brass leg tables, the Miro looked livelier.

"Well?" He was waiting for her approval.

"I like it." She sat on the leather couch. His vest was open and his tie unknotted, he must have had a busy day. She hoped her timing wasn't bad, maybe he'd had an irritating afternoon.

"Now what's on your mind at this late hour?" He slid a crystal cigarette box across the coffee table to her. "Dany, are you sure you feel all right?"

"Yes, yes. Only I . . . but I wish you understood French. Do you?"

"Now where would I have learned French, Dany? I didn't get through high school. Why?"

"In French I could say it easily. I had rehearsed a speech and, well, whenever something important is happening I revert to French. When I'm nervous."

Mac leaned forward to light her cigarette. "All right, this is important. How can you be nervous with me? Now say it slowly to yourself in French and then translate it."

"Have you ever wanted something more than anything in the world and did you make up your mind that you'd do any-

273

thing for it?"

Mac laughed. "Oh, you know it, kid." He was smiling. "Now, Dany, you didn't say that to yourself in French, did you?"

"No. No, I just said it."

"Okay. See, it's simple. Just come out with it, Dany. I think you need a drink."

"Mac, on West Forty-fifth Street there is a house. A double brownstone is for sale that will make the most perfect atelier. The best workrooms. I can have the most successful costume house in the world if I have this house." She took a long pull on her cigarette. "Thank you, no, I don't need a drink."

He folded his arms across his chest, sitting back and waiting.

"This is what was going to be difficult . . ."

Mac shrugged, grinning and gesturing for her to go on.

"I have been to the bank and they turned me down on the financing for this house. I have some debts, they say. Not many but though my business seems very successful I don't show a great profit."

Dany wondered what he was thinking. She wished he had the slave trader look now, then she might be able to say what she had come for. If he were undressing her with his eyes it might be easier. She didn't know how to flirt, she had to go on talking. "Mac, a few months ago I asked you if all the women you . . . if they always volunteered." How would Renee play this scene, what would she do now? "I want to say that if you are interested I will volunteer. I will if you can arrange to make it possible for me to have the brownstone house. If you'd lend me the money."

He wasn't smiling and she had no idea what he was thinking. His dark eyes seemed wider but she wasn't sure what he was going to say. Or do. She was sorry, this was a mistake. She shouldn't have tried.

"Dany, Dany." He was shaking his head as if he didn't believe what she had said. "You're not a whore, Dany. Do you think I'd. . . . Listen, I ought to be pretty goddamned an-

274

gry. What makes you think I'd be willing to hop into your bed?" He frowned at her. "I can pay for whatever I want but usually I don't. Not in advance, at any rate! And later, well, that's another matter. I send flowers, a string of pearls. Maybe even a diamond or two, a bunch of emeralds. I've done all that because I'm a very generous guy, Dany. When I want to give the gift. Understand? No obligations, though. Never. You're too good to have to make this sort of offer. Dany, you've been to one bank? That's all? Do you know how many banks there are in this city? I'll find you a bank. You'll get your house. Christ, how you manage where you are I can't understand." He stood in front of her and took her hands, pulling her up from the couch and he took her chin in his hand as if she were five years old. The way she held Veronique when she wanted to make a point. "Something important, you said. You were right, something important is going on with us. When you want to, say you're ready, Dany. But not as a payment for anything."

He held her hands and she couldn't say another word.

"Now, how about going over to the Stork for a drink. You look rather pale, my girl."

Dany didn't like the Stork Club when Arthur Bellamy used to insist on going there. God, had it been six years now! She knew why he considered it classy but the quiet, smaller places serving good, simple food that Peggy found were far more attractive. Who needed all the racket and showing off? What was gained unless a few men had a business meeting, a deal to make or they wanted to look at the pretty Powers models who frequented the place? To be seen, that was the purpose. It was a man's place, not unlike a private club.

Mac called it his neighborhood saloon. It was right up the street from his office, what could be more convenient?

And his table was ready in an instant, his favorite scotch was available in the rather quiet Cub room before the dinner crowd arrived.

"Okay, now will you tell me your version of the Harcourt party the other night?"

"Oh dear, you heard," Dany sipped the cocktail Mac

275

urged her to try. A bourbon toddy, not one of those popular fruit salad drinks, simply the fine stuff; good bourbon, bitters, sugar and a twist of lemon. "Gossip doesn't take long, does it? I've always thought it originated in the fitting room, the talk, but it spreads fastest from a party, I guess."

"Why are you so naive? This is a barracuda world we're in. Columnists get paid to print what dirt they hear on the telephone, at parties or in restaurants. Like this place. Do you know how many people exist mainly to see their names in a paper? Well, you made Kilgallen's column today. No names, one of her blind items. 'What highly respected member of the theatrical costume world and what attractive European . . .' Well, Dany, who in the know would have trouble guessing? Anyway, Evans Morley had told me about it. You saw him at the party, didn't you?"

"Yes, but not until later."

"Don't be upset. It won't hurt to have your name in a column, especially if you're the injured party."

"Don't tease me, please. I'm not sure I can be adult enough to stand that. *Injured?*" Dany told Mac about Joe Albert. "You know the beginning when I met that man, subcontracting for Hy Immerman's show." Dany told Mac about the first time in Boston when she saw Joe and Jack at rehearsal, for the first time she talked about Jack Albert. She told all of it. "And he is probably marrying a girl his father has picked for him. Mac, I don't think I've ever felt so dirty. Joe Albert's face!"

"Forget it, the bastard's not worth it. Want another drink?"

"No, I must go. I like to have dinner with my daughter and it's getting late. Look at the time!"

"Let me take you both out one night. Can we do that?"

"If you'd really want to."

"Where would she like to go? The Circus will be in soon. Coney Island, the Palisades? We can do it when we're back from New Haven. That's in six weeks, you know? I'm wondering if I'm not waving the flag too obviously with this one. *Our Stars and Stripes,* but why not? A lot of laughs, pretty girls to look at and some old-fashioned, bold sentimentality." Mac was seeing it on stage, Dany knew he imagined it all happening and it wasn't going into rehearsal until next week. Mac was impatient, he had the same spirit she remembered during the first days with Gerard and Charlotte in Paris. "But I don't want this writer, Harlingman, getting carried away with politics. Well, we'll see in a few weeks. Nothing wrong with some high-toned patriotism, is there?"

"I think it's a good idea," Dany said. "Tom Thornton brings me the sketches to see at the end of the week. Mac, even if Veronique doesn't want to go to the Palisades, I do. Everytime I've been on Riverside Drive I've longed to go over there, on top of those cliffs with all the twinkling lights."

"Then we'll do it. I worked over there when I was just a kid, selling hot dogs at a counter. I must have been fourteen and then I moved up in the world. I sold tickets for a ride on the Ferris wheel, then the loop-the-loop. You can learn a lot watching people when they're waiting on line for one of those scenic railway or carousel rides. You see a stubborn, determined look behind the smiles. They've made up their minds to have a good time. I guess I've been selling the same thing ever since. A ride on the merry-go-round or $4.40 for the best seat to see Jolson or Durante. It's all the same, isn't it? Whet their appetites, arouse their curiosity. They don't mind spending their money for a ride, do they?"

Tom Thornton couldn't stop talking. He flipped his sketches across Dany's table, describing the details with as many gestures as words. "Gingham, naive and innocent. But I'd like to blanch it a bit and then overdye it to this shade of blue. Rickrack, everything edged in rickrack. Calico. Artless but with a bit of European sophistication in these paisleys. Americana, that's what it is!

"Now, there they are, Dany. Tell me, you're the only one I believe. Did the Pacific get to me? I hope not, my limpy leg is bad enough. But not my sketching hand. I said that to myself over and over. The truth, Dany, have I been away too long?"

"These are the best drawings you've ever done." They were, Dany thought. Tom's designs were light and airy, charming and romantic and comparable to Louis Ostier at his best. Dany could never think of anything more flattering than that. "Will you give me a sketch when we're finished?"

"Chérie, bien sûr!" Tom said, making a joke of his exaggerated hard accent. "Brooks does all the men and the ladies' chorus. You get the leading ladies! I hear this new girl, Norma White, is the best!"

"They say. Tom, are you recovered? I worried about you managing the stairs."

"Dany, I'm fine! But I may play the limp for a bit of sympathy when we get to dress rehearsal. Never can tell and Mac Roth can be rough, I hear."

"You hear?" She wanted to know who was talking. Certainly not Evans Morley, he wasn't that tactless. "Who, Tom?"

"Mac's secretary. Norman O'Hare. We were in college together. Iowa! He's been with Mac for years now and he says he's the most generous boss, personally, but then he gets tight about the office. Stationery, telephone bills, the petty cash. Can you imagine? The guy who hired the Duc de Verdura to make an emerald pin for Dolores Del Rio before she did his first movie! Norman knows everything. Funny, we weren't friendly at school. Now I'm his new confidant. Kind of his hero!"

"Chéri, you are a hero. You fought—"

"No one would believe it, would they? I hear Owen Patterson's in the Air Force. Wearing custom-made uniforms, I bet. Did he have a ghost pilot do his flight training for him, the way I did his designs?"

"You're above all that now," Dany said. It still hurt Tom; she knew it. It always hurt but you learned to hide the pain, to tuck it away in a separate little drawer. Funny, Dany thought, how many drawers there were for all the distasteful memories.

"Yes. Look at me," Tom said. "I'm out of the navy and I'm doing a big musical. And talking too much. Nothing changes after all! How can you resist talking when you're working for a legend? Norman keeps his secret phone book, not a private number in the whole country that Mac doesn't have. With some mighty suspicious names listed. From Hollywood to Washington. And every available woman around. He knows all the beauties. From call girl to rich divorcée. And all the wealthy widows. Sweetie, imagine how many widows there have been these past few years!"

It was indiscreet for Tom to know all this, to be talking. Dany didn't want to listen, it was hard putting all the pieces together. Like a difficult jigsaw puzzle. Mac, the kid full of ideas and ambition working in an amusement park and becoming a top producer. The charm boy with women everywhere. Alix had told stories. Peggy had a few, too. Now Tom Thornton, he had more to say than anyone about Mac Roth.

"And there's a Mrs. Roth. She lives on Washington Heights, near Fort Tryon Park. A quiet woman with a quiet life and he doesn't see her. She won't divorce him."

Dany might have known; it would be one of the designers who got all the dirt.

Mac hadn't exaggerated, there were many banks in the city and, it seemed, he knew at least one officer at all of them. Dany went to lower Broadway near Wall Street, downtown to Park Avenue and uptown on Madison, over to Seventh Avenue in the garment district. She filled out forms and applications and as soon as she returned to the atelier she called Mac at his office to report her feelings about the meetings. Two weeks of confusion and perplexity, wondering and worrying about mortgage rates and percentages that she found confusing.

"You haven't heard anything yet?" Mac asked when he called. "Have you seen your mail? Not a word? I'll get that Barnaby guy down at Chase. What's he fooling around for? And Mayer at Barden Trust, what's with these guys?"

Dany was accused of impatience for all of her life but now that she saw Mac's temper and testiness she realized she was saintly by comparison.

"It's just as well, there'd be no time to think about the house with the new orders coming in," she said.

"Dany, don't placate me," Mac said. "I don't believe you anyway. You're more anxious than you let on and I know it, *Madame* Mounet."

He was right but she didn't want him to know it. He'd call her naive again, she mustn't think she could fool him.

"Listen, how would you like to bring Veronique over to Toots Shor's for dinner, we can give her an early meal."

"How would you like to walk over to Rumpelmayer's at four o'clock instead? Your favorite restaurants aren't exactly ideal for a little girl out of kindergarten on Friday afternoon. She'd prefer an ice cream soda, *Monsieur* Roth."

He wasn't used to children but he said Veronique wasn't a child, she was a person, a very young person. Veronique loved hearing that and Mac became her hero.

He promised her the circus, the zoo, the beach and all the rides at Palisades and at Steeplechase in Coney Island after *Our Stars and Stripes* opened in New Haven.

"I have to be in Washington for a couple of days, then out to the Coast to organize these USO tours before I come up to Connecticut." Mac waited until Katie had Veronique ready for bed. "Do you give old fellas like me a kiss good night?" he asked and Veronique's arms were around his neck in a second. A loud kiss on his cheek.

"She not five, she's fifteen," Mac said later.

"Oh, she's five," Dany said. "Almost six. You're her new favorite. She doesn't have the opportunity to meet many men in Maman's atelier."

"I get it. It's not that it's me, only the fact that I'm a man?"

Dany looked at him, knowing that he was teasing and she wondered why the afternoon had just happened as naturally as it had. Unplanned and comfortable, a few hours with Veronique and every minute enjoyable and relaxed.

"Since you're almost flattering me why not let me take you to Twenty-One for dinner?"

They talked about what was happening in the Pacific and in Europe, about the rigid work schedule ahead of them. After the third show opened in the fall Mac would have proved his point. Someone besides Ziegfeld could have three hits on Broadway at one time. And then time to get back to the movies. He had to raise a lot of money for that project. "Speaking of projects, I'll get to the banks for you before I go away. You'd better have the new shop for all the work you're going to have."

"Mac, not *shop,* please. Atelier. Workroom maybe, but never the *shop!*"

"Atelier. Mounet atelier! It rhymes. Listen to me now. Serious, okay? And let me say this quickly. I don't think in French like you do and this is something I don't talk about very often." He slowly sipped his coffee before going on. "Dany, for fifteen years I've lived alone. By myself. With many, many attractive women coming in and out of my life. But I have a wife.

"I married her when I was twenty, running a vaudeville tour in the Mid-West and I haven't seen her since she decided that I was a gambler, a wastrel, a crook and a spendthrift. So she lives uptown by herself. Like a widow, no, a spinster. Like some suspicious old maid and she isn't very pleasant. Take my word for it, Dany, I'm not looking for sympathy and I don't usually go around talking about her but I wanted you to know."

And she was pleased to hear him telling the truth, she wasn't listening to fitting room gossip now. This was without malice, without that sharp but delicious taste that secrets had.

"Because, Madame Mounet, I think about you all the time these days and we have some thinking to do together, you and I."

Tom Thornton groaned and sank lower in his seat. "This

281

act is longer than *Strange Interlude!*"

Dany told him to be quiet. "Hush, Tom. You must learn how to whisper. Everyone will hear you!"

"Talk about flag-waving! Only we've made the wrong flag. Maybe I should have designed cossack shirts and peasant blouses. Dany, technically it's smooth as silk but how serious can this book be?"

Evans came down the aisle to sit beside Dany. "They say it's supposed to be satire." He sighed and stretched his legs over the seat in front of him.

"Satire!" Tom Thornton exclaimed, his surprised voice ringing through the theatre.

"Do you think they can hear you over at the Yale Bowl, Tom?" Mac called out from his place in the center row with the director and the set and lighting designers. "Satire is one thing but do we need social significance with it? In wartime, especially when we're winning? I want everyone on stage when we're through. If we ever get through with this!"

It was almost an hour later when the curtain came down and quickly snapped up again. The stage manager kept the company on stage, calling out for everybody to stay where they were. Mr. Roth was going to give his notes before any of the other departments.

"Thanks everyone," Mac began. "All of you on stage for working as hard as you have. I'm sorry to say you'll be working harder in the next few days. The next few weeks. You'll be learning new lines and new songs because what we've got here right now, what you all played just now has to be thrown out like a lot of garbage."

Voices interrupted him from the back of the orchestra, from the side aisle of the theatre. The composer and the lyricist, the book writer were on their feet coming toward Mac. "Mr. Roth, how dare you—"

"Mac, this the most insulting and ob—"

"I know what I'm saying is objectionable! When I want to do a musical about the romance of Communism I'll call you guys back. Now I don't give a good flying fuck how offensive this is. I'm offensive and I'm tired of all your hurt egos on display here these past few days. We haven't come to New Haven for psychiatry sessions. So I want you three off your collective couch and quit telling me about the artistry that's being lost here. It ain't working, got it? And if I have to call for another writer I will. This can work if we all pull together. Or I'm on the phone to New York and we start having that group of good play doctors up here to help. Starting tomorrow!" Mac sat down, turning to the stage managers and his secretary who were nodding affirmation. He whispered some quick notes and pushed his seat up, sitting on the edge of it. "Now, if Mr. Harlingman will agree, the director can give his notes and we'll dismiss the company. Then break for an hour and we'll meet in my room to try to fix some of this before an audience comes marching down these aisles tomorrow night." He turned around, spotting Dany six rows behind him. He gave her a broad wink. "How was that, Madame?" He mouthed the words. "Did I tell them?"

Dany came down the aisle with Tom. "Did you! Mac, now you need a martini."

"I want a potato pancake, let's go across to Kaysey's. And a beer, you have the martini. Well, I have work to do. Do you? Stay up and wait for me. I'll get them out by one-thirty or two o'clock, the latest. Then we can have some champagne."

"To toast the future?" Dany asked.

"Maria, it's done," Dany said. "A *fait accompli*, Maria. I can buy the house! We're going to move. I'll be making mortgage payments for the rest of my life but I don't care!"

"At last. *Bocca al lupo*," Maria said. "Oh, I do wish you good luck!"

"Now for renovating and finding workmen. Let's hope the money lasts to do all of it."

Dany had toasted the future with Mac a week ago and he said he never welshed on a promise. Welsh was a word she never heard but it meant she'd have a deal at a bank, enough to buy and renovate the house. And now she was going to have it. The brownstone, the new atelier. It was true, it was going to be hers. Only the bank to be paid every month. She didn't know what influence Mac had with the director of the loans and mortgages department but papers were waiting for her signature when she walked in to keep her morning appointment.

Now she held the stack of sketches to show to Maria from Tom for two new scenes in *Our Stars and Stripes,* from Carl Brandon for Mac's next musical. It was really a revue, no messages, no flag-waving. A big, happy show and Mac was aiming for Irving Berlin to do it and if not he was going to Cole Porter or Jerome Kern.

"Names, stars!" Mac had said. "Listen, if I don't have the best — songs, sketches, dances dressed up with classy sets and lighting, and the most glamorous clothes — what have I got? I'm selling a dinner at the Colony not a sandwich at the Automat."

Our Stars and Stripes was going to stay on the road for another month, until all the revisions were in, until the cast was secure with the new material. As secure as one could be, no point in skepticism, Mac had said, but an extra two weeks in Detroit wouldn't hurt.

Dany handed Maria the drawings. "Look at these hats Carl has done. You'll need new space just to make the brims."

Dany couldn't wait to tell Peggy when she got in from Washington later, to tell Veronique when Katie brought her in from school. And Alix, where was she this afternoon? "Oh Maria, think of it. My own house. And we have to decide on an opening date. The only way to do it. Pick a date and that's what we work toward. Curtain up! I want theatre carpenters, scene painters. They'll understand deadlines. Evans will help and Carl and Tom. They'll know who to recommend."

"And Mac Roth, *cara?*"

"Of course. Maria, what are you thinking?"

"That perhaps Mac Roth won't want to live in a brownstone on West Forty-fifth Street."

"He won't. But it will not matter. Do you think I'm . . . we're . . . that he might be considering—"

"That it is serious. And I'm happy for you."

"My clairvoyant Maria," Dany said.

Dany touched the pin on the lapel of her suit jacket. Before she went to the New Haven train station, when she waited outside the Taft Hotel for the taxi, Mac had given her the box.

"This isn't for Christmas or your birthday. By the way, when is your birthday? I thought you needed a little surprise and I hope you like it."

"Mac!" The most graceful stem of diamonds with ruby rosebuds. "Mac, I can't accept this." She wasn't able to say anything more and the cab was pulling up to the curb.

"Yes, you can. Hold on to it. You never know when I may want to borrow it back."

After the first dress rehearsal and the meeting in his room he had ordered the bottle of champagne. They toasted the future. And he didn't like champagne. "I asked you to say when you were ready, remember? That day in my office before we went into rehearsal. Our life is going to be a series of rehearsal dates, before, during and after. Remember B.R.?"

Dany remembered. She read his mind and she didn't have to wonder about the mental undressing, he was more romantic than anyone on earth. Mac had his own style, true style. The way Charlotte and Gerard had it. Mac was poised and easy, not graceful like Gerard. Oh, maybe without the polish, the finesse but who was ever going to be exactly like. . . . And generosity, Mac behaved as if he'd always had all the money in the world and he loved spending it.

It would have been childish and coy if she told Mac she wasn't ready. It wasn't the most perfect setting, the hotel room wasn't the most elegant and it was after two in the morning, but she was ready.

Mac's fingers were slow and light over her cheek, moving over her neck. Funny, his workman hands slid tenderly over her skin. Afterward, when the intensity was over, his body was gentle as he nestled closer to her.

285

"This is what is meant by pure pleasure." He looked satisfied, pleased with himself.

"The way you feel after a steak at Toots Shor's?"

"Come on, Dany, what kind of comparison is that?"

"I wonder." It was more than pleasure and she didn't want to say that. Silence was something they understood and she knew he admired her as the independent woman who wouldn't make demands, who agreed that this was nothing more than pure, uninvolved sex. What they had been building to since they'd first met. And she didn't want to admit to herself but, oh God, being with Mac was more than pleasure.

Now Maria pushed the stack of drawings aside. "I'm not clairvoyant but I can tell. It's written on your face. You think of him all the time, don't you?"

Was it ever like this for Charlotte, Dany wanted to know. Had Charlotte reacted this way when she went off to Genoa or Marseilles to find whatever anonymous pleasure she was seeking? Or during those first months when she was pregnant, did Charlotte find a new emotion then, realizing at last how much she loved Gerard? Did she feel the drumbeat, the unbearable excitement Dany felt when she saw Mac come into the workroom after a day at rehearsals, when she met him at his office or in a restaurant.

When Mac took her hand, when she touched him, tenderness merged with fervor. She wasn't sure she could look at him without wanting to be in his arms. Demons were watching over them, she was sure of it. Gentle laughter turned to abandon, she became a jungle cat without shame and she felt pain when she had to say good night, goodbye.

Dany rolled and unrolled the floor plans across her worktable every few hours. She pushed aside the muslin she was cutting, the satin she was about to drape to look again at the space there on the blueprints, to check, to make sure. Shelves, cabinets, storage bins. Were they placed properly? Were there enough of them? The wiring, the sockets. The

286

lighting must be bright and steam irons in the middle of the floor; was that a good idea?

"Too much work in this room! I'm turning down the next order that comes in, this is impossible. No more work until we're on Forty-fifth Street!" She said it over and over but she needed the work. Delays were expensive and it was taking too long to move.

"Forget it, the opening will be postponed! Maria, can you imagine this? We cannot get into the house on time!"

Dany lost her temper and quickly she apologized. To Katie and Maria, to a seamstress, to anyone who was in her way. "This is not the kind of extravagance I love, this spending and waiting! Time, everything takes time! I planned on getting in before summer, now we'll be lucky if it's August!"

Mac was in Chicago to get the backing he needed for the revue, from old friends who owed him, Mac said and it was about time for an expensive, lavish musical to try out there. Then he was off to Hollywood again. He'd added new war bond tours to his schedule and organizing another committee for the USO meant stopping in Washington on the way home.

"Mac, what is it like down there?" Dany asked when he called. She didn't want an answer, she wished she'd asked a different question. Who was he seeing, what attractive name from his phone book? Dany called it his widow book, ever since Tom Thornton had talked about it. And she'd heard Mac talking to his secretary. One evening last week he had called his office from her worktable.

"Norman, call Chicago and ask Mrs. Thomas if she will have lunch at the Pump Room on Thursday. And try Eileen Simkin in Santa Barbara, see if she wants to go to Chasen's on Saturday night. And the Democratic dinner in Washington, I almost forgot about it."

"What is it like?" Mac repeated. "Always the same, maybe a lot worse. Rumors flying, everyone nervous. I can't wait to get home. Listen, Madame, I'm thinking about taking a house up in Westchester. Maybe around Mount Kisco, will you like that? Walks on a country road, riding lessons

287

for Veronique. Dany, what do you think?"

She thought it was stupid to be suspicious. He wanted a house for the summer and she had to deal with workmen to get her own house finished. Mac wouldn't recognize delays, he'd have Evans and his office staff handle lateness and deferrals. He'd start another project as a diversion. Why be possessive? He liked women around him, good-looking women. Riding lessons for Veronique, what an idea. Veronique would be in camp in July and away from the chaos of moving and organizing. The child had never known a summer away from Peggy's house in Oyster Bay, the change was going to be healthy. Riding lessons. Veronique loved to swim but she wasn't very athletic. Dany didn't worry about it, and yet there was something. Gerard. Had he been a coward? After his suicide, Dany thought about it and wondered. She had to watch Veronique, to see that the child didn't inherit that one dreadful quality, that odious weakness. Veronique must never be afraid, she mustn't know about cowardice. It couldn't be a hereditary trait, not when Dany was her mother! It was one thing to lie about Simon, that wasn't difficult. Now Veronique knew it all, her father was a hero. He was Pasteur, Hippocrates and St. Francis melded into one fantastic being. The fragile one who died too young. Dr. Simon Mounet. No, Veronique mustn't be a coward about anything!

Mac didn't stay in the city for more than ten days at a time and the summer was long and more hectic than Dany ever imagined. She was at the house on Forty-fifth Street every morning to let the workmen in, then at the end of the day she rode across town once more, holding her breath, saying silent prayers. Let them get done with it. Break through the walls and be finished with the new partitions. Finish, done, please! Let's see some progress today!

Dany's evenings were spent on the telephone. Peggy calling from Washington, she was there all the time now and depending on Dany for gossip, relying on her for news of the theatre and the brownstone. "Mac Roth, what's new there? And my darling Veronique, does she miss me?"

Alix called from Hollywood, complaining about the ordeals of her first movie. "Maybe my last! I'm four inches taller than my leading man. They say I mustn't worry. Haven't I seen Bogart and Ladd? What's that to do with it, I asked? And Dany, they didn't get Adrian for my clothes! You couldn't come out, could you? Why didn't I have costume approval in my contract? Agents! What do they know? Why didn't I think? When do you move into the house? How's Mac Roth, are you seriously. . . ."

And Mac called when he was able to get through from London, when he got away from the Signal Corps documentary he wanted so desperately to do. He called from Chicago after his backers' meetings. And when he was back on the Coast, he called every night.

"Madame Mounet? Why don't you find time to go up to the country, see if you like that empty house I'm paying for this summer. Spend a few days in it if you can. Look around, see what changes you'd make—"

"Mac, why are you asking me this?" Dany didn't recognize the tone of his voice, he sounded hoarse.

"Because I think I'm going to buy it. I'm making a very good deal out here with this new group for a lot of money, and lots of plans! They're all immigrants and smart, Dany. We'll make pictures, here, in Europe, all over the world. Big pictures, after the war, Dany. And that may be real soon."

Soon? It had become a habit, this war. Worse, it had become a routine, one that was easily forgotten with the pace of work. She had forced that and it helped. Not totally but for hours at a time. Until she was alone or when she looked at Veronique. The war over, and impossible questions were perhaps going to vanish with it. That was her wish, but was it possible?

"We're leaving here in a week. I thought I'd better go along." Mac wasn't hoarse, he didn't have laryngitis. He was nervous! "This is the biggest USO show ever done and maybe I can nail Hope or Grable to come back to Broadway while I'm out there. Besides, I've never seen Hawaii. Now, listen carefully, Dany. I'm getting a divorce. Don't ask what

289

kind of settlement I'm agreeing to. I'm agreeing. That's a tribute to you, Dany. So how will you like the sound of Madame Mac Roth?"

A house in the country! And how often would he be in it? Mac didn't stay in the city for a month at a time. He had meetings everywhere and that wasn't going to stop. A traditional house not far from the city! And why? Mac wanted stature now. Dany was sure of it. And he wanted her as part of that stature. She didn't want a house in Mount Kisco, not even for weekends. Not now!

Forty-fifth Street was nearly ready; in only a few days the bedrooms would be painted. They could sleep in their new rooms. She and Katie waited to welcome Veronique home from camp.

And the revue. Carl's sketches were piling up on her table, making the show would be the baptism of the workroom. The new atelier. She'd had one meeting with Benny, the Romanian tailor. She had to have the men's department, she had to have the best. That was Benny, Joe Albert's tailor. Dany reached for a cigarette as she thought about it. Benny was full of humility but he knew how to drive a bargain. He wanted too much money, but she'd made a vow about Joe Albert. Now she was going to steal his best tailor. It didn't matter what salary Benny was asking for, she had to hire him.

Madame Mac Roth.

Oh, Mac, why now? She had dreamed of this, imagined it since the night in New Haven but the reality was something else. She hadn't expected him to, and now to answer Mac. And she hadn't been able to. When he came home, she had said, they'd talk about it then.

Dany paid the cab driver at Washington Square. She wanted to walk through the park to Maria's Village apartment. The tree lined street didn't look like New York at all,

290

the low red brick houses with the curlicue rails across the white window frames seemed to spell happiness before she went up the stairs. Maria's apartment made Dany think of France, the spare, simple rooms reminded her of the Mounets' house in Amiens.

Was that house still there? When would she hear from them? The interrupting flash of questions again, it never stopped.

Fred Mennino was intelligent and kind, allowing Maria to talk too much and enjoying her run-on chatter. He laughed when Dany and Maria were together, they usually spoke at the same time.

Before dinner Maria came into the parlor from the kitchen to ask if they wanted another drink. She stood next to Fred in his favorite wingback chair, laying her hand on his shoulder, her fingers touching his neck. That gesture, the loving, light caress said more about caring than any words.

"Are you thinking about Mac?" Maria asked.

"I'm caught, Maria, you're clairvoyant again!" Dany said.

"Maybe," Maria said, looking at Fred before she went on. "How long will it take for you to make up your mind? Do you intend to make suffering a part of your daily diet? You can have someone, someone who cares. Do you know how much that means, Dany? What are you waiting for?"

"You're right," Dany said. Maria made it quite apparent that somehow everything could be simple if faced without procrastination. Dany hadn't ever behaved any other way but . . . Madame Mac Roth! "Doesn't it sound funny? Madame Mac Roth? He's calling when he gets back to California. Maria, I'll tell him then. I'll say yes."

A house in the country and where would they live in the city? *Her* work, *her* house, *her* daughter, and what did Mac expect her to do? Dany could hear Charlotte's voice, saying those last words before she left New York. Be extravagant, dream! How approving Charlotte would be right now. This was as reckless as extravagance could ever be!

The taxi turned at the square to go up Fifth Avenue. Not many more nights to ride to Fifty-fifth Street, Dany thought.

"Mind if I put on the radio, ma'am?" the driver asked. "The late news."

She wasn't aware of the announcement for a second, the voice was clearer after she heard him say Pacific.

". . . en route to Los Angeles from Honolulu. The crash was approximately three hundred miles off the coast. Aboard were Army and Naval personnel, members of a USO troupe returning after entertaining in Pearl Harbor and the Broadway and Hollywood producer, Mac Roth. Mr. Roth had . . ."

Ten days can go by as if the clocks had stopped clicking, without any perception of time. It had been like a coma with all the necessary moves in a sleepwalker's tempo. Dany was in the house on Forty-fifth Street. She wasn't sure how it had been accomplished but Maria and Fred had been in and out, Peggy was there and not in Washington, Katie gave orders to workmen as efficiently as she disciplined Veronique. It seemed everyone was passing by in a slow motion movie and Dany sat alone in the dark, watching them.

The shadows cast through the skylight at the far end of the new workroom were fading. The pattern of stripes on the floor was disappearing with the end of the twilight. The dressmaker dummies stood alone, their silhouettes melting off the floor. Dany sat at her new table watching the vanishing light, aware of the uncomfortable silence.

No sounds, none. Not yet. Tomorrow morning there was to be a service at Temple Emanu-El and Dany knew what sounds she'd hear then. She heard them in her head before tomorrow came. A service, a funeral without a coffin, without Mac. Was he ever going to be found out there in the Pacific?

She wasn't going uptown tomorrow. Absolutely not. To listen to eulogies glorifying Mac? Memories and reminiscences that weren't hers. She had her own eulogy for Mac. Her own memory. She'd never tell anyone, she'd hold on to her own pictures. Mac's eyes, the appraiser's eyes and his frown, his mocking laugh. All that was hers, only hers.

Dark suits and black dresses on a hot August morning. But she'd been wearing black for how long now? At work, at rehearsals. Mac had teased about her black lingerie and how he'd laughed when she told him why. Blue had been her color until the night at the Paris Opera when she met Karinska who always wore blue. Dany had taken to black after that night. It was her color. Indeed!

She had no heart to join the line of women proud to appear at the synagogue, longing to be recognized. Names from Mac's phone book. The showgirls, his dates from the Stork Club, the divorcées, the widows flashing their bereavement.

"Oh, look, there's Bootsy," Dany could hear the whispers in the crowded temple. "And Sondra. Did you know about her? I had no idea! And over there, no, not on your right. Down front to the left. Isabel what's her name."

And the real widow, the wife he never saw. Was she going to be there? To sit alone, to say a prayer. The widow Roth in that mob tomorrow morning, that swarm of photographers and autograph hunters.

Did it matter if she went to the temple in the morning, Dany wondered. Wasn't it a case of being seen in the right places? No, she didn't have to prove anything. No one had the chance to learn that she was going to be *Madame* Mac Roth. Only Maria and Fred Mennino. And Peggy. They knew.

Now in a day or two it was going to start, she knew the pattern all too well. She'd hear the telephone and think it was Mac calling. The front door would ring; a delivery boy and she'd try to guess. Had Mac sent flowers, champagne? A gift box from Cartier. No, from now on the packages delivered were going to be the customary boxes of thread and zippers and seambinding, the rolls of fabric, the bolts of muslin, the everyday staples to keep the workroom going.

She had to put sound in the room again. Mac hated the dismal silence as much as she did. The darkness without

293

shadows. He'd want the steady roar day after day, week after week. He'd love to hear the voices jabbering in strange languages, the sewing machines turning at full speed. A racket in the room. Mac wanted that as much as she did. The noise of perfection.

This house was going to stand for quality. Dany knew it. She was going to put magic in these rooms, she had to. For Veronique. Up the stairs would be their home and down here a magical playroom, flashing like the fireworks over the Seine. How distant a memory that was but she remembered. Dany swore to herself, nothing was going to touch her here.

Nobody would touch her ever again. Renee had said it once. She didn't want to see Dany as one of those pinched Parisian women behind a cash register, parsimonious and bitter, on a pension and getting drier and drier by the year. What a laugh! Dany was already in black. No cash register and she wasn't going to grow pinched with age. By God, no! But she wasn't lucky. Not at all. Not for that. Dany shut her eyes. She never prayed but she was good at making vows. No more love, she'd do without it. No touching, no reaching out in the night to feel another body. No, never another man.

Renee. Was it three days ago when the mist had cleared, when the slow motion stopped for a while? Dany remembered Peggy coming by to talk. Paris was liberated. The Americans were in Paris, the city was free. All of France was free! It will be good for you to get out, Peggy was saying, come with them to Rockefeller Plaza to sing the "Marseillaise." Bless Peggy, dear Peggy, she was taking Veronique and Katie.

Did Renee look like one of the pinched, shriveled Parisians? Was she thin and starved and emaciated? Was Renee alive?

"Maman?" Dany jumped, startled to hear a voice. "Maman, I've been calling you. Are you all right? Can I come in?"

How small Veronique seemed standing at the door down the long stretch of the workroom. "Yes, *chérie,* I'm all right.

You can come in. This is your home, too, my darling." Dany walked to the front of the room. "But isn't it dark in here? Let's put on some lights." Dany pulled Veronique as close to her as she could, holding her tight. "You never had your riding lessons, Veronique!" The child looked up at her, wide eyes sleepy and confused. The things you almost had, my baby. The things you'll never know. Your father a suicide in France and you don't know who he was. You have a brother in England, *chérie,* and you'll never know him either. You can't. You mustn't know about that. And you almost had the most loving stepfather. Dany held Veronique. She didn't want to let her go.

Seven

1980

Veronique came down the stairs to the workroom early in the morning. It would be an hour before anyone arrived, an hour to assemble Belinda Jones's notes and organize the routine for the day. Picking up the costumes at the St. James, fixing them and getting them back for the afternoon rehearsal. There wasn't much to change; Belinda's work had been accepted with enthusiasm. Veronique had to admit it, the costumes looked wonderful. Fortunately. Now to get on with Elsa's play, start the fabric lists for the shoppers and with luck she might be able to begin muslins with Ryan later in the afternoon. Maybe she could stop thinking about David Wilfrid's play that she hadn't read yet, this mysterious script that dealt with Dany's early days in Paris.

Veronique went to set up the coffee machine the way Nancy usually did before the crew came in to work. Wouldn't Nancy be surprised; Veronique rarely came in before nine. She could hear her comment; "Mmm, the apple doesn't fall far from the tree after all." Veronique lit a cigarette, waiting for the coffee to brew. She hadn't been able to sleep for two nights now, not since David Wilfrid left the fitting room with Elsa late Monday afternoon. He'd called twice yesterday but she was at rehearsal with Belinda. When she called him back he was out and she knew his first reading with the cast had probably gone on too long.

Charlotte Dessaux was David Wilfrid's mother. Veronique couldn't forget his voice; the brusque but gentle accent. She wasn't able to get his face out of her mind; the wide cheekbones, the dark eyes.

The phone was ringing. Veronique poured her coffee and ran to her table to pick up the call. "Dany Mounet, good morning," she announced the way Nancy always did. "Hello. No, it's not too early."

"I didn't want to miss you again," David Wilfrid was saying. "Look, if you have a date tonight break it. I'll pick you up at eight o'clock. Let's have dinner, you choose the place. And I'll have the script for you."

Did anyone ever say no to him, Veronique asked herself.

"Thank you," David said as they walked down the three steps into the cool calm of the small Italian restaurant. "I've been here four days and I've been taken twice to, it is Le Cirque, isn't it? Good food but too posh for me and last night I went to a counter for a sandwich after rehearsal. This is nice and they're not going to ask me to wear a dreadful necktie, are they?"

"Not here," Veronique said. "There's a garden in back if you'd like."

"Would you mind if we stayed here? I like this soft light and eating in a barroom seems less like a ceremonial rite, doesn't it?"

He held her arm as they were led to a table. "Here you are," he said, giving Veronique a manila envelope. "The play. Will you read it as soon as you can? I can't wait to hear what you'll say.

"Barney Wilfrid was my uncle's name," David was saying. "He claimed he came from an old line of theatre people and for hours, days, weeks, as long as you'd allow, he'd go on about the generations of Wilfrid forebears. Our ancestors. Theatre people, he'd say, we are THEATRE PEOPLE! In capital letters."

Some people can make magic of the past, Veronique thought; a family history becomes legend and David was creating his legend now. His black eyes were warm with memory, holding her attention.

"I doubt that the family tree went very far back with his theatre people; more likely in the last century they were shopkeepers dealing in threads, cloth and such things. Cotton was the commodity that kept Birmingham and the North Country going during the Victorian years. But someone along the way was stagestruck and a new branch of Wilfrids came into existence. Barney owned a group of variety houses, you called it vaudeville here, I think. In England those theatres lasted a longer time than in America. Well into the sixties, I reckon. He was a beautiful man, Barney Wilfrid." David hailed the waiter. "Shall we have another bottle of wine? Veronique, you smoke too much." He took her hand, laying his palm across hers as a warning not to light another cigarette and he didn't let go for a while.

"Jenny was his wife, my father's lovely shining sister who took me from France when I was a month old and I became a Wilfrid. With a huge family of aunts and uncles and cousins spread across the North Country and quite a few in London, too. All Wilfrids and Jenny was the foreigner who had come from Paris to marry Barney. What a marriage it was, there have never been two people happier and more devoted. I was brought up in box offices, backstage and in green rooms. Do you think it is justice that a renegade appears in such happy families? Someone who shakes things up a bit?"

"I don't know about renegades," Veronique said. "Hardly at all. Our past is nothing, only a house on Forty-fifth Street. There were no relatives, I had no cousins to play and fight with. Dany was orphaned as a child, my father's people perished in the war. Oh, there were friends, astonishingly good friends, but I can barely remember anything before our brownstone. I know Dany's stories of the struggles to make a successful business. There was a time when Dany was quite poor," Veronique laughed. "You must hear my mother say 'You never starved in Paris, *chérie!*' David, do you realize how strange this is? Charlotte Dessaux made it possible for Dany to be a success! And Dany didn't know about you, David?"

"*And* I didn't know about your mother. Read the play, Veronique, then we'll talk about Paris." David tasted the wine, nodding approval to the waiter. "Tell me about growing up in your house."

"My house. I don't think I ever considered it mine. It's always been 'the house,' Dany's house. Not mine," Veronique said. "She lives one flight up the stairs in a cluttered apartment with rooms all red and rose and pink. I've teased her, saying they were rooms blushing with memory. It's very pretty and I have the top floor. No clutter. No blushing rooms. Just beige and ivory and very plain."

"Do you mean casual and unaffected?" David asked. "I don't think you've ever been plain."

"I'll take that as a compliment," Veronique said. "It is — well, understated. I went to very good schools here in the city. Dany saw to that, no expenses spared but no classroom was nearly as good as Maman's workroom. The house filled with a steady parade of actresses and actors. *The people of the theatre.*" Veronique laughed, thinking of those early days on Forty-fifth Street. "After two years of college in New England I said I wanted to work with my mother. I'd learn more at home than in any class. I used to bring my friends to see the 'atelier,' as Dany loves to call it, after school. A stagestruck kid showing off and I usually had great crushes on one of the leading men or a dancer in the Ballet. That's not much of a story, is it?" Veronique asked. "One house, one job. But there was another place. Would you like to see where I was born? Where we lived when Dany came from Paris. It's not far, we can walk after dinner."

"I'd like that," David said. "Be my tour guide, Veronique. I've never been here before."

They walked to Fifty-fifth Street to see the old red brick house where Dany had her first workroom. "Up there on the second floor," Veronique said. "Of course, there weren't many skyscrapers around here then. Only rows of houses like this in all the side streets, milliners and dressmakers and very smart restaurants. Chic little cabarets. I don't remember coffee shops and all these fast food places. It was more a

299

residential neighborhood and I remember lots of little shops, everywhere, in all these houses." They turned into Park Avenue and Veronique described the apartment buildings that had lined the avenue before the office towers pressed in.

David said he was reminded of London when they walked uptown, turning off Madison Avenue towards the park. "What a lovely night. Tell me, did you have a nanny who took you here to play?"

"I did! I've almost forgotten. Katie lived with us until I went to nursery school." The warm June breeze feathered through the trees along Fifth Avenue. "She went back to Ireland, to Cork where she'd been born and she died there." Veronique saw the swings, the seesaw, she remembered the children's zoo. "But my playground was really the workroom. Other kids had dollhouses, I had an enormous room filled with dressmaker dummies."

"Would you like a nightcap? Do you drink after dinner?"

"No, thank you. And, yes, I do. Sometimes too much, I'm afraid," she said. "You have rehearsal in the morning. Let's find a cab and I can drop you at your hotel."

David's hands touched her cheeks with a gentle caress. "Sometimes you look like a child of twelve."

"This child of twelve has a script to read and I have a feeling I'm going to read it in one sitting."

"Not much of a bedtime story for a little girl," David said. "Think of it, Veronique. What wonderful toys we had, dressing rooms and workrooms, stages and props and costumes of silk and satin. Magic curtains and spotlights."

Veronique looked at his eyes sparkling with merriment. "Dany would love to hear you saying that."

"All the other kids were deprived without such toys!" He waved for a taxi coming down the avenue. "I'm going to call you tomorrow at the lunch break." He opened the car door, touching her cheek again before he kissed her. "And I'll see you tomorrow night?"

Eight

1980

Veronique reached for Elsa's sketches, holding them as if they were perishable pieces of parchment that might crumble in her hands. It was customary to cover all designers' sketches with glassine, they took such a beating going from one hand to another during the making of a show. These drawings Elsa had made deserved preservation under glass.

At two in the morning Veronique finished reading David's manuscript and then unable to sleep she'd read it again, turning the pages quickly, hypnotized by the story unfolding in a Nice courtroom with flashbacks to a villa in Villefranche and an apartment in Paris.

He had written a play about real people; Charlotte and Gerard Dessaux, the couple Dany had painted as two idyllic fantasy figures when Veronique was a little girl. They had been Titania and Oberon, these two people who were David's parents but what he was telling was not a fairy tale. In August, 1939, Gerard Dessaux had killed his wife.

Veronique looked at Elsa's sketch of the woman in the white gypsy dress. The bright poppy red and cerise accents were to be made of ribbons and crochet pompoms. Was this startling color scheme to be an example of the character's bizarre chic or was it Elsa's metaphor for blood? Had Charlotte Dessaux really fallen to the wet, mossy floor of her garden in a dress such as this? Was she found there behind the Villefranche villa in this fine *broderie anglaise* batiste dress with the claret red seeping through the cloth in quick, narrow rivulets of blood? Veronique put the sketch down, the drawing felt like a piece of that bloodstained cotton.

What would Dany think of Elsa's drawings? More important, would she believe David's play? Veronique pressed her cigarette out in the ashtray. Last night he had said she smoked too much but this wasn't the right time to stop. And yet she had to try. How much warmer and cared for could she feel after that moment when he covered her hand as a warning. She had been touched. His firm fingers, the wide palm, his strong but gentle hand. Oh, it had been so long since she'd been touched.

David's play wasn't about hatred but he'd written with malice, a vivid picture of deception in pre-war Paris. Now forty years later she was a part of his play, Veronique was sure of it. Yes, there was an epilogue to this.

Call, David, she said to herself, please call before your lunch break, before you go to rehearsal. Veronique couldn't bear waiting to talk to him. She dialed the hotel number and the operator said Mr. Wilfrid had just walked out of the lobby.

Now she had to unroll the muslin waiting at the end of her table, drape and coddle it into a shape for Elsa's approval. She had to chalk the eyelet pattern and mark the spaces for the trimming and ribbon. This dress was like the one in a photograph upstairs in Dany's bedroom. Charlotte Dessaux in a peasant dress that Dany had probably made back in the thirties. Without this dress would there have been a company called Dany Mounet?

Drawings were always looked at with a dressmaker's eye, sketches were mere indications for a costume to be brought to life for the stage and sometimes they were charming drawings framed for the apartment wall or for the house in Watermill. Now these beautiful sketches on the table were examples of doubt and mystery. What had Dany been hiding all these years? Every drawing seemed like a question mark, a puzzle waiting to be solved. And, oh God, Veronique thought, how she hated puzzles.

"Well? We-el-ll?" Veronique knew Ryan would be full of questions. It wasn't easy to ignore him when he sensed there was gossip in the air.

"Well, what?"

"How was last night?" Ryan asked. "That's what."

"I read David Wilfrid's play and I didn't sleep very much at all."

"Gee, it doesn't show. You look as fresh as Sandra Dee after her first date with Troy Donahue. How was dinner? Where did you go?" Ryan's questions began. "He *is* very attractive, you know. Ve-er-rry sexy. How was it?"

"Ryan! I never ask you how it was. Don't pry, please."

"Pry? It's absolutely emanating from you, this unnatural glow. You're shining like a Metro musical and you tell me not to pry? I've never seen you react so positively to anyone."

"Oh, Ryan, don't be idiotic. The man has written a startling play, that's all," Veronique said. She wanted this conversation to be as trivial as their usual morning gossip. Truly she didn't want to tell Ryan anything at all. Not yet.

"Veronique." Nancy's voice came over the intercom. "Telephone."

"David, good morning." Veronique looked at Ryan. He wouldn't leave the table now, the imp. "I just called you. Yes, I've read it, twice. And, oh, it's so good, David. Do I have questions to ask you! Yes, I can be ready. Thank you, I'll pick you up at seven."

Ryan's eyebrows were hitting his hairline. "Yes, darling?" Veronique couldn't resist teasing him now. "Anything you want to know?" She was smiling. "And are we going to start to work this morning?"

David was waiting in front of the rehearsal studio when Veronique's cab pulled up.

"Don't let him go," he called out as she opened the car door. "We finished a bit early. Hello, I'm awfully glad to see you. Where are we going?"

His T-shirt and jeans would not have been too welcome at Caravelle. Apparently he disliked dressing as much as she did. She was glad she had reserved a table at Alfredo's.

"You're going to see Greenwich Village and have more Italian food since you love it so much. How did it go today?"

"Rather well, I'd say. They read through it again. I think it's a great cast and they were on their feet for the first time. You can tell much more when they start moving about."

"Cross-examining by the defense and the prosecution?" Veronique asked. "I hope you're ready for my interrogation, I have so many questions for you."

"Ask away," David said. "You look very pretty. I have a feeling you always look very pretty." He took her hand and held it until they reached Hudson Street. He reached for his billfold. "Now help me. I get confused about tipping these fellows."

"You have written quite a play." Veronique added ice to her glass of Frascati. "David, there hasn't been a courtroom drama on Broadway in years. It has to be a huge success."

"I hope you're clairvoyant. Are you? I've heard about your critics. Not much different than ours, I'm sure."

"They'll love it. Honesty and truth don't have to be written about in esoteric terms. You've made a tragedy that's full of suspense and," Veronique hesitated, "it's glamorous. Doesn't everyone want to enter an exciting world they've never been in? Isn't that why people line up at the box office? And, David, I promise you the clothes will be beautiful."

"My darling girl," David said, "I appreciate your enthusiasm. Now eat your linguini."

"David," she couldn't wait any longer, "it's all true, isn't it?" Her cross-examination had to begin.

"It's true all right. Try doing research in France for something that happened forty years ago. I spent six months there and I was a nuisance to the police, worse to the staff at Nice Matin where I dug through all the old newspaper files. Of course I changed names but it's true, all right."

"When did you first find out? How?"

"Don't all kids love to ask questions? Maybe I was more inquisitive than most. I had Aunt Jen and Uncle Barney. That's what I called them, not Mum and Dad, and I wanted to know why I had no mother and father."

"You were hurt," Veronique said. "Naturally, how could you not be?"

"At first all I knew was that my parents had died in the South of France just before the war broke out. The Riviera. Well, that was quite an exotic fact for a smart little kid."

Veronique could see a little boy with big, dark eyes. A smart, beguiling little kid.

"The Wilfrid house was full of love, warmth and affection. There were kisses good morning and kisses good night. Nothing was concealed in that house, British reticence was an unknown trait to Aunt Jen and Uncle Barney."

"I've been accused of that British reticence," Veronique said, "and I've been asked where it came from."

"There's a difference between reticence and propriety. I think you have a strain of reserve. A defensive primness." The little boy had grown up again. The dark eyes were flirting. "Where *did* it come from, Veronique?"

"I'll tell you some other time. I want to be the district attorney tonight, David Wilfrid." She didn't want to scoff at her supposed primness now, she wondered if her eyes told him that flirting was unnecessary. "You were talking about your family."

"Yes. Aunt Jen. She had photographs all over the house. In the sitting room, on the piano, on tables. You've seen that kind of overstuffed room. Old furniture and treasured relics, all reminders and loving memories. Pictures of the Wilfrids, the aunts and uncles and cousins. And Charlotte and Gerard." David poured the last bit of wine in the bottle. "In a family album. You saw some of them the other day.

They were seductive, those pictures. They set me to wondering. Thinking about those incredibly glamorous and, I don't know, obscenely rich people. I must have been in my early teens then and I asked why my parents looked so different, not like any of the Wilfrids. Uncle Barney told me and he was very gentle. Charlotte and Gerard Dessaux lived in a different grand world. I remember he used a phrase, 'alien to us' and then I heard the story of the murder. My father had killed my mother in a rage of jealousy because he suspected her of being unfaithful."

"You were angry." She saw it on his face, how clearly the emotions showed, the bitterness didn't ever completely go away. "You'd been cheated of your real parents and suddenly you found someone to hate. Now you could blame your dead father."

"I thought you made beautiful costumes. You read minds beautifully, too."

"No, not usually. But I do know how you felt. Is that odd?"

"Not odd at all." David took her hand, slowly caressing the length of her fingers. "I thought that infidelity was as common to them in their world as champagne and caviar. In that life in Villefranche and Monte Carlo, villas and yachts, cabanas at the Lido. Unfaithful? It seemed awfully Victorian to me and I thought only of Gerard's treachery, his ultimate dishonesty and it enraged me. I was a kid full of high flown and progressive ideals. Rather precocious, you know." He grinned. "He killed her in the garden. He slashed at her with a rake. What an entrance into the world I made. An ambulance speeding along the Corniche, a bleeding pregnant woman, a premature birth. Headlines. 'Eminent producer kills beautiful wife!' "

"David." Veronique could not say anything more. "David."

"I had my villain. What a little brat I must have been when I asked Uncle Barney if it was common for those chichi fashion magazines of the thirties to print pictures of wealthy Jews."

"You guessed that they denied being Jewish?" Veronique asked.

"Once I asked Aunt Jen if my parents had been religious. She gave me an odd and surprised look and her hand touched my cheek. It was a way she had, when she touched me, that soothing pat on the cheek that said don't be hurt. What did I really know? 'They were Jewish, weren't they?' I asked and Aunt Jen shrugged her shoulders." He imitated a guttural French accent. "She said, 'They didn't deny it but they didn't admit it.' Veronique, shall we have coffee? Dessert?"

"Expresso, please." How curious this was. David's past, layers of memory, disconnected wires now waiting to be spliced. "Are you very religious?"

"No, not at all," David said. "But don't you see? It had nothing to do with church or prayers. It had to do with being positive; about knowing who you are and what you are. Charlotte and Gerard didn't do that. There was no prejudice in that group of creative people. In Paris? Who'd care? Their life was a sham because they avoided one essential truth."

"You were surrounded by all the love of the Wilfrids and yet you felt deserted?"

"At the same time I was fascinated. When I was young the answers to my questions were quite simple. They became more complicated as I grew older, I guess. Look, I don't believe it was necessary for Gerard to go to a synagogue in Paris every Friday night and Saturday morning. But Aunt Jenny lit her candles on Friday night without saying the prayers. She didn't even know the prayers, she only knew that the ritual established something valid. A sense of belonging, a feeling of heritage. Think of what poor Gerard felt at the end, think of his guilt. The unceasing remorse after his influence bought him a verdict of not guilty. To commit suicide. Talk about being your own victim! Well, he did give me one hell of a curtain, didn't he?"

"Yes, David. Your father gave you a play and your research gave you the facts." Veronique stopped. Oh, how she wanted a cigarette now. "But there's more. I know it. I can feel it."

"You're skeptical, aren't you, Veronique?"

"If Dany didn't talk about any of this for all these years, there is more. If she has hidden things from me they are things hidden from you, too."

"I thought I was done with it. I thought I'd found some objectivity now that I was in New York to get the play on again." He gripped her hand. "How could I have known that I was going to meet you, that your mother had known Charlotte and Gerard. Your mother had come to New York and war had just broken out. What more could there be, Veronique?"

"Something. I thought I knew her and that I understood her silences, her maddening way of putting off any serious discussions. For years I thought I was good at filling in the blanks with Dany after she'd make one of her clever, delaying gestures, her way of dropping the curtain. My mother was brought up in a convent. She learned discipline there and, I suppose, her talent for reticence was developed then." Veronique folded and refolded her napkin, smoothing it out carefully before she caught herself. "Who's nervous? Who misses the cigarette I'd usually be smoking now? Can reticence be hereditary, I wonder? Oh, damn it, David, maybe I haven't known her at all."

"I'm sorry I've raked up all this. I'm tired of the past." He leaned forward, taking her hands and lifting them to his lips. "Let me take you home, Veronique. Not to your door but upstairs to your apartment. To your uncluttered rooms and let me undress you and see you and feel you. I love you, Veronique. I think I knew it the minute I walked into your workroom. I love you."

Nine

"Well, isn't it a sunny morning!" Nancy said, hearing Elsa bubble with superlatives. She took some of the muslins out of Veronique's hands.

"It's going to be heavenly, Veronique. I couldn't be happier!" Elsa was saying. "Lawrence, help. Don't let Nancy carry all the patterns!"

Lawrence Purcell, Elsa's assistant, was dismayed by the wave of enthusiasm that had emanated from the fitting room all morning.

"The taupe suit will be superb, won't it?"

"I can't wait to see it in the fabric, Veronique, though she could wear the toile!"

"And the cinnamon dress!"

"Perfect, Veronique, just perfect."

"Don't you think it will be a surprise for the audience to see how lavish the clothes were in 1939?"

"I hope so. I want them to get that Marie Antoinette analogy. You know, let them eat cake, the last big party before the deluge!"

The fabrics were dropped in a heap on Veronique's worktable.

"Would you like a cup of tea?" Veronique asked.

"I'd love it. The Arnold girl, that body! And her style, she moves like an angel. She'll be a star. I can always tell." Elsa's

309

exuberance was nonstop. "How refreshing to see someone that young arrive for fittings looking like she'd just stepped out of a bath. At Arden's!"

Ryan brought the tea. "She's a terrific actress. I saw her in a play off-Broadway last year. A flop but she was awfully good."

"Do you think she sounds like the original Charlotte?"

"You'll have to ask Dany when she gets home," Veronique said, hoping Elsa wasn't becoming too nosy. Don't spoil this mood, Veronique thought, it's all too rare.

"Have you heard from mother?" Elsa asked.

Elsa said *mother* with the smug familiarity of a possessive aunt. "We agreed not to call each other unless it was really important. She cabled that she'd arrived safely." Veronique knew that Elsa still thought of her as the teenage girl she'd first met in the fifties.

"Isn't Lydia Castleman a wonder?" Elsa had to bring the conversation around to her costumes again. Her ego had to go on being fed. "The old girl sure knows how to wear clothes."

"Not bad. I understand why she loves to tell her age. Eighty-five. She's truly a miracle."

"Well darling, you know that the real Renee Hugo was a legend in Paris. Isn't it funny how I'm using the real names?"

"Who was she?" Lawrence asked. He was precise and efficient, an expert with minutely detailed lists and charts marked with every measurement and specification for the entire company but he never recognized the personality under the costume. Dany called him "the librarian." Elsa waited until he was out of earshot before she called him her "Wasp butterfly."

"Was? She's still alive," Nancy said. She couldn't tear herself away. This talk was more delicious than the Danish and coffee sitting on her desk.

"Yes, she is," Veronique said. "Dany is going to be with her next week. She lives in a village outside of Aix. Renee has been retired for years."

"Veronique, you look extraordinarily well today." Elsa made it sound like another question. "Lawrence, why are you burrowing around in all that muslin?"

"I can't find my glasses, maybe they're in the fitting room."

Veronique picked up her cup of tea, looking at the time. Hours to go before seeing David. Had she ever felt better than she did today? This idiotic happiness, a mist of soft spring rain fluttering over the workroom. David's voice murmuring in her ear. A present, she'd been given a present and she couldn't let the pleasure of it go, not yet. Though she wished it wasn't so apparent to everyone who looked at her.

"Now decide on the crêpe and not the silk jersey, Elsa," Veronique said. "You did see that Lydia is a wee bit fat."

"You sounded just like mother when you said that. You're right, forget it and dye up the canton crêpe. Where is that piece of it?" Veronique reached into the bin and Elsa took the cloth, tossing it across the table.

"Yummy, no?" She draped the end of it over her shoulder. "I feel like the Duchess of Windsor." Elsa was basking in the joy she'd made this morning. Not like the Duchess at all, Veronique thought, but her blonde hair pulled back into the neat chignon, her white silk blouse tucked into the faintly oyster shantung trousers was as chic as a *Vogue* cover. "Think of it, Dany with Renee Hugo. The memories of Paris in the twenties and thirties. And before! Jouvet and Guitry, Giraudoux and Cocteau and Bébé Bérard!"

Lawrence came back wearing his glasses, followed by Mario Bertani, the second assistant Elsa had hired to deal with accessories.

"Did you have to go to an optician to find them? Ah, Mario, what did you find? Let's see."

Lawrence unwrapped the boxes, lining up the shoes on the table. "Look at the character in these brogans!" he said. "And you found the cork wedgies, pure 1939. Look, Miss Groueff, aren't they perfect for the housekeeper!"

311

"Lawrence dear, control yourself. What is this, the Stanislavsky school of shoe shopping? They're only shoes. Let's hope they fit. Let's go over to Benny," Elsa said. "Thank you, Mario, you've made a good start."

"She's positively euphoric today," Ryan said to Veronique. "And so are you, Miss Mounet."

"You'd better sort out these patterns before they get lost." Veronique was going to ignore Ryan for as long as she was able to do. No inquisitive questions from him for a while.

"If we were in an elevator 'Stardust' might be playing," Ryan went on.

"Veronique!" Elsa's voice was a drum roll calling attention from Benny's table.

"Look at these lapels, aren't they perfect?" Elsa asked. "No one cuts a suit like you do, Benny dear. Now when will you start your fittings?"

"I'm waiting for buttons," Benny said. "And the silk floss for stitching the pockets. Besides, the pants are not back from the pantsmaker."

"Oh, Benny, you'll have it all tomorrow," Veronique said. "Why not schedule the fittings now and have Lawrence call it in to rehearsal." It was the way Benny worked; he always found reasons to delay the fittings but the result was an impeccably tailored suit.

"Why do you procrastinate?" Elsa asked. "You can fit the jackets without the trousers. Tell Lawrence when."

"Can I tell you later?"

"When I'm having hysterics in Boston?" Elsa pinched Benny's sallow cheek. He loved to be coaxed. "Please, darling? Start the fittings. Can we order lunch in, Veronique? I have to work on the hats with Andy. Wouldn't Dany be pleased to see how smoothly it's all going?"

"Yes, she would," Veronique answered. "It's the kind of day Dany loves."

"Veronique, I'm curious," Elsa said, "and I keep wondering. How well did Dany know the Dessaux couple?"

* * *

"The summer days at home are very long," David said. "Evening comes earlier here, you have a true twilight." A bit of sunshine still sparked the Gramercy Park street. The last shadows of the day were fading to a deep grey. "Is it always this lovely?"

"No," Veronique said. "But it *is* lovely now because, I'm seeing it through your eyes. This is my favorite part of the city. An oasis. I've often thought about living down here. There are quite a few neighborhoods that feel like villages, small towns, but I like this best. The park, the old slate sidewalks. It's cheerless on Forty-fifth Street but I've never lived on another street. Let's walk some more, you aren't tired, are you?"

"No. I'm waiting for you to tell me what happened today. I know, the costumes will be ravishing but you're holding something back."

"You're a man of perception." She hadn't been able to shake the feeling of heaviness. "Elsa is curious and asking questions, alluding to things in her supposedly cute way and I can't tell her that I don't know. I haven't the answers myself. Elsa is a very inquisitive woman."

"A bit of a *yente?*"

"I'm afraid so." Veronique laughed. "I think all designers are fishwives." The weight on her back disappeared when David's arm went across her shoulders.

"Gossip is a barbiturate for show folk. It relieves the tension," David said.

"Mmm, Dany thrives on it, too." Veronique said. "The tension, that is, though she does enjoy a bit of gossip."

"Tell Elsa you don't know anything. And don't magnify all this, my darling."

"I wonder if Dany has kept secrets or if she lied about certain things when she came over here."

"Your mother didn't have to tell you about an old murder case," David said. "Why would she be compelled to talk about a scandal involving two people a thousand miles away?"

"Why not?"

"Perhaps she wanted to preserve an attractive memory, what she knew before the murder. People do that all the time. Memory is a convenient tranquilizer too, you know."

"Not for me," Veronique said.

"Come now, my girl. In what way would it have affected your life?"

"I'm not sure," Veronique said. "But doubting, what's worse than doubting?"

"You're talking about now. When you were a little girl it wouldn't have mattered. Don't you see?" His voice was tender but imploring. "I grew up with doubts, Veronique. An artichoke has to be peeled leaf by leaf before you get to the spiny choke. That's cut away and then you reach the delicate heart. I knew about a murder but I didn't know my parents. Uncle Barney gave me one fact. At first I was obsessed by it and ashamed of my hatred for those two people I'd never known. What a legacy they left me. Shame and loathing.

"After University I went over to Europe, to Italy, Greece and Holland, playing very seriously for a long time. I told Aunt Jen that I needed to be on my own for a while. For a while turned out to be two years! God, how selfish we are at twenty-two."

"I was twenty-two when I asked Maman if I could do the upstairs rooms into an apartment," Veronique said. "I wanted to live alone but I guess I wasn't courageous enough to really leave the nest."

"Yes. I didn't have the courage to go to France. Until one morning in Amsterdam when I woke with a monumental hangover and some friends called to invite me to St. Tropez. The ideal spot for one who'd become accustomed to hangovers! Why not, I thought. The sun might help me dry out. I stayed sober for weeks and I knew it wasn't a terribly long drive to Villefranche. For me taking that drive required courage. That's when the last leaves were pulled off the artichoke.

"I wanted to experience what I imagined was a Dessaux holiday. I checked into La Reserve, expecting some sort of revelation, I suppose. I went to the casinos and looked up a

314

few people who led me to other people. Titles, rich backgrounds, their sort of crowd. I waited for a flash of déjà vu but there was nothing. I didn't like it at all until I went driving off alone again. Veronique, have you ever been to Provence?"

"Once," she answered.

"Well then, you remember. The color of it, those hills and the aroma of lemon trees. Veronique, you have so many things to tell me. When? Don't hold back."

"The lemon trees, David. Go on," Veronique said, hoping he wasn't going to ask her questions. Not yet. She wanted to listen to him.

"Well, after the warmth of the sea and that indescribable sky I was homesick. Suddenly I missed Aunt Jen and Barney and I knew I was ready to go home." David stopped, leaning against the park fence. "I have to tell you everything, don't I? I want you to know it all. But if I'd written this play and it opened on Broadway, if you weren't involved with the making of it and you went to see it, what would it have ticked off for you?"

"I don't know. We wouldn't have met and I wouldn't be standing here in Gramercy Square wanting to kiss you. Oh, David. I can't believe I said that!"

"I'm glad you did!" His eyes were light now that he wasn't thinking of the past. "See how easy it can be? Speak up. Say what you feel."

She began to speak but his lips stopped her. Enigmas be damned! She did feel better than she'd ever felt.

"David, I have an idea. Can you skip rehearsal on Saturday? We could drive to Watermill for the weekend. We can have two days on the beach!"

Ten

"The city does seem far away when you look at this," David said. From the driveway bordered with low pines to the tan fields stretching beyond the road he saw flat land.

"Beautiful, isn't it?" Veronique said, letting the front door slam behind her, trying to balance a pile of cushions for the terrace furniture. "After the irritation and tension in the city this is the most satisfying sight I know. These fields, the wheat color, are better than hills and mountains. I'm always restless with high trees and all those green leaves over my head."

"You, too?" David asked. "I'm excitable enough under ordinary circumstances but unless all the majesty of green mountains is far off in the distance I'm as high-strung as a diva on opening night. Give me miles of beach and the sea and I'm so relaxed I fall to pieces. And I'm happy as I'm falling. Is the beach close by?"

"Would you like to walk to it, David? We can be there in five minutes."

"If you don't think it's too late."

"I love it at this hour and we can see the sunset," Veronique said. "We can swim tomorrow, if you like cold water.

"Cold? Nothing is going to be cold for the next two days."

"Oh, David, aren't you glad we're here?" Veronique stood behind him, her arms around his chest.

"Glad, are you?" He turned to her, smiling and running his hand through her hair. "I like your hair loose this way. Come on, let's have our walk or I'll be making another suggestion. I'll make it before the evening's over anyway."

"And you rarely come here, how can you stay away?" David asked when they came back from the beach. The doors to the terrace were open and a strong breeze was swinging the cotton curtains.

"We work." Veronique looked through the cabinet under bookcases. "Oh, David, there's no gin. Will you have vodka or rum? There's rum."

"Rum will do nicely. But why, Veronique?"

"Well, we *have* been working this summer. Haven't you noticed?" She brought the drinks out to the terrace. "Dany gets out for a weekend now and then. For the past few years, I've been going to Ryan's house at Fire Island. That's another group, a completely different atmosphere. Here it's Dany's friends, their parties. They entertain and change clothes three times a day. I haven't wanted that regimented sort of social life for. . . . I never really wanted it."

"But this house is so informal and comfortable. And you love it, don't you?"

"Yes, I do but I've hated being alone. Until the past few months. If Dany hadn't gone away I had planned to come out here, to test myself. To force myself to think about me, just me and—"

"That's changed now, you know?"

"I know." And she didn't have to explain, she said to herself, not when she saw David's eyes. "What a lovely feeling. In spite of the suspicion and the questions, I've never felt this way before. Do you know what it's like, David, when I look at you? When I come to rehearsal and wait for you out there in the dark and you turn to find me. You sense it, I can feel you reaching for me."

"My darling, I'm too far away from you now." He moved to her chaise, snuggling against her. "I'm awfully glad we're

317

together. I'm glad it's taken this long for us to reach this point in our lives. Do you realize I'm going to be forty-one in a few weeks?"

"Careful. You're out with an older woman."

"I see us young and very important because we're together." They held each other, saying nothing, watching the evening sky. "Now either we have another drink or we go to dinner. Which?"

"Dinner," Veronique said. "Will you go marketing with me in the morning? We need to put some food in the larder."

"I'm not leaving you, not for a second."

"Good. Now can you bear a long drive? I want you to see Montauk and we're going to have the best lobsters you've ever tasted."

"Have you ever thought about being a tour guide?" David asked when they drove back to the house. "You know the best restaurants, you show me beautiful scenery and you enjoy every second of it."

"You're my first foreign visitor I'm happy to say." She parked the car in front of the house. "What a heavenly night. It should be sunny tomorrow, look at the sky."

"Shall we have a nightcap under the stars?"

"David, it *is* too bad you're not romantic." They went to the living room. "I know we have brandy or framboise, poire? Dany loves having after-dinner drinks."

"Framboise in the garden. Is that romantic enough for us?"

"David, it's remarkable. We're instinctively drawn to the same things. And we like the same food. The beach, this flat land. I never knew anyone who said that mountains made him nervous. I'm making a list. Didn't you make lists when you were a boy?"

"Yes," he mumbled, his lips against her shoulders, moving under her open shirt. "I love seeing you like this, happy and feeling good about *you*. Isn't that nice?"

"You've done that, made this possible." She rubbed her

318

cheek against his, her hair covering his face. "I'm without shame now," she said. "Hasn't it taken a long time for me to be this way."

"Veronique."

"David."

"Ver-rron-ique." He rolled the *r's* brusquely, laughing with her. "Shall we make love on your mother's lawn? Under the stars?"

"Beneath this velvet sky? We're playing a scene. What's it from?"

"Don't know, something very Thirties. Or shall we go in? This grass is getting very wet."

"David, we can have black coffee now and a big breakfast after we've shopped," Veronique called out. "Where are you?"

He cam into the kitchen carrying a bunch of pale pink roses. "I stole these for you. From your neighbor's bushes across the road."

"You're not a thief. They grow wild all around here. Did you see anybody?"

"No car in the driveway, I'm sure no one is home. Pretty, aren't they?"

She took a vase from the shelf. "Thank you. You don't mind black coffee, do you?"

"It's how I have it. Can we go right away? What a day! The colors of this house in daylight, Veronique! As happy as we are."

"You approve? I did it years ago, soon after Dany bought it. It was dark and drab when we first saw it and if Dany had her way she'd have made it all rose and red like her apartment in New York. I said we had to complement the beige around us. There were more potato fields then, with soft pastels to reflect the sunlight."

"Does your mother know everyone in the theatre? I was looking at the pictures in the library."

"She calls it her den. She's been working for a very long

319

time. I think she *has* known everybody."

"I love it. Gielgud, Gertrude Lawrence. I wish I could have seen the Lunts. You have to tell me who many of them are. She has to be very sentimental, your old mum."

"She is in her own way but she doesn't like to admit it. Wait till you see what she has saved in the city; playbills, books, more autographed pictures." Veronique put the vase on the kitchen table. "We know about one picture, don't we?"

"Veronique, not that again—"

"No, absolutely not," she said. "You do love all this affectionate collecting, don't you? What is your house like?"

"House? My small flat in London. I save things, too. You'll see. Maybe not your taste but I have an odd group of stuff. Pictures, sculpture. I inherited most of the Dessaux collection, what wasn't confiscated by the Nazis. A lot of it is in storage in Paris. I'm up in Blackpool much of the time with Aunt Jen. She keeps the theatre going and I try to lend a hand. I'm not much with management, I assure you. And the desolated look on her face when I say goodbye. What a hideous feeling to leave someone old alone in a room."

"You won't have that feeling with Dany. She wouldn't allow you to see it."

David frowned for a moment. "We'll have to find a larger flat now."

"*We* will?"

"Of course we will. You're coming back with me, you know. I'm going to show you my country, the places I love. The way you've been showing me here."

Veronique was wide-eyed. She lowered her head, staring into her coffee cup.

"Veronique, my darling, haven't you thought about it?" He covered her hand with his. "Where we're going from here?"

"Maybe I've been afraid to think about it."

"No need to fear. Success or failure, whatever happens to the play, we're in this together. You and I." He wasn't teasing now, he laughed with relief. "You're stuck with me, my girl."

He had said it. They were together. "My girl." What a special sound the two words had.

Veronique drove along the back roads for as long as she could before turning onto the highway. "This was farmland, David. Do you turn old barns into new houses at home?"

"But we don't make them into fake Palladian villas," David said. "How long have you had your house?"

"Dany bought it in the Fifties when I was in college. Alix Harcourt had a house in Southampton on Gin Lane. We'll drive over there later. You must see it, it's one of the richest roads in the world and you'll see the village. Alix wanted Dany to have an investment. You can't imagine what all this property is worth now. Alix really wanted a friend nearby. Her husband was quite stuffy and his old family house was terribly formal. Dany created another atmosphere, obviously. It was too small to do any other way. I spoke up quite a bit back then. When we finished Alix said she'd rather live with *us.*"

"I saw her once, in a Lonsdale play in London."

"You did! Dany has made her costumes forever, since Alix starred in her first play. Alix has always known exactly what she wants to wear but she listens to Dany. Well, she divorced Southampton and the house. She married again and that gave her a palatial villa in Cap Ferrat, where Dany has been all week. Alix still has the house there but not the husband. Auntie Alix. Oh, David, I have so much to tell you!" Veronique drove into a gravel driveway. "Here's the vegetable market."

"And a perfect day for a picnic on the beach."

"I'll get what's on the list, you pick whatever you'd like to have." Veronique took lettuce and endive, makings for a salad.

David went in and out of the stalls touching things with the delight of a boy in a toy shop. He picked up an eggplant with surprise. "White?" he asked. Purple broccoli, yellow tomatoes, brown peppers and ruby lettuce. "Rather esoteric, wouldn't you say? The land of the gourmet. Where are the real vegetables?"

"Veronique!" The voice was familiar before Veronique turned.

"Belinda, how are you?"

"I was going to call you" Belinda Jones said. "To ask if you were coming out while Dany is away."

Veronique introduced David. "Hello, I can't wait to see your play," Belinda said. "What a surprise! Listen, will you come over for dinner? You can see I'm buying out this place and we're not even vegetarians! Veronique, you've never met Kenny."

"Thank you," Veronique thought quickly. "We have dinner plans."

"Then come for drinks, please?"

Veronique tried to signal David with her eyes but he was no help. "We have an early reservation," Veronique lied. She was a rotten liar and she wondered if Belinda could tell.

"Well, come at six thirty. Six o'clock if you'd like."

"What an agreeably round woman," David said as they drove home. "We didn't think quickly enough to get out of it, did we? She was happy to see you."

"Yes. I've never seen her away from the workroom. She seems different, maybe because I'm different today. Dany is fond of her but I never liked her very much. She hasn't been married for long. I wonder what he's like."

"My darling, we'll go for one drink."

"If we weren't going back to work I would start painting again," Veronique said. "Look at this beach. I thought I wanted to do watercolors, loose, free Japanese landscapes but now I'd stretch big canvasses and work in oil. Big paintings, David! Big, brave limpid seascapes! Am I having sunstroke from this perfect day?"

"Whatever it is I like it." David shut the picnic basket. "No more food until dinner time, I've eaten like a hog. The rather Victorian flower paintings are yours then. The ones in the bedroom?"

The old Veronique. "I couldn't work that way again,

322

not anymore."

"But they're good. You're talented, my girl."

"Mmm." Veronique stretched on the terrycloth mat letting her hand rest on David's thigh. "When I was in a drawing class at school a teacher used to criticize my work. I remember the old man who posed for us, he wore an old tweed jacket and I drew all the wrinkles in his sleeves where his arm bent at the elbow. The teacher asked what the lines meant; little tumors she called them. I said I was trying to capture the age of his coat, the threadbare quality and she said it was wrong. She said I wasn't neat. What kind of inhibition did that lead to? I haven't thought of this in years.

"Not only did I have to conform to get a passing grade but maybe there should be no wrinkles in my own sleeves. They must always be perfectly pressed. Neat, clean and precise. No Jackson Pollack squiggles. Instead accurate, little flower pictures. That accuracy was good in the workroom, Dany maintained a standard of quality from the start. But it affected my way of living too. Nothing messy, nothing careless. There wasn't enough rebel in me." Veronique leaned over to touch David's face. "Except, David, shall I tell you about it?"

Eleven

The girl running up the subway stairs, rushing for the bus, desperately hailing the taxi with her hands clutching the shopping bags filled with pieces of fabric, was serious and determined to be treated with respect. She wanted to do the job better than anyone; she did not want to be treated as the boss's daughter. From the West Fifties to the lower East Side; from the East Forties to Fifty-seventh Street, Veronique raced to the fabric shops to collect samples of cloth, swatches of color, half yard lengths of special silk to show Dany and the designer.

"I promise I'll give you an order tomorrow." She tried to entice a fabric salesman. "We will need at least fifty or sixty yards. I'll pay you for the half yard. You know the designer won't be able to visualize this from a tiny swatch." Veronique looked hurt and disappointed. The salesman relented. The length of printed chiffon she was fingering was cut for her.

"Take this other sample, too," the salesman said. "The georgette is not as nice but it'll make you look good to bring back more than what you were asked to get. Take, take; besides how can I resist a beautiful girl like you? And don't forget to say hello to your mother." Sometimes it was easier than Veronique had anticipated.

When Veronique had come home from Bennington at

324

Christmas holiday she had told Dany she was unhappy and impatient at college. She wasn't learning any more than what she could learn in the workrooms.

"Will you hire me, Maman?" she had asked after listing her reasons not to return to Vermont after the spring semester.

"Why not?" Dany had replied. "Don't expect any special treatment. You may be my daughter but you'll have to start like all the others, as a shopper."

"What will you pay me?" Veronique asked.

"What the other shoppers get which will probably be cheaper than having you come in from Bennington every weekend to go off to the theatre and the ballet."

"By the way, do you think I can get to see *Giselle* tomorrow night?" Veronique asked.

"Sometimes I think you'd hitchhike in to see *Giselle*."

"To see Erik Bruhn, not *Giselle*," Veronique replied.

Dany seemed pleased. Veronique knew that the prestigious school in Vermont hadn't impressed Dany. It had been Peggy and Alix who thought Bennington was the proper college. Dany would have preferred Pratt or Parsons, an art education for her daughter who painted and sketched, who might want to become a costume designer.

"Dahling, after she has finished four years at Bennington she will be able to go anywhere, do anything!" Alix had exclaimed two years ago, with the peculiar sense of snobbery nurtured by the insecure feelings of a childhood spent at public schools in the Bronx.

Veronique knew Dany had her own insecurities. How very American for an immigrant to dream of a superior and distinguished education for a daughter, but it was an unhappy year for Veronique. She was completely disinterested in any weekend activities at school. She strode into the workroom on a late Friday afternoon; hugging Nancy Elmont, stopping to kiss Maria Mennino and greeting everybody in the workroom with an exuberance purposely noisy to allay Dany's possible reprimands.

"You're here again?" Dany chided as she reached up to kiss Veronique. A casual embrace. Veronique thought it was a sign of independence not to show affection these days and she was sure her mother agreed. "Haven't you stopped growing? Are you sure you don't want to be a model, *chérie?* You have the height. God knows you wouldn't need false eyelashes! You'd make a lot of money, my darling."

"No, Maman, far too superficial for me." Veronique meant it. She plainly wasn't interested in anything not related to the workroom, the excitement of the theatre. She knew she was photogenic and she'd heard Auntie Alix talking in the fitting room one day.

"That child's gray eyes, those raspberry lips! My dear, she doesn't need a drop of makeup. Oh, to be that young!"

Veronique heard it but she didn't really believe Auntie Alix. Through the winter and spring Veronique came barging into the house hungry for the new plays, the ballet, a new modern dance company, the art exhibits. She satisfied her curiosity for two days. On Sunday she packed her canvas satchel and, glum and dejected, she returned to Vermont.

Now Veronique was pleased to be working in the atelier. How Maman loved the sound of that word!

"Be grateful that your Aunt Peggy is in London. And that Alix is making the picture in Rome or you'd be hearing criticism," Dany said. "Oh, I'd get scolded for hiring you but the streets and the shops in Paris were an education for me. Why shouldn't my daughter learn the same way here?"

"And things move faster in New York, don't they, Maman?"

After six months Veronique knew every fabric resource, every shop where there were goods for the making of a costume. She bargained whenever she could, she was methodical and organized. When the new fall season began

326

there was more work in the shop than Dany had had in years.

"If you found two new shoppers I could supervise them, spend more time ordering by phone and help you out with many other things," Veronique suggested one evening as she and Dany ate their dinner. "I'd love to start draping."

"You love to start everything, *chérie,* but do you have the patience to finish anything?" Dany teased her but it wasn't a bad idea. "Let's look at the list of possible new names in the morning. You have a practical eye, Veronique."

Veronique saw Dany's eyes, she knew her mother liked hearing her daughter speak up. If Veronique was away at school Dany would go upstairs too late in the evening, fix a light snack and read in bed after a long day. Now, at the end of the day, Dany suggested dinner at one of the nearby restaurants. "Where, *chérie?* Du Midi, Pierre au Tunnel? One of our little French places? Twenty years ago Arthur Bellamy named this business House of Mounet. I wonder how he knew I'd be having a partner."

"From what I've heard Arthur Bellamy thought you might be changing your name to Bellamy." Veronique couldn't resist a little gibe.

"Fresh! Has Maria been gossiping with you again? You are aware, my child, of the name of this business? Dany Mounet. Arthuer Bellamy, poor dear, was quite pretentious."

"But he did have romantic ideas?"

"Never mind." Dany ran her fingers through her hair and lifted her chin rather saucily, making Veronique smile. Paris has never left her, Veronique thought. She's as seductive as some Montparnasse demimondaine that Lautrec would have wanted to paint.

"We have designers crawling out of the woodwork," Dany said pointing to the blackboard on the workroom wall. "Look at that list. The fitting schedule is overwhelming. We need more fitting rooms!"

"You should have refused the Shakespeare Company. Is there any profit in doing those alterations? You say you hate doing that kind of work, don't you?" Veronique asked.

"*Chérie,* how can I refuse Evans Morley. He has been a friend for more than twenty years. He hasn't had a job in ages and if Equity insists on American actors to be extras we have to fix the stock costumes coming in from Canada so they can be worn here. I simply cannot say no to Evans. We will do it cheaply and it will help him. You know how general managers hate to spend money."

"Cheap. If you can do it in a week and if you don't get carried away with extra labor," Veronique said, adding *"Maman"* rather gently.

"Well, partner," Dany replied, "I thought you might take care of it in your section."

Veronique now had a corner in the back of the workroom where she made accessories; belts, appliques, trimmings for the finishing touches on the costumes being made in the busy room. It was easy to acclimate since Dany was treating her as an associate. A minor one but nevertheless . . .

"You can do it all," Dany said. "What can it be? It's *Coriolanus;* tunics, lots of tunics. Chlamys and chiton. Those words! It will be easy and I'll help you with the fittings. I can't give it to Benny and the tailors; Elsa Groueff will be sulking and bitching if Benny works on anything but her gangster suits for that speakeasy musical she's doing. Why are we so busy?" Dany's hand went grandly to her brow in a broad gesture. "Sometimes I think it was easier to starve in Paris."

"Of course, Maman, of course," Veronique said, laughing to herself. Dany may have been poor in Paris but she never starved.

The Canadian wardrobe master arrived with the stage

managers when the cartons of costumes came in from Canada. As the boxes were emptied Dany examined every item. "Burlap! Homespun! They should be raw silk or at least heavy linen! My dears, I don't want you to worry for a second. I will fix them so you will not recognize them."

"They only require refitting, Madame Mounet," the wardrobe master said as Veronique came into the back shipping space.

"Remember, Maman, you said cheap," Veronique whispered.

The man bending over the last box of costumes looked up and smiled at Veronique.

"Here are the last of them. These do look like silk, don't they?"

"Young man, they look like reprocessed wool!" Dany snapped. "We haven't met. I am Dany Mounet and this is my daughter, Veronique."

"I'm very pleased to meet you both. I'm Howard Cronin, the assistant stage manager."

A stage manager. Veronique thought he should be in white flannels playing croquet on a Newport lawn or in hiking tweeds roaming a Scottish highland. Or in an early Victorian library, all mahogany and burgundy velvet, at a long desk poring over some leather bound tome, straw color hair falling over his forehead and squinting at the words he read because he was terribly myopic. The narrow tortoise glasses framed bright grey eyes made larger by the thickness of the lenses.

"I have the measurements of the people we've hired."

"We won't need them if you send them in for fitting. One will be enough, I should think," Dany said.

How odd for Dany to be so curt and abrupt. Why doesn't she like this fellow, Veronique wondered.

He didn't flirt with Veronique but the following week when the *Coriolanus* costumes were being refurbished Howard Cronin stopped by whenever he got away from rehearsals. He came into the workroom with minor notes, details that were ordinarily handled by telephone. How many seats did Dany want for opening night, dress rehearsal was moved back to 3 P.M. not at 2 P.M. He came in carrying his Mark Cross briefcase, wearing rumpled chinos and a grey shetland jacket that fell loosely from his shoulders as if it were on a hanger on a clothing rack.

It was obvious to Veronique that he liked her; he hung about with no apparent reason when he came to the workroom. He said he was fascinated by the work going on; intrigued with the twenties costumes being made for Elsa Groueff, the Western costumes for the musical Hale Walker was working on. He was awed by the arrival of Alix Harcourt late one afternoon when she was to have her first fittings for the Lonsdale revival she was starring in.

He seemed reluctant to leave the shop that day; lingering at Veronique's table as she tried to work, watching her trace a pattern, cut a design shape in brown paper that he didn't understand. Finally he said, "There's an opening night party at Sardi's. If you don't have a date I'd like to take you." He hesitated a bit and added, "I'm sure your mother has been invited. I've never been to Sardi's." At last, Veronique thought.

"I'd like that. Thank you." She was delighted. "I'll be sitting with mother but I have no date for afterward." She hadn't had any dates since she left Bennington. No one interested her and she had seen only a few of her old Dalton chums since she'd started working.

Dany seemed apathetic when Veronique told her of Howard's invitation. "If you'd like that, *chérie*. It will be a very small party, though they always say that. I said we'd go with Evans Morley and Alix who will have one of her young beauties in tow, I suppose."

"Don't you think Howard Cronin is a beauty, too?" Veronique asked.

"I am afraid so, *chérie*," said Dany and she walked to the fitting room.

330

* * *

Heads turned as Veronique and Howard walked into Sardi's. He wore his ill-fitting, hired dinner jacket with the same carelessness he wore his rumpled tweeds. Veronique had copied a Claire McCardell denim dress she had seen in *Vogue*. At the first round table they joined Dany, Evans Morley, Alix and her dark, sleek escort; the most popular of the young male models discovered by Alix when she was lecturing at Stella Adler's acting classes. When John Fletcher joined the group there was the expected deafening applause for the master of the English classic theatre. After a round of drinks, he suggested they go upstairs to the party.

"Might as well take advantage of being given a gratis supper, don't you think?"

"They don't say he has his first shilling for nothing," Alix whispered as they left the table.

The clamor of anticipation filled the second floor of Sardi's crowded with noisy members of the company; edging around the tables, drinks held precariously, trying to find places to sit for supper before the morning newspapers were brought in and the reviews from the critics would tell them if they might have a successful run or even an extended engagement.

"Everybody is here! *Tout* New York! Celeste, darling! There's Hank with Nedda and Josh. Mmm, Victoria and Mickey are together again," Alix was waving, throwing kisses and pushing efficiently as she led the way through the pack. "There's our table, John."

It was unexpected to see Howard impressed and uneasy in the throng of celebrities. He guided Veronique to a table away from the Fletcher group when one of the production staff called out that there was room at his table.

"Well, we know they can't knock the play," Paul, the stage manager, was saying.

"No, but if Atkinson decides to compare it to a produc-

331

tion he saw in London in 1934 we can be in trouble," Paul's date said. "It *is* good. Why, it really is an old-fashioned melodrama and isn't that what they always want to see?"

Veronique recognized the blind optimism that was like religion to everyone working in the theatre. She had been aware of this pie in the sky attitude since she began to listen to fitting room talk as a child. It was always the first time; it had never happened before and with blind faith the actor hoped for the best. It was stimulating to listen to the discussions, scenes analyzed and picked apart, some bit recalled with relished laughter.

"If 'they' knew what 'they' wanted to see there'd be standing room only at every theatre on Broadway," Howard said. "A drink, Veronique? I'm ready for a beer."

The press agent called for attention; he was going to read the *Times* review. There were sighs of relief. If the review hadn't been favorable it would not be read aloud this way.

"The production was admirable."

There were murmurs of satisfaction.

"The performance was noteworthy. The acting was distinguished."

Sighs of pleasure sounded through the room.

"John Fletcher is superb. He is our foremost Shakespearean actor."

There was cheering and shouting; apprehension vanished.

"Well, now we can relax," Paul said. "Who wants to hear some good jazz? Gerry Mulligan is playing at Nick Condon's down in the Village."

"We'd love it," Howard answered. "Want to, Veronique?"

There was hesitancy in his voice but his eyes were imploring; as if he were saying please, don't say no, don't disappoint me.

They went to the Village to listen to music and they met

for hamburgers the following night after the performance. They went out with the group of actors from Canada; the young crowd who hoped to stay in New York and find work on Broadway after the run of *Coriolanus*. They went out for drinks, late meals and endless talk about their favorite subject; the theatre. To Downey's and Ralphs, new places for Veronique; coffee houses on MacDougal Street and cheap little restaurants in Chinatown. She was happy being a part of the circle; listening and laughing at their intense arguments.

"How can you say Brecht isn't commercial? You read the reviews but you haven't read the plays."

"There are poets and there are playwrights. Tennessee is a poet."

"I can remember my own childhood and the tawdriness I grew up in; I don't need John Osborne to remind me of it. I want to see more Giraudoux and Anouilh."

"They do not translate into English," Veronique said with authority. She had read the original French plays after seeing *Time Remembered* with Dany.

"Veronique is right," Howard said. "There is a lightness necessary in French comedy. The actors' feet must not touch the floor of the stage. It should be light; like floating feathers." He had a way of listening as if he were disinterested but then he would make his comment and there was no more discussion; the subject was changed. He sat slouched in his chair, his long legs stretched out at the side of the table, drinking his beer and receiving attention. He didn't seem to demand the spotlight but it found him.

Was he unaware of the admiring glances as they sat at the bar at Downey's; as they walked through Shubert Alley, Veronique wondered. He didn't have to talk; looking at him was enough. She loved his offhand manner; the unflappable attitude; the way his El Greco hands reached to snuff out his cigarette as he made his point in an argument.

Every night the circle grew larger; more friends joined

333

the group as they sat at longer tables, talking louder and staying out later. They played "Association" and "Botticelli" and Howard introduced his favorite game.

"I'll sing you the verse and you have to name the song."

"Oh Christ, Howard, it's not fair," Paul groaned. "You know every show tune that's been written."

"Let's try. Aw, come on." Howard was like a kid whose electric trains were being taken away. "Guess this one. It's Cole Porter." He sang in a low scratchy voice.

"You don't let me lead you astray enough.

"You don't live enough, you don't dare enough,

"You don't give enough,

"You don't care enough,

"You don't make my sad life sunny enough.

"Yet, sweetheart, funny enough . . . ?"

He waited for the refrain.

No one could guess the song. "Does it matter?" Paul asked. "I think he's trying to tell you something, Veronique."

Disapproval was a word Veronique had never been aware of. Dany hadn't believed in it, reason was its substitute. Veronique grew up surrounded by adults and sewing machines and fitting rooms. As a child Dany had taught her to feel the blades of a pair of scissors. You used them to cut cloth not fingers. Condemnation and reproach were words unknown to Veronique until she learned them from her schoolmates.

And now Dany was disapproving. In the kitchen every morning they usually talked about the day ahead. The fittings, the schedules, the workroom gossip. Small talk, cheerful and trivial conversation. They were as casual as roommates before going off to work.

Veronique knew she was staying out too late but she was ready every morning at seven and longing to tell Dany about the night before. She wanted to reveal the word

334

games they had played, the discussions about the theatre and Giraudoux and Anouilh, but most importantly she wanted to talk about Howard and her confused feelings.

"You should go to the Bon Soir, Maman. Jimmy Daniels is the singer there. He does all the songs you love. Cole Porter, Coward and French music you must remember. You know he worked in Paris in the thirties."

"Yes, I've heard of him." Dany's response was cold and unresponsive. "I never had time to go to Le Boeuf Sur La Toit. I was working too hard."

It was as if a door had been slammed shut; a phone receiver had clicked off. Dany had taken her breakfast tray to the sink, to wash her cup and plates. She turned her back to Veronique and then left the room. The conversation was ended. Dany did not want to listen and Veronique sat staring at the pink Limoges coffee cup and her half-eaten croissant; ignored and rejected.

There was no chance to talk about playing the verse and song game; no opportunity to repeat Paul's perplexing comment after Howard had sung the Cole Porter verse and it was impossible to tell Dany how confused she was. There was nothing to do but clean her own breakfast dishes and follow Dany to the workroom and begin the day's work.

If she was not to understand why she was being shut out by her mother then she would go her own way; if questions were not to be answered then there would be no asking, Veronique decided. She would find work to be busy with until it was time to meet Howard at the stage door after the evening performance. She would be happy to join in the word games, the bottle party they had been invited to. Though she wondered why they never did anything alone, she would enjoy the last week before *Coriolanus* closed.

They went to a cold water flat for a Charades party and to Mulberry Street for a spaghetti supper and sat at their table in the back of Ralph's drinking too much beer. The week was going by too quickly.

At 2 A.M. in the morning as they walked across Forty-fifth Street, Howard said, "John Fletcher is giving a small closing night party on Saturday but I thought that afterward we might go down to Nick's and listen to Miles Davis. Would you like that, Veronique?"

It was cold standing on the stoop of the brownstone and she wished she had the courage to ask him in but she couldn't. "I'd like that," she said feeling awkward and clumsy. She wanted to say something more, something tantalizing but she couldn't.

"Good." He stepped forward, pressing her against the front door, almost leaning on her, his wool scarf grazing her cheek; with his hands clenched deep in his jacket pockets. He bent to kiss her lightly then he turned and went down the brownstone steps. "See you tomorrow night," he said.

As she opened the front door and went upstairs to the apartment she wondered if Dany was awake. She wanted to tell her mother that she felt like an inadequate child.

John Fletcher's party for the company and crew was a respectable and muted gathering in a small Central Park West apartment. A waiter served drinks from a makeshift bar set up in the small kitchen; one of the company dressers sliced ham and stirred a large pot of baking beans as actors came in and out asking for more ice, club soda, a splash of water.

"We can slip out quietly when the food is served," Howard whispered. "I've left our coats on top of the heap in the bedroom. I'll give you a signal when we're ready."

"That was easy," Veronique said as they came out onto the avenue to look for a taxi. "But shouldn't we have said good night?"

"And risk six people wanting to join us?" Howard asked. He grabbed her hand as he hailed a cab.

The supple beat of the music hit them the moment they entered Nick's.

"A champagne cocktail has always meant Scott and Zelda, speakeasies and glamor. And I've never had one," Howard said. "Let's celebrate and have them."

"What are we celebrating?" Veronique asked.

"Us."

"Then we should have them." With caviar and pâté, Veronique thought, on a Porthault table cloth, with crystal goblets. Extravagance as only Dany dished it up in a moment of caprice; excessiveness to go with the satin smooth riffs Miles Davis was playing. Veronique wished Dany could see her, excited and happy sitting in the smoky glow of amber spotlights. *Us.* He had said *us.*

They stayed until closing time, when the harsh hard lights reminded them that he was due at the theatre early in the morning for the pack-out. Howard picked up the swizzle sticks after paying the check. "Half for you, half for me," he said giving Veronique three of them. "Mementos."

"Remembrance." As if I needed them, she said to herself.

"Would you like to see where I live?" Howard asked. "Bank Street is only a few blocks from here."

"This is it," Howard said, flipping the light switch. He said it as an apology. The room was small and square, the cracked, chipped bottle green walls were lined with shelves of books and record albums. "I have to start packing tomorrow," Howard said, stepping over a valise and going to the kitchenette behind a bamboo blind. A ladder back chair was piled with more books and magazines, a club chair with a blue admiral's blanket over it was covered with sweaters and shirts. Other valises were in front of the sofa bed, open and made up with pressed white linens. "A beer, Veronique? It's all I can offer you."

"No thanks," Veronique said, looking out the window parallel to the street lamps. "You're very neat, aren't you?"

"I try. This place is so small I have to be neat," Howard

said. "Wasn't it a terrific evening? You know that you looked great at the party when you danced with Fletcher?"

"And nervous. He has hands like the tentacles of an octopus."

Howard put his beer on the side table and stretched out on the bed, pulling off his turtleneck sweater. He reached up to Veronique. "You're very pretty," he whispered.

"You are, too." He was kissing her, holding her shoulders and not moving, then slowly he pulled her on top of him. She could hear the music again, the light, sparkling jazz from the club floating in and out. Her hands ran through his flaxen hair, then he grabbed her wrists, sliding her hands along his arms, over his chest.

"Undress, Veronique. Pretty Veronique." His lips were on her neck, her ears. He began to unbutton her shirt. "Please take off your clothes. Please." His mouth was on her breasts, her nipples, his fingers dancing over her back. "My beauty," he murmured, moving her onto her back and kneeling over her. He clicked off the lamp and Veronique opened her eyes. The shadows on the ceiling were almost blue, a silvery gray on his hairy, blonde chest. He was over her, quite still for a moment. She shut her eyes again, her hands roaming his long, narrow body. Slow, slow. Savoring every motion. He was over her, sliding languidly, touching, caressing. Silent. Lowering himself toward her and she moved naturally and easily as if she was doing something she'd done many times before.

"I don't know how to say goodbye. I haven't ever said it except to Dany, when I went away to school or to camp." Veronique wanted to get up from the lunch counter, to leave her sandwich uneaten and run back to work.

"I've spent most of my life saying goodbye," Howard said. "This isn't a teary, sad farewell, Veronique. We'll be together in a couple of weeks. Now finish your lunch."

"If Dany will let me come out to Chicago. We have so much work in the room and she isn't awfully enthusiastic about us, you know."

"But she allows you independence," he said. "Do you realize how admirable that is?"

It was not the time to discuss Dany's disapproval; he was leaving and she had to return to the shop to make knotted fringe for Elsa Groueff's flapper dress and crochet edging for Hale Walker's Western skirts. Instead she would have liked to postpone this departure. She wanted to touch Howard and ask why he knew about goodbyes.

They finished lunch silently and she held his arm as he paid the check; she clung to him as he waited for change and they hugged and kissed as they reached the street.

"I'll call you after the opening," he said, turning to go back to the theatre.

"We need another blackboard; there is no room for the fitting lists. My God, how will we get it all finished?" Dany came out of the fitting room full of apprehension, her arms laden with crêpe de chine dresses. "Those children are all losing weight. We could not have cut all the dresses too big. They are being overworked, there must be too much dancing in the show. We need more fitting rooms. Nancy, buy another blackboard!"

"Madame," Nancy said, "if you didn't rewrite my schedules in such large letters you'd have room enough with one blackboard." Nancy was used to playing out this scene. She was completely unperturbed.

"If I don't rewrite your little bookkeeper's hand I cannot see from my table. Veronique, I need more apricot crêpe, they've added two more girls to the speakeasy number. Where is the dyer's delivery? Hale will have an absolute fit if he can't approve his shirt fabrics."

"Maria wants you to look at the new hat shapes," Nancy interrupted.

"Why do I have to look at them? Elsa changes everything I suggest anyway! We have to talk about the out of

339

town, Nancy. Let's go over it at tea. I'm working late tonight. Tonight? Every night this week. Veronique, will you work tonight, please? Philadelphia for Elsa, Detroit with Hale and Alix opens in Wilmington. Of all the dreary towns for a tryout, Wilmington!"

"Madame, there are Du Ponts in Wilmington. It will be very glamorous. You know Miss Harcourt always opens in Wilmington. Now, please go to see Maria."

"The Du Ponts impress Alix, not me! Now, if they came up with a replacement for dacron or orlon even nylon, any *on!*" Dany said. "Yes?" she looked at Veronique.

"I didn't say anything. Yet," Veronique answered. How happy Dany was when the workroom was frantic.

"When you want me I'll be working with Maria!" Dany walked toward the millinery department. "No one pays attention to me!"

Veronique didn't want Dany to see her impatience but she wondered when Howard would call. She knew there could be problems hanging the scenery in a new theatre but he said he'd call after the opening. That was last night. Veronique knew she mustn't walk around the workroom looking despondent but it was difficult to hide her feelings. Maria had been aware of the bad mood earlier in the morning.

"*Bambina,* what's wrong? Such an *aspetto triste,* don't let your mama see you fretting this way, *cara.*"

"Maria, she doesn't want to listen to me anyway." Veronique hadn't been able to say more and now she wondered if Maria was going to give some motherly advice to Dany.

At tea Elsa asked about the out of town schedules. "You must let the office know how many people will be going to Philadelphia, Dany."

"I know, I know. Nancy is going to call in the morning. You'll want everybody, won't you, Elsa? Remember, I don't want to hear a word about the expense! Benny will take another tailor and Maria needs her assistant. I'm going to want Veronique. It will be your first out of town, *chérie,* and what a beginning! On Elsa's show." Dany was going to make a roundabout point, Veronique was waiting for it. "We'll hire the usual local women down there when we want them. And I'll have to go directly to Detroit afterward. Don't worry, Elsa, I'm only sending a few people. Hale doesn't have your kind of budget. Who ever does? Veronique, you'll have to come right back from Philadelphia to start swatching for the ice show. In a few days I'll be back and then Veronique, we'll go to Wilmington for Auntie Alix."

Dany was purposely steering her away from Chicago. How long was she going to go on without acknowledging Howard?

"Work, work, work!" Dany was saying. "No Thanksgiving in Watermill. I forget what the house looks like. Do you think we can get there for Christmas, *chérie,* or will we be having roast goose at this worktable?"

"I don't care about the holidays, here or anywhere!" Veronique couldn't believe she heard herself. "All I know is that I'm going to Chicago this weekend. I promised Howard and I can leave from Philadelphia. I'll fly back here on Monday morning. Early!" She was practically shouting.

When they worked overtime the constant hum that usually pervaded the room accelerated, becoming a strident roar that seemed to stimulate action. Everyone moved faster, everything snapped with heightened animation. Voices were louder, talk was sharper. Veronique whipped her needle through the thin silk taffeta trimming for Elsa's gossamer tea gowns, she heard the drone of the machines but there was no accompaniment of voices. Determination was rippling through the room but it was a muted whirr. A hush.

Dany stood at her table draping muslin for the last of the twenties dresses, working silently. Veronique thought of apologizing but at the same time she was thinking of

341

Howard, the phone call she'd place when they finished working. She was sorry, she knew she was responsible for the pall that had come over the room after her surprising outburst. In all her life she had never been disrespectful to Dany. There had never been a reason for it. Yet the idea that she'd frightened everyone gave her a small tingle of pleasure.

At 1 A.M. Veronique called Howard, knowing he would be out, but leaving a message and it was close to 3 A.M. when her phone rang.

No, he didn't wake her. Yes, she understood that it was difficult setting up in a new theatre. She was happy that the reviews were even better than they had been in New York. Yes, she planned to leave for Chicago on Friday. No, she was fine; it was late and they were working very hard. Yes, of course, she was looking forward to coming out. No, she was not angry.

Of course she was angry and hurt, but when she heard him vaguely apologizing the hurt feelings subsided into a purr and she truly could not wait to see him.

The four days in Philadelphia were frantic. She had to remember all the details for the group in Chicago. Why was disorder funny, she wondered. The shedding angora sweaters made the singers cough; the cloche hats covered the dancers' eyes and made two girls trip through the Charleston. The star's entrance at the top of the drawing room staircase and the miscued setpiece rolling off before she began her opening line. Yes, she was going to have amusing stories for Howard.

For three days in the basement of the Shubert Theatre they worked from early morning until late in the night. When a break was called for lunch or dinner Veronique ran to the corner delicatessen for sandwiches. She sewed and fitted and helped Maria and Dany. In the clamor of preparing for dress rehearsal Dany forgot her animosity and she talked to Veronique, suggesting that she sit next to Elsa and take notes while Dany sat behind them.

"Isn't Elsa a miracle, *chérie?* A nervous miracle but hasn't she made it look splendid?" And later after notes were given to the wardrobe staff in the basement she asked, "What time tomorrow does your plane leave?"

The next day, closing up the portable sewing machines and packing their findings, Veronique was looking at the clock when Maria came to hug her and said, "Have a lovely time, *bambina.*" Dany surprised her by saying "Be a good girl, *chérie.*"

Howard was waiting in the lobby as Veronique came through the doors of the Blackstone Hotel, a smart figure in an obviously new Burberry trenchcoat and pressed gray flannels, a red paisley tie and a navy blue blazer.

"You look wonderful," she said as their arms wrapped around each other. "Are you auditioning for a new role?"

"The new clothes? To celebrate your arrival. Are you tired, hungry? It's not too late for you, is it? There's a party for some of our company and for the ballet troupe that just opened. Everyone is waiting to see you."

It wasn't what she expected but she knew they would go. He took her to the desk to register. "They didn't have an adjoining room but we are on the same floor. Why not check your bag and we can pick it up later. You can clean up at the party." He had it all planned. She was bewildered but she could not say no and he seemed to be in a hurry.

It was not the kind of party they went to in New York; not at all the kind of apartment they usually went to, not a cold water flat in a walk-up tenement where they brought shopping bags holding cans of beer and pints of scotch.

It was a luxurious apartment overlooking the lake; a rich mixture of Empire furniture, suede sofas and Breuer chairs. Veronique guessed there were at least a hundred people gathered in the enormous rooms. The host was a jolly round man wearing a charcoal pin striped suit with a red carnation in his lapel. He greeted her effusively.

"My dear, at last! I've heard so much about you. I'm Urban Powell. Did you have a good flight? I'm sure you will know more people here than I do. And more intimately since Howard has told me that everyone appears in your fitting rooms sooner or later. Doesn't our boy look stunning in his new clothes?"

Veronique was sure she didn't like the man. "It's my mother's business and I've only been working for her a few years." Looking into the room she did see some familiar faces from the ballet company. She felt uncomfortable in her cardigan sweater. The other women were in cocktail dresses—taffeta, jersey, *peau de soie*. They were all in black and wearing pearls. Then she realized how many more men there were in the crowded rooms.

"There's a matinee tomorrow, I have to be up early." Howard tipped the bellboy for Veronique's luggage. "But let me stay with you." He loosened his tie. "I've missed you."

It was what she'd wanted to hear for the last three hours, what she'd been thinking of for weeks.

"Veronique, I'm so glad you're here," he said. His fingers stroked her hair, his mouth on her neck, her lips. She had been longing to touch him and if he wasn't going to worry about how early he had to be up in the morning neither would she.

"Why isn't room service listed as one of man's greatest inventions? I wish I didn't have to work." Howard drank the last of his coffee. "We're meeting at the stage door at 5:30 A.M. You will be all right on your own, won't you?"

"I'll be fine," she said and, feeling content, she was sure she would be.

She walked through the frigid streets, shopped and spent the late afternoon in the hotel room staring out the window at the Chicago skyline and thinking of the pleasure of the night before. She found her way to the theatre, and the restaurant they went to was very much like Downey's. They chattered through the meal as they had in New York; gossip, news read in *Variety* and they were overjoyed with Veronique's tales of rehearsals in Philadelphia.

"What will be playing when we get to Philly? Three months to go and it'll be goodbye *Coriolanus*," Paul said. "If we don't go back to Canada it will be the unemployment lines for spring of 1960, won't it?"

"Paul, we have five cities before then. Don't get gloomy on us," Howard replied.

"Have you met our happy optimist, Veronique?" Paul asked. "Did you know those glasses he wears are rose colored? Guaranteed to see only bright futures with sunny skies and lovely moonlight."

"But it's a lovely way to be," Veronique said. Paul enjoyed ribbing Howard, sometimes she thought he wasn't kidding.

She saw the evening performance and later they went to Paul's hotel room. It was shabby and run-down but there were sandwiches and beer, a record player and the word games. Veronique was comparing it to the room at the Blackstone when Paul said, "Out of the technicolor and into the black and white again, huh, Howard? How can you make the transition, isn't it like running the film backward?"

"I don't understand. Paul, what do you mean?" Veronique asked.

She had never seen Howard give anyone a dirty look before but he was annoyed with Paul. "I moved over to the Blackstone for the weekend with you," he said.

A double room in an ordinary hotel would have been more romantic than two singles in a deluxe place like the Blackstone. Technicolor, Veronique asked herself. Then someone suggested they play a round of Charades before calling it a night. Howard's team won and he couldn't hide his complacency.

"Can you afford staying here, Howard?" she asked when they came into the Blackstone. "I wouldn't have minded staying at the other place."

"I would have. It wasn't good enough for you. Don't worry. This isn't exactly the Ritz, you know." He wrapped her in his arms.

They slept without making love; he clung to her all night like a puppy seeking protection.

An elaborate breakfast brought by room service brightened Sunday morning. They were going to the Art Institute to look at paintings and he had reservations for lunch at the Pump Room. He had gone to his room to shower and change clothes. An hour later he knocked at her door in his blazer and flannels with a pink shirt and navy dotted tie; she smiled.

"You look a treat," she said, not able to resist using one of Alix's pet Britishisms.

Veronique couldn't make him change his mind about an expensive lunch. After he ordered Bloody Mary's in the lush aura of the restaurant she asked, "Would you like to be rich, Howard?"

"Yes," he answered quickly. "Very rich. But how? Not as a stage manager or anything else in the theatre, God knows. Last summer at Jacob's Pillow, we had our palms read by one of the dancers there. She told me I'd never be rich but I would always be surrounded by money and rich people. Maybe that is my fate." The drinks were brought and he clinked her glass. "What about you, Veronique?"

"I've never thought of it before. I've never had to, I guess. Dany has made such a special world for herself and me. Being rich has never seemed too important to me." As she thought about Dany's extravagance and how appealing it would be to Howard, a captain brought champagne cocktails to the table.

"I'm sorry, we didn't —" Howard began.

"Compliments of Mr. Powell," the captain said.

Veronique looked across the restaurant; a man was waving. Urban Powell, the host at the party on Friday night. He was blowing kisses and his three companions waved as if they knew her. "Howard," Veronique said. "They seem very pleased to see you."

Howard raised his glass in thanks. Veronique thought he was blushing.

Driving out to the airport in a taxi he asked about San Francisco. "I hope you will be able to come out to California. We play L.A. for two weeks and San Francisco for a month."

"I know but we have six months of very heavy work ahead of us." She was perplexed and melancholy and not prepared to say goodbye again. She insisted upon paying the cab driver. She held his hand as they went to the check-in counter.

"Howard, what did you mean in New York when you said you had spent your life saying goodbye?"

"Saying goodbye to people began very early for me." He hesitated and lit a cigarette. "My mother died when I was four years old. I hardly remember her except for a hospital bed and a chilly room and a frail, little person who clung to me and said goodbye. And after she was gone my father had three wives. And three divorces. I liked his wives, the last one was on the stage in England for a while. She knew John Fletcher and helped me get this job."

Did sadness suit him, Veronique wondered. His gray eyes were moist.

"I went to many different schools and we moved a lot. Teachers and friends and houses to say goodbye to. And all my stepmothers. I was on my own in many different places so, you see, many more goodbyes."

"And all of the people you said goodbye to, Howard?" Veronique asked. "Did they love you?"

"I hope not, Veronique. Look, they're beginning to board your plane." He held his hands over her cheeks and kissed her. "But could I help it if they did?"

* * *

347

Veronique spread the sketches over the worktable and reached for one of the color cards piled in front of her. Carefully she compared the bright colors painted on the sketches to the satin squares lined up in the cardboard folders. It was the beginning; the way to see what was available from the large fabric suppliers before sending the shoppers out to search for specific cloths or deciding that a color was absolutely unavailable and it would have to be dyed. She was struck by the blatancy of Carl Brandon's figures; there was not an iota of subtlety on the designs in front of her. Was this why there was the word "kitsch"? But when the primary colors, in shiny satins and sequins and beads whirled across the ice rinks in the enormous arenas around the country the broad strokes of brilliant vulgarity drew raging applause.

She was awfully glad to be asking herself questions about the right shade of cherry red rather than thinking of all the puzzling, enigmatic thoughts she had plagued herself with on the plane from Chicago and through a night of fitful sleep.

"Detroit is not my idea of the dream city of America!" Dany came into the workroom in the early afternoon. "It snowed and I have never known such cold. Am I glad to be home! I'll take my bags up later. It looks like we have done two major hits. Elsa's show had brilliant reviews and Hale's needs some work but it is enchanting! I think it can be another *Oklahoma*." She was full of energy and eager to talk. "Tell me what has been going on; did Maximilian send the sables for Alix's sleeves?" She said hello to everyone moving quickly in and out of the workroom aisles. "The flight was horrendous, there is snow everywhere. So bumpy! Did you start selecting colors, Veronique? What do I have to look at?" At last a direct question, but did Veronique want to talk about it now? "We should work every night this week. We must be in Wilmington on Thursday."

It was a happy prospect for Veronique; perhaps it

348

would keep her from thinking about Howard.

Alix paused for a moment on the landing then descended the curving staircase. She knew the pause was necessary for the *oohs* and *ahs* to be expected from the women in the audience admiring her sable trimmed emerald velvet gown.

The set was furnished in the style imagined to be typical of an elegant drawing room. The actors in smart evening clothes spoke in clipped British accents and Alix dominated the stage using the lisping voice that had become her trademark.

Veronique sat at the back of the orchestra laughing at the mannered, witty dialogue. This group watching dress rehearsal seemed small after the huge assemblage in Philadelphia for Elsa's musical but they responded to the talk on stage with the same appreciation that delighted Veronique.

Alix's voice in her dressing room was quite different, the lisp was gone and the tone was throatier. "Dany, darling, the neckline of the cocktail suit pulls across the back. I feel like I'm choking. A few notches and maybe a softer facing? It will help, won't it?"

"I suggested a wider neckline but you wanted it this way."

"I thought I did. I thought claustrophobia of the neck was better than showing this scrawny, aging wattle." Alix grimaced at her image in the mirror. "Age, age!"

"Save your voice for tonight's rehearsal. Don't wear the suit in the second act and Veronique will stay in and work on it."

"If you put the jacket on before you go to dinner, Auntie Alix, I can mark it," Veronique said.

"Ta, darling." Alix was wiping cold cream off her face. "Now tell me about that attractive boy you are seeing and what was Chicago like? And, Veronique, sweetheart, since

349

you are running off for weekends with handsome young men I think you are too old to go on calling me Auntie. After all, we may be competing for the attentions of the same good-looking fellows from now on. Don't you agree? I saw you two in Downey's one night. You are quite a gorgeous pair. If I hadn't seen the glow in your eyes I'd think you were brother and sister."

"Mmm, maybe too beautiful," Dany said giving Alix one of her change-the-subject looks.

"I haven't heard from him in weeks." Veronique didn't want to go on about Howard but she thought Alix would be a far more willing listener than Dany.

"That dreadful ingenue in that awful pink taffeta will step on your laugh in the last scene if you are not careful, darling," Dany knew how to switch the conversation.

"You saw it, too? She has more confidence than talent, that little one." Alix was in her glory, talking about her performance.

Since she was a little girl, Veronique had heard these two go over the smallest details of a performance like a pair of plotting Mata Haris. She was relieved to listen to them now. There would be no talk of Howard.

Veronique knew it was silly and childish to wait for Howard to call. Somehow she felt she had to remain aloof but it was hurting. Sitting in Alix's dressing room, ripping and sewing the jacket she checked the time in San Francisco and realized that curtain was up out there. She would wait until she was home tomorrow and call him before he went off to the theatre.

It was after midnight when the curtain came down on dress rehearsal. Notes were given in Alix's dressing room. Alix was smiling and agreeable as she listened to Nevil Caine, the director. Yes, she knew what was needed for the first act curtain line; she understood what he wanted before the third act denouement. With more aplomb than she used on stage, Alix asked Nevil to sit down. It was time for the star to give a few notes of her own.

350

"No, no, Dany, you do not have to leave. We are all part of the same company, aren't we? If everything on this production was done with the artistry and perfection that you two have given my wardrobe we would be without problems and we could open in New York tomorrow night. Now, my darling Nevil, your direction is impeccable," Alix said as she walked to the little club chair he sat in and towered above him. "However, I was playing Coward and Behrman and Barry when you were a little boy aspiring to the Royal Academy. If my fellow actors do not feed me my lines with a sense of what is to follow, the beat and the meter of this fragile little piece is completely lost. I hope you are going to the other dressing rooms after this to read them what is called the riot act." Nevil tried to get up. "Nevil, I am not finished. That little angel in the third act is wearing the most unfortunate dress. You must get that what's-her-name costume supervisor to shop for a new one. But before she does, you, tomorrow morning, should call New York and get some actresses to audition for the part. The new dress will have to be worn by a new actress. For whom did that little dear undress to get the part, anyway? Not you, darling! I am not allowing that little bitch to play further than this week in Wilmington!" Alix called for her dresser to unzip her green dress. "Now shut your eyes for a moment and let me change. Thank God this day is over! Who is hungry? Shall we have sandwiches and a little wine in my rooms?"

"Alix, we are leaving first thing in the morning," Dany said.

"Oh darling, no. You can't stay for the opening? You'll miss the Du Pont's little party. It's going to be terribly chic. Please? Well, you both need some food and a bit of wine. This child has worked through the dinner break." She put her arm around Veronique and kissed her cheek. "We'll talk about the old days, get a little tipsy and then I will let you go."

"I am hungry, Maman," Veronique said. Listening to

351

Alix reminisce was better than champagne.

The Wilmington train was late but Carl Brandon was not at all annoyed when Dany and Veronique walked into the atelier. He had been waiting an hour but he was happy telling Nancy the latest jokes. She was his perfect foil; her priggishness leading him to more and more outrageous stories.

"Honey, I'm so happy to see you and I know how those trains from the South are. Late, always late like all Southerners. I'm the exception to that rule but I've been having the best little visit with Nancy." His drawl was as heavy as it had been when Dany had met him in the early Forties.

Veronique could never guess how old Carl was; no one could. Dany said he was either an old forty or a very young sixty. Despite the winter weather he was wearing a pale blue gabardine suit. Veronique was sure it had been made in Dallas. It was more appropriate for the rodeo than for a cold December day in New York. She could not remember Carl dressed any other way, this was his uniform. The Western cut suit, the matching shirt and string tie, the thin suede boots only a shade darker than his suit. Veronique did not know why Carl embarrassed her, but he always had. Now for some peculiar reason he reminded her of someone and she could not remember who.

"Why darlin', this is all marvelous!" he said as the huge boards of color swatches were spread out on Dany's worktable. "They could use you at Brooks, Veronique. They present colors to me in a great heap and it takes days to make a decision." He patted Veronique's cheek and she hoped her wince didn't show. "This is gonna be easy. What fun!"

He didn't hesitate for a second as he bent over the boards choosing the bright shades Veronique had lined up. "Honey, you can start the patterns and order the fabrics. Suppose I come in every morning at eleven and we work for a few hours, then I can go to Brooks in the afternoon. Before you know it six weeks will have flown by and we'll be off to Sioux City for the fittings and then I can be off to New Orleans for Mardi Gras. Can you believe we are going to Iowa? Why, nobody I know has ever been to Iowa but they say the new auditorium there is spectacular! Do you think they'll have corn in February? You'll have your measurements for the new skaters in the next few days and we'll use the same old girl they've hired for years to fit on. And, honey, wait until you see the new boy they chose for the try-ons. He is divine, absolutely divine!"

Dany slapped Carl's arm. "Behave yourself, Carl."

"Oh, don't worry darlin'. He's much too 'nellie' for me. Can we start choosing feathers and beads tomorrow? Now, can I take you two ladies to lunch?"

Veronique was sorry she had called Howard when she put the phone down late that afternoon. How could he be that disinterested? What was worse or more deflating than a voice saying hello in an offhand tone? *"I'm fine."* The blasé sound, quite unlike him. "I suppose you're busy as ever. Talk to you soon." Yes, she thought after she hung up, we'll talk when you're in L.A. but only if *you* call. She walked from Nancy's desk back to the workroom and asked Dany if she could work late, she wanted to begin the selection of trimmings for the next day. She wanted to forget the tone of Howard's voice and she didn't want to be gloomy sitting at a restaurant table with Dany.

Carl was in the workroom every morning promptly at eleven and the work went smoothly, without crisis. Satin, velvet, crêpe leotards, sequinned and beaded, embroidered and encrusted in every possible design lined the workroom racks, stretch wool jumpsuits hung from the pipes over the tailors' worktables like glaring traffic lights.

There was no coolness in Howard's voice when he called

from Los Angeles, he was cheery and hoping to convince her to fly out for a few days. The next week he called from Denver and then from Washington.

"Will you come to Philly in two weeks?"

"Howard, I don't see how I can. We're trying to finish the ice show and you'll be back after you close down there, won't you?"

"No, Veronique. I'm going up to Toronto to see my father," Howard said. He said it as if she knew, she hadn't any idea that his father was in Toronto. "I won't get to New York for weeks. I may go with Ballet Theatre for their tour. I have to talk to them next week. They're looking for another stage manager."

"Howard, the road again?"

"I have to work, don't I? Aw, come on, Veronique, say you'll come to Philadelphia."

"We'll be in Iowa in two weeks." She wasn't sure but she was longing to see him. Why fool herself? Howard's blond hair, his long, thin body. "Well, maybe, if I can fly from Sioux City."

"Great! Check the airline and call me tomorrow, will you?"

"Howard, we don't have to stay at the Barclay or one of those expensive hotels—"

"We're getting a rate at the Bellevue. Don't worry."

"Calling Iowa flat is an understatement," Dany said. "Why are we waiting? I hate this place. The room is cold, the breakfast eggs always have those dreadful grits on the plate and look at the lobby! This is a hotel?"

"It isn't that bad, Maman." Veronique was impatient too but she didn't want Dany to know it. It was the third day they would walk through the dry, frigid air to the vast auditorium where the company played the current show at night and every day stood obediently as Carl's costumes were yanked and pulled, pinned and stretched to fit over

354

their bodies like gaudy second skins.

Veronique was looking forward to the weekend with Howard. If the costumes were approved by the producers and the choreographer she could be in Philadelphia on Friday night. Carl was eager to go to New Orleans; Dany was tired and wanted to be in New York. There was an uneasy nervousness in the air.

What a strange breed they were; these skaters who performed like athletes attempting ballet in costumes that looked like the circus or a cabaret revue.

Carl Brandon managed to keep the atmosphere light. He darted through the muslin-hung partitions that became fitting rooms for the two costume houses. He'd flit past the sewing machines and worktables out to the huge rink balancing with an acrobat's agility to watch the skaters practice in pounds of bugle bead fringe and ostrich feathers. He kissed the skaters, pinched their behinds and told dirty jokes in his drawl that became more southern as the pressure mounted.

When the skaters prepared to glide onto the ice in costumes made by Brooks, Dany was full of compliments and praise.

"Magnifique, mes enfants," she called out. *"C'est un tableau. Carl, ils sont ravissants. Divin, divin!"*

Veronique looked over to Maria's worktable covered with coq feathered turbans and they shared a conspiratorial wink.

How impressive it was for a diva to be backstage in Sioux City, Iowa giving a performance in French. It was an opportunity Dany could not afford to miss. The Mounet personality was not to be ignored. There were not two enemy camps behind the ice rink but there was a definite feeling of détente; a deferential politeness existed between the competing costume houses. Dany made sure they knew there was a star among them.

"Veronique, did you see that terrible appliqué embroidery?" Dany asked when the skaters had gone by. "And

355

the weight of those leotards! Ours are as light as fairy wings!"

The night before Carl had taken the Brooks staff to dinner. Tonight he invited Dany and her group.

"The house manager has recommended a wonderful steak house not very far from town. And they have liquor, not that three point beer we've been drinking. Can you all be ready at eight?"

Whether it was diplomacy or Southern hospitality didn't matter; Veronique appreciated Carl's generosity.

They walked into an ordinary looking roadhouse with formica table tops and a long lunch counter. Carl thought they were in the wrong place but he showed the cashier the card he had been given and she pointed to a door at the back behind a narrow row of booths.

"Why, honey, it's like the old speakeasy days," Carl said, ringing the buzzer on the mahogany door.

A tuxedoed captain checked Carl's name and led them into a bar room badly decorated with maple furniture, leather and hunting prints. Their coats were taken and they walked into a dining room brightened by brass chandeliers and red table linens.

"Well, this is right nice. Let's have cocktails and a leisurely dinner," Carl said. "Now, name your poison."

Dany, Maria and Benny liked the sweetness of the whiskey sours and Veronique was happy with her Coke, but Carl thought his bourbon sour was too sugary.

"No problem. If you all look at the menus I'll go to the bar and have this changed. I'll be right back."

Veronique watched Carl at the bar explaining how to fix his drink. In a second he was shaking hands with three middle-aged men in workclothes who looked like farmers. They stood at the bar circling a young fellow in a workshirt and denims. He was rugged and energetic looking though he was spare and sinewy. The older men seemed proud to be introducing him to Carl, as if they were showing off a trophy. Carl spoke for a moment and returned to the table.

"Now the bartender knows how to make a sour sour. What are we all having for dinner?"

During the meal Veronique watched the laughing group at the bar as they downed their neat whiskies. Their voices grew louder and more raucous as they affectionately jostled and poked the young man who amiably accepted their attention.

The service was slow but the dinner was delicious. Carl regaled them with spicy gossip about the skaters and the intrigues of changing relationships as the tour of the ice show went on year after year.

"Thank you, Carl, but we cannot have brandies." Dany reminded them of the time and how much work waited for them in the morning. "I am sure a taxi can be called for us and you can stay if you feel like drinking."

"I promise I will not get drunk but I do like my bourbon, you know." Carl paid the bill and as they stood at the front of the bar room waiting for their coats, he said good night. In a second he was back at the bar, inviting his new friends to join him with a nightcap, moving a barstool next to the handsome young fellow and earnestly starting to chat.

In a flash Veronique remembered. Carl reminded her of that man in Chicago. Urban Powell, the man who sent the champagne cocktails to the table when she was with Howard at the Pump Room.

"Waiting for you in the Variety Club on the second floor. Howard."

Veronique crumbled the note and thanked the desk clerk. She walked across the lobby to the elevator. It was late and she was weary. The flight had seemed endless, to Chicago, a waitover, then another plane that stopped in Cincinnati before arriving in Philadelphia an hour behind schedule. Veronique sighed. She didn't believe in premoni-

357

tions but she wondered if this trip were an error in judgment.

Pressing the bell at the door of the Variety Club, she thought, another bar, another place that looked like a speakeasy. But she didn't feel like a John Held flapper and she wasn't sure what these places were like in the twenties, anyway. There was Howard in his rumpled tweed jacket and his unpressed flannels, holding a beer, smoking a cigarette. She stood in the vestibule and he looked up from his glass, smiling. Her disagreeable premonition was forgotten. He looked tired and more disheveled than usual but he felt good as he wrapped his arms around her.

"I got tired of waiting in the lobby. The plane was late, right? Oh, you look fine," he said as they stopped kissing. "Mighty fine. Are you hungry? Want a drink?"

"No, thanks. I feel as if I've been in these clothes for a month. What a long trip!"

"Look, have a shower and come back down here. Then we can have a drink and go to the all night place for sandwiches." He kissed her again. "I'll be at the bar."

He was drinking scotch when she came back. They moved to a table in the back room, noisy and bright with jolly people from the shows playing in town, a group at the piano singing songs from "Fiorello."

"Would you like a scotch?" Howard held her hand; he kept kissing her. "It'll pick you up."

"Why not?" Somehow she thought this was the time to try it.

They talked until closing time. He wanted to know all about Iowa and the ice show but he avoided most of her questions. "If this job with the ballet company doesn't work out I'll worry later, but I like the road. I know nobody likes touring but I do. There's always something new, a new town with new places to see and new people to meet. The vagabond existence, I suppose, but maybe I'm a gypsy."

Veronique asked about Paul and the group from the

play.

"No, he's not coming in. He has a new girl and they went somewhere with her friends." The other pals had gone to some big party on Rittenhouse Square.

"Didn't you want to go with them?" Veronique asked.

"I was waiting for you," Howard said. "Ready to go? Veronique, aren't you hungry?"

"No, not at all." She was feeling buoyant and light, as if she were on a raft floating over rippling waves. If this was what scotch did, it wasn't bad at all. There was a delicious sense of mischief when they kissed in the elevator going up to her room. Was this what Alix called "a little bit tipsy"?

She was like a greedy child, impetuous and full of curiosity, loving the feeling of breathless craving without any sense of time. She had no idea how long they'd been in bed but suddenly the fog rolled back. Howard's hands were cold. The mist evaporated. He felt dry against the shiny, warm oiliness of her body. Daylight quickly filled the room. He had been acting she was sure of it. He'd been giving a performance.

Veronique was awake early and she wanted to go to the dining room for the proper breakfast Howard loved so much. It wasn't easy waking him, he was like a spoiled boy buried under the blankets. She didn't want to be snappish but too many thoughts were clicking in her head and she didn't want them there. Getting out of the room was all she could think of. Tomorrow was Sunday and he was flying to Toronto. She was taking the morning train to New York.

As a child she had never liked puzzles. She was short-tempered and impatient with the riddles that fascinated other kids. She controlled her temper now but she had a feeling that the solution to a puzzle did not come easily, solving mysteries had nothing to do with maturity.

Veronique remembered the first nights when they had gathered at Downey's and Ralph's; the actors' hangouts

359

where the gang met for drinks after the performance. Was it so long ago? The Variety Club had the same atmosphere but now the group came in and out, stopping for a last drink, a final goodbye before leaving Philadelphia.

"I'm sure you will find a new job in no time at all and I'll be seeing you in the fitting room in a few weeks." Veronique was reassuring but she wondered if they would ever see each other again; if their paths would ever cross. Making rounds and doing auditions was a gloomy prospect for any actor.

It was a relief when Paul suggested playing games. As usual, Howard won the Verse and Song game; softly crooning the words to some seldom sung Broadway show tune.

"Let's play Association," Paul said. "Then somebody else can win besides Howard."

They played a few rounds and Paul's date was very good at guessing the famous personality that had been described when she asked the abstract questions.

"You're too smart, Linda." Paul was pleased that she was bright and relaxed. It wasn't easy being a new face in a crowd that had been on tour for months. "We'll try to stump you this time. Turn away for a minute, please."

Linda walked away while they tried to choose a new name for her to guess. Howard wanted cigarettes and went to the machine next to the bar.

"How about Eleanor Roosevelt? Cole Porter?"

"Joe Kennedy? Mary Martin?" Names were suggested in whispers.

Howard had stopped at the bar. Veronique saw him gesture to the bartender, accepting the offer of a drink from a swarthy, foreign looking man.

"Veronique," Paul said, snapping his fingers at her for attention. "We're choosing Howard. I don't think he'll be back for this round."

"Sorry," Veronique said. "I wasn't listening."

Linda came back to the table and asked "What color is

360

this person?"

"Earth colors. Autumn leaves," came the answers.

"What period in history?"

"This moment. Edwardian London, the Mauve decade."

"La Belle Epoque," Paul answered.

"I don't have to ask for a place then, do I?" Linda hesitated for a second. "What drink?"

"Port," was the response. "A fine old Port. Tawny."

"What cloth, what sort of fabric?"

"Mmm, cashmere, silk. Expensive!"

"What form of travel does he remind you of?" Linda stopped. "It is a man, isn't it?"

"First class. First class anything."

"What kind of literature?" Linda was asking the questions faster now.

It was Paul's turn again. "Rimbaud. Proust." Then he added, "Maybe a bit of Jean Genet."

Would she like this person? Did any of them like this person, Veronique wondered. Over at the bar Howard was enjoying his conversation with the stranger.

"Come on, Veronique. Pay attention," Paul said. "What car?"

"Sorry." Veronique couldn't take her eyes away from the bar, another drink was being ordered. "Well, I might have said a limousine but why has it taken me so long to know . . . it's definitely a convertible."

"I have it!" Linda cried out. "Howard, it's Howard, isn't it?"

Veronique stood up, walked through the room, past the bar to the coatroom and out to the elevators. The sound in her head was a siren, a shrill alarm clock and beyond the ringing were dim voices, faintly calling her. Don't go, Veronique! Oh, please don't leave! Please . . . but she had to keep moving. The ringing persisted.

"Veronique! Wait a minute!" It was Paul coming after her in the hallway.

"Leave me alone. I'm fine—"

"I know that but listen to me. What you just saw at the bar, Veronique—"

"Doesn't he ever stop, Paul? What is he like when I'm not around?"

"You're too good for all this and I've wanted to talk to you—"

"You don't have to—"

The night in Sioux City, that night in the restaurant with Carl Brandon. The farmhand in the jeans and the admiring older men. Why did she understand it now?

"Howard's a confused guy. He can't help himself, Veronique."

"Why? Why?"

She shut the door to her room, emptied the drawers of her clothes and began to pack her valise. The knock on the door stopped the screeching in her head. Howard came in and without a word sat on the bed, watching her pull clothes from the closet.

"I don't know what we have been doing." She found her voice at last. "And I don't think you will tell me but I have to get out of here." She gasped for breath, her voice was low. "I have to get away from you, Howard. Somehow, I feel ashamed and embarrassed and I don't know why." She glared at him, sitting on the bed staring at his reflection in the closet door mirror. "Your friends were just describing you in a game. It wasn't very flattering and a comparative stranger was able to guess that it was you!" She turned her back to him, reaching for her dresses in the closet.

"Veronique, I want to tell you but I'm not sure I can. There has been so much that I've been trying to change." He said it like a pleading little boy. "You really don't know me. I've been trying to be someone that I can't possibly be."

"All the romantic things I thought about you are nothing but weakness. And you're a cheat, Howard. You can't resist a glance from any stranger at a bar! You have to be

362

constantly admired. Is that why you liked me around? For my admiration, too? How dishonest! Not to me but for yourself!"

"Veronique," his voice was a whisper. "I thought—"

"That I made you look better? Was that a part of it too? It isn't what you are or what you can't be. What you are doing at this very minute is the dreadful part, Howard. And you aren't aware of it! Somewhere along the way, Howard, you'll have to admire someone else. You'll just have to! You're sitting here talking to me but you're looking at yourself in the mirror. Howard, you're not looking at me . . . you're looking at yourself!"

Veronique walked away from the closet, put her clothes in the valise and snapped it shut. She picked up her shoulder bag, the valise and dropped the room key on the bed. At the door she turned and he was still staring at himself in the mirror.

Veronique walked into the apartment on Sunday morning. The little red light was lit under the coffee maker; she knew Dany must be in bed reading the *Times*. She knocked at the bedroom door and Dany called out.

"Veronique?"

"Yes, it's me." She went in. Dany was on the bed, in her robe, with the Sunday papers spread out around her, the discarded sections tossed on the floor.

"You're very early."

"I took the last train out of Philadelphia." She didn't know what to say, what to hide, how much truth could she tell. It wasn't sympathy she wanted and it was difficult to admit stupidity. But that's what it was. Plain naive stupidity. Maybe Dany would begin, maybe she'd ask a question.

"Are you all right, *chérie?*"

"Yes," Veronique began. "No, I'm not. Oh, Maman!" And if she cried Dany would be annoyed. We don't cry, she'd say, but Veronique couldn't stop. She could hardly say maman. Her voice cracking and spilling into gasps and it was impossible to move. She didn't want to run off to her room, she didn't want to sit. She wanted to stand there and keep on sobbing. Then the words were spewing out, she was telling Dany about last night. The man at the Variety Club bar, the association game. She told Dany about her doubts and the questions she'd been afraid to ask. Why she found Carl Brandon embarrassing and he'd reminded her of someone—the host at the party in Chicago. Her suspicions after the incident at the Iowa restaurant.

Dany got up from her bed and took Veronique by the shoulders, moving her to the little boudoir chair in front of the fireplace.

"I knew," Dany said.

"You knew? Why didn't you tell me?"

"How could I? Would you have listened? Haven't you always been free to learn in your own way? The way I gave you the scissors when you were little. Remember?"

"I can't get his face out of my mind." Veronique was limp and exhausted. "Oh, Maman, the look on his face, like a lost poet."

"Are you going to defend him because he looked poetic?" Dany sounded angry. "Don't defend him. And save me from the poets, Veronique! Frightened, timid people. Relentlessly selfish and spoiled. Beautiful, yes, but what do you do with that beauty? He is not hanging on the wall at the Louvre waiting to be admired."

"Maybe he'll change. Maybe he'll learn."

"Change?" Dany touched Veronique's shoulder. "Oh, *chérie* don't become one of those women who think they're so alluring they can change the man. Never! He won't change. Find a cynic, Veronique. Cynics wear armor to hide their vulnerability. I know. I almost spent my life with one. They can survive because under their skepticism they're filled with wonder. You laugh with the cynics.

Oh, how I used to laugh with Mac. Have you been laughing with Howard?"

"No, there wasn't much laughter." Veronique was almost apologizing. "But the look of him, that mystery. Not knowing what was beneath that splendid look."

"Nothing! A lazy, timid beauty waiting for the next bidder. Maybe the true poet can be under the cynic's armor but timidity is what hurts, Veronique. Lying back and waiting. Experience is breathing and experimenting! I don't know why I knew so positively when I first saw Howard Cronin but I'd seen him many times before. Beautiful and waiting for admiration." Dany knelt and held Veronique's face tenderly. "Admiration from the wrong direction. You deserve admiration yourself, my darling. I always say we don't cry. You can cry now and get it over with. But I'd prefer if you didn't. He's not worth your tears. I wish you weren't so hurt, Veronique."

Twelve

Veronique brushed sand off her forehead and wiped her sunglasses with the edge of her towel. "It may not have been conscious but I never allowed anything sloppy in my life after Howard. I didn't indulge in what I considered to be careless behavior. Instead I became an onlooker."

"And you didn't want anything to be yours, Veronique? Dany collected the warm memories, not you."

"And apparently she's hidden a few, too." Veronique looked over her glasses at David. "So you don't think my memories are warm and cherished?"

"Do you? You've said it yourself, you wanted a monochrome apartment with none of your mother's blushing colors. And, my darling, out here in your house the gallery of photographs is all Dany's, not yours."

"You think I went too far by refusing to collect? Maybe it was another form of rebellion."

"A sterile one," David said. "And after this fellow, Howard, there was no one at all?"

"Auntie Alix entered the scene! She'd just divorced her Hampton husband and in the accountancy firm handling her settlement she met her idea of the perfect Mr. Right-for-me. Have you ever known anyone who has no color? Someone incredibly nice, kind and intelligent and, well, colorless."

"You're describing thousands of people. And you know that you're wrong. You probably didn't want to see the color."

"Clever David." Veronique leaned over to kiss his cheek. "Do you believe me, running on this way?"

"High time," David said. "Go on."

"Not much to tell. His name was Myron. Can you imagine? I couldn't bear the name and I couldn't think of anything else to call him. I tried Ron but it didn't fit him. Really! Now I'd think what's wrong with Myron. But I was young, a baby recovering from Howard Cronin. Though I did enjoy going out with Myron and his friends who were all older, much older. Business friends, colleagues and they treated me as an exotic sprite. Myron's nymph. I thought about Lolita but Myron wasn't that much older. He only behaved that way to adapt to his friends. Winters in Palm Beach, summers here in Southampton. A life of utter conformity. His club, his house full of his family's furniture. Even in bed he was very proper and we weren't in bed that often." Veronique opened the thermos to pour some iced tea. "Not before we were married, not before the engagement was announced.

"Alix opened in a play that winter. Not a hit but it was Christopher Fry and she was superb in it. I knew some of the cast. They'd been in the *Coriolanus* company and I went out with them a few times. It was fun. I hadn't realized how much I'd missed the evenings of dishing and listening to theatre people talk. Myron's group, well, they were civilians."

"You weren't used to squares, after all," David said.

"I'd been trying but it wasn't working. Myron had proposed and I almost said yes. Until those evenings sitting around a table and talking show biz!" Veronique laughed. "Not very mature, thinking that way. But, David, a life on Fifth Avenue and in Florida! Not working unless I became a decorator or dabbled in watercolors. I couldn't do it. I think Dany was relieved. She was afraid I might accept Myron though she wouldn't admit it. And I started to see more of the old crowd at night after their shows. Drinking too much and then it was summer. Weekends at Fire Island at the Pines where everyone was as handsome as Howard. Too much tequila, marijuana and watching. The boys, the girls, whoever. I became the supreme voyeur. There you have it. Do you wonder why I haven't talked about my *warm* memories?"

"Veronique, I wouldn't call them colorless!" David said. "And Dany, she never gave you any motherly advice?"

"She'd always gone on about that clear sense of independence she'd given me."

"She was right but how do you think she's seen your life? Now I mean."

"With unspoken disapproval, I guess. I've shut everyone out until the past few weeks. Until you, David Wilfrid. Oh, I had my friends but for years I haven't allowed anyone to come near me."

"And I'm near you now." David lifted the sunglasses from her eyes, his lips moving over her face. "Come on into the ocean with me. I want to feel you wet and salty, messy and sloppy. And I promise you it will be beautiful."

Veronique and David were puzzled standing at the open doorway. Belinda's directions to find the house were clear; the third white house with gray shutters past the railroad tracks, on the right side after the tennis court.

368

David shrugged. "Hello?"

"Hi," came a voice from somewhere in the back.

"Hello! I'll be right down!" Belinda called from up the stairs.

"Hi, I'm Kenny Zeller." The enormous man coming to greet them looked like a bouncer in a gangster movie, his white sweat shirt and loose tennis shorts accentuated his tremendous bulk. Not a bouncer, Veronique thought, a bodyguard. "Glad you could come over. Let's go out in the back, we'll stay by the pool." He led them through a small living room into a huge kitchen and out to a garden. "I'm sorry but she insisted I watch the oven while she was dressing and I didn't hear the car."

"I apologize!" Belinda was panting, coming out behind them and trying to finish the yarn bow holding her hair back. "I was so busy cooking all afternoon I lost track of the time. I'm happy to see you. Tell Kenny what you're drinking."

"You have a lovely garden." David admired the pots of geraniums, the daisies and day lilies surrounding the wooden deck.

"Isn't it terrific? Kenny does it. I cook and he gardens, when we're not playing tennis. I just started lessons this year. I'm not very good but I love it."

"You're good." Kenny brought their drinks from the small bungalow at the end of the liver-shaped pool.

"Not yet," Belinda laughed as she took her glass. "We're the two biggest players the instructor has ever seen. The oven! I almost forgot! Veronique, will you help me in the kitchen?"

The big room was a hodgepodge of rustic furniture, formica counters and provincial tile walls with old copper pots and baskets dangling on hooks from the ceiling beams.

"Kenny's terrific. We've just had our second anniversary. I can't believe it." Belinda opened the oven, taking

369

out a pan of small pancakes. "Veronique, this David Wilfrid is divine! Do you mind, there's a bowl of cream there in the fridge. These have to be eaten while they're hot. Wait till you taste them!"

Veronique watched Belinda quickly arrange an iron-stone platter with the food. Belinda was so noncommittal in the workroom it was a jolt to see her bouncy and ebullient in the kitchen.

"Kenny lived here with his first wife. She died four years ago; it wasn't easy at first but I love it now," Belinda whispered. "Grab those napkins, please."

Veronique followed her out to the garden.

"Now try one of these, David. Put a dab of sour cream on top."

"It's a potato pancake!" David exclaimed.

"Kenny's mother taught me. Isn't it the best thing you've ever put in your mouth?"

"The lady here is turning out to be a damn good cook," Kenny said proudly.

"I was always a good cook, good old Wasp cuisine, but now I'm a champ at ethnic. Oh, I wish you were staying for dinner, I've made stuffed cabbage. Have you ever tasted that?"

"Long ago in my house in Blackpool."

"Blackpool?" Kenny didn't know where it was.

David asked for another drink. He told them about the Wilfrids and the tradition of their theatre; he described growing up in a house where a line reading or rehearsal might be interrupted by Aunt Jenny serving up her Alsatian dishes, the cooking that was her way of maintaining that sense of tradition.

"All my life I wanted to do something creative but I had to take over my father's business," Kenny said. "And I had no talent. Making maternity dresses, that's creative?"

"When you do it better than your father it sure is,

370

sweetheart," Belinda said.

"I'm trying to talk my wife into designing for me but she's scared."

"Belinda, that should be exciting," Veronique said.

"No thanks. Nothing to do with another fitting room. I'm frightened enough now, but at least I have Dany to talk for me. I love doing my sketches but then I'd like to go to sleep and wake up after all the costumes are on the stage and the curtain is coming down. I don't want to be the boss's wife in another fitting room. No, I want to try something new where I can work by myself. Now that I'm in the awesome of my life."

"Autumn, honey." Kenny rested his big hand on Belinda's knee. "She does it all the time!"

"What did I do now?"

"Autumn," Kenny corrected. "Autumn of my life."

Belinda giggled. "I *do* do it all the time, don't I? Want to tell David about my spelling?"

"Are you aware of that?" Veronique asked.

"Aware! Kenny wants to be creative and I want to learn how to spell!" Belinda blew a kiss to Kenny. "He understands me and that's all that matters."

"It's true," Veronique said. "Having someone who understands."

"You don't care about seeing your work come to life?" David asked.

"Later, on the stage. I can do without the nit-picking in the fitting room," Belinda said.

"Aren't we a peculiar lot? I know a set designer in London who won't read the script," David said. "He asks to have the play described to him and he does a remarkably good job without ever reading it."

"Want to go to London, Belinda?" Kenny asked.

"Oh, I read the script. It's the making of the costumes that I can't stand!" Belinda said.

"Strange," Veronique said. "I hate the fitting room

too. The noise, the endless fussing and the chatter."

"Chatter! At least you think quickly," Belinda said. "You and your mother! I have to keep quiet because I can't think fast enough." She ate the last pancake. "One avant-garde ballet, that would be stimulating. Something minimalist. I'd like that."

"If you'd get paid," Kenny said.

"If you had a proper budget," Veronique added.

"Designed in point of spree, maybe." Kenny seemed delighted to rib Belinda.

"What's that?" David asked.

"You know all of her mistakes, Kenny?" Veronique asked. "Do you know what *point d'esprit* is, David?"

"The net with all the dots woven in?"

"Very good!" Belinda said.

"But Belinda makes it sound like a summer resort!" Kenny said.

"We really must go, David," Veronique said. "Look at the time."

"You didn't see the house. When are you coming out again?" Belinda asked.

"Next week we do the dress parade and then off to Boston," Veronique said. "Cross your fingers! Three weeks, then into New York."

"And home, right after the opening," David said. "I'm taking Veronique home to England."

"Oh, marvelous! Marvelous!" Belinda exclaimed.

"She loved hearing about England." Belinda and Kenny were waving as Veronique and David drove away. "Belinda loves to be the first to get the news," Veronique said.

"I had a good time," David said.

"So did I. They look like a couple of grizzly bears and they're really angora kittens."

"Kittens who are mad for each other."

"Yes," Veronique said. "That's the way it's meant to

be, isn't it?"

"It is, my darling. It is."

"No tricks, David, and no hunger. No grasping and clinging—"

"Us," David said. "Eyes together, lips meeting. One being, Veronique. *Us,* together."

Veronique drank the last of her coffee, put the morning paper to the side of her worktable and stared at the blackboard: Mon., Tues., Wed., Fittings, *Villa Affair*. Thurs., Dress Parade, *Villa Affair*.

Final fittings, showing the clothes to the producers, the director, and David. Next week dress rehearsal. Boston in July would be hot, she remembered it was always hot up there. Veronique congratulated herself for not having a cigarette. It wasn't fair to cheat or to break her promise to David. Almost three weeks without a cigarette. It had been easier than she expected. Whenever she inadvertently reached for the pack she immediately imagined David's hand covering hers, his signal not to take one and after a few deep breaths the yearning disappeared, the feel of David's hand lingered.

David's play. Dany had promised Elsa she'd be back for the out-of-town opening. Dany, bubbling with excitement and full of small talk about Alix and the Riviera, stories about Renee.

Veronique wanted the week to fly by. Dany was going to be surprised when she saw the stage in Boston. She'd say she wouldn't have taken the holiday if she'd known. A play set in the Thirties with a small cast, Elsa's exquisite sketches brought to reality. And, oh, are there questions waiting for you, Maman! And important things for you to hear! In six weeks, she would be leaving for London with David! It didn't seem possible to think of it without doubt. But Veronique was sure, absolutely certain. She longed for a cigarette now, laughing to herself. Why did she think it was going to be easy? With Dany?

Ryan came to the table with his usual container of yogurt. "Good morning. Do you know how marvelous you look? What a weekend by the sea will do!"

"Yes, I think I do know. And I'm not hiding it, am I? That's what's marvelous."

"Sweetie, it should happen to me." Ryan put his hands together at his chest in a gesture of prayer.

"It will. Want to check the beading department before anything else? They know Thursday is dress parade, don't they?" She squeezed Ryan's arm as they walked to the embroidery frames. To think only a few weeks ago she was accused of being prim!

"I almost forgot, at the last minute on Friday Elsa asked to make the blue dress looser." Ryan turned the frame to see the gun metal beading. "She asked if you'd look at some old *Stage* magazine pictures. She wants to achieve that utter nonchalance, the look of the dress about to fall from the shoulder. Poised but unposed! Are you ready for that one?" Ryan was impersonating Elsa's precise, high-toned voice.

"What is she talking about? It either falls off the shoulders or it doesn't. Damn, where are the pictures?" Veronique asked.

"I have the magazine on my table. Look at it, you'll think of something."

"I thought I'd seen all of the research." Veronique went back to her table. Designers! Why was Elsa worrying now? At the last minute.

How fascinating to see Renee Hugo in a dark bias-cut satin gown, a candid shot from a club like El Morocco and the other pictures. They were taken in Dany's first fitting room up the stairs on Fifty-fifth Street. In 1939. The story at the side of the page was about the revival of that first play, the comedy Arthur Bellamy produced.

"We were privileged to be invited to the studio of costumier Dany Mounet. There in her fitting room that looks like a comfortable Parisian salon we watched the master designer Louis Ostier supervise his elegantly witty costumes for Renee Hugo. It is not often that New York gets to see a production that originated in a French boulevard theatre. The turn of the century farce played there last season to packed houses and the word is out; the 'succés fou' will be repeated here on Broadway in December. The members of the French production staff are enamored of our town. Madame Mounet says she felt she had been here before, in another life perhaps. When Arthur Bellamy commissioned her to come to our shores last year Dany Mounet said it was a blessing from the Gods. 'My husband had died in December and I . . .'"

Where had this magazine been? Dany always said she hated interviews. This was why. The words on the page jumped like the letters on an optical chart. December! Veronique looked up, Elsa had arrived, she was talking to Nancy at the doorway to the workroom. Deciding what kind of sandwich to order. She'd be coming over in a second to ask if Veronique was going to lunch with her.

Veronique wanted to run out of the room, out to the street. She couldn't go screaming out of the workroom like a deranged woman but she wanted to. She wanted to yell out to everyone, to Nancy and Elsa and Ryan, to all of them.

December! Veronique wanted to shout. Simon Mounet died eleven months before she was born. Simon Mounet wasn't her father!

"Veronique, what's happened?" David asked when he telephoned. "What's wrong?"

"Can I meet you later at your hotel? It's insane, David, but I discovered something new today. Another hidden fact. I have to get out of this house. I have to breathe!"

"Tell me. Look, I can leave the theatre now," David said.

"But I can't. Day after tomorrow is dress parade and—"

"You said it was all quite organized."

"It is but Elsa keeps fussing and the way she's been eyeing me all day you'd think it was her life. I'll meet you at the Wyndham at five."

Veronique gave him the magazine as soon as she walked into his room. She sat, watching him as he read the old article, waiting for his reaction. She reached for her bag and David looked up.

"Veronique, please don't have a cigarette."

"I stopped carrying them. I want my handkerchief. Well, do you see? The time? Simon Mounet died in December."

David listened to her as he opened the bottle of wine chilling in the ice bucket.

"Veronique, you never had a father. Simon Mounet was whatever you wanted him to be. You didn't know a father except for the stories your mother told you."

"That's right," Veronique said. "A loving, dedicated, fragile man who died before I was born. He was going to be a brilliant doctor. I heard all that but why didn't she tell me about my real father? She never told the truth! Charlotte and Gerard perished in the war . . . lies! Lies and secrets. Soon after Simon died she was with another man. Who was he?"

"My darling, does it matter now?"

"David! He could be alive somewhere—"

376

"I doubt it. A lie hurts more than a secret. Secrets evaporate, they lose importance but lies can come back to plague the liar. Unless the ones who knew the truth are dead. Dany may have been that lucky."

"No." Veronique grabbed the magazine. "Because there is this. She always said she hated publicity and didn't need it. No interviews! Because of this. An old magazine buried in the files of a library."

"Your mother had to have reasons. If I hadn't written this play, if we hadn't met you'd know none of this. You would have gone on as you were a month ago. Dany would have nothing to tell. All right, she'll tell you now. She'll tell us. Getting to this point hasn't been so bad, has it? She's a remarkable woman, your mother. She created a successful business, she made a place for herself in a world she loves very much and you're none the worse for it, I'd say."

"An imagined, fantasy world."

"Have your wine and listen. I have more of Uncle Barney and Aunt Jenny in me than whatever I may have inherited from my mother and my father. We grew up in different houses, Veronique, we were raised in different ways but we were loved. You weren't Oliver Twist out in the streets stealing for Fagin."

"David!" She had to interrupt him. "You know who your parents were."

"Yes. Look what I found out." He pulled his chair closer to hers. "We have been ready for this in some strange way. Some alchemist has mixed a brew that has brought us together."

"That is why I must know. Dany isn't one for magic potions. Why have we lived this way? A lovely, busy life in a very attractive world, not truly superficial but maybe it was. With so many things locked up. Protecting each other from hurt when we should have talked and helped each other.

377

"All those costumes year after year. A house full of fabrics and dressmaker dummies. The ideal place for hiding. For silences. A no-man's-land between the workroom and the stage door of the theatre. No real world existed. Do you know that when there was a meeting to negotiate prices Dany sent Nancy. Dany didn't like going out very much, not to face a discussion about budgets, figures, facts! I wasn't permitted to go. 'You've no head for business, my darling,' she'd say. I found seclusion in the workroom too. I made it my haven after Howard. Then Myron. Later I took up with the old gang of gypsies. Ryan and his crowd. Was that a real world? But I chose it and we know why."

"Go on." David said it very softly.

"Oh yes, I went to Europe. Twice. All shut up and tight, trying to have a good time. I loved the scenery and museums, the ballet, the opera. *Otello* in the courtyard of the Doge's Palace. But Venice without a lover? I didn't find a gondolier, one of the boys I was with did that."

"Veronique. You were adamant, you weren't allowing any possibilities for a lover."

"David, you always know! After the opera one night we went to a club, Ciro's, I think it was. A late night place where you could have a good supper, drinks. They had a dance floor. The bar was, you know, quite a gay bar. I saw a group of people, very typical somehow. An attractive man, Italian and not young. Open collar, turned back cuffs over his navy blazer, a fine gold chain around his neck. Tan, very tan, with white hair. He must have been devastating when he was younger. And a woman, a hawk of a woman. Truly avaricious and the two of them were hovering over this very good-looking, very blond fellow. It took a second but I recognized him. Only his hair was blonder and he was older. A layer of youth like a film of makeup on an old face. It

378

was Howard. Quite drunk, all three of them. I didn't say a word, I wrapped my scarf over my head as if I were going to church and walked through the bar. Right past them."

She leaned forward, kneeling on the floor, burying her head against David's chest. "I've been on the periphery of everything in life. Just outside and I don't mean on the edge. Oh no, I took no chances there—where danger is. Just outside. Watching. That's all I've been doing. Maybe I've always known that pieces were missing." She looked up at him, unable to control her tears. "Do you want some weepy, frail thing around your neck now?"

"You weren't a weepy thing this weekend, my love."

"Dany used to say we don't cry. Maybe I held back these tears by taking seclusion in the workroom."

"Was that Dany's fault, Veronique?" David asked.

"No, goddamn it!" She stopped for a second. "But if only she'd talked to me. If she had told me. The two of us, hiding. She dropped her own curtain after Mac Roth was killed. I realized that but there was more. And I was hurt. Oh, David, how many straws can be the last?"

He was smiling at her, beginning to laugh.

"You're going to make fun of me?" She started to laugh, too. "I'm better now."

"You're fine," David said.

"All the questions. At the fittings I think of the real people and I wonder where the connections were. Where they are now."

"Veronique, it isn't like tragedy in the theatre. Everyone dead on stage at the final curtain. Swords and blood and poison. Tragic happenings are assimilated, we're tough and we absorb. We're affected but we go on and we improve. Dany will be back in ten days. You'll know everything then. You'll talk to her as you never have before."

"I can't wait. I want to know now."

"Pick up the phone." David looked at his watch. "It's just past midnight there. Go on, make the call. Ask Dany to come home."

Thirteen

1980

"Renee! You look beautiful!" Dany called out before the driver opened the car door.

"You too, little one." Renee came down the chipped stone path. Her step was vigorous, the same long strides, as though she were making an entrance and the audience was applauding. "Oh, I'm so happy you are here at last."

"Twenty years, Renee. It's been twenty years."

Was Renee lying too? The scent of Muguet de Bois was strong as ever but the pale powder failed to hide the crosshatch webbing around her cupid's bow lips, little pouches of flesh were pulling the round cheeks toward the shortened neck. Yes, she was older but her hair remained short and lacquered black, her eyes were young and alert and still edged with kohl. The pale blue voile falling loose over her body was neither dress nor peignoir. When you're fat, you're fat. Dany remembered their first meeting at the Ritz more than forty years ago. The canary voice had more rasp now.

"Don't worry about your baggage. Selene, where are you? She will take care of everything. Madame Mounet is here, come fetch the luggage!" Renee trilled instructions, dismissing the chauffeur. "Here it is, this is where I live." The wrought iron gate squeaked in its rusty hinges. "Not much larger than the green rooms in some of the theatres I've played, but I love it. I have to love it, it was all I could afford. Oh, I am thrilled to see you, little one!" Renee squeezed Dany's hand and led her to the house.

The thin woman rushing past them to the car grinned, showing too many teeth. "Bonjour, Madame," she smiled.

"This is Selene. She takes care of me. She cooks like a dream. You will see."

The path was bordered with marguerites and overgrown with nasturtium and roses. Mimosa and wisteria poured over trellises beyond the house clashing with drooping bougainvillea; all of it excessive and haphazard.

"I go nowhere. Where is there to go? I've seen it all and this is enough. A good table and the gardens. Have you ever seen such a garden? I have grapes! I read, I have the telephone, and I eat. That is obvious, isn't it? I walk to the village and they know me there. I am still the star when I go marketing. Can you believe? Yes, me! I market!"

The front room had low ceilings and it was small and cluttered. Books and magazines were stacked on tables as shaky as the front gate. Portfolios and folders leaned against the sides of the faded toile-covered sofa, watercolor landscapes and drawings were scattered on the whitewashed walls and the soft chairs were a blue cotton almost matching the Provence sky. Flowers crammed in round porcelain bowls were everywhere. It was a room full of carelessness and affection, clearly it was Renee's house.

"Do you want a nap? A bath?" Renee asked.

"I dozed in the car. A bath will be nice, but later, *chérie.*"

382

"Good. Don't bother unpacking, Selene will do it."

The bedroom was tiny and precise as a doll's house. Obviously Selene had been at the room that morning; it was as fresh as the carnations on the bed tables and the color of the garden pinks.

"Do you still drink Cristal, Renee? I brought you a case of it."

"Divine! And we have foie gras. How luxurious of you and to have been driven by limousine!"

"In Paris, I stayed at the Ritz. Why not, after all these years?"

"Exactly, *chérie*. We will have drinks on the terrace. There should be a glorious sunset to welcome you to Aix."

Renee was right. Selene did know how to cook. A bit heavy on the garlic, but a delicious dinner. Fried anchovies. Why couldn't you get them in Watermill? The soft breeze through the orchard cooled the little terrace but it was too pleasant to go in for a shawl. Two old ladies having coffee on a summer night, Dany thought. In no way would she give in to the slight chill in the air.

"Have another bit of mousse, little one?" Renee took a large spoonful for herself and poured more coffee. "So, my beautiful goddaughter, how is she?"

"Beautiful, but not very happy. That is why I came to France. One reason, anyway. I wanted to leave her alone for a while. To run the business by herself. I thought the responsibility of the workroom would be good for her," Dany said. She drank her coffee. "Veronique doesn't love the business the way I did. The way I do. She is waspish and very impatient lately."

"How I wish I could know her. A goddaughter on a

383

telephone every ten years! There's no one in her life?" Renee asked.

"No, not for years. If there were I'd know about it. We live in the same house, we work together every day. Somehow she never seemed interested or she wouldn't allow herself to be. Remember when you were in Hollywood, Renee? Does it seem possible that was the last time we saw each other?"

"It was an impossible time, that hurried dinner at the noisy restaurant everyone said was chic. Le Bistro! And it wasn't." Renee wiped the chocolate mousse she had spilled off her bosom. "I had to be at the studio for makeup at dawn and you were rushing off for fittings in the dressing room of some theatre. What did we talk about? The theatre! What we always talked about and there were other things, weren't there?"

"Well, that's when Veronique asked to have the top floor of the house for her own apartment," Dany said. "Maybe it was selfish of me to give it to her. But it kept us close together and she didn't want to live anywhere else. Never in all these years have I heard the sound of a man's shoes going up those stairs."

"She has friends, doesn't she?" Renee asked. "She is not a recluse?"

"No. She has quite a lot of friends. And what a *lot!*" Dany jeered. "People from the workroom, actors, dancers, all the gypsies. The boys who are too young and too pretty. She overromanticized that first affair; then I suppose she was afraid of any relationship. There is a safety with the boys, a kind of protection."

"She has her young, pretty group. What's wrong with that?" Renee lit a cigarette. "Have a Gitane, they make them with filters now. At least she is not one of those foolish women out to seduce, to conquer and cure the man who prefers other men. We've seen that one." Re-

384

nee took a deep puff of the cigarette. Dany wondered who Renee was thinking of. "Bent on setting a trap and after she has succeeded she is miserable and mean, furious because most likely it was only for one time. Then she is irate and greedy. She wants more and she is spiteful and jealous. How unattractive!" Retirement had not diminished Renee's relish in telling a story.

"And she is always the one, that woman, who is so terribly offended when the normal man, staid and perhaps dull and awfully average, tries to seduce her. In a restaurant, his leg rubs under the table; in a cafe, he sends her a drink and with flirting eyes offers a toast, later his hands move too fast in the back of the taxi and she makes oh such sanctimonious protests. Veronique is not one of those aggressive women."

"No," Dany said. She had to laugh, the man Renee had described reminded her of Myron. "Veronique is not one of those."

"*Chérie,* if she ever does find a man, watch out! You must not be so critical, little one."

"I wanted Veronique to be happier, to have more than I did," Dany said.

"You've never talked like this to Veronique, have you?"

"We never talk seriously. She avoids it." Dany stopped for a moment. "Or I do."

"Precisely. You don't talk. You never did." Renee pursed her lips and shook her head. "Tst, tst. Tell me, little one, in all these years you have not had some clandestine episode? Some secret escapade?" Renee's laugh was as raucous as ever and mischievous. "You can tell me, you know."

"No, I swear." Dany was surprised. "I *did* write that to you. All about Mac. And what might have been. Now, Renee, have you?"

"Hah, no! Not for years." Renee laughed. "But I am older than you and look at me! Not that I wouldn't have liked to. Someone young and far too handsome, the kind of handsome that hurts. Now I think there's a scrim that drops very softly over my eyes when I look in the mirror. It diffuses this third act face, hiding the truth from me and I like it that way because when I apply the lipstick or brush my hair I see through that scrim and I'm thirty-two. Since I see thirty-two, I feel thirty-two. But I knew, *chérie,* I knew. The young lover would not have had the scrim."

"So we settle for a blur, is that it? Life becomes a pair of old eyes seeing the world in soft focus like some avant-garde photographer," Dany said. "I've been thinking about old age since they gave me that silly award a few weeks ago. It's another reason why I came over here. I don't know. Something has been making me restless, driving me and I keep thinking about the past. I'm not dissatisfied, I haven't been for years but maybe I haven't taken the time to think."

"You see? You have had a scrim of your own," Renee said.

"Do you think so?" Dany took a cigarette and poured some wine. "Let's finish this before we go to bed."

"And then we can open another bottle," Renee said, happy to stay up and go on talking.

"When we were driving here today, I wondered. Had I come to France to visit cemeteries. In Paris, I went to Père Lachaise to see the graves of Venard and Ostier. They are not together, as you know, but they may as well be," Dany said. "Disheveled, uncared for graves. It's disgraceful, the condition of that cemetery. No place for quiet tears or recollection when you are surrounded by graffiti and broken bottles. Don't the Parisians care for their dead? I thought here is the hero and the collaborator, both more unkempt than they were in life. It does not matter at all now."

"What matters is that we remember, *chérie,*" Renee said quietly.

"Yes. And I went to Amiens. Oh, what a sad and forlorn town. I put flowers on the Mounet graves and I walked away thinking how fortunate I was. I might have been one of those widows in a black suit and a hat with a veil if I hadn't gone to New York. Why don't you see those women anywhere else but in France? I went to church and thanked God; for what would my life have been had I stayed? A pension from a shirt factory?"

Dany looked at Renee's hand holding her cigarette between the thumb and the forefinger, short puffs of smoke curling into the dark air. She was a van Dongen portrait but the subject had grown old. Don't go away, Dany thought. Please, Renee, stay here for a long, long time.

"Then two days ago," Dany said, "I went to the little cemetery in Beaulieu with flowers for that marble shrine. It is a lovely spot, isn't it? Calm and cooled by the sea. Charlotte and Gerard would have approved of what you selected. Then when I wanted to cry, I couldn't. Because I was told very early that I mustn't cry? Is this what happens at the end of one's life? This crawling melancholy lurking around me. There is more to living, isn't there, Renee? I've never thought about any of this before. There is more, but what is it?"

"Little one," Renee said. "If you knew the ending, why would you sit through the play?"

"Come out! Have your coffee here." Renee called from the terrace. "I'm up early every morning. I get hungry." Renee pouted as if she needed an excuse. "Do

387

you want eggs? I always have an egg. Just one. I'll call Selene and she'll fix you what you like."

"This is fine," Dany said. "I'm not one for a big breakfast. This looks delicious." The round table was covered with a pale pink cloth, stitched daisies floating across the cotton into an elaborate border. Jars of jam, a bowl of fruit and a pitcher of juice were in a provincial style of ceramic. Moustier, it was called, Dany remembered. She lifted the napkin from a basket; the croissants were warm. "Perfect, and this butter. We don't have this at home."

"And you don't have this sky." Renee tore her croissant in half, smearing raspberry preserve on it and a small shower of crumbs fell to the tablecloth. "Look at this day!"

"It's glorious," Dany said. How neatly Simon used to break his breakfast rolls, she remembered. Carelessness and self-indulgence went hand in hand and Renee paid no attention. All that sugar, but Renee never could resist a sweet. "You have more color here than we have at the beach at Watermill. And these butterflies!"

"You know that butterflies are supposed to be our loved ones come back? If it's true, this garden is full of my past. But I'm not happy with ghosts," Renee said. "Wait until you see the countryside. I thought we'd drive into Aix for lunch. You are a tourist, after all, and I must show you the sights. Wear something light. It gets very hot in the afternoon."

"Do you still drive, Renee?"

"Do you see a horse and buggy in the road? Of course, I drive!" Renee laughed.

Renee was cautious behind the wheel. She handled the car as meticulously and effortlessly as she had held the stage when she was acting. "I'm impressed," Dany said. "I've always been impressed by you."

388

"Why, *chérie,*" Renee smiled. "You are giving me a rave review?"

"I am indeed, haven't I always? Do you know how I used to copy you? If it worked for you on the stage or when you walked into a room, then I would try to emulate you. I did your walk, your gestures and when I knew it would be impressive, I made my accent very heavy; that ooh-la-la French that Americans find beguiling. It was a marvelous way to disarm a tough producer when I was working on prices for a new show."

"Ah-hah, so I am responsible for part of the Mounet panache! I am happy to hear that."

"Veronique laughs at me to this day," Dany said. "She catches me at some particular affectation and she giggles. I act as if I don't understand why she is laughing. The twinkle, the way she lets me know that she is in on the joke. Her gray eyes are—"

"Yes. Little one? Go on. Her eyes?"

Dany ignored Renee's insinuating look. "Oh, just twinkling."

Renee stopped the car, pulling up to a siding on the road. "Dany, my mother ran a cafe in Lyon and I helped her at the cash register when I was seven. I knew how to do arithmetic before I went to school. Unless, you were carrying a baby for eleven months it wasn't possible for Veronique to be Simon's daughter." The sunlight dappled the grass under the canopy of plane trees, flickering and soundless. "So don't tell me about Veronique's twinkling grey eyes. I know. She has Gerard's mischievous, merry eyes."

"Why did you never say anything?"

"Because I knew you didn't want to be discovered." Renee put her hand on Dany's shoulder. "We are French, aren't we? There is something about secrets with us."

"Then I don't have to tell you about it? Even now?"

Dany asked.

"*Chérie,* if you had one of those escapades I asked you about last night and you wanted to keep the memory for yourself, wouldn't I understand?" Renee said.

"Yes, Renee. I think you understand more than anyone I've ever known."

Renee started the car. A warm breeze bathed Dany's cheeks when she opened the window. She watched the shadows of the fluttering leaves, the quivering patterns of sunshine on the roadway. She felt easier than she had since she came to France three weeks ago. They were silent as they drove into Aix.

"Have the turbot. Sauce Nantua! Pale pink with those little crayfish. My mouth is watering!" Renee clutched the menu to her bosom, impatient and eager to order lunch. "Lapin is a specialty here and they have oysters in curry, little one!"

"Or a salad Nicoise. I'm thinking of the desserts Selene will surprise us with tonight." Dany looked at the wide veranda of the restaurant, crowded with round tables covered with aquamarine linen, clear crystal, heavy cutlery and yellow roses in small, fat Faience bowls. The canvas umbrellas were greener against the brilliant blue sky.

"A cool white wine, yes? Nothing too sweet, I promise." Renee was carefully planning the meal. "Oh, let's have champagne."

"Yes, let's," Dany agreed. The sense of relief, the happy colors, the bright day called for it. "Definitely champagne."

Renee waved to the captain. They discussed the possibilities of hors d'oeuvres and entrees; two generals plotting the strategies of their next campaign. "Now then." Renee put her elbows on the table, clasping her hands as a cushion for her chin. She pouted. "You said you did not have to tell me but I am absolutely busting to know. May I ask when it happened, *chérie?*"

"Why not?" Dany answered. "May I have a cigarette?"

"You may chain-smoke if you like but tell me, tell me!"

"Do you remember a costume ball you went to with Louis Ostier? You were Helen of Troy and you didn't like wearing black."

"Of course I remember." Dishes of shrimp, olives, artichokes, mussels and mushrooms were placed in the center of the table. Renee purred. "You little devil!"

"There was nothing flirtatious, nothing. It just happened. Charlotte was down here looking for a villa and Gerard was to take me to dinner. He had that desolate look, the hollow expression he got when Charlotte was away. It happened, that's all. We were in the workroom and he touched me. I don't know to this day, but I think that I thought I was offering a gesture of mercy. What egotism! To think—"

"You're not eating, *chérie,*" Renee said softly. "Have I upset you?"

"No, on the contrary. I'm relieved. This is what has been gnawing at me, I suppose. Forty years, Renee! It seems like I have kept this to myself forever. Remember the night when Veronique was born? And the day when they came to say goodbye, one by one. First Louis and then Robert. I was so grateful to you, being there when Gerard came in. Robert was worried about the war and Louis was nervous and timid about the very privacy of motherhood, as if he was intruding in some secret place. Then I watched you when Gerard came in. And I wondered was I fooling Renee or was she on to me? Why didn't I realize you were too good an actress to let me know that you were suspicious?"

"I was loving every second of the scene and flattered,"

Renee said. "After all, I was to be the godmother!"

"You know it's almost as if I were talking about someone else. A simpleminded girl deciding to carry out a lie. The widow of a doctor who had not lived to see his baby born. The timing was perfect though. It was going to be easier in America. I was convincing, wasn't I?"

"You were," Renee said.

"I think I believed it myself that first year. Simon was Veronique's father. I said it over and over."

"You would have been a very good actress."

"Oh, how I dreamed about that when we first came to Paris," Dany said. "To be an actress. Well, I have been, haven't I? The myth I created for Veronique about Simon. I hardly knew him. I realized that later when I was embellishing the story. The way I did the embroidery for a costume. Another row of paillettes, a line of bugle beads and a few more rhinestones. You make it richer with more detail. I did that with stories about Simon and Paris and myself. The creature I made up! I wonder if I really knew him. Excessive, lavish Dany Mounet! There wasn't enough icing on any cake. And such certainty! I seem to have lost it these past few weeks and if I didn't have it I knew how to fake it!"

"I loathe certainty. All those terribly sure of themselves people. No, no; vacillation is attractive. It keeps me going, it stimulates me. What is certainty?" Renee noisily chewed a black olive. "Except death, which I am strongly avoiding. Taste these mushrooms, *chérie*. They're divine!

"Dany, you could not have become anyone else. Not a widow in Amiens, not a dressmaker in Paris. You'd have found your way into the theatre somehow. You'd have met another group of people and learned from them. I don't believe in any of that 'might have been another

392

way' philosophy. There is some invisible magician who touches us with his scepter. We do not invent ourselves, little one. It is just that some of us are clever enough to see what is offered and we find the oyster with the pearl in it!"

Dany laughed. "Oh, darling Renee. How lucky I am to know you!" She was back in Paris in those early days, fascinated by Renee and her worldly chatter. "That must have been the magician's finest touch, having us meet."

"Merci, merci." Renee blew a kiss into the air. "Now get on with your lunch."

"Tell me, Renee, what do you think was your favorite performance?"

"Ah, what a question." Renee lit a cigarette. "I smoke too much, but at this age what does it matter? And it keeps me away from another helping of food. Have this last bit of mussels, the vinaigrette is delicious. My favorite? Does that mean my best? It has to, though the critics may not have agreed. But there were so many! The grand roles and the classics, remember Phedre with all the suffering? And the comedies, the Feydeau and Anouilh with his ephemeral bubbles." Renee inhaled deeply, her fingers extended as she blew a smoke ring. "The best I've ever been? It was not on the stage or in the movies. It was here in Aix in the garden of my house."

"Renee, what on earth do you mean?"

"A young man came to see me. About two years ago. To ask me questions and I knew I must not give him the answers. Come, finish your lunch and I will tell you about it when we get home." She crushed out the cigarette in the ashtray. "Maybe all the secrets have to be told today."

"Are you comfortable?" Renee asked.

393

The webbing of the plastic chair was hot from the afternoon sun, but it didn't matter. "Yes, I'm fine, thank you," Dany said.

Renee stretched out in the other chaise, kicking off her sandals. "A letter came one day from a David Wilfrid. He was staying in Nice for a month and he wanted an interview, to talk to me about his father. He would drive over here one afternoon and he gave the date. Rather a brash note. No question about convenience or if the time was suitable. The note was so curt he could have sent a telegram. There was no return address on his letter. I had no way to write to him, to lie, to say I would not be home that day. That week. Ever! I didn't want the meeting and yet I was curious. How could I not be? I wanted to see what the boy looked like. But I didn't want an interview. You see, I recognized his name instantly."

"You did? Who was he?"

"Gerard's sister was married to a man named Wilfrid," Renee said. "This must be the son. It had to be."

"Renee!" Dany sat up. This wasn't the trivial gossip that used to surprise her when she was alone with Renee. This was what she never expected to hear, what she hoped would never happen. The paths never would cross, she had believed that for how long, for how many years? "I never knew the name. I could have asked but I didn't want to know. The son? Renee, he is Veronique's half brother!"

"Wait, *chérie*," Renee said. "I told you there were secrets."

"But what?" Dany exclaimed. "What did he want. The sister lived in England. Why didn't the boy stay there?"

"He is a writer. He was working on a play about his parents and his father's trial. He had been doing re-

394

search in Nice; he had found the old newspaper files but there was no one he could talk to. No one was still alive except me."

"You said you gave your best performance. Why, Renee?"

"I did." Renee reached for a Gitane. The pack was empty, she crumpled it and dropped it in the ashtray. "Selene!" She called to the kitchen. "Be an angel and bring us cigarettes!" Renee stood up and walked to the trellis wall, touching the mimosa, picking off a branch of dried wisteria. Selene brought the cigarettes, greeting them with her toothy grin.

"You will eat at eight o'clock as always, madame?" she asked.

Renee looked at Dany. *"Comme toujours?"* Dany nodded; food was not on her mind. "Can we eat at nine o'clock tonight, Selene?" Renee asked. "Do you mind?"

"No, madame, not at all. Be careful, it is getting chilly," she smiled.

"Thank you, Selene." Renee moved a chair from the table nearer to Dany. "Do I look my age, Dany, do I? Well, you have not seen me without makeup, *chérie*. And that day he came here, I did not wear any. A bit of pale powder, nothing more. I never played in anything avant-garde, nothing experimental. But, Dany, I missed something. There is much to be said for improvisational theatre. We had it right here on this terrace that afternoon.

"I played a senile woman, a wee bit deaf but with moments of lucidity." Renee began to play the part again. "I should have had a white wig and a tattered parasol. I never played *The Madwoman of Chaillot*, but I always wanted to. I had no props or accoutrements, but what a performance I gave! Oh yes, I wore my reading glasses all afternoon and he was a lovely blur, this David

395

Wilfrid. Ah, if I were forty years younger, I thought. There would have been a seduction scene in this garden instead of an interrogation. Dark eyes, shining black like a coq feather and sunburned skin smooth as lacquer. A marvelous voice, very British but rather brusque. Ah, little one, what an attractive man!

"We had tea. I thought it was appropriate and Selene made strawberry tarts. I thought cucumber sandwiches might be going too far. He spoke French quite well though a bit harsh, like the Alsatians. Alsace, that's where they came from, the Dessaux family, I remembered.

"Thank God it was a warm afternoon. I didn't want him in the house, not with all the pictures and photo albums, the clear reminders of my illustrious but faded past! That may have led to too many more questions. I wanted to get it over with. He was very kind and considerate.

"And he began. 'Can you tell me what you remember about my parents, Charlotte and Gerard Dessaux?' he asked.

" 'Who?' I was suddenly very deaf and quite vague.

"He asked again. 'They were your friends before the war. He produced many of the plays you were in.'

"I took a long time to answer. 'Dessaux? Oh yes, the producer. Yes, I knew him.'

" 'What kind of man was he?'

" 'He was kind,' I said. 'Very kind with great style. There's no style anymore.'

" 'Do you remember the trial?'

" 'I was never in a play about a trial. Every play is a trial. You'll find that out, young man.' "

"Renee, so you pretended to be a deaf old woman," Dany interrupted. "But I don't see why. What were you hiding?"

"Before Gerard died, before that terrible time in Villefranche, he made me promise that I would never tell a soul. And I haven't. I gave David Wilfrid nothing more enlightening about Charlotte's murder than what he had found in the newspaper files." Renee shivered, hugging herself against the strong breeze that rolled over the garden. "What I had promised not to tell was that Gerard was not David Wilfrid's father." She reached for her sandals. "It is getting chilly, *chérie.* Shall we go inside? I think tonight I would like a martini before dinner. A very, very cold one."

The fading sun filled the living room with pale violet light and faint blue shadows. Renee lit the lamps. "Selene likes to save on electricity," she said.

"Renee, please go on with the story. What is all this after so many years?" Dany said. "I'll make the drinks. Do you want vodka or gin?"

"Oh, gin of course. You'll have one too, won't you?" Renee asked. "There a Bombay on the shelf under the table."

The tole tray was set up very professionally; bowls of nuts and olives, lemon and lime on a small cutting board. Dany dropped ice into the cocktail shaker. Wouldn't you know Renee had kept this? Dany remembered the sterling tray in Charlotte's apartment and the cocktail shaker with the silver top, the conical glasses with the thin, thin stems. Not those big glasses made for all the ice everyone in New York always wanted. This was for the perfect cocktail, the way the bartender made them at the Ritz.

"Three olives, please, *chérie.*" Renee said, standing at the table as Dany shook the drinks. "I stir mine, but no matter. Now sit down and listen, little one."

"The child was not Gerard's?" Dany asked. "When I used to think of Charlotte's letter! Her elation, the pleasure of becoming a mother!"

"She was telling you the truth. She was happier than I had ever seen her—for a while," Renee said.

"Do you think that Charlotte suspected Gerard was Veronique's father?"

"Not for a second, *chérie*. If she had any idea, she would have told you the truth. No, she didn't know about it, I'm sure. Charlotte was, and you know I loved her dearly, but Charlotte was thinking only of herself then. Maybe she did that all the time. Oh, she cared about people, Gerard and me and you, but first came Charlotte." Renee sipped her drink. "Isn't that the way most of us are, *chérie?*"

"Maybe, maybe." Dany wondered, was it true? Hopeless egotism, was it a flaw or an inherent trait driving all of them forward? Was it a weakness of her own? "I can't understand it yet. I want to know everything, but Renee, for all those years, the terror I felt and how I wondered. Veronique had a brother in England and she knew nothing of his existence. I wanted it that way. What other way was there?" The sting of the gin was good, too good, Dany thought. She would have to mix another. "Well, go on."

"I warned Charlotte when she went to Villefranche to supervise the redecoration of the villa that winter. I had never given her advice before. She would always confide in me and I would listen but I never interfered. Oh, I'd nod and be sympathetic or I'd shake my head in disapproval, but this time I told her to be careful. No trips to Marseilles, no drives to Genoa. What motherly advice! How pompous of me but I couldn't help myself. I worried. Remember how worried I was before we went to New York?

"Never mind, it happened in another way. She went to see some paintings at a studio up in Cagnes. Everyone

398

was painting somewhere on the Riviera in those days. Matisse and Picasso, Leger, English groups, everybody! She met a young Italian sculptor. He was living across the border in San Remo. His name was Tino, I never heard his surname. I don't know if he ever used it. He was simply called Tino. I have a snapshot of him somewhere, in one of those folders I've saved, crammed with the past. Everybody's past! Always the witness! That is what I would have called my book if I had written it. But why bother? No one has to know what I've seen. Isn't it enough that I've seen it and thank God I can remember it all!" Renee preened, fluttering her eyelashes. She tucked her legs under her and snuggled into the sofa.

"Well, *chérie,* it was not one of her anonymous episodes. This was an affair. Charlotte was mad about him. The villa reflected Tino. His taste, his abstract, odd ideas about natural form and using things found in the earth. Suddenly she was doing a sparse, uncluttered house. Not my taste particularly, but what a house it was! If only it hadn't been shut by the police when you came over."

"She sent me pictures of it," Dany said. "I have them someplace. I've kept my photo albums, too. Charlotte had said she wanted a showplace."

"It was cool and comfortable. And very sleek. She found things nobody had seen. Metal benches and pieces of wood, old vines and roots that became bases for tables. It was nothing like what Sert was doing or Ostier or even Bérard. That Tino, he was very creative. I first met him at a party in Menton. How can I describe him? He had a rawness, a rough crusty sense of style. He was like a workman, a stonecutter with a book of poetry in his back pocket."

"Would you like another martini, Renee?" Dany

asked. "I would."

"I was hoping you'd want one. I wouldn't dream of letting you drink alone, *chérie!*" Renee leaned back against the soft blue cushions, closing her eyes. "One long holiday, those months before the war." She opened her eyes and took the drink from Dany. "Like a grand, expensive ball with endless champagne and no hangovers. In September we suffered. Remember? God, how we paid for all our foolishness. I was very busy that spring and very popular. I had finished the Duvuvier film and I was very thin. You can guess why! Well, it didn't last terribly long. By the time Charlotte came up to Paris, I was eating again." Renee squealed with laughter.

She was savoring the taste of memory. What seasoning was she adding, Dany wondered. Renee's sense of theatrics was too sharp. Could she resist her own spices? Her chronology went off now and then.

"I'll never forget it," Renee said. "June. You've never seen such rain! Hail and windstorms for weeks. Paris was frantic and wet. Parties! One after the other; the blue and white ball, the circus party, a ribbon ball! Truly mad. And Charlotte came from Villefranche to see the doctor. She was pregnant. She was carrying Tino's child.

"I don't know what she said to Gerard, but he became another person. I saw the change. No man had ever been more thoughtful or kind. You know that. Now he was positively solicitous. Charlotte wanted that child and she wanted Gerard to be the father. Simple, she thought. She would break away from this Tino, if Gerard agreed to let her have the baby. It was too late for an abortion anyway. Gerard became the proud papa-to-be, accepting congratulations. I don't know what whispering went on, what gossip, and if there wasn't any it was a miracle in that crowd! They saw everybody; whether it was Elsie Mendl or Cocteau, no matter. Gossip was as much a part of their diet as our vitamins are now. Not that we don't add a bit of idle chatter these days. But I heard nothing. Gerard was quieter, distant, and . . . I don't know . . ." Renee lit a cigarette and blew a smoke ring. "Yes! He was an elegant, reticent robot going through the motions of what was expected. Oh, how I longed to tell you, Dany! You saw how defeated he was and your visit was so brief. Yet in spite of everything, *chérie,* though the doctor said she was fragile and weak, Charlotte was glowing!"

"Glowing?" Dany asked. "Did I glow? No, I was like some farmwoman in the Somme, walking up a long flight of stairs, up to the little studio, working. I didn't think about the joys and rapture of becoming a mother. Like some healthy animal, I'd have my baby and get on with my life. I had no lofty view of motherhood."

"You never knew fear, little one. Didn't we always tell you that?" Renee went to the bar tray to take some more olives.

"Yes, you did." Dany got up to put an ice cube in her glass. "Until this past month. Did all my bravery bring me here? I've been like a frightened child looking for something. No, more like a frightened old woman, because I didn't know what I was looking for!"

They stood at the narrow table, holding their drinks. Dany looked at Renee, the kohl liner had smeared onto her cheeks, there was more lipstick on the rim of her glass than on her lips, but her eyes were clear and bright; she was not tired. It wasn't pleasant telling all this but there was pleasure in sharing it. Dany wanted to touch Renee, to pat her hand, to hug her, some sign of tenderness and affection. They stared at each other and Renee blinked her eyes for a second. Dany knew that no

401

gestures were necessary.

"Charlotte asked me to spend the summer with them. No, *chérie,* she didn't invite me, she pleaded with me." Renee sat down again, leaning forward on the sofa, her shoulders hunched and tense. "I had to come to Villefranche. I went down in July. The house was finished and Gerard was only coming on occasional weekends. He was working very hard, checking his theatres and converting many of them into movie houses. If he was deliberately avoiding being with her in the villa, we will never know.

"All the luxurious goings-on of Paris moved down to Monte Carlo. It didn't stop; they merely changed houses. Massine and Kochno and the ballet company. Dali was designing one ballet, Matisse another. Louis was there and Bébé, Chanel and Schiaparelli. But those two were never together, they had their own coteries. Lunches, picnics at the beach and the titles! Princesses and Duchesses and Maharanis. Charlotte loved flitting from group to group. Then the doctor ordered her to be very quiet. He said she must rest or she might lose the baby. And, Dany, how she wanted that baby.

"We were quiet and rather isolated then. Gerard came for a few days at a time and he was so agreeable and stylish; his neat jackets and white trousers, the perfect shirts, and always affable. But, *chérie,* such utter sadness and resignation. As if a jail sentence had already been given. What a trio. Me! Eating again and their food was wonderful! Leave it to Charlotte to have found one of the best cooks on the Riviera. Getting fat after another scrapped love affair. I was not feeling my best, but I covered up my feelings. Another Hugo performance! Oh, what a group we were. Charlotte obeyed the doctor, she rested and read and watched us swim. Now it was as if she was doing penance, going through a kind of absolution for her errant ways. I'm sure she thought about a life in a little remote Italian town with Tino. She may have fancied that and she did adore him, but she loved Gerard more and in a different way. What Gerard was thinking was a mystery. I never knew until much later.

"Tino's friends were poor, living in houses scattered over the hills, rented studios in St. Paul and Eze and Cagnes. I don't know how often she saw him alone but he did like to drink at a bar, Jimmy's in Cagnes. She may have seen him there. It was a popular hangout. He was forbidden to come to the villa. But he did arrive one afternoon after Gerard had gone back to Paris.

"You know that time in the summer when the sun is relentless and there is nothing to do but have a siesta. You think there will never be a breeze again. The air is gone, you are living in an oven. The soundless heat. It's strange, that silence. Even the birds have taken a nap, maybe you hear a lonely cricket. The noise of wheels on the road, a distant voice would echo and bounce across the gardens. I felt like an eavesdropper. Charlotte had come into my room after Tino arrived. I was on the bed reading. 'Renee, you are not going out, are you? Stay in sight, please? Out on the balcony. He won't stay long.' I wondered if she had any premonition; but, no, it was impossible. 'Sit out on the balcony,' she pleaded.

"I would have stayed in my room or in the salon. I sat out on my little balcony and I watched them walking around that lovely garden, along the back path that led down to the road to the sea. I didn't know what they were saying, then suddenly very clearly I would hear a scrap of conversation. Sometimes Tino's hand would let go of her waist and move into the air. I've never seen a gesture of such futility. What a pair they were! Charlotte, blond and tanned from the sun that bathed us every day on the terraces, her eyes more lavender than ever and she was wearing fisherman's smocks over her growing belly. Marvelous faded blue they were. She was rather a sight, all the same. Thin and bony as ever but with the round, full belly! He wasn't very tall, and talk about suntan! He could have been carved out of Carrera marble, *chérie;* not a bit of waste on him. He was something beautiful to see. They both were until his Italian temper flared. *'Carissima,'* the way he said that word. How much love and adoration can be expressed by one word. Well, an Italian word!

" 'The hospital in Genoa will be fine. I'll find a house. High up over the sea and away from this world here. In the Cinque Terra. We'll bring the baby home to live there. It will be enough for us.'

"I heard that as if they were standing next to me and then . . . nothing. They must have turned onto the purple path and the bougainvillea was thick enough to absorb their voices. A few minutes of that hot silence again and suddenly — *'Maldetto!'*; *'Brutta bestia!'* *'Merda!'*

" 'I'm not good enough for you! No, I'm not rich enough to be the father of your child!' Garbled, raging words of temper. It was quite a while before Charlotte came back to the garden and she was alone. She waved to me and I went downstairs. We walked to the terrace that overlooked the sea. I saw her cheek, red from the palm of Tino's hand. He had slapped her.

"We stood looking out at the still, incredibly calm sea, in that late, hot sun. 'Where was he when I was eighteen; when I was young enough to care as much as he does now.' That is all she said. We didn't see Tino for two weeks after that. In fact I never saw him again."

"But he did come back?" Dany was startled by the rasp in her voice.

"We never knew, we could not be sure." Renee walked across the room, picking up some anemone petals that had fallen from the vase on the table. She looked at the fragile crimson petals in her hand and let them slowly fall into an ashtray. "If you go over something every day of your life, you don't forget. Why I went out for lunch and cards that afternoon, I'll never know. No one seemed to be home when I got back. No one worked in the late afternoon, the two servants usually went home and Marie, the cook, always slept after lunch.

"I was wearing a new Lanvin suit I had bought in Monte Carlo. Pongee, natural pongee and a little beret, white with silly straw pompoms. Very chic. I went to my room and wondered if Charlotte was out in the sun. It was breezy, windy in fact and she loved to sit out and watch the sea.

"She could stare for hours at the water with the salty air blowing against her. I called to her before I stepped out on the balcony.

"Dany, the first movie I did for Chabrol wasn't as brilliantly cut. Talk about split seconds! There was no sense of time. Everything that happened then seemed to be fragments, sensations without reactions.

" 'Charlotte!' I called out again. And why? She could have been in her room having a nap.

"Gerard was standing in the garden. Absolutely still, a statue! Not moving. He was numb. 'Gerard, you've arrived early!' I was happy to see him. Then I saw the edge of white cotton behind the rose bed. Those lush, silvery pink roses. Charlotte's favorite. I went to the edge of the little balcony. I saw her on the ground, her dress covered with blood. Gerard looked up at me. Dumb, not a word. Immaculate in his pale gray flannel suit and then I saw that he was holding a rake, the teeth were red with the blood.

"Over to the right, where her room opened on to the side of the garden came Marie's voice. 'Monsieur Dessaux, I called for an ambulance! I called the police.' She whispered it, but how loud and clear that whisper was.

"By the time I ran down to the garden we heard the ambulance arrive. And the police. I leaned down to touch her. She was alive. Gerard didn't speak. He just kept looking at me, saying nothing. He couldn't, and I don't think we said a word to each other until we were at the hospital."

"Tino. It was Tino who killed Charlotte?" Dany asked, moving to the sofa to sit next to Renee. The letters she had received, those few reports from Renee and Louis Ostier were all untrue. It would have been easier without knowing any of this, it wasn't important now. Wasn't it all too late? But no, Renee had to tell. To have kept silent for all these years. The burden of a well-kept secret. No, Renee had to tell her. There was no one else and when were they going to see each other again? Dany answered herself quickly. Soon, no more distances, or never again? "Where was he, this Tino?" Dany asked.

"He must have crossed the border back to San Remo. Little one, it was the last week in August! Ten days later, well, you were there. And, Dany, all the things I couldn't tell!"

"But you weren't sure? Were there no fingerprints on the rake?" Dany was impatient. Was there no solution, even now?

"Oh, I was sure!" Renee said. "The stretcher was wheeled out to meet us at the door of the hospital. Charlotte opened her eyes once, looking up with fright and wonder. She didn't recognize us. 'Tino' she whispered. No, there were no fingerprints, little one. I don't believe that Tino ever struck her with the rake. I think he must have slapped her and she fell. That damned

406

rake collapsed a lung. It pushed into her ribs so hard the blood could not get out of her heart. It was a miracle that she bore the baby!"

Dany didn't remember a time when Renee was quiet, without a bit of reminiscence or an amusing anecdote. Now she was quiet at the dinner table. And she wasn't hungry.

"We must eat this if it kills us," Renee whispered. "She will be hurt. She worries." Renee nodded her head toward the kitchen.

"I know," Dany said. It was the first time she had seen Selene not smiling. Like a dog knowing that its master was disturbed, Selene's eyes had been wide with concern and her big white teeth had not been showing as she had served the meal. Dany looked at the slices of chicken on the plate, knowing how insulted Selene would be if she didn't clean up every bit.

Renee's look of helplessness made them both laugh. "Good," Renee said. "Force yourself."

"What a terrible responsibility for you, Renee. All through the trial and for all these years. How good of you to have honored Gerard's wishes."

"Very simple. I had taken an oath. And I loved that man. Like a brother, a member of my family and I had no family. Except for Gerard and Charlotte, Louis, Venard and you, that was my family. Aren't there always secrets in all families?" Renee said. "Especially in the theatre?"

"In the theatre though everyone talks too much," Dany said it very gently. "I wish you and Veronique could know each other, could spend time together."

"Why hasn't she come here? The only time she was in Paris I was shooting that flop in Morocco. The waste, little one! Three of us working, working. Slaves to our art! But now she'll have to come, my travelling days are over. I'm too lazy and too fat!"

Dany laughed now. "We'll see about that. Do you remember those last few months, the trial?"

"Bien sûr, of course." Now Renee tore at her chicken wing with gusto. "There was the infant in the hospital and Gerard in jail. It didn't take long to put him there. What had that fool Marie said to the police? Or more important, what didn't she say? How deeply did she sleep that afternoon? It was a lovely day for a siesta with the breeze blowing but not to have heard Tino and Charlotte in the garden? They couldn't have been too far away. Charlotte hadn't run, the path would have been covered with blood. I wondered later, much later, how anti-Semitic Marie might have been because when the trial began the press went mad playing up the fact that Charlotte and Gerard were Jewish."

"And we never knew! Why did they hide it?"

"Doesn't everyone appreciate a round of applause, especially in the theatre? Isn't that why we were there in the first place? No matter what you did, in whatever area, you hoped there was applause waiting for you. Gerard produced his plays with elegance, he was known for his selectivity and his infallible eye. Well, I think he was afraid of rejection and criticism. Prejudice. He chose to deny what he was, that was detestable but he couldn't bear the thought of ostracism. Neither could Charlotte. Can you see them being left out of anything, any place?

"Judgment is so easy when you're reading a newspaper editorial or a magazine article. You make up your mind very quickly which side you're on. Left or right, pro or con. Traitor or hero?" Renee intoned. "It's simple if you don't know the party concerned! Robert Venard became a hero in the resistance. How many knew why? To avenge the death of his young lover who was killed in

Sedan months before Dunkirk. And Louis Ostier? The German uniform was so splendid he spent five years infatuated with those uniforms and ruined his life. It wasn't any easier to judge those who left France or those who stayed. What a muddle all of it was!

"Charlotte had been Gerard's *raison d'être* and his life had no value without her. Can you imagine thinking that little of yourself? To be without any will. Have you ever seen complete defeat, *chérie?*"

"Renee! We don't forget!" Dany said. She remembered the flat in Passy and Simon's warped acceptance of defeat: "Not a pretty sight." And she could see Gerard that day in Nice. That futile day.

"Not pretty at all." Renee put down her knife and fork. "Silence may be bearable although I never liked it. Silence represented unpleasantness to me, discomfort. Something repressed. Speak up, I always wanted to say! Talk about what's on your mind. Say it! I've never been pleased by serenity. Serenity and silence don't necessarily go hand in hand, anyway.

"The lawyer complained that Gerard hadn't given him facts. The finest criminal lawyer in France, and he saved Gerard! Too late, but he was exonerated. Lack of evidence. What a laugh, after all!"

"Renee, if I had stayed—"

"You would never have been able to get out of France if you'd stayed. The hysteria when the war began! I think everyone we knew was running back to Paris. They had to. I waited for the trial and for Gerard's sister to come from England. It was not easy, little one! That September when Europe was going berserk!

"Then before his sister arrived Gerard spoke to me. 'I'm an expert in duplicity,' he said. 'I've lived with it long enough. Now I'm going to end with it. What a last act this drama has. Or is it one of my boulevard farces?

Either the jury will find me guilty, the cuckold gone mad with rage, or innocent, the cuckold justified. I get the punishment either way. I married Charlotte the way I bought a painting, a work of art at auction. Was it fair? We lied to ourselves and everyone we knew. Renee, when I read the news reports, when I heard the ghoulish stories coming out of Germany these past six years, I should have known our duplicitous life couldn't last. But what mastermind of the theatre would have predicted this?'

" 'It is over,' he said. 'That is all. The boy will be brought up in England. There is honesty in my sister's house. That means he will have freedom. Only you will have to keep the secret, Renee. Dangerous things, secrets, and I hold you to the keeping of it. Jenny must never know. The boy must never know. It will not be a good thing to be a Jew in France now. Was it ever good, anyway?'

" 'But, Gerard, the child is not completely a Jew.' I said. His eyebrows went up. Up to the sky! That look, how do I describe that look? 'So?' Gerard whispered. Was that some final irony? More duplicity?'

"Renee, you kept your word. That is the most honorable act I've ever known. And yet — "

"What, *chérie?* Do you know that I'd not have told you today if we hadn't talked about Veronique? Never would I have uttered a word! Trains of thought, hah! It was all leading to this, wasn't it? The subconscious takes us into strange alleys, no?"

"A minute ago you spoke of irony. If you told the boy, what is his name? Wilfrid? If you told him the truth when he was here, it might have been more constructive."

"But Gerard didn't want him to know!"

"And Tino, did you try to find him? After the war

did you look for him?"

"Yes. When I went to Italy to do the Fellini movie. The supreme accomplishment for a fat character actress! You get to do a small role in a Fellini movie. I tried to find Tino. Italian bureaucracy makes the French look like wizards at statistics! It was very difficult. A sculptor named Tino. One name in San Remo. Files were checked, not a thing. He must have had another name. San Remo was very small; he must have been killed in the war. Oh, if I found him I might not have kept the secret. For what, little one? If I'd found him, if an investigator came up with something, for what? My own curiosity?"

"So this Wilfrid fellow will never know." Dany thought about it. Was it quite just? She wasn't sure at all. "No, I suppose it doesn't matter now. He had his home in England. He had the family. That's what Gerard wanted, wasn't it?"

"And a good plot for a play. Gerard didn't think of that, I'm sure. The Wilfrid boy was seeking confirmation, an affirmation for what he took to be the truth. I wasn't going to dissuade him. He had his facts. He's a good writer. He made it better than the truth. The degenerate monster and his decadent wife."

"How do you know, Renee? That he is good?"

"He sent me a script. I have it around somewhere. Maybe my performance as an addled old woman wasn't that convincing. Oh, maybe it was pure conceit on his part, but he did send it to me. He used the words from the newspaper reports, the luxurious villa, the decadent affair—"

"What?"

"Little one, what is wrong? All I was going to say was that he called his play *The Villa Affair.*"

"Renee, you can't mean it? The play we're making in

411

New York, the play Veronique is working on is called *The Villa Affair!*"

Renee waited. It seemed a long time before she spoke again. "I'll find the script. I'll give it to you, *chérie*. You can read it for yourself."

Fourteen

1980

"This is Renee, Renee Hugo." The voice Veronique heard when she answered her phone didn't belong to an old, old woman. It might have been some secretary reading her boss's memo. "Your mother has left. She's on her way home." Not the sound of the addled woman David had described.

"She was trying to get on the Concorde."

A silence, Veronique wasn't sure what she wanted to say.

"We've spent our lives missing one another. Do you realize I haven't seen you since I wheeled your baby carriage in Central Park? Life has taken us in different directions, my dear Veronique." Another brief silence, then the warm voice of an intimate friend. "Listen carefully and forgive me, I'm old but I'm not one to meddle. Perhaps I'm too old for that!"

She laughed and Veronique was reminded of Dany's imitations of her. A lovely laugh, the fluttering of bird's wings. "Veronique, there have been secrets that I've kept. A lifetime of unspoken facts. Be patient with your mother when she comes home. But talk, the two of you must talk. It isn't fair for me to tell you all of it now. Dany has to do that, these are things she did not know until yesterday."

413

"Renee, it doesn't matter what the facts are." Veronique heard herself, she sounded older than Renee. "What is important is that she talks to me, that we face each other."

"Absolutely, my dear Veronique. That is correct." And Renee went on talking.

"Watch what you're doing to that dress," Veronique said. "Don't stretch it." Ryan was at the pressing table holding the iron like a weapon ready to use in an attack. "Be gentle, we must have perfection today."

"Why are you carrying on?" Ryan guided the iron an inch away from the blue silk, steaming the folds at the waistline. "This isn't a musical with hundreds of costumes. Calm yourself, Veronique."

"Where is Elsa? And Nancy, does she have enough coffee for everyone?" Veronique reached into the lining of the dress on the form. "Get under here, shrink the facing a bit. Are the fitting rooms clean? Benny's suits! Elsa wants them lined up before she—"

"Hold on, will you?" Ryan exclaimed. "It's only a play. We'll be finished in a couple of hours. Why are you so uptight?"

"Perfection, remember?" Veronique expected it this morning. Every morning but particularly today. She hadn't told anyone that Dany was coming home, that she'd be arriving sometime today. "We mustn't forget anything. I hate it when we're missing something and it's too late to look for it." It was better this way, to get on with the day. Business as usual. Ryan was right, Veronique knew it. She had to control herself. "Are Phyllis Arnold's dresses in the fitting room?"

"Right where they're supposed to be, darling," Ryan answered. "Honestly, Veronique!"

"I'm glad you've put the iron down." Veronique tried to smile. At Ryan, of all people, the only one who could read her mind, except for David. David who had walked into this room just three weeks ago. "Look at the time! It's almost eleven!"

"And, sweetheart, it's only a dress parade," Ryan said.

Bless Nancy. The fitting rooms were arranged, gloves, jewelry, accessories were meticulously lined up on the tables in front of the mirrors. Nancy and Lawrence must have seen to that. Yes, only a dress parade. Another play to be delivered. Routine to Ryan and Benny, to Elsa and the rest of the staff. With the customary suspense spreading through the workroom. Normal. And nervewracking.

Veronique moved the potted fern away from the mirrors. The lush green plant looked better near the door. The delicate fronds shook as she placed it on the floor. She took the card from her blouse pocket.

"Darling, this is to remind you to stay cool today. Love, David."

Cool. Veronique saw herself in the mirror. Better than yesterday, she thought, when she sat alone in her room and heard the operator calling from Aix. Her pallor was gone, the angry face had vanished. How often did this happen? To move through a day, giving instructions. Going through the motions and hoping she was hiding successfully. Quickly blinking her eyes, turning her mind to computer. Not another soul in the house had to know, not yet.

She checked herself in the mirror. Was her ego so great today that she was pinned to the image in the glass? No matter, she had color after the weekend in the sun, her ivory blouse heightened her tan. The pallor was gone. She had energy. Confidence. And David was responsible for it. David, what was he doing at this moment? They hadn't talked this morning. He didn't know her phone rang at three in the morning. She was in that heavy sleep of escape before she recognized the sound. She thought he was calling to see if she was all right. Then she heard the operator's matter of fact voice. France—a call from Aix.

"Veronique, here you are!" Elsa came into the room. "I was wondering about the lights, shall we go dim or will it be a nuisance later when we want them bright? Oh, let's have them up. After all, we're showing clothes. Beautifully detailed clothes for the stage. Not costumes." Elsa took a pill from her bag. "These pains! Oh God, my tummy! You'd think I'd never done a show before. And it looks superb. Doesn't it, Veronique?" Her nervous fingers danced in the air. "I need water. Lawrence dear," she called out, "may I have a glass of water! Why is it so terrifying? Until they're here and dressed and we've begun. We'll have strong, clear light today and next week they can have shadows and mood when they're on stage. Oh, will I have my stomach pains then!"

Lawrence gave her a glass, shrugging his shoulders. "Miss Groueff, I have to check the shoes for you." He shook his head, a sign of futility and he walked out of the room.

"Benny, no," Elsa shouted. "Not in here." He was wheeling in a rack of suits. "The men will dress in the small rooms."

"Since there are more men than women in the cast I thought we'd—"

"No, darling." Elsa tried not to sound annoyed. "Miss Arnold and Lydia Castleman are in this room."

"I just thought—"

"Really, Benny!" Elsa steered the rack toward the

416

smaller fitting rooms.

It was easy not to think with Elsa in the room, Veronique said to herself.

"We're the first ones here?" The stage manager came in with his assistant. "Good morning, everyone. Eleven o'clock on the dot. The theatre's four blocks away and the actors are late. Is everything ready here?"

"Naturally." Elsa's grin was patronizing. "Are you ready?"

"I'd like to check some prop clothes," he said. "Can you spare Lawrence for a few minutes? Ah, good morning, Miss Castleman."

"Good morning, my dears," Lydia's usual jolly, let's-get-on-with-it attitude wasn't apparent today. "Where do I go, Miss Groueff?" She stretched her neck, offering her cheeks for automatic kisses.

Veronique led the way to the room behind the big mirror. The unexpected performance, as always. Who could predict an actor's mood? "We have you in here next to Miss Arnold."

In minutes the fitting room was buzzing, the icy formality and over-polite greetings were quickly forgotten and a loud, forced cheerfulness took over. Either way it was too much, Veronique thought, but understandable. This really was Elsa's morning and her anxiety was reasonable. The actors had to wear the clothes for only a few minutes and next week on the stage in Boston was time enough for discontent and egocentrics. For the complaints about collars and waistlines, for the motivations involving the shape of a hat or the color of a tie.

She hadn't seen David come in but the director, Elliot Youngman, was whispering to him. Last minute notes, a new idea? Elliot motioned to the producers, bringing them into a huddle. And Fay and Oscar Nye were smiling in agreement.

417

If the producers were cheerful, Elsa could relax. The camaraderie meant an easy morning. Without stress. Veronique knew they could begin.

David moved through the crowd to greet Elsa. "I'll say thank you now. For all your care and splendid work. I'm not waiting, you'll hear it from the others later." He turned to Veronique, his arms bracing her shoulders. "Cool?" he asked.

"Cool," she answered. Who but David would know how much a few kind words meant to Elsa at this moment. "Thank you for my present," Veronique said.

She watched him move around the room. A few encouraging words to the actors, small talk to ease the pressure. She remembered the afternoon he came into the workroom, sweating and impatient. She'd thought he looked like a boxer, an athlete ready to run on a Rugby field. She couldn't imagine the world without him. He had led her to confidence and she was never going to lose it now. She was going to remain calm. "Well," Veronique said to Elsa. "Shall we start?"

The first two actors stepped onto the platform in front of the mirrors. At the opening of the play, when the lights came up, they were the first to be seen. The prosecutor and the defense attorney. In ordinary clothes that had to tell who they were. Nondescript. The most difficult aspect of designing, Elsa always said. The character was a man from Nice in a dark suit. Almost black but blue, the suit he wore every day, summer and winter. Wrinkled from the heat and worn-out. It hadn't fit properly when he bought it. Tailoring a suit that had to tell so much to the audience was difficult. The actor playing the role was too heavy for clothes that might have been found on a rack in a thrift shop. Benny had

418

cut the wool after it had been washed and carefully sprayed in places to give it age. Now, here it was, an old suit, shiny from too many pressings and too tight. After all, the character had been thinner then.

The second actor, playing the lawyer from Paris, was in flannel, a middle tone of grey and double breasted. The cloth was expensive, the fit perfect and obviously custom-made but his tie was a dull, dark brown and his shirt collar was unstarched. The jurors, the local trades-people and workers must not be put off by Parisian style. This man must not alienate the panel by looking too rich.

Benny followed the line of actors in front of the mirrors. The jurors in workclothes, plain and functional but dramatized by Elsa's palette. A monochrome mix of earth tones and greys, the colors of newspapers, the rotogravure of the Thirties. Damn them, Veronique said to herself, why was it the small-part actors who picked, signalling for the director's attention, to let him know there was something wrong with a costume. Benny was there, ready, at the actor's side, with his scissors and his pins.

Frank Berger stepped forward, the tall, bony man with the long nose and cold grey eyes. The Gerard. In a casual navy blazer, a silk shirt open at the neck and folded flat over the collar of his jacket. Smart, gracious Gerard, not disheveled after driving from Paris to the Villefranche villa. There are people who don't wrinkle their clothes, Elsa had said, people who never perspire. This man was one of those people.

"Oh, it's marvelous!" Faye Nye exclaimed.

"Elsa, they look great," said Elliot Youngman.

Nancy's squeal stunned all of them in the room. The doors were open and her surprised cry was loud. "Madame!"

"Hel-ll-lo, hel-ll-lo!"

As if on cue from the director everyone stood up. Veronique wished she could see David's face but his back was turned. Was Dany going to receive a standing ovation? She was a marvel, looking as if she'd just stepped out of her dressing room and come down the stairs from her apartment. Fresh, full of energy and ready for another day in the workroom.

"Damn the traffic! It took as long to come over the Triboro as it did to cross the Atlantic! I was on the Concorde!" She stayed at the back of the fitting room for a moment. "No, I don't want to interrupt. This has never happened to me before! To be on this side of the room for a dress parade. Me, the observer!" She walked in, stopping for kisses from Fay and Oscar Nye. "Hello, hello!" She was delighted with the attention. "Let me sit and watch. I'll make notes. Remember when I first took notes for you in Philadelphia, Elsa? At the Shubert? How long ago that was but I'll never tell. *Jamais, jamais!*"

Veronique couldn't take her eyes off her. Dany made the grand entrance but she was nervous. She was using French words. A sure sign, Veronique knew. Dany was nervous as she embraced Elsa, waiting a second before hugging Veronique. Hasty and casual pecks on the cheek. *"Chérie!"*

"Maman!" Veronique hoped she sounded surprised. She realized the company was standing, awkwardly watching and waiting to resume.

"Now, now," Dany said, "you must go on. Please!"

"Mother, do you know Frank Berger?" Veronique asked. Calm, she had told herself, and cool, as David had said. "And this is Elliot Youngman."

Elsa was holding David's arm. "You two haven't met."

"Maman," Veronique was at his side in an instant. "This is David Wilfrid. The author."

Was Renee ever wrong? His firm handshake, the look of him! Renee had said it. A stonecutter, the suntanned workman, smooth as marble. Charlotte's son. Dany understood why Renee had wished she were younger. David Wilfrid didn't let go of her hand. And his dark eyes were as shiny as lacquer. Had she ever recovered from such eyes? As she expected, in a flash of memory, there would be a smile. A foxy smile, warm at the same time. Yes, he was smiling at her and it seemed to be an accomplice's smile. He was telling her that he knew something.

"No, *non merci,* I'll sit here behind you," Dany said. "This is your play. It's as if I've just come in, one of those pests who makes everyone stand up so she can get to her seat after the curtain's gone up! Now, you've all worked very hard. Please, I mustn't hold you up any longer. Do go on." Dany leaned over to Faye and Oscar. "This is delicious, you realize I know nothing about this play, *quelle surprise!*"

Nothing. Oh, Veronique, three weeks ago Elsa Groueff was bringing a play into the workroom. How lucky to have an order during the summer. A little play. Dany looked at Veronique as the chatter and noise of appraisal and approval went on about her.

"Will you please open your tie, Walter," Elsa asked. "A bit sloppier, you know?"

"Can Sam take off the vest and let his shirt hang out?" Elliot wanted to know.

Suggestions, notes. Nit-picking ideas made after weeks of rehearsing, nervous tension mounting before the looming horizon that was Boston. Three weeks and forty years later.

Veronique was thinner. No, that wasn't it. She had vi-

421

tality. Not waspish like she was before Dany went away. She was at ease and supple. Dany's cat that never purred was beautiful. At every word, every comment that was uttered she looked at David Wilfrid. The air between them seemed to pulsate.

Oh, Renee, how you called it a few days ago. You said watch out when Veronique finds the man, and it was quite evident. Renee should be sitting in the fitting room now. To hear this low, humming wave; to breathe this essence, a light perfume filling the room. A magnet in Veronique's eyes, her hand on Ryan's shoulder as she whispered a note. Veronique who never touched anyone that easily. A quick sizzle of vitality in David Wilfrid's shoulders as he moved to the edge of his seat. They were reaching to each other, he was holding her.

"Perfect!" someone said. Was he the stage manager?

Phyllis Arnold stepped forward in a white dress, a gypsy's dress of cotton eyelet trimmed with ribbons. It was stained to simulate blood. The dress Charlotte wore when she was found in the garden.

"Bravo, Elsa!" It was Oscar Nye, how kind for the producer to give praise.

Dany stared at the actress on the platform. She looked nothing like Charlotte Dessaux but she was attractive and she had the cool, natural elegance and the pale complexion. That dress, how could Elsa know when she was designing the play? Where did she find her research? How many copies were there of the photograph in the silver frame on the table upstairs in the bedroom? Dany remembered; the dress had nothing to do with the Thirties. It was one of the peasant styles Charlotte had loved when she came back from Italy. How long ago, those dresses being sewn in the small Passy apartment. Before Renee Hugo, before knowing that an exciting, other world was there in the pile of pleating and embroidery and peasant cottons.

David Wilfrid wrote a play based on newspaper clippings and stories told to him by Gerard's sister. He'd made a melodrama, a good one, Dany thought. But the play she read on the plane was not about the people she knew. Not her Charlotte and not Gerard. Dany watched Veronique cinching in the sash at the actress's waist. What questions did Veronique have after discovering this world she'd never been told about? Was there an inevitable question, Dany wondered. But why? David Wilfrid didn't now Veronique's grey eyes were like Gerard's.

Elliot Youngman signalled David and they walked to the side of the room. The director had a thought, a new bit of business, perhaps. A short, whispered conversation, David shaking his head in assent. Another idea. David taking Elliot's arm, holding his elbow. A firm but gentle clasp as he listened and agreed. He didn't let go. That was Charlotte's gesture, the tender control of her hand when she spoke to someone. Especially Gerard. David was holding Elliot's arm the same way. The recognition was startling. He *was* Charlotte's son.

Dany turned when David and Elliot came back to their seats. She felt the stare, her eyes met Veronique's. In all the time in the same house, working side by side, Veronique had never stared that way. A look of certainty. Dany wanted to turn away but it wasn't possible. No, Dany kept her eyes on Veronique, hoping she was letting her know. Too many glances had been avoided for too long, too many confrontations had been evaded.

Veronique went to the dressing room; in a minute Lydia Castleman came out wearing purple, a shade lighter than aubergine. A dress and tunic, a satin tam with coq feathers. She was followed by Phyllis Arnold in a taupe suit of fine wool. Was Elsa Groueff mad to use cashmere? Was there a limitless budget to make these clothes? But it was a suit Charlotte might have worn. The blouse was lilac. Had there ever been a time when Charlotte hadn't worn something lavender. Her favorite color. A scarf, a kerchief, amethysts. Always a touch of lavender.

Dany looked at the actresses in their costumes and she saw Charlotte with Renee at lunch in the little bistro behind the Odeon, at cocktails on a rainy afternoon at the Ritz.

Charlotte used to admire Dany's fearlessness. Did Charlotte know fear when she travelled to Barcelona or Amsterdam or Marseilles? Memory should blur, but nothing was dim or shadowy, nothing had faded or washed away. The actors in the room were jolting the past into sharp clarity today. These memories began a few weeks ago in France and now it was unmistakable. Dany hadn't forgotten.

On the plane, all the way across the ocean, Dany had thought about what Renee had said. Through the clouds and the startling blue sky Dany thought about Charlotte. She wanted a villa, a place in that world of Monte Carlo and dukes and duchesses, maharajahs and ranees. She'd revered all that before she met the sculptor, Tino.

"No, Elliot dear, this isn't the second flashback of the play," Elsa was saying. "This will be the Maxime's scene." She was using her schoolteacher voice. "We're going in sequence, as in the play. You understand, don't you, David?"

"Yes," David said. "May we get on with it now?"

"Sorry, I was ahead of myself," Elliot apologized. "I

was thinking of the other party scene. Okay, can we move a little faster, gang?"

Veronique agreed with Elliot, but was it possible? All these dresses, suits, and coats. How fast can clothes be changed?

"I'm too old to rush," Lydia said when they returned to the dressing room. "If they'd stop talking so much out there we'd be moving faster."

"Let's try," Ryan said. "Are you with us, Miss Mounet?"

Ryan was jittery too. Veronique had heard the edge in David's voice a minute ago. Agitation. Was it going to spread through the group? But this is merely a prelude, Veronique thought. She helped Lydia button her jacket before sending her forward again.

Maman, what will you say later? Do you realize three people are going to talk? David will be there, too.

Now the dresses for the second party scene. How many parties were given, Veronique wondered. *You've never starved in Paris, chérie!* How often had she heard Dany utter those words? Had she truly been hungry in those days?

"Elsa, do you like Lydia all bundled up in her cape?" Elliot asked.

"Lydia!" Elsa shouted. "We agreed you'd enter with it falling off your shoulder—"

"My dear, I know how to wear my clothes. After all, back in the Thirties I told Valentina what to do and Molyneux—"

"But this isn't how Miss Groueff wants you to wear it," Veronique said.

"I know, I know. Elsa knows her business, but I'm in the Lydia Castleman business. I know better!"

"Not today, Miss Castleman." Veronique pulled the silk tie at Lydia's neck, slipping the satin cape to expose one shoulder. "Now look—" Veronique turned the side mirror. "See how dramatic it is?"

"Oh, Lydia, so much better, darling!" Fay Nye clapped her hands.

"Now that's just swell," Elliot called out. "Hooray!" And he applauded.

Lydia turned from the mirrors, letting the cape slide lower from her shoulder and bowed in appreciation as if the idea had been her own.

Dany stared at Veronique. What assurance, the poise as she took charge. Her slightly mischievous expression. Dany saw Gerard walking through the crowded bar during the entr'acte at the theatre. She thought of the first opening night party in Paris. Gerard had that same expression.

Oh, the ego of Lydia Castleman, her ridiculous shenanigans! And this was trickery, Dany thought. This dress parade was baiting her. David Wilfrid had captured more than what was going to be on stage. The opulent clothes were luring her into places she'd wanted to forget. The nights riding back to the flat in Passy, to Simon and his notebooks.

These velvets and jerseys, the dinner jackets and tail suits, these coats Elsa had designed made her remember. The years after she'd bought this house, after Mac was lost in the Pacific. Learning the questionable pleasure of self-indulgence. It helped her hide, to avoid the hurt. Buying rare books and keeping good wine, flowers and antique paisley, expensive old chairs to cover in older brocade. Ruby red and pink and cerise, colors to forget with. The luxury of fine floral-printed linens to cover her big bed where she'd always sleep alone. In a second, simply one moment, she knew she was old, but she had never seen so clearly. Charlotte used to tell her to collect things. Oh, what an evasion that was!

Veronique hadn't collected things. She wasn't meant to hide. Veronique had learned that from her mother. The workroom had belonged to her for three weeks. This had been *her* atelier and she had realized Elsa's designs perfectly. She wasn't hiding today.

Yes, Dany saw Gerard's eyes. The same shape, the same brush of dark lashes. But the bold stare Dany had just seen wasn't inherited from Gerard. It was what Charlotte and Renee had admired. No fear, they used to say. Veronique *was* her daughter.

Dany looked at David sitting in front of her, his dark hair curling too low over the collar of his polo shirt, Charlotte's son. She wanted to yell. *He's not your brother, chérie!* Hah, if anyone had known the frightening picture of a boy growing up in England, in a place she never wanted to acknowledge. David Wilfrid had to be . . . oh dear, he was going to be forty-one. Yes, the waste of fear, such a joke! What would Charlotte have said?

Now the actor in a dark overcoat stood in front of the mirrors. Frank Berger with a homburg and fawn gloves, a sable collar on his coat. This was some devil's prank. Gerard, coming to the atelier on the Left Bank that winter night. Was there a prop bouquet of blue flowers ready for the actor? David Wilfrid didn't know about that night. David didn't know about long, slender fingers that had rolled up a bolt of cloth and carefully folded a length of velvet before she felt that hand. The clothes were what Gerard would have worn but Frank Berger's hands were wrong. Fleshy hands without bones. Not graceful hands.

Veronique helped Phyllis Arnold out of the mauve

chiffon dress, the last of the costumes. Fay and Oscar Nye were applauding when she came through the dressing room door.

"Brava, Elsa!" Elliot Youngman was beaming. "And your work, Veronique, the end, the absolute end!" He had kisses for everyone, he was shaking Benny's hand. Even Ryan was grinning. And David? Was Oscar Nye going to go on talking to him forever?

Veronique sighed. They had done it. Finally.

Dany had allowed all of them to move ahead of her. Oh no, Veronique said to herself, don't defer this, Maman, not now. Then, as if Dany had heard, she barged ahead. The long stride that didn't slow with time. Dany was in front of Fay and Oscar, stepping onto the little stage.

"Elsa, it is divine, my darling. *C'est ravissant, vraiment!*"

"Dany, I'm thrilled that you're home!" Elsa was choking with emotion. "I'd have been miserable if it had gone this brilliantly and you weren't here. Are you proud of this daughter of yours?"

"*Bien sûr.* Of course, would I have gone away if I didn't know she'd do it beautifully?" Dany's voice was husky. She reached for Veronique's hand as Elsa went on talking.

"*Oui,* France was wonderful, Elsa. And, Veronique, I have many, many things—"

"To talk about." Veronique had to finish the sentence. "I know." She had asked Ryan to carry on without her, Nancy was going to help him clear and get back to the workroom. "Shall we go upstairs?"

Veronique turned on the landing at Dany's door. "No, come up to me. There'll be more sun in my place." Uncluttered. Veronique wanted to take two steps at a time. And brighter in her simple apartment.

428

᠁"Darling, did Renee call to say when I was arriving? I had very little time, you know?" Dany's voice was lighter now. A bit of a trill, cheerful and slightly giddy. She turned to David behind her on the stairs. "What a rush but I'm used to rushing." She tripped, almost falling backward. David caught her, helped her gain her balance.

"Maman, are you all right?"

"I'm fine, fine. Who's used to this extra flight? What else did Renee have to say, *chérie?*"

Veronique was at the door. "We didn't talk for very long." Sunlight was pouring into the room. She held the door open. She'd never seen David this quiet before. He followed her into the living room. This was her time, David knew it and he was letting her have center stage. "But I know more this morning than I've known in more than forty years.

"There's coffee, I made it before I went downstairs this morning," Veronique said. "No, Maman? David?"

Dany was leaning on the parson's table, her fingers moving back and forth, leaving print marks on the beige patina.

"Maman, Gerard Dessaux asked you a question many years ago—" Veronique took David's hand, she had to be holding him now. There were going to be surprises for him, too. This was a day for shocks.

"That question wasn't going to change his life. He'd decided about his life before he talked to you. He asked you if I was his daughter." Veronique gripped David's hand, her nails digging into his palm. "You didn't answer him, instead you nodded your head. But you didn't answer, Maman. And he knew, he knew you couldn't lie and so you didn't speak." She looked at David. Was he expecting her to know more than he did? Oh, how she'd always hated puzzles, guessing games. "He knew that I was his daughter."

Veronique longed for sky, the stretch of endless beach. The horizon, anything clear and distant, not the faces in front of her now. "He told Renee. He said he didn't have your courage to go on creating new things, making another life. Oh, Maman, no silences, not ever again."

"No, *chérie*, no." Dany was trying not to blink, her voice was cracking. "Never, never."

Veronique let go of David's hand, she wanted her arms around him before she went on. "You can cry if you want to, Maman." Suddenly Veronique felt a small laugh rising from her throat. She wanted to hold Dany, too. "But I'd prefer it if you didn't."